WHS McIntyre is a partner in Scotland's oldest law firm Russel + Aitken, specialising in criminal defence. William has been instructed in many interesting and high-profile cases over the years and now turns fact into fiction with his string of legal thrillers, The Best Defence Series, featuring defence lawyer, Robbie Munro.

The books, which are stand alone or can be read in series, have been well received by many fellow professionals, on both sides of the Bar, due to their accuracy in law and procedure and Robbie's frank, if sardonic, view on the idiosyncrasies of the Scots criminal justice system.

William is married with four sons.

More in the Best Defence Series:

Killer Contract

Fourth in the Best Defence Series

WHS McIntyre

William H.S. McIntyre
Copyright ©

www.bestdefence.biz

I intend to live forever, or die trying.
~ Groucho Marx ~

Chapter 1

It was the court case of the year; the decade. In fact, as we were only a few years in, the millennium: Lawrence 'Larry' Kirkslap, Scotland's most flamboyant entrepreneur, standing trial for the murder of Violet Hepburn; a good time gal who, according to all the evidence, had met with a very bad end.

It's always a good start to any murder defence if the alleged victim's body cannot be found; however, over the previous four weeks, the Crown had laid before the jury a gilt-edged prosecution case, studded with gems of circumstantial evidence. A circumstantial case is often likened to the making of a rope, where strands of evidence are gathered to form a cord strong enough to support a conviction. By all accounts, if you weaved together the strands of evidence against Larry Kirkslap, you could have made a noose to hang an elephant.

And yet, to watch Kirkslap stride out through the big bronze doors of Edinburgh High Court and onto the Royal Mile, you would never have thought he'd been sitting in the dock for over a month. Florid-faced and smiling, he waved to photographers, joked with the journalists, and there, by his side, jogging to keep up, his lawyer: Andy bleeding Imray.

I punched a cushion.

'Oh, stop it, Robbie.' Jill flopped down on the sofa beside me. 'It's your own fault, you've said it often enough: if you'd stayed with Caldwell & Craig, you'd be dealing with all the rich clients too.'

'Yes, but Andy? Dealing with a case like that? What does he know about anything?' If my old firm, Caldwell and Craig, was an albatross in the world of legal seagulls, Andy was a barely-hatched chick.

'You should be happy for him,' Jill said. 'I'm sure it'll be fine. After all, you taught him everything you know.'

'Don't say it.'

She did. 'Not that it would have taken very long.'

After I'd watched the news report and struck Jill on the head with a cushion, I was flicking through the Wednesday night channels, looking for the second half of a Champions League match, when ordered to halt. Jill was an ardent fan of U.S. medical soaps. In the one I'd inadvertently stumbled across, a patient was busy having a heart attack. White-coated actors charged about with crash-carts, wielding heart defibrillator paddles and shouting, 'clear!' It was all very glossy and highly dramatic. There was probably a U.K. version in which a bored NHS 24 call-centre operator told someone it was only indigestion.

After a momentary pause, during which, at the third attempt, the patient was shocked back into the land of the living, I continued onwards through the adverts in search of football, until Jill snatched the TV controls from me and held them above her head.

'My house, my remote,' she said.

'I see. Then by that law, it's your house and these are all your plants.' I wafted a careless hand at the various pot plants scattered about. 'They're going to be very thirsty when you come back from Switzerland in six weeks' time.'

'You wouldn't really let my plants die?'

Some single women kept cats. Jill had a room full of house plants with names I'd never heard of before, all, apparently, in need of frequent TLC and lashings of H2O while she was away on business.

'You've been to my office,' I said.

Jill shuddered. She was thinking of my umbrella plant. 'Is that thing even alive?'

The answer to that was: barely and purely out of spite. The only moisture the plant ever received was the bottom of a cup of coffee, the only mineral sustenance, the ash of smoker-clients whom I made stub their cigarettes out in the pot of rock hard soil. And yet the umbrella plant remained; even, occasionally, sprouting a tiny, defiant green leaf. Its survival was an inspiration to us all at Munro & Co; an encouragement to keep on going, no matter how tough things became. Secretly, I admired its tenacity to endure despite life's many hardships. Mostly I just ignored it. That was what worried Jill.

'You'd better not neglect my plants when I'm away. I want you through here regularly. Just follow the instructions I gave you. That's not going to be a problem is it?'

I vaguely recalled a piece of paper Jill had given to me a few days earlier, containing descriptions and locations of various plants as well as some stuff about dead-heading, watering from the base up and other confusing horticultural terminology.

'Depends,' I said.

'On what?'

I reached up and grabbed the remote from her hand. 'On whether you let me watch the football in peace.'

Jill curled an arm around my neck. Nippy to sweetie in under fifteen seconds. 'Watch football?' she said, her lips close to my ear, making me shiver, but in a good way. 'Is that really what you want to do on the last evening before I fly off for a month and a half?' She put her other hand inside the neck of my shirt and stoked my chest. She stood, took my hand, pulled me from the couch and tried, successfully as it happened, to drag me off in the direction of the bedroom. Suddenly, I realised how close we'd become over the few months we'd been together, how much I'd miss Jill when she was away. The football I could catch up with later on the highlights programme.

'Will you miss me when I'm not here?' she asked.

I switched off the telly and threw the remote onto a nearby armchair.

'Oh, probably,' I said.

Chapter 2

'Bad idea.' Joanna snapped shut the small velvet box and handed it back to me.

The partner and staff of Munro & Co., all three of us, had gathered for an impromptu meeting in my room, Monday morning.

'Don't you like it?' I asked.

'It's lovely, but it's not the actual ring that's the problem - it's the whole concept.' So said Joanna Jordan, former Procurator Fiscal-depute, now my assistant: poacher turned gamekeeper, or perhaps it was the other way around. She'd not taken long to form a double-act with my secretary when it came to organising my professional and now, it seemed, private life. I was beginning to wish I'd never asked for a female opinion. They had so many.

I opened the box again. 'Look at the size of that diamond. That's a full carat. Nearly.'

'What Joanna is trying to say,' Grace-Mary said, 'is that buying an engagement ring is a nice thought...'

'But?'

'But it smacks of arrogance,' Joanna clarified further.

'I wouldn't say it was arrogant,' Grace-Mary said, 'but, yes, definitely a teeny-wee bit presumptuous.'

Joanna nodded. 'It's like you were saying: I'm going to ask you to marry me, but as we both know you're going to say yes, I've just gone ahead and bought the ring. Now off you go, doll, smack on the arse, there's probably a pile of ironing to do.'

'Hold on,' I said. 'Let's assume for just one nano-second that Jill doesn't think I'm arrogant.' I turned what I hoped was a steely gaze on Joanna. 'Let's say, purely for the

4

purpose of argument, that she loves me *and* she loves the ring.'

The staff stared at each other clearly struggling to come to grips with my naiveté.

Joanna sighed. 'Love's got nothing to do with it, Robbie. And it doesn't matter how nice the ring is. You're going to have to face it, there's no way Jill, or any self-respecting wife-to-be, is going to let you think you made the correct choice in something as significant as an engagement ring. That only happens in the movies.'

Grace-Mary screwed up her face in sympathy with Joanna's words. 'It wouldn't be fair on you if she did. To simply accept the ring would lay down a misleading marker—'

'Set a false precedent,' Joanna said. Obviously she thought that translating things into legal jargon would help me understand. It didn't.

'And that precedent would be?' I dared to ask.

'That you actually knew what you were doing and didn't require the expert guidance of your wife in all matters of any importance,' Grace-Mary explained. She lifted a wire basket of mail from my desk and took it over to the filing cabinet. 'When are you going to shift this monstrosity?' She gave the cabinet a kick. 'It would be much better against that other wall out of the way, and there's no time like the present.'

'So,' Joanna clapped her hands together, 'are we done here?'

'No, not quite.' I opened a drawer and threw the subject of our discussion into it. From one of the piles on my desk I extracted a file and handed it to her.

'What's this?'

'A wee trial for you. I can't do it. I've got a jury starting in Falkirk.'

Joanna opened the file and grimaced. 'Indecent exposure?'

'Don't worry it's dead straightforward. The accused is in his own bedroom. How is he supposed to know that passing school girls are going to look in?'

She skimmed through the papers. 'Maybe if he didn't press his genitals against the window they wouldn't.'

'He'd had a shower and was drying himself.'

'Yeah, right.' Joanna was having difficulty remembering that she was a defence agent now.

'Don't worry,' I told her. 'As ever with these types of cases it will all come down to—'

'Credibility and reliability?'

'No,' I said. 'Flaccid or erect. Now get going.'

'Are you serious?' Grace-Mary asked, after Joanna had left for court, more in hope than anticipation of finding a limp penis. 'You're really going to ask Jill to marry you? What's the plan? Romantic dinner somewhere nice?' She yanked open a filing cabinet drawer. 'My Frank proposed to me at an England/Scotland game. I should have known something was up. I'd never been to a football match before and then he whisks me off for the Wembley weekend in nineteen eighty-one. Scotland got a penalty and Jim went down on one knee. I thought he was saying a prayer at first.' She stared down at the fourth finger of her left hand where there was only a simple gold band. 'It was a lovely engagement ring until I lost the diamond on holiday. We were always going to have it replaced... then Frank took ill... I don't even know where the ring is now.'

'John Robertson, wasn't it?' I asked, in an attempt to evade the risk of emotional dialogue.

'Who?'

'Who scored the penalty that won the match.'

Grace-Mary looked up from her finger. I thought her eyes looked a little red-rimmed. 'Frank had a tenner on England. He always bet against Scotland. It was his idea of an insurance policy.'

'Must have made a few quid in his time,' I said.

Grace-Mary gave me a wry look, cleared her throat. 'Talking of which, where are you getting the money to buy an engagement ring?'

'There are two ways of making a profit,' I said. 'Increasing sales or decreasing overheads.'

'And?'

'I've done a deal that will help us cut-back on the rent.'

'A deal with Jake Turpie?' Grace-Mary knew Munro & Co.'s landlord as well as I did. Jake was a scrap dealer, a money lender, a part-time, second-hand car salesman and a full-time, first-rate psycho.

'Yeah, I'm doing Deek Pudney's trial in lieu of three months' rent.'

'And if he's found guilty...?'

I didn't like to think about it.

Grace-Mary took a letter from the wire basket and slipped the edge into a paper punch. 'I'll tell you what - an all-expenses paid trip to the bottom of Linlithgow Loch.'

I lifted my briefcase. 'Relax. Have some confidence in me.'

'I will and I do.' Grace-Mary slammed her hand down on the paper punch. 'But take your swim-suit with you just in case.'

Chapter 3

Tuesday. Day two of a trial that had started off badly, and was going downhill faster than the Weight Watchers bobsleigh team. The only light relief was the new bar officer. Someone in Scottish Courts HR had outdone themselves. Stacey was pretty, young, female and blonde; not the usual gruff, male ex-cop supplementing a police pension, and, unlike the normal geriatric recruit, seemed quite at home with digital technology. A press of a button and the monitor screens around Courtroom 1 of Falkirk Sheriff Court illuminated.

'Should have pled at the first diet,' the Procurator Fiscal chirped across the well of the court to me. She smiled in the general direction of the jury box; more stony faces than Easter Island. One of them, beard, tweed jacket, shirt and tie, I just knew would end up as foreman. He had the look of a headmaster. Facial hair and the teaching profession never bode well for us purveyors of a reasonable doubt.

I glanced around at my client, sitting impassively in the dock. Shaved head, steel grey suit over a black turtleneck, Deek Pudney was eighteen stones of gristle and bad intentions, the right hand of Jake Turpie who was sitting watching the proceedings from the back row of the public benches.

Normally, in any court case in which Jake held an interest, a defence lawyer could be assured of one of two things: either the witnesses wouldn't show up, or the witnesses wouldn't speak up; both excellent lines of defence, but neither available on this occasion.

Deek was charged with assault; a very bad assault on an undercover police officer, codename 'Joe'. Undercover Joe's duties concerned the tracking down of heroin suppliers, and he'd found what he considered a fool-proof method. In full Junkie mode, Joe would roll up at a Sheriff Court near you, usually on an afternoon when there were Drug Treatment and Testing Order reviews taking place, come over all pathetic and rattling with the assembled junkies and ask where he could 'get'. A phone call later, he'd have a name and a meeting point. Joe would then buy a tenner bag and put a tail on his provider, whose house would promptly be raided by the drug squad. Bingo: one ready-to-go prosecution. Entrapment only worked as a defence if the dealer had been persuaded by Joe to do something he wouldn't have done otherwise, and, nine times out of ten, a search produced bags of smack, digital scales, tick-lists, text messages and all the other paraphernalia required to establish an on-going concern in the supply of diamorphine.

Yes, undercover Joe had it all worked out, or thought he had, until poor directions and an ignorance of the local geography led him to Jake's henchman loitering on a Street corner in Bo'ness. How undercover Joe could have confused shaven-headed, suit-wearing, muscle-bound Deek as a Junkie, I'd never understood: unless he thought he'd struck gold and been referred, not to the usual street-dealer, selling to feed his own habit, but Mr Big. That was a mistake. As was Joe's refusal to take no for an answer. Deek was a tall man, but his temper was about as short as his neck.

With a press of another button, a CCTV recording played. The time display at the bottom left of the screen showed 13:46. Broad daylight; not a good time to be committing crime: an excellent one for optimum video quality.

One or two jurors put hands to face as digitalised Deek straight-armed Joe and then with a raised knee caught him again on his way down to the pavement. Had the film show stopped there I might just have managed to argue that Deek had felt threatened having been accosted by the pseudo-junkie; however, other requirements of a defence of self-defence were the use of necessary and proportionate force. I guessed that stamping in turn on each of now unconscious, undercover-Joe's elbows and doing the same to each knee might come under the heading of cruel excess.

The recording concluded at 13:48 and with it the Crown case. The CCTV operator, a couple of cops and a consultant orthopaedic surgeon had given evidence as had Joe himself, though not from the witness box: from a wheelchair, one leg and two arms still in plaster two months after the incident.

When court adjourned for the day, Deek having been carted back off to Barlinnie, I found Jake waiting outside for me. The decidedly unamused features of Munro & Co.'s landlord were, as ever, situated above the oil-stained boiler suit that was his choice of apparel for every occasion.

'How's it looking?' he asked.

I wondered if Jake had been watching the same trial as me. 'It's looking like five years - that's if Deek's lucky and escapes a remit to the High Court for sentencing.'

'Would serve him right. The man's an idiot. Getting into fights with the polis?' Jake hawked and spat in the gutter. 'And getting caught on telly? Mad.'

He was taking the news well. To reach a deal on my fee, I'd had to step into the realms of tentative optimism in my pre-trial discussions with Jake, and feared he might be harbouring unrealistic expectations. We walked towards the rear of the court where my beat-up Alfa and Jake's muddy Transit van were parked. One or two of the jurors, including beardy, were already outside, lighting up cigarettes.

'So what's the plan?' Jake asked.

'The plan?'

'Aye, to get him off.'

I stopped.

'He's not getting off. Did you not see the video?'

Jake stared blankly at me for a moment or two. 'How about we get some witnesses to say it was the cop that attacked Deek?' he said at last.

'What? And hire Steven Spielberg to shoot a different movie?'

Jake's left eyelid twitched ominously. I decided to rein in the sarcasm, even though he appeared to be having trouble coming to grips with the patently obvious.

'The CCTV evidence is very strong. Sometimes you just have to put your hands up,' I said, lamely.

'Aye, other people do. Not me and not Deek. Understand? I've a business to run. People owe me money. I've not the time to collect it myself. That's Deek's job and I can't just find someone else with his... experience. Not just like that.'

I could see why, even with the unemployment figures, Deek's would be a vacancy hard to fill.

'I'm sorry, Jake. But it looks like you're going to have to put a postcard in the Job Centre window.'

'Funny.' Jake laughed. Something he almost never did except when hurting people. He stopped abruptly. 'But, really. You'll think of something, Robbie, because Deek's going nowhere except back to working for me.' He gave the side of my face a playful and yet solid scud with the flat of a grimy hand. 'Whatever it takes.'

Chapter 4

'Going badly is it?'

It was nice to see my dad smiling. He was at the back of his house, up a ladder poking about at a row of slates above the rain gutter.

'CCTV,' I said. 'It doesn't cross-examine well.'

He clambered down. 'I'll bet the rain's been getting in there all winter. Slates missing, sarking practically non-existent and there's no felt, only horsehair.'

'That's what you get for buying a cottage, away out in the wilds.'

'It's only three or four miles from Lithgae Cross and a fat lot of good you were helping me to buy it. What's the matter? Conveyancing too difficult for you? I had to pay that lawyer a fortune in fees.'

We'd had this conversation before. My practice was purely criminal defence. Never mind the extra professional indemnity premium involved in property law, I'd long forgotten anything I ever knew about conveyancing; something I was pretty pleased about when I'd heard of my dad's intention to flit. I didn't see him as the ideal client.

'Still it was good of you to kick-start Scotland's property market,' I said. 'Why don't you help the ailing construction industry and have someone sort the roof for you? Before you break your neck.'

I followed him inside. The internal layout was not dissimilar to his old place. Back door leading into the kitchen, and from there to a livingroom with a bay window and a real coal fire below an impressively carved ancient mantelpiece. I think it was the fireplace that had swung it for the old man. That and the great big Belfast sink in the kitchen.

'It's my birthday next month,' he said, with a vague wave of the hand, a gesture which I'd come to recognise as a direct order to make a cup of tea.

My dad and I were both April babies. It was a month that saw the ritual exchange of malt whiskies between father and son. 'Which Islay distillery is to have the privilege this year?' I asked. 'You decide the malt and I'll decide the age of it.'

'I'm not wanting whisky this year.' And, having made that startling announcement, he sat down at the kitchen table and picked up the newspaper. 'I want a surprise party.'

Overlooking the whole lack-of–surprise side of things, I wondered what had got into my old man, who usually moaned about attending any formal social event to which he was invited.

'You had a party when you retired.'

'That was ages ago.'

'Seven years.'

'Ach, that was different. It was work related. Anyway, I can hardly remember it.'

Not surprising given the amount of drink that had been taken. Anyone who could remember my dad's retirement do, hadn't actually been there.

He folded the newspaper to the crossword. 'I'll let you have a list of folk to invite. After that it's just a case of organising food and nibbles. Maybe a balloon or two. You don't have to go crazy with bunting, and if you're worried about music—'

'I wasn't planning to lose any sleep.'

'...get the number of the Red River Trio from Brendan down at the Red Corner.' He filled in an answer and then scratched the top of his head with the pen while considering the next question. 'And tell your brother to show face. Maybe bring a couple of his football pals with him.'

'Venue?' I enquired, rinsing out the teapot with boiling water before dropping in a couple of teabags.

'Here of course. It'll be like a housewarming and my birthday rolled into one.' He looked at the ceiling, tapping his lower lip with the ballpoint. 'I'll need to get that roof fixed though.' He got up and from an overhead cupboard brought down his favourite enormous teacup and a mug for me. 'You back at Falkirk tomorrow?'

He wanted a favour. 'Yes, but I'll be very busy.' Busy on the receiving end of a guilty verdict and trying to dodge the wrath of Jake Turpie.

'Too busy to nip into the wee DIY shop next door to the court?' From somewhere my dad produced a packet of Tunnock's teacakes and slid one across the table at me. 'When you're there, pick us up a roll of felt and tin of that tarry stuff, will you?'

Chapter 5

Next morning, crack of eight-thirty, I came across Joanna and Grace-Mary in my room, poring over the court diary, trying to decipher my handwriting.

'Is that supposed to be a 'G'?' Joanna asked.

'I know,' Grace-Mary agreed, 'It looks more like a squiggly 'S', doesn't it?'

My bad handwriting was just one of the many reasons why Grace-Mary favoured the typed word. The dubious benefits of a computer diary had been the topic of many a frank discussion, usually with my secretary doing most of the discussing, and I was concerned that she was now grooming an IT acolyte.

'So, Joanna,' I butted in, 'how did the flashing trial go, yesterday?'

She looked up at me through narrowed eyes.

'Erect, was it?'

'You could have run a flag up it and saluted.'

'Oh, well. Not to worry.' I stepped between them and took the diary. There were far too many empty spaces. The drop in prosecutions across Scotland was really beginning to bite. Too many people were on the receiving end of fixed-fines that they could conveniently not bother to pay. I closed the diary and sat down behind my desk. 'Anyway, don't let me keep you,' I said.

'From what?' Joanna asked.

'From your next trial.' I tapped a finger on the front cover of the diary. 'At *Slassow* District Court?' Only I found that reference to my handwriting amusing.

Joanna pulled a face. 'Not Glasgow District, Robbie. It's a dump. When I was a Fiscal they used to threaten you with six months transfer there if you didn't toe the line. Believe me never was a line so well toed.'

'Tell me you're not asking Joanna to do the dog case?' Grace-Mary pleaded on behalf of my assistant. 'Not Billy Fitzpatrick?' She lifted the diary and turned to the date as though it might be wrong. It wasn't.

'Dog case?' Joanna brightened. 'Suppose it might be all right. I've got some good dangerous dog authorities tucked away somewhere that should come in handy.'

'It's not so much a dangerous dog case,' I said, as she was about to leave in search of law books. 'More of a domestic breach, slash, section forty-seven combo.'

'Section forty-seven? An offensive weapon? What's that got to do with dogs?'

'Nothing,' Grace-Mary said.

'Not that section forty-seven,' I said. 'The other one.'

It took Joanna's finely-tuned legal mind a few seconds to sift through the various legislative possibilities. 'The Civic Government Act? What? Urinating in a public place?'

Grace-Mary folded her arms. 'Not *urinating*. Try again.'

'Stop being so melodramatic,' I told my secretary. 'What's the problem? It's just a wee domestic. Billy's new burd locked him out because she thought he was drunk.'

Grace-Mary pulled the case file from a cabinet. 'The man's never sober.'

'And so he knocked on the door a few times.'

'With his boots,' Grace-Mary clarified.

'Perhaps slightly too loudly for that time of night.'

'At what point does the dog appear in this story?' Joanna enquired.

'It appeared from nowhere,' I said.

Joanna cocked an eyebrow. 'And?'

'And did plop-plops on the front door mat.' Grace-Mary closed her eyes and held out the offending file.

'Plop-plops?' Joanna took it from her. 'A big dog done it and ran away? Really, Robbie? Is that the best defence your client can come up with?'

It was and he'd needed help coming up with even that. 'Look don't start,' I said, noticing that Joanna had rolled up the file in her hand and was gripping it as though she wanted to swat something. 'You're not a Fiscal now. Put the old tin helmet on, fix bayonets and be glad your old employers are actually prosecuting something. I'd go myself, but there's still a day left in Deek Pudney's trial.'

A voice from the doorway. 'Do you think I'll get in trouble if I print this?'

The three of us turned to see Kaye Mitchell standing holding up a mocked-up front page. Kaye was editor of the Linlithgow Gazette and one of Jill's best pals. Presumably because of my romantic affiliation with her friend, she seemed to think that made me her free legal help-line, and the fact that my office was practically next door to hers meant that visits were not infrequent, and usually when I was dashing out of the door or had a client waiting to see me. Kaye had never troubled to see the inside of my waiting room, a drab room with a couple of wobbly wooden chairs usually occupied by one alleged criminal or another, and not for those of a nervous disposition or with concerns over health and safety.

'What do you think? Is it Corntonvale-here-I-come or will I get away with community service?' She glanced about the room. 'I could start here. When did this place last get a coat of paint?'

Kaye and Jill had been classmates, the year below me, and when, apparently, how to be nippy was part of the school curriculum.

The phone rang in reception and Grace-Mary went off to answer it.

'It's not called community service anymore,' I said, dragging the conversation away from the decorative state of my room; something Grace-Mary was always harping on about, threatening to get her retired brother-in-law in to 'smarten the place up a bit,' and no doubt supplement his state pension to the detriment of Munro & Co's already poor standing with the bank. 'It's now a community payback order.'

'There a difference?'

Not that I had noticed. To my mind it was just the Scottish Government tinkering with the criminal justice system by re-branding sentencing disposals to make the voters think something was being done.

'Let me have a look.' I took the sheet of paper and read the headline: *'Linlithgow's Burke and Hare'*. 'What's it about?' I felt obliged to ask, though I didn't want to. It was a quarter to nine, I had to be at Falkirk Sheriff Court by ten and my jury speech was a work of fiction still in progress.

'The two boys that tried to rob the tomb. Have you not heard?'

Boys from Linlithgow charged with a crime and I hadn't been instructed? What was the world coming to? 'Have they been convicted?'

'Not yet.'

'Charged?'

'They're up in court later in the week. They were caught red-handed, I heard, and so I expect they'll be pleading guilty.'

Why Kaye, after years of court reporting, thought that guilt and a guilty plea went hand in hand, I didn't know. 'I think you'd be safer waiting until they do before you go convicting them in your paper,' I said.

Joanna stuffed Billy Fitzpatrick's case-file in her enormous handbag and pushed past Kaye out of the room.

'What's wrong with her?' Kaye asked. 'And don't say time of the month or I'll belt you.'

'She's not enamoured with the quality of work she's getting here.'

'Maybe she should leave. Look at the case Andy got. Larry Kirkslap? Now that's what I call a quality client. You been following the trial? Completely done out of the park, of course, but—'

'Do you mind?' As unsubtly as possibly I stared at Kaye and then at the door. 'I'm busy. I have some work to do for one of my lesser quality clients. Millionaire entrepreneurs or not, everyone gets the same gold standard of service at Munro & Co.' After a brief hunt around I located Deek Pudney's file. It had fallen off the side of my desk and the insides had spilled across the floor.

'How's Jill doing?' Kaye asked, ignoring my invitation to leave. 'Six weeks in Berne? All right for some.'

I stooped to gather Deek's paperwork. 'She's working.'

'Course she is.' Kaye sat down. 'How are you two doing - romantically? Can't be easy. I know what these long distance relationships are like. I've time for a quick coffee, if you want to talk.'

'I've got to go, Kaye.' I put Deek's file in my briefcase. I could mull over my jury speech in the car and jot something down when I got to the court. 'Grace-Mary will make you a cup of coffee if you ask her nicely.'

And then it dawned on me. If Kaye and my secretary got chatting, it would be only a matter of time until the engagement ring was mentioned, and I didn't want word filtering back to Jill. It was almost nine o'clock. Falkirk Sheriff Court was twenty minutes away.

'Tell you what,' I said. 'Why don't we go down to Sandy's and chat about my love-life over a proper cup of coffee?'

Kaye crumpled the front page and lobbed the ball of paper over my head, nearly into the waste paper bin. 'Let's go,' she said, linking an arm through mine.

Deek Pudney would just have to settle for Munro & Co.'s bronze standard of service.

Chapter 6

Grant Goodwin was a Stoke City fan. Somebody had to be. More importantly, he was Sheriff Clerk and even more importantly he owed me a tenner. A few months   back, Grant had been in unusually buoyant mood following a famous win over Manchester United at the Potteries, and I'd felt it time to put into practice a gambling theory I'd been working on - or, at least, my dad had.

The old man had noticed that in those games where a footballing minnow took a bite out of a championship-contending shark, the minnows went on to do badly in their next game. Whether it was over-confidence at having just beaten a blue-chip team, or because they were knackered after their efforts the week before, they almost always lost. With Stoke sitting comfortably mid-table and their next match also a home game and against some bottom-feeder or other, Grant had been happy to shake hands on a bet. He even gave me the draw.

'You'll get your money,' he said, after I'd brought back bad memories of the nil-nil with Norwich City, just like I had the last few times I'd been at Falkirk. I was hoping to clarify the precise date of payment when Stacey the bar officer entered the courtroom, jurors following on behind. We'd had the speeches and the Sheriff's charge and the jury had been out for forty-five minutes; a lot longer than I'd thought it would take them to come up with a unanimous guilty; however, they hadn't reached a decision yet and were simply being brought back so as to be given permission to have lunch.

In days long past, the jury was not allowed to eat or drink while it considered its verdict: it helped speed things up. Nowadays, it was something of an anachronism, but many old-school judges still insisted on the jury returning so as to be formally told they could break bread.

'Lunch has been provided,' the Sheriff intoned. 'You may temporarily cease your deliberations, eat and recommence at one-forty-five.'

'All rise!' bellowed the bar officer. Fifteen slightly bemused jurors who had only just sat down were led off again, while his Lordship rose from the bench to something better than soup and sarnies.

'What was all that about?'

I turned to see the decidedly unhappy features of Jake Turpie. I told him, but he still didn't understand. 'It's not actually the law, more like a tradition nowadays, but most Sheriffs don't like to take any chances.' Not this close to a conviction they didn't.

I turned to catch sight of a black gown disappearing out of the side door as Grant slipped into the private corridor that served the shrieval chambers.

A tap on the shoulder. Jake again. 'I hope I'm not going to be disappointed,' he said, giving me a stare so cold it could have sunk the Titanic.

If by disappointed he meant not seeing Big Deek for the next few years, I had some bad news for him. It could wait. I returned a smile that could have been filed under 'sickly', muttered something about how you never knew with a jury, and we walked down the stairs, parting company in the lobby where I took a sharp left through the security door into the sanctuary of the agents' room.

Inside, discarded black gowns were flung about the place, while their former wearers gathered around a big table stacked with case files, eating Panini's from the court café. Conversation ranged widely, from football to the latest Supreme Court ruling to cruel and unusual ways of torturing senior members of the Scottish Legal Aid Board. Time flew by. The loudspeaker in the ceiling announced that the custody court was about to start in Court 3. Those around the table reached for their gowns, while continuing discussions that had moved on to cult children's TV programme the Banana Splits.

It was then that I remembered the roofing materials my dad had asked me to pick up. It was almost two o'clock. It wouldn't take the jury much longer to reach a decision. They'd probably only stalled this far for the free lunch. I didn't want to hang around after the trial was over in case I bumped into Jake again; better to nip along and buy the stuff now before the jury came back with a verdict.

So, leaving behind great legal minds that were now desperately trying to recall the name of the donkey in Arabian Knights, I broke into an amble and headed for the DIY store; the sort of place where you could spend hours browsing, finding things you never knew you needed, while wondering how you'd managed to do without them. Unfortunately, my plans to be in and out of the place in under five minutes were derailed by a young lad in a 'Chaos in Kavos' T-shirt, who was the only member of staff on duty, and whose idea of hardware probably had a lot more to with the latest graphics card than hammers and chisels. When I went in, ringing the bell above the door, he was negotiating with an old guy in dungarees for the sale of a pound of two-inch brads. Once the pair of them had worked out that a pound was about half a kilo and the customer had explained that a brad was the same as a nail, but different, the shop assistant disappeared through the back, not returning for fully ten minutes. When he did materialise, carrying a heavy looking cardboard box, the flakes of pastry he brushed from the side of his mouth suggested that he might have stumbled across a bridie during the course of the great brad hunt.

It was a good twenty minutes later, then, that I left the shop carrying a tin of bitumen and a roll of roofing-felt which was a lot heavier than it looked. As I struggled back to my car, I could see, down to my left, some smokers congregated

22

at the back door of the court. I could make out two G4S officers, white shirts, red and blue striped ties, a social worker, Stacey the new court officer and three jurors, including beardy, all puffing away. If the foreman-to-be of the jury was still mulling things over, I had plenty of time. I put the stuff in the boot of my car, collected my gown and case file from the agents' room and wandered up the stairs to a deserted Court 1; deserted except for a certain Sheriff Clerk, in shirt sleeves, black court gown hung over the back of his chair, writing up the minutes.

'Oh, it's you,' he said.

I rubbed thumb and index finger.

'You don't give up, do you?' He sighed and made a pretence of patting himself down. 'My wallet's downstairs in my jacket. I'll get your money later.' He glanced at the red digits of the clock above the witness box: 14:27. 'I'd nip down just now but the jury will be back any moment. Don't know what they're thinking about to be honest.' He unhooked his gown from the back of his chair.

I took my seat in the well of the court. 'You've got bags of time,' I said. 'Half the jury are at the back door having a smoke.'

Grant, wrestling with his gown, one arm in and trying to catch the baggy sleeve with his other hand, looked up at me, grinning. 'Yeah, right.'

I wasn't sure why he'd found what I'd said funny. His grin faded. He studied my face closely. 'I'll... I'll just fetch your money,' he said, eventually. Standing up, he cast his gown aside and shot out of the door.

23

Chapter 7

Deek Pudney crushed my hand in his great hairy mitt. In his other he clutched a TESCO carrier bag containing the few personal belongings he hadn't left behind at Barlinnie Prison. We were outside Falkirk Sheriff Court and Deek was breathing in his first lungfuls of fresh air in three months. Jake was waiting for us in the pub. The Roman Bar was situated less than fifty yards from the front door of the court, and many accused persons and witnesses found it a handy place to relax while waiting for their case to call. I'd had clients who'd become so relaxed they'd had difficulty returning to court.

I walked in beneath the shadow of the recently-liberated Deek, to find Jake sitting at the bar drinking a glass of ginger beer. 'You!' He chucked a bunch of keys at Deek. They bounced of his chest and landed at his feet. 'Wait in the van.'

The big man stared longingly at the rows of beer taps then picked up the keys and about-turned.

'Eejit,' Jake muttered as Deek retreated and I pulled up a stool next to him. Wherever Jake sat there were always seats available in the immediate vicinity. 'You see what I've got to work with? The man's not done a hand's turn for three months and he thinks he can just stroll in here for a pint?'

I shouted up a lager tops. In a place like the Roman Bar that was probably considered a cocktail.

'He with you, Mr Turpie?' the barman set a pint in front of me, suds slopping down the side of the tumbler onto a sodden beer mat.

Jake nodded and there was no further talk of payment, which was good because I'd spent all my money on tar and roofing felt.

Jake was quiet, staring at his drink, turning the tall glass this way and that. He was thinking about something. Never a good sign. 'Three months free rent?' he exclaimed, at last.

I knew what was coming.

'What? For a two—'

'Three.'

'...day trial?' Jake gulped down half his ginger beer with one swift, angry, flick of the wrist.

I drank an inch. The lager-tops was good and cold. 'It takes Lionel Messi two seconds to score a goal,' I told my landlord, 'and he earns more in a week than I do in a year. You're paying for my expertise. We agreed: three months rent-free. Remember that thing we did with our hands? That was called a handshake.'

Everything with Jake was done on a hand shake. He didn't trust anything to paper.

'You got him off, I suppose,' he grunted, finishing his drink.

I summoned up as much modesty as I could muster. 'All in a day's work. Had to be my speech that swung it.' Truth was, there hadn't been an awful lot to say. I'd just given them the usual smoke and mirror stuff with some scales of justice thrown in. A female juror in the front row had spent most of my speech tidying up her cuticles, while the young man beside her practised his doodling skills on the pad of paper he'd been given to note the evidence. Even as I reached a crescendo, banging on about the presumption of innocence, no-one seemed particularly bothered and Beardy had failed to stifle a yawn.

'You always were lucky,' Jake said.

'Lucky? You saw the CCTV.' I took another sip from my pint. 'Luck had nothing to do with it.'

And it was true. The victory had not been down to luck, nor, I had to concede, but didn't, down to my jury speech. Although in Deek's case the witnesses had shown up and spoken up, someone in authority had cocked-up. That person was an inexperienced court officer called Stacey who had yet to be introduced to section 99 of the Criminal Procedure (Scotland) Act 1995; a section with which I hadn't been entirely familiar with myself.

In any trial, the average jury spent a lot of time in the jury room. At coffee breaks, lunch or when there was legal argument in court, the jurors were removed from the courtroom, and, during those downtimes, court officers would escort the tobacco addicts outside for a nicotine fix. That is until the jury was asked to retire and consider its verdict. At that stage in proceedings, Section 99 applied; a section that was drafted in the days of smoke-filled jury rooms; legislation that prohibited jurors from leaving the jury room other than for exceptional circumstances. Choking for a smoke didn't count. Unfortunately, for one shiny new court officer, for the Crown and, admittedly in this case, for the interests of justice, Section 99(3) said that, if it happened, *'the accused shall be acquitted'*. No ifs, buts or maybes. *(see author's note at end)*

The first I knew about it was when Grant Goodwin called me and the PF into chambers. Sheriff Marcus Blue was one of the nicest men to don a horsehair wig. The last time I'd been at Falkirk he'd found the case against my client not proven and then told the accused not to do it again. Sheriff Blue wasn't a soft sentencer, but you couldn't ask for a fairer judge.

As the clerk led us into the room, I noticed the blonde-haired court officer, was already there, palely loitering by the side of the Sheriff's desk.

'We all make mistakes,' Sheriff Blue pronounced, after he'd put the PF and myself in the picture. 'What's important is that we learn from them. Isn't that right?' Stacey smiled thinly, blinking back tears. 'Good, then there's no need to prolong the agony, or,' he looked me in the eye, 'to seek unwanted publicity.' He swivelled in his chair to face the Sheriff Clerk. 'Mr Goodwin?'

The Clerk opened the door and the bar officer drifted out of the room leaving behind a trail of perfume. I had a feeling an ex-cop would have made a less dignified exit, courtesy of a foot up his back-side.

Audience over, we returned to court, the PF muttering under her breath and Grant Goodwin saying something about me having all the luck. It was a moment to savour and so magnanimous did I feel at that moment that I almost told the Clerk to forget the tenner he owed me. Almost.

Chapter 8

Hang a thief when he's young and he'll not steal when he's old.
The words of the 18th Century judge Lord Braxfield. He had
a kindred spirit in Sheriff Albert Brechin, West Lothian's
most senior Sheriff, a judge not troubled by doubts, especially
reasonable ones, and Scotland's best advert for the jury
system.

'Your client is guilty, Mr Munro.' Brechin waved a thick
sheaf of papers at me. 'I'll not bother to read the schedule of
previous convictions, I'll weigh it later.'

Forty-eight hours on, and the glowing ash on my
smoking jury success had lengthened and crumbled as I was
brought back to earth with a conviction. Fortunately for my
latest client, though the Sheriff's spirit was willing, his
sentencing powers on a summary case were limited.

'Appeal it, Robbie!' my client yelled to me as he was led
away to the cells below.

'And get us out on interim lib!'

Bail pending an appeal? Perhaps he'd like a note of next
week's winning lottery numbers too.

High up on the bench, Sheriff Brechin grunted in
satisfaction, pushed back his chair and climbed to his feet.

'All rise!' the court officer called to the deserted
courtroom. The witnesses and any spectators had already
left. Apart from the Clerk, a court officer and me, the place
was empty. Lunch-time on a fine Friday afternoon in March,
the townsfolk of Livingston had better things to do than
watch another toe-rag get his comeuppance.

I waited until the court officer had led the Sheriff off to
his chambers, then removed my black gown and draped it
over a shoulder. Ten past one. The trial had lasted nearly

three hours; longer than anticipated, mainly due to Brechin's infuriating habit of having the evidence given at dictation speed so that he could note it down, which he did using a fountain pen that moved very slowly and required regular replenishment. The legal aid fixed fee for a trial was capped at one-hundred pounds. Take off overheads, tax etcetera and I'd be lucky to have made enough money to cover the cost of petrol back to Linlithgow, something that was no longer a chargeable outlay. Sometimes I felt I should register myself as a charity. To make things worse, before I could grab a bite to eat I'd also have to draft an appeal for my client and lodge it with the Sheriff Clerk. A top class, twenty-first century service for a third-rate, twentieth century fee.

I quickly dashed off a note of appeal against sentence. I wasn't wasting my time with an application for a stated case. There had been sufficient prosecution evidence to convict, and, not unusually, Sheriff Brechin had accepted it whole-heartedly. A twelve month sentence was, however, on the severe side. I charged along to the Clerk's office, where I could see only one Depute hovering around in the vicinity of the public counter. I called him over and slipped the paperwork under the security glass.

'You always were an optimist,' he said, and then noticed the foot-note. 'Oh, and an application for interim liberation too? I'm sure Sheriff Brechin won't mind me interrupting his lunch to give that request his full consideration. Do you want to wait for the result?'

I might have been an optimist but I wasn't clinically insane. There'd be no interim lib today. My client would have to take his chances with the Appeal Court. I gathered gown and briefcase and set off in the direction of Munro & Co., whose offices were conveniently situated for Linlithgow Sheriff Court. That is until they'd moved the Sheriff Court to Livingston. Now I had a ten mile trip each way.

But even the vindictiveness of Sheriff Albert Brechin couldn't keep me in a bad mood. The sun was nearly shining, three rent-free months lay ahead and I had a tee-time booked for four o'clock. On the way back to work, I decided to drop into Sandy's café for a crispy bacon roll just to keep my strength up.

'Ciao, Robbie. Tuo padre è qui,' Sandy called to me from behind the counter. There were one or two customers scattered about and he liked to keep up appearances at the establishment which, despite the signage, only the proprietor ever called, Bistro Alessandro.

I looked around for my dad. A man usually not easy to miss.

'He's in the...' Sandy's Italian vocabulary was beginning to feel the strain.

At that moment my dad walked out of the toilet. 'The bagno,' he told Sandy.

I didn't think so. I was fairly sure that bagno was bathroom, something Sandy's basic plumbing facilities did not remotely constitute. 'Is it not just toilette?' I ventured.

'That's French, not Italian,' said my dad and Sandy in unison.

'No, he's right enough,' another customer spoke up in support of me. 'It's the same as the French except there's no S at the end.'

'Oy!' Sandy shouted. 'Who's the bleeding Italian here?' He turned to my dad. 'Would you like anything to eat Mr Munro? Or did you just call in to inspect the bog and abuse my native tongue?'

My dad gave him a friendly pat on the cheek and ordered a cup of tea and a roll on square sausage before sitting down at my table. 'What's this I've been hearing?' he asked.

'You hear a lot of things, Dad. You'll have to narrow it down for me.'

'About you buying engagement rings.'

I didn't even bother to ask who'd told him. Over thirty years as one of Lothian & Borders' finest had left him with a network of spies; Grace-Mary chief among them.

'A bit presumptuous of you isn't it?' he said, another expert in the female psyche. My dad leaned back in his chair as Sandy brought us our drinks. 'What if she doesn't like it? Jewellery. Women are terribly fussy about it. And shoes.' He took a sip of tea. 'In fact,' he'd obviously given the matter some thought, 'most things. What you going to do if she says no?' He smiled at the thought.

'Dad, this is strictly top secret. I'm not having Jill come back from Switzerland and being the only person in Linlithgow who doesn't know I want to marry her.'

'How is she, anyway? Have you heard?'

'She flew out Thursday afternoon. She's lost her mobile, but phoned to say she'd landed safely. They've put her up in a really nice hotel and given her a guide to show her around, help her settle in.'

The food arrived and my dad took a bite out of his roll. 'How long's she away for?' he asked through a mouthful of bread and sausage.

'Six weeks.'

'That long?'

'It's this new job of hers. She's going to be based in Edinburgh, but the head office is in Berne and she has to go there for training.'

'Lot of rich blokes in the pharmaceutical business. Six weeks? You never know who she'll meet over there.'

Jill was the daughter of my dad's best friend, the late Vincent Green, and I, so far as my dad had always been concerned, a subject not worthy of her attention. He disapproved of our getting together on the basis that my track record in affairs of the heart ranked somewhere between poor and hilarious and Jill deserved better. I let him dream on about rich, handsome Swiss men sweeping my girlfriend off her feet, while I checked the inside of my roll. The crispiness of the bacon was never in doubt, but Sandy was known to skimp on the brown sauce and occasionally to top up his HP sauce bottles with vinegar to make them go further.

'Dad could you do me a favour?' I asked when satisfied that my sauce quotient was up to scratch.

He lowered his brow. 'Possibly... Nothing to do with one of your clients is it?'

'It's Jill's plants.'

'What kind of plants?'

'I don't know... house plants.'

'What about them?'

'They need watered.'

'And you want me to go all the way through to Corstorphine for the sake of some flowers?'

'I promised her. The bus practically goes past the door. You just need to get off a couple of stops before the Zoo and—'

'I know where she lives.' He sighed. 'How do I get in?'

'There's a key. In the garden, at the side of the house, you'll see a clay frog. The back door key is under it.'

'Alarm?'

'Inside the back door there's a wee table with a plant on it. The doofer for the alarm is on a ledge underneath. You just press it once to disarm and once to arm when you leave.'

My dad's roll was now a few stray crumbs on a white side-plate. 'You having another?' I asked, rhetorically.

My dad glanced up at the clock on the wall, beneath which Sandy was standing at the counter, flicking through what looked suspiciously like an English/Italian dictionary. 'What's wrong you're not at court? You're usually flying about all over the place. Business slow or were you just passing and thought you'd drop in to delegate gardening duties?'

'I had a case in Livingston but it's finished. My new assistant is off dealing with other stuff for me.' In the current climate, with booming crime but falling prosecutions, it had been a financial gamble to take on Joanna; even though I'd assumed it would be short term while she looked for another public sector job. That had been nearly six months ago. Since then she had settled into her role as defence agent, and the fact that I could now divide up my caseload meant that I was called upon less and less to perform my being-in-two-places-at-the-same-time routine. Whereas, I'd always harboured some concerns about the advocacy skills of my former assistant, Andy Imray, Joanna was a safe pair of hands. Those clients who moaned initially when told I couldn't conduct their case, never complained when met by a tall, slim, attractive brunette who knew her way around a courtroom. It also meant that I could pull rank and side-step some of the stinkier trials.

'I see your old assistant is doing all right for himself,' my dad said, busy trying to attract Sandy's attention by holding up his empty side plate and pointing at it. 'He's got that big case on the go just now in the High Court. Seen him on telly last night.'

'Larry Kirkslap? That man's obviously got more money than sense. I mean, Caldwell & Craig? Do me a favour. What does that lot know about criminal law?' I tore a chunk out of my bacon roll.

'You weren't saying that when you were working there. Best law firm ever back then, according to you.'

And I'd been quite correct. After all I'd been the criminal law partner until C&C had decided that crime soiled the livery, or, at least, legally-aided clients did.

'Same again, is it, Mr Munro?' Sandy called over, having eventually taken the hint. He placed his dictionary under the counter. 'What about you, Robbie?'

I had most of my roll left, but shouted up another. Better safe than sorry. 'How many criminal lawyers do you know dad?'

'Too many.'

'Okay, let me put it this way. Just say you got yourself in bother.' He was about to protest, but I put up a hand. 'Who would you trust to get you off? Me —'

'You?'

'Okay, not me. How about Paul Sharp?'

'The weirdo? The one who dresses like Georgie Fame?'

'Paul is an experienced criminal lawyer. He's been around for years. Be honest, who would you instruct? Paul or Andy?'

His refusal to answer was answer enough.

'These rich clients,' I said, munching my way through the rest of my roll. 'They don't know what they're doing. They assume you get what you pay for and so they go to the biggest, most expensive law firm when they get into trouble. The really big legal outfits never darken the door of the criminal courts. Andy's got potential, but he'll not learn his trade doing the occasional, high-profile work that comes his way at C and C. He needs to work his way up through the leagues. Spend some time in the JP and Sheriff courts before charging into a mega-murder trial.'

I popped the final morsel of roll into my mouth and explained how it was all very well for Andy to be swanning around the High Court, but what about the client? He needed someone who knew the angles, the legal loop-holes and technicalities of criminal defence work. Larry Kirkslap would learn the hard way and have a life sentence to mull over his choice of lawyer.

I was all set to expand further, with reference to Deek Pudney's acquittal, when Sandy emerged from the kitchen carrying a plate.

My dad made way for the next batch of rolls. 'By the way, Sandy, Robbie's getting these. And don't give him any tick, let him show you the colour of his money.' He picked up a roll. 'Your boy, Andy, seems to have done all right for himself, though.'

'In what way?' I asked my dad, once I'd assured Sandy that I'd square him up later. Much later.

'Have you not heard?' My dad's teeth were already embedded in his second roll. He chewed for a moment or two, savouring the food and the news he was about to impart. 'Kirkslap was acquitted. It was on the lunchtime news, just now. Andy, your hopeless ex-assistant, got him off on some kind of loop-hole or technicality.'

Chapter 9

'You do have to admit it puts your smoking jury case into perspective,' Paul said, as I thrashed about in the long stuff, looking for my drive. My golfing companion's fascination for Sixties' fashion extended even to golf-wear: white nylon polo-neck under a lemon pullover and on his bottom half, hound's-tooth slacks and matching black-white spikes. I felt drab in my ancient chino's and washed out navy polo shirt.

Paul selected a weapon from his golf bag and joined me amidst the foliage. 'Terrific win and Andy couldn't have picked a bigger client.' He laughed. ' And as for the Crown case - talk about a stone-waller? You could have seen it from the moon; there was masses of top quality circumstantial evidence.'

'He got lucky,' I said, realising how jealous I sounded. 'How could the judge forget to swear-in the jury before the trial?'

'It happened to me once,' Paul said. 'No-one noticed until after the first witness had given evidence. Nothing important just the police photographer. All they did was restart the trial, swear-in the jury and take his evidence again. It was just routine stuff anyway.'

'Think they'll just do the same here?' I gave the shrubbery an extra hard whack with my seven-iron.

'I'm not so sure. No-one noticed until after the jury came back with its guilty verdict. They could re-indict, but if the Crown is out of time and the Appeal Court think Kirkslap's tholed his assize or think he couldn't receive a fair trial, Andy could be on the receiving end of a giant win bonus. You know his client's reputation. The man's a party animal and not shy when it comes to throwing money about.'

Paul killed a bunch of thistles with a series of swipes to reveal my golf ball, resting in the roots of a gorse bush. A couple of whacks failed to dislodge it. I declared it unplayable. 'I'll take a drop,' I said, hooking the ball out with my club and punting it onto the centre of the fairway. Rounds of golf with Paul were fairly relaxed affairs. He might dress like Bernard Gallacher, but that was where any similarity ended.

Paul lined up his second shot from the edge of the fairway. He still had a hundred and fifty yards to go to the flag. He swung, hit mostly grass and watched as his golf ball hopped, skipped and jumped along the fairway and into a greenside bunker.

'Shame,' I said, lining up my own shot. 'It looked so good in the air.' I hit what for me was a sweet shot that landed on the edge of the same sand trap, took a friendly bounce and rolled to the middle of the green.

Paul snorted in disgust. 'Remember you're four to there... at least,' he said. His familiarity with the rules of golf was as vague as my own.

I shoved my club back into the bag and we set off down the fairway.

'By the way,' Paul said, 'I've got a nice wee cut-in for you. It's a bail undertaking on Monday.'

Whenever Paul or I had a case involving two accused, we shared them to avoid a conflict of interest. It wasn't a good idea to act for both in case the clients started pointing the finger at each other during the course of the trial.

'It's for those two boys who tried to break into the mausoleum, you know, over at Ecclesmachan. It was in the Gazette today.' Kaye must have gone ahead and published right enough. 'Violation of a sepulchre.'

'Not a crime you see in court every day,' I said.

'You're welcome,' Paul said, attempting to dislodge himself from the sand. On his third blow, the ball blasted from the sand, hurtled over the green without touching grass and ended up a pitching-wedge away in the rough.

The standard of play didn't improve greatly. We shook hands in the gloaming on the ninth green. As the scoring had been somewhat uncertain throughout, we decided to call it a halved game.

'I want to show you something,' I said to Paul, as we were changing out of our spikes.

'If that's not the most disconcerting thing to say to another man in the changing rooms, it's definitely in the top one,' Paul replied.

'Shut up and look at this.' I shoved my mobile phone under his nose. The display showed a picture I'd taken of the engagement ring I'd bought for Jill.

'Robbie, this is all so sudden—'

'Very funny. It's for Jill.'

'How long has it been?'

'Five, nearly six, months.'

'Fast worker. How old is she?'

'A year younger than me.'

'You know, she might just be desperate enough. Her biological clock will be boinging away like crazy. They could probably use it at the start of News at Ten. Have you two talked about having—'

'Just try and concentrate. The ring.' I pushed the image on the phone closer to his face. 'What do you think?'

'I think it's a stoater.'

'Really?'

'Really.'

'Not a mistake? Grace-Mary and Joanna seem to think that presenting Jill with it is arrogant.'

'Well...'

'You think it is too?'

'No...'

'Good.'

'Slightly desperate perhaps.'

'Desperate?'

'You know, please, please marry me - see I've bought you a lovely ring, desperate. You want to play it more cool. Women can sense desperation a mile off - it's very unattractive in a man.'

Who knew proposing was so difficult? 'When did men stop buying engagement rings?' I asked.

'They never started. You've watched too many old movies.'

'So what do I do with it?'

'Take it back to the shop. Let her pick one herself - *if* she says yes.' I didn't miss the slight emphasis he'd placed on the if. 'You know what women are like. It could be the Star of India and she wouldn't like it. They're never happy unless they're complaining about something.'

'I can't take it back. I got a special deal for cash.'

'Well,' Paul said, shoes laced and striding off to the clubhouse, 'you better hope Jill likes the desperate, arrogant type.'

There was no escaping Larry Kirkslap's case, not even at the nineteenth where the enormous TV in the corner of the room, that usually showed nothing but sports, was tuned into a news programme.

It seemed the jury had come back with a majority guilty verdict, but before the Advocate depute could move for sentence, defence counsel had advised the court that there was some doubt as to whether the jury had taken the oath, to *well and truly try the accused in accordance with the evidence.*

Andy took up the story from there during his interview with a BBC reporter. 'There was a lot of head-scratching as everyone tried to think back to the start of the trial. Then the jury was sent out, the recording of the first day's proceedings was played and sure enough: no oath.'

'So the error had gone unnoticed for twenty-one days? When was it you realised there might have been an oversight?' asked the man with the microphone.

Andy smiled. 'Day one.'

'Nice one, Andy,' I said, after they'd wrapped up and moved on to a story about salmon fisheries.

Paul put down his pint tumbler and winced. 'Ooh, not sure if he should have said that.'

'Why not? So, he kept it up his sleeve in case it came in useful, which, by the way, it did - big time.'

Paul disagreed. 'If he realised there was an error in the court procedures he should have mentioned it straight-away.'

I almost choked on my pint. Was Paul being serious? 'He's a defence lawyer. If I taught him one thing at Munro & Co., it's that you do your best for the client. There's enough people out to get an accused without his own lawyer joining in.'

'It doesn't matter what you think, Robbie. Andy's an officer of the court. The powers that be won't like this at all.'

'But his client will like it.' So far as I was concerned that was the main thing. 'And there's nothing anyone can do about that.'

Chapter **10**

'They sacked you?'

Andy was an early Monday morning visitor to Munro & Co. Joanna hadn't arrived at the office yet and Grace-Mary, who had put the kettle on for an emergency cup of tea, was now hovering in the background, a concerned expression on her face.

My former assistant, sitting opposite me, nodded. 'Gross misconduct, bringing the firm into disrepute.'

'By getting your client a great result?'

'Unprofessional, underhand and unbecoming an employee of Caldwell & Craig, is what Mrs Sinclair said.'

Maggie Sinclair, senior partner of Caldwell & Craig, lived by a strict set of business and moral rules that she applied whenever it suited her, and always to people other than herself. She was the one who'd persuaded the partners that crime didn't pay and been directly responsible for my departure, and, indirectly, for the setting up of Munro & Co.

'We're quite busy just now, aren't we, Robbie?' Grace-Mary said. 'We're bound to be able to give Andy something to do. Tide him over until he finds something else. Something better than here,' she added, unnecessarily I thought.

Was that why Andy was here? Looking for his old job back? I had to put a halt to such talk. Joanna was pulling her weight, but she still felt like a luxury I could ill afford. My work load didn't justify bringing on board another assistant. I had a note of Maggie Sinclair's direct-dial number and thus managed to circumvent Caldwell & Craig's tank-trap of a receptionist. 'What's wrong with you, Maggie? Are you crazy or something?'

'Perfectly sane, Robbie. Thanks for asking. Now what can I do for you?'

'Not for me: for Andy. How could you fire him, especially after he's secured such a famous victory?'

'It's precisely because of his, I'd call it, infamous victory, that his employment here has been terminated. When I took Andy on to deal with clients who'd fallen foul of the law, I was thinking of things like corporate manslaughter, fraud, insider-trading; normal, respectable crimes. Not murder. How he managed to persuade me to take on Larry Kirkslap's case—'

'Apart from the money?'

'...I'll never know,' she continued unfazed. 'But his indiscretion on prime time television was totally unacceptable. You must see that. Setting free a murderer, not letting the judge know he had made a mistake and being pleased about it afterwards? It's dishonourable.'

I didn't buy it. Give me a dishonourable victory over an honourable loss any day of the week.

'Larry Kirkslap's case is over...'

Now we were getting closer to the truth. Before the Kirkslap case came along, Andy had seen little or no action at C & C. The problem with rich clients was that they didn't get into trouble often enough. You needed regular bampots, a good turnover of proper criminals, if you were going to get anywhere in criminal law, but Legal Aid rates couldn't sustain a blue chip firm like Caldwell & Craig, whose hourly rate was greater than the five hundred pounds the Scottish Legal Aid Board deemed sufficient funding on which to defend an entire prosecution. That was the reason I'd been ousted and later replaced by a less expensive model in the shape of my former assistant. To Maggie's mind, now that Larry Kirkslap's case was over, and with no other high-earning criminal cases on the horizon, what was the point of keeping Andy on? Except that Maggie didn't seem to realise that the case was far from over.

'The case is over,' I agreed. 'For the time being, at any rate.'

'...and so is Andrew's career at Caldwell & Craig.' She paused. 'What do you mean, for the time being?'

'I mean there's bound to be a re-trial.'

Andy leaned forward, elbows on my desk. 'Do you think so?'

'What are you talking about?' Maggie demanded.

Did Maggie really think that the High Court of Justiciary would sit back and do nothing after one of its brethren had cocked-up so supremely? No chance. While it was the Clerk of Court's responsibility to administer the oath to the jury, the buck stopped at the person wearing the horse-hair wig and red jersey. The Appeal Court wouldn't let a little thing like a judicial oversight get in the way of a conviction. They'd rubber-stamp any Crown appeal and Larry Kirkslap would be back in the dock in no time at all.

'You really think there might be a retrial?' Maggie's coolish tone had warmed up somewhat, and I knew why. I put my hand over the mouthpiece and suggested that Andy and Grace-Mary go get a cup of tea. They left; Andy with his head held low.

'Are you still there Robbie? What do you mean a retrial? Kirkslap got off on a technicality. The court mucked the whole thing up. How can they have a retrial?'

For a moment there was silence as, from afar off, we both heard the ching-ching of the same cash register.

'Maybe...' Maggie's tone of voice lightened. 'Maybe for once, you're right, Robbie.' She laughed. 'Perhaps I have been too hasty—'

If Maggie was having second thoughts it had to be because she knew Kirkslap would follow Andy. Sure Caldwell & Craig could easily employ somebody else, but did they have time? Had Andy formed a strong relationship with the client? Why would the accused want to go to anyone other than the lawyer who had already had him acquitted?

43

'Well, if that's your final word on the matter, Maggie…' I said.

'Didn't you hear me, Robbie, I said—'

'Still, I know how precious the name of the Firm is to you, so I suppose Andy will just have to abide by your decision. He always did say you were a miserable old cow,' I added, burning any remaining bridges.

Grace-Mary and Andy returned clutching mugs of tea, my former assistant wearing a hesitant, but hopeful, expression.

I replaced the receiver. 'Sorry, Andy.'

'That's okay,' he said, with a helpless shrug. 'At least you tried.'

'So, what are your plans now?' Grace-Mary asked him.

'Dunno. I'll have to start looking around for another job. I can't set up on my own, I've not been qualified long enough.'

'You know, Andy,' I said. 'What Grace-Mary was saying earlier… there may be a way we could squeeze you in here, temporarily.'

Andy looked around the room, no doubt recalling the extravagant surroundings of his recently departed office at Caldwell & Craig. I should have taken up Grace-Mary's offer and had her brother-in-law give the place a freshen-up. Maybe even taken down some of the more stubborn Christmas decorations that remained sticky-taped to a corner of the ceiling. If only I could bring Andy on-board, with the fees from Larry Kirkslap's retrial I could practically gold-leaf the interior.

'It's kind of you, Robbie,' Andy said, 'but I think I'd rather stay in Glasgow, or even move through to Edinburgh. I thought you might ask around for me, see if anyone is hiring. I like Linlithgow but it's so— '

'What's it today?' Joanna demanded, striding into the room, slinging her bag from her shoulder and dropping it on my desk. 'Invisible dogs or erect penises?' She noticed Andy. 'Hello. What are you doing here?'

Andy swept a quiff of hair from his face and re-adjusted his designer frames. 'Hello, Joanna,' he said. 'I could ask you the same question.'

'I work here,' she replied, turning a suspicious eye on me. 'Don't I?'

'Sorry, Andy,' I said. 'Did I not mention that Joanna had joined us?'

'No... I don't think you did.' Andy smiled and took Joanna's outstretched hand in his. 'I miss all the gossip at court and I've been so busy with Larry Kirkslap's case.'

Joanna gave him a smile. 'Well done on that, by the way. Took some guts to say you'd spotted the mistake right at the beginning and not let on.'

Andy blushed.

I inhaled deeply. 'What *is* that you're wearing, Andy? Joanna, give us a woman's opinion.' I ignored Grace-Mary's throat clearing. 'What do you think of Andy's aftershave?'

'Aftershave?'

'Yeah, I think I might invest in some myself.'

I propelled her at Andy. She moved in close. A hand resting on his shoulder, she took a cautious little sniff. 'Er... very nice,' she said.

Andy was now bright red to the roots of his dark hair below which a thin film of sweat had begun to bead.

'What's it called?' I asked, as Joanna stepped away.

'Soap,' Andy said, voice husky, eyes still fixed on Joanna.

'They don't half think of the names these days, do they?' I said. 'Soap. Make a note of that will you, Grace-Mary? It's my birthday soon. Anyway, Joanna, Andy's here because I've offered him a job. He'd be helping you out with a few things. You'd both need to work closely as a team. Spend a lot of time together.'

Andy gulped.

'Unfortunately, Andy doesn't think it would work. He's a big city lawyer now and—'

'Hold on there, Robbie. I didn't say no. I am out of a job after all and... well... you know I have a great attachment to Linlithgow, to you and Grace-Mary.' With some difficulty Andy tore his gaze from Joanna's lovely form, walked over to the window and stared out at Linlithgow High Street. 'I'd love to come back and work here. It would be just like old times.'

I slapped him on the back. It would be just like the same old salary too.

Chapter **11**

'Nail-sick.' My dad stepped off the last rung of the ladder and wiped his hands on his trousers, leaving streaks of black on tan corduroy. 'Three hundred and sixty quid. That's how much I spent on a survey before I bought this place. No point taking any chances, I thought. I'm not going to trust the seller's home report, I'll have my own man take a look.' He kicked the ladders and the top rails slid along the guttering. 'He must have been blind. And you,' he jabbed a finger at me. 'If you were a real lawyer, doing proper legal work, you'd sue him for the cost of a new roof.'

I grabbed the ladders before they slid off the side of the building. 'Surveyors always have disclaimers on their reports,' I told him. 'It's those real lawyers who make them bullet-proof so that people like you can't sue them.'

I laid the ladders down along the gable end of the cottage and followed him inside to the kitchen.

'What are you going to do now?' he asked.

I wasn't planning on doing anything. I'd only come round after work to bring him his DIY materials and make sure he didn't take a header off the roof. Now that he'd realised his roof was going to need some professional attention and not just a roll of felt and a tin of sticky- black gloop, I could relax.

'Well?' My dad rummaged about in the cupboard under the sink.

'Well what? I'm a lawyer. Not a *real* one, I know, but, still, I don't fix roofs for a living.'

'I'm not talking about the roof. I'm talking about my birthday party. Where are you having it now? You can't have it here until I get the roof fixed, your flat's too wee and

47

goodness knows where Malky's staying these days. I've not heard from your brother in weeks.' He emerged from under the sink with a bottle of Oban. My dad's usual taste in whisky had temporarily migrated one hundred miles northeast from his beloved Islay. He took down a glass and poured himself a dram. 'A wee bit fiery at first, but it grows on you.' He put the cork back in the bottle. 'You're driving,' he said. 'The kettle's over there.'

There was a pile of unwashed dishes. I found a mug, rinsed it under the tap and was reaching for the kettle when my dad's phone rang. It was Jill. She'd been away nearly two weeks and I was missing her like crazy.

'How's it going?' I asked.

'Fine, apart from the fact that I still can't find my mobile. I've either lost it on the way over here or left it at home. I never realised how much I relied on it. I don't have anybody's number, just the one's I can remember. You haven't come across it while you've been watering the plants have you?'

I hadn't for reasons into which I thought it best not to delve too deeply. 'How are you coping with the language?'

'Okay, really. Everyone speaks German, though I can get by on English, or, if I have to, French. Josh has been a great help. He speaks, English, German, Italian, French and probably a few other languages. He's a downhiller racer. He nearly made it to the Winter Olympics once. As soon as I told him that I was a keen skier he was booking us in for a weekend at Zermatt.'

'Zermatt?'

'The resort on the glacier. There's snow up there all year round and Josh says—'

'Josh?'

A sigh that had started somewhere due north of the Alps, travelled a stretch of Western Europe and into my ear. 'Do you never listen to me? I told you about him. He's kind of like my guide while I'm here.'

Jill had said something about someone. As I recalled she'd referred to him as a human resources liaison officer, and I'd imagined a middle-aged guy in a lab-coat, ticking things off on a clipboard. There had been absolutely no mention of Olympian downhill-racers or trips to Alpine ski-resorts.

'Anyway, got to go. I'm using a borrowed phone and Josh and some of the gang have arranged a fondue night. Cheese and chocolate,' Jill giggled, 'not mixed together. Separate. You'd love it. Say hi to your dad for me and I'll give you a call in a couple of days.'

Please do, I thought, if it doesn't interrupt your skiing or ingestion of molten chocolate too much. Who was this guy, Josh? And how much was a flight to Switzerland?

'Jill doing fine is she?' my dad asked.

'She says hi.'

'What's with the face?'

'Nothing.' I splashed some fourteen-year-old single malt into the mug.

'Told you.' My dad took the mug from me and poured the contents into his glass. 'What's he called? Fritz? If it's Hans tell him to keep them to himself.' He laughed alone, collapsing into a coughing fit that could only be cured by another wee half. 'Germans. Troublemakers. Always have been.'

'He's Swiss—'

'Same thing,' said my dad, robbing Switzerland of a thousand years of history. 'Like nothing better than a good war.'

'...and Switzerland haven't been in a war since... ages.'

'They speak German and their banks are full of Nazi gold. Just because they're smart or cowards, or both, doesn't mean they're not troublemakers. Germans?' he snorted. 'They're as bad as the Irish. The Germans would start a fight in an empty house. Remember your great Uncle Pete?

49

Remember what they did to him when he was a POW in Burma?'

'That was the Japanese, Dad.'

'Huns, Nips, it's all the same. They fought on the same side.'

'He's called Josh, which is probably short for Joshua, so he could very well be Jewish.'

My dad helped himself to his third dram in a row. 'Sticking up for him now are you? I doubt if he'll need your help. If he's Jewish he could probably buy and sell the pair of us.'

'All I'm saying is that if he is a Jew, and he may not be, I don't think he'd appreciate being referred to as a Hun or a Nazi. And what have you suddenly got against Jews? Your pal, Ben, short for Benjamin, is one. Where did you think he got that nose?' I didn't want to discuss it any more. I put the cork back in the bottle and replaced it under the sink next to the bleach and a packet of yellow scouring-pads. My dad had always kept his whisky there. When we were boys, Malky and I had been banned from going anywhere near the cupboard under the sink because that's where the poison was kept.

But my dad wasn't quite finished; the big problem with the rest of the world being something of a specialist subject. 'Let's face it,' he said, raising his glass and studying the whisky as the light from the window caught the golden liquid. 'The Jews aren't exactly innocent, are they? Or the Arabs. I mean, when it comes to bother, there's no-one does it like the Middle-East. Yeah, sure, Europe flares up now and again, mainly, like I say, because of the Krauts, but it's all over in a few years and everyone's friends again until the next time. The Jews and Arabs have been at it for thousands of years. Someone's really needing to have a serious word.'

I wasn't sure why the United Nations bothered with the Road Map to Peace, when all they needed was ex-Sergeant

Alex Munro, the Palestinian and Israeli leaders, a truncheon and a police interview room.

'And Ben's all right. He's as Scottish as you or me.'

'So, it doesn't matter what race or religion a person is?' I said. 'Just so long as they're Scottish?'

'It's not like that. I've known Ben for years. We're playing dominos tomorrow night. Semi-final.'

And that, I supposed, was the nub of it. Race, nationality and religion weren't really the problem. It was the foreigners you didn't know that were the problem.

He ran hot water into the sink and added a squirt of washing-up liquid.

'You don't have to take off your watch,' I told him. It was an Omega Seamaster that Malky and I had bought him on his retirement. 'It's water-proof to six hundred metres.'

'Thanks for the advice, Jacques Cousteau. I'll wash, you dry, then you can give me a lift down the Red Corner. I'll need to find the name of someone to take a look at my roof.'

'You can get the bus or a taxi back here, then,' I said. 'I'm not hanging about the pub while you and your cronies talk about slates.'

'Away, it's not like I'm having a night on the tiles,' he said to his own great amusement. 'Give me your mobile and I'll call you at the house when I'm ready.' He flicked my legs with a tea towel. 'After all, it's not like you've got a date or anything.' He threw the towel in my face. 'Unlike your girlfriend.'

Chapter 12

In 1313, William Binnock of Ecclesmachan helped re-capture the then castle, not yet palace, of Linlithgow from the English. For his brave deeds, Robert the Bruce granted him lands to the east of the town that became known as the Binny Estate. It was upon this land that in 1872 a Mr Stewart, a naval captain, the latest in a line of feudal proprietors, had constructed a splendid mausoleum. Asked why he did so, when there was a Kirk churchyard nearby, he is said to have replied, *'in the great day of resurrection, I wish to rise from my own property.'*

Fast forward one hundred and fifty years or so and upon this ancient and long sealed resting place, under cover of darkness and armed with various house-breaking implements, descended Nathan and Danny Boyd, brothers from the nearby village of Philipstoun. By the sounds of things they weren't exactly Indiana Jones material. A farmer, noticing strange lights in the fields and suspecting badger-baiters, had summoned the police. The Boyd brothers were caught red-handed.

Paul Sharp was waiting for me in the cafe at Livingston Civic Centre, twelve noon on Tuesday. We walked together across the grey flagstone vestibule to the wooden benches where sat my soon-to-be client, Danny Boyd. Paul introduced us, and after a consultation with my new client, his mother hovering in the background, I swiftly gathered that the boy wasn't the brightest. At sixteen years of age, Danny was the younger of the brothers by two years and second-named accused on the summary complaint, a copy of which was later served on each of them by a police officer once we'd climbed the flight of stairs to the Sheriff Court. Paul and I had a brief discussion about the two boys in the corridor outside Courtroom 4.

'Nearest thing West Lothian has got to hillbillies,' he said. 'Someone else must have been using the Boyd brain cell that night. Both caught in the act, didn't ask for lawyers when interviewed and made extremely helpful comments to the police upon arrest.'

It looked like a straight guilty plea from both; however, where there are two accused, and to avoid a trial, the Procurator Fiscal would often take a guilty plea from one or other. In this case I thought we might persuade the PF to drop the charge against the younger of the two Boyd boys, if his brother pled.

Even though it would do me out of a fee, I made that suggestion to Hugh Ogilvie, the PF. He wasn't interested.

'I need both of them to plead,' he said. 'That pair are lucky not to be on petition. Violation of a sepulchre? They used to hang you for that.'

But the shadow of the noose would not pass over either boy: not even shades of the prison house. Neither accused had a prior conviction, and so an order to perform unpaid work in the community seemed a certainty.

I took young Danny's details and had him sign a legal aid form. Danny was a school-leaver, though, strictly speaking, you had to have gone to school in the first place before you could officially leave. Sixteen and unemployed, he had no income, capital or educational qualifications. His father was dead and the family income was derived from a small-holding that he and Nathan helped their mother to run, producing organic vegetables, eggs, home-baking and preserves for onward sale to local farm shops and garden centres. Though Danny was financially eligible for legal aid, I knew I'd still have a fight with the Scottish Legal Aid Board because there was no likelihood of loss of liberty or livelihood; the two main criteria that SLAB used to determine whether it was in the interests of justice to provide legal representation via the public purse. It wasn't uncommon to do the work and only later have SLAB tell you that you weren't being paid for it. Better to plead not guilty and put the case off for a while. That way I could at least know if legal aid was going to be granted before I did the work, and, anyway, there was still a good chance that on a later date another, more reasonable, PF would accept Danny's not guilty plea.

Sheriff Lawrence Dalrymple read the complaint, took the pleas of not guilty and studied the two lads in the dock over his half-moons. 'We'll fix an early trial diet in view of the age of your client, Mr Munro. They can both be bailed, standard conditions.' Much to the dismay of the reporters, the court appearance was over in a minute or two and the wheels of justice turned in the direction of a boring-old drink-driver.

Kaye Mitchell was waiting for me back at my office. 'What a waste of time,' she said. 'How am I supposed to turn that into a story? Nothing happened!'

She would just have to wait for the trial. Reporters hated that because a trial held the possibility of a not guilty verdict and an acquittal wasn't really much of a story. My phone rang. Grace-Mary patched Malky through to me.

'What kind of whisky are you getting Dad for his birthday?' he asked. 'Last time I saw him he was banging on about Springbank eighteen-year-old being the greatest dram ever. Do you know how much it is for a bottle? Eighty quid!' he said, before I could hazard a guess. 'You could buy a house in Campbeltown for eighty quid. I was thinking we could go half—'

'He doesn't want whisky, this year.' The phone went dead. 'Did you hear me?'

'No, it sounded like you said he didn't want whisky this year.'

'He wants a birthday party, but it's to be a surprise.'

'And who's going to organise that?'

'You are,' I said. 'I'm snowed under at work just now.'

'What about me?'

'What about you?'

'You think you're the only one who's snowed under?'

Besides letting a Sunday newspaper use his by-line for a ghost-written sports column, Malky's worked involved chuntering on about football on a local radio phone-in for one hour, three nights a week. Occupationally, we weren't talking avalanche-warning.

'Come on, Malky. It'll be easier if you organise it,' I said. 'Seeing how there's a hole in Dad's roof and we're going to have to hold it at your place. Where is your place, by the way?'

'I'm sort of between places. I'm staying with Jorge Kleinman just now.'

'The one who played with you at Rangers?' Jorge Kleinman had been the subject of more transfers than an Airfix Spitfire. He had to be loaded. His flat was probably the size of Ibrox Park, just with less of a mortgage.

'How many Jorge Kleinmans do you know? Of course it's that Jorge Kleinman.'

'Good, because Dad was hoping some of your football chums would turn up. If we have it at Jorge's place, it'll kill two birds with one stone. See if you can dig up some more has-beens.'

'Least I never wuz a never-wuzzer,' he said.

'Whatever. Just remember: even although you and Jorge will be there, that won't be enough balloons.'

Chapter 13

Gleann Iucha. The people of Linlithgow didn't speak Gaelic. It was unlikely they ever had, even back in the day when a young Mary Queen of Scots was toddling about up at the Palace. Those folk from much further north and west who did speak Gaelic also spoke English; however, in case there was someone - a hermit living in a cave on a Western Isle, perhaps - who spoke only Gaelic, and, just in case that person ever decided to holiday on the mainland, the Scottish Government had kindly arranged for all Scotland's railway stations to display the name of each town or city in both languages. To those at Holyrood, a lost teuchter on the Scotrail line was an unthinkable proposition.

'You'll like Mike,' Andy said, as, Wednesday afternoon, we stood on the Glasgow bound platform, me pondering the Gaelic signage and the size of my recently received Council Tax bill, my assistant staring down the track towards Edinburgh. 'He's a good guy. Specialises in intellectual property rights and was in right at the beginning of P45 Apps along with Larry and Zack.

I didn't know who Zack was, but you didn't need to own a smart phone or tablet to know that Larry Kirkslap was CEO of P45 Apps Ltd, a controversial games company that had taken the mobile world by storm. Kirkslap had been a male model in his teens and early twenties. He'd modelled designer wear, advertised male-fragrances, even had a nearly-hit single, and then the eighties came along; he'd been forced to find real jobs. Kirkslap had used his undoubted charms to sell high performance cars, double-glazing, insurance, toiletries, machine parts, vacuum cleaners, the list went on and on, the quality of product, along with his public profile, down and down. Then came 2008; the credit-crunch. For the first time in forty years Larry found himself unemployed.

'So he invented the P45 games suite,' Andy said.

Unlike millions of others, I was yet to become addicted to the P45 craze. Put simply, which wasn't hard to do, they were a series of basic parlour games, no doubt dredged up from Kirkslap's childhood, adapted for mobile equipment and used to play friends or random individuals for money; the loser paying via extra charges on his or her phone bill. It was basic, puerile and highly addictive. A good player could end up in credit and run his phone for free or upgrade to better equipment. Some made fortunes. Others lost fortunes. The players decided the stakes in advance and from each game P45 took a cut. Kirkslap's company also received commission from the mobile phone companies who benefitted from the extra phone usage.

'He invented a multi-million pound series of apps just like that?'

'More or less.' Andy enlightened me further. 'The games were Larry's idea, his business partner, Zack Swarovski, was the software engineer who redesigned them. The beauty of the games is that they cost very little to play, but are played by a great many people. And it's not like pitting your wits and life-savings against a computer programme pretending to be another on-line poker player. You are playing against actual people and the games are ones everybody can play. Your granny has as much chance of winning as you have. They're cheap, cheerful and fun.'

It sounded too easy to me. Why hadn't somebody else done it? Gambling on kids' games could hardly be copyrightable. Then again, what I didn't know about intellectual property rights you could have written on the back of a cinema screen.

'P45's success is mainly down to Zack's designs, but also partly due to Mike Summers.'

'Mike's the guy we're meeting?'

'Yeah, he's the company secretary. He was an assistant with the law firm that Larry and Zack first consulted. Now he works for P45 full-time, handling all the company's legal issues. I'd hate to think what they're paying him, but whatever it is, it's got to be worth it. Mike not only carried out the incorporation of P45, he established the intellectual property rights and negotiated tie-ins with the mobile phone companies and, most recently, a lot of major social networking sites. Once the big guns were on-board, things took off globally. At the last count, the company had twenty million customers, here and in the States. Once it rolls out in the Far-East, who knows where it will go? Zack heads a team of app-designers working on add-ons and updates round the clock. With Larry fronting the show and Zack the IT brains, it's a great team.'

The platform trembled as the three o'clock pulled into Gleann Iucha.

'This Mike, you say all he's looking for today is some advice as to whether there will be a re-trial?'

Andy nodded. 'Yeah, I've already told him the Crown will at least try to have the case re-raised and he wants to know what's going to be involved: costs, timescales, etcetera. I know and you know that a Crown appeal could run on for longer than the trial did.'

'If there is an appeal.'

'Why wouldn't there be? My big worry is how Mike is going to take the news that I'm no longer with Caldwell & Craig.'

'So long as he knows you're the reason his boss is walking around in a three-piece suit and not stripy pyjamas.'

'He knows all right. He also knows that I lost the case and that Larry's liberty is all down to a stroke of good fortune. He's not daft and he's only giving us half an hour. We need to treat this as an audition.'

The train slowed to a halt, doors opened and passengers alighted, pushing by us until there was only one man left standing on the platform. Mid to late forties, I guessed, he was tall, muscular and carrying an iPad in a black leather case.

'Mike. Good to see you again,' Andy said as we approached. 'This is Mr Munro, I mentioned him to you on the phone.'

'Robbie,' I put out a hand.

Mike hesitated. Peered at me. 'Robbie Munro?'

'Yes,' I said. It was my turn to be hesitant.

'It's me, Mike.'

He who was known as Mike, grabbed my hand and shook it violently. He pressed the iPad case to his chest. 'Mike, Mike Summers. Okay, I've lost some hair, put on a few pounds, but...' he patted my stomach and laughed, 'I see you've been eating well yourself.'

I almost laughed too.

'We were at Uni together,' Mike said.

I really wanted to remember him.

'We were in the same conveyancing tutorial class for the Diploma.'

I cast my mind back fifteen or so years. For me, the required attendance at conveyancing tutorials had tended to be more of a theoretical proposition than a practical outcome.

'I used to give you my notes,' he added, although I was still coming to grips with the *we were at Uni together* part. If that was correct, then this Mike guy had to have been a mature student, because he had to be ten years older than me. His beaming smile began to dim and I sensed Andy's laser-like stare boring into the side of my head. The audition wasn't going too well, and we hadn't passed the introductions stage yet. I reassembled my facial features to suggest slow-dawning recognition.

'And you used to complain about my handwriting,' he said, encouraging my thought process. 'I think you still have one of my conveyancing folders. You borrowed it for the re-sit.'

I'd always thought there was something slightly creepy about mature students. Maybe creepy wasn't the right word, but there was something unfair about them competing for qualifications with a bunch of teenagers let loose from home for the first time, and for whom studies were the least important aspect of their University life. Still, the old guys always took the best lecture notes, and I did vaguely recall a red ring-binder of conveyancing materials that I had memorised, regurgitated and spent the rest of my legal career trying to forget.

'Mike!' I said, having given up on remembering who he was. 'Great to see you.' We shook hands again. He had a firm grip. 'I'll not ask how's business.' I rubbed the lapel of his suit between a thumb and forefinger.

He shrugged modestly. 'I've just been reading about your smoking jury case.'

I was unaware that my victory had made any of the newspapers given the coverage the collapse of Larry Kirkslap's trial had received. 'It was nothing,' I said, truthfully, whilst failing to sound modest.

He opened the leather case, and with a few swishes of his fingers brought up an article on his iPad, using the METRO app. Who needed an electronic device to read a free newspaper?

'Trust you.' Mike held the iPad, facing me. *No Smoke Without Trial*, was the rather confusing headline, but at least I'd received a decent name-check. 'Still up to all the dodges, eh? Just like Andy, here.'

'To know the dodges, you have to know the law,' Andy piped up. 'I've joined Robbie at Munro & Co. As you can see, Robbie and I know what's required to secure an acquittal even when things look hopeless.'

Mike closed his iPad, looked at his chunky wristwatch. 'I'm afraid I've not got much time. I'm meeting Larry in

Glasgow in an hour. He's taken a suite at Carnbooth House. I'll have to leap on the next train that comes in.'

That gave us about twenty minutes.

'No time to go to our offices, then,' Andy said, sounding relieved.

'No, let's walk and talk.' Mike marched off towards the stairs leading to ground level, and we hurried after him down Station Brae to the High Street, taking a right turn past the Star & Garter Inn, built 1759, gutted by fire 2010, restored 2013. The pavement was narrow. Andy manoeuvred himself so that he was side by side with Mike, while I tagged along at the rear. 'As you know, the reason I'm here is to ask if you think there will be a retrial.'

Andy shook his head. 'Difficult to say. What is certain is that the Crown won't just let it go. They're bound to lodge a bill of advocation. We'll have to lodge a challenge, instruct a top appeal Q.C. —'

'But would such a challenge be successful?' I detected a note of impatience in Mike's voice. 'If not, I don't see the point in dragging things out and racking up lots of legal costs.'

I wasn't sure if Kirkslap would necessarily view things the same way. Dragging things out might seem like a great idea to him. Certainly the racking up of legal fees part appealed to me, but Munro & Co. had yet to be given the nod.

'What about you, Robbie? Do you think the Crown would win an appeal?' Mike broke his stride, letting Andy walk on and leaving me shoulder to shoulder with my old University chum.

'The Crown doesn't need to appeal. Kirkslap wasn't acquitted. The trial judge had to reject the guilty verdict, but the case was deserted pro loco et tempore, not simpliciter. The Crown will regroup and slap a new indictment on him any day now. That's what I think.'

Andy looked slightly miffed when my opinion did not concur with his own.

'Will the Crown be allowed another bite at the cherry?' Mike asked.

By this time we had reached the traffic lights at the railway bridge. 'Why not?' I said. 'The problem with the trial wasn't the fault of the prosecution. The Crown prosecutes in the public interest, and it's hardly in the interest of the public for a murderer to go free just because fifteen jurors weren't made to promise to do their jobs properly.'

'Can't we argue double-jeopardy?' Mike asked. 'Say that Larry's tholed his assize?'

Unlike my conveyancing knowledge, years of intellectual property rights law had obviously not completely erased my old Uni-chum's memory of criminal procedure, but, unfortunately, that's what Scottish criminal procedure was now: a memory. Once upon a time, due process was jealously guarded by the judiciary. A prosecution had to be done properly or the accused got the benefit. Those days were long gone. Section 300A of the Criminal Procedure (Scotland) Act 1995 allowed the remedy of just about any procedural irregularity. You could have powered Parliament House if only there had been some way to rig up an electrical turbine to the judges of yesteryear who were spinning in their graves.

'Does that go for your smoking jury client too?' Mike asked.

I didn't think the Crown would bother to appeal that. Deek Pudney had only beat up a cop. He hadn't killed a young woman and dumped her body in the woods.

Our small party proceeded on its circular route, under the railway bridge, up the hill and into the car park at the rear of the railway station. We talked some more until the train was due, Andy and I trying to sell Munro & Co., Mike holding his cards as close as the leather encased iPad he kept clamped to his chest.

'Do you two actually think you could handle a retrial?' Mike said, when we were back on the Glasgow bound platform again.

'Definitely,' Andy said.

The rails began to hum as the three–thirty rolled into town.

'Without the experience, support and resources of Caldwell and Craig behind you?'

I had a feeling the case was slipping away, and that our sales pitch had been a waste of time. 'We both used to work at Caldwell & Craig. When it comes to crime,' I jerked a thumb at Andy and them myself, 'we *are* the experience of Caldwell & Craig. We have an ex-PF providing support and Larry Kirkslap's financial resources are all the resources that we're going to need. This time around we'll know exactly what the Crown case will be. We can study the first trial, discover where the Crown landed its biggest hits and dodge them in the re-match.'

'And the result?'

The train slowed to a halt.

'Who can tell? It sounds like it was a strong Crown case, but with me, Andy and —'

'Robbie, it's been great seeing you again. Andy, thanks for everything.' Mike shook hands with each of us in turn. 'No disrespect.' He looked around the small railway station, mid-way between Scotland's two main cities, where only every second train felt the need to stop. 'But I think Larry's interests would be best served by a larger legal outfit handling the case.' The train doors parted. Mike stepped between them and onto the train. With a farewell wave of his iPad he was gone.

'That's that then,' Andy said, as we trudged back down the stairs from the station.

And it very nearly was.

I'd given my dad a loan of my phone on Monday evening and he hadn't given it back to me yet. Andy let me borrow his. I punched in 141, then the number.

'And do you know who has stolen your iPad, Sheriff?' asked the British Transport Police receptionist at Queen Street Station, once the main switchboard had patched me through.

'Robbie, stop it,' Andy hissed in my ear. 'You're going to get us both the jail.'

My finest Albert Brechin impersonation didn't provide a name, just an highly accurate description of Mike Summers.

'He's on the three-thirty from Linlithgow,' I said, trying to keep Andy from yanking his phone out of my hand. 'If you hold onto him, I can be there inside an hour to identify my property.'

'Robbie!' Andy realised that the ticket-seller was giving us funny looks. He pulled me outside. 'I'm having no part of this. A false report to the police—'

'That's right,' I said, 'to buy us some time. Do you want this case or not?'

'Not if it means breaking the law.'

'Not breaking—'

'Wasting the time of the police, malicious mischief, attempting to pervert—'

'Okay, okay,' I said cutting short the list of crimes before we got to high treason, 'we're bending it a little, but all in the interests of justice.' Had the boy learned nothing during his time with me?

'This is not about what's in the interests of justice. This is about what's in the interests of Robbie Munro.'

I'd always had difficulty distinguishing between the two, but now was not the time for a jurisprudential discussion. 'Are you coming or not? We'll need to run. My car is parked back at the office.'

I had trotted a few paces before noticing that Andy was still at the entrance door to the station. I jogged back.

'It's no good, Robbie,' he said. 'I should have known it would be like this. I can't work this way. Let Kirkslap go where he wants. He's stuffed anyway. Someone else can get him a life sentence. At least I'll be known as the lawyer who got him off.' He glanced up at the timetable on the wall. 'Thanks for the job offer, but I'm hot property just now. I think I'll catch the next train back to Glasgow and see if anyone is hiring.' He laughed. 'Before I start to cool down.' He stuck out a hand. 'Sorry to disappoint you, Robbie, but it's for the best. You know that. I've got my career to think about, and it's just not going to happen here. Say bye to Grace-Mary for me. Who knows? Maybe I'll catch up with you and Joanna in court one of these days.'

I didn't know what to say. We shook hands. Andy re-entered the foyer and set off for the west bound platform.

As soon as he was out of sight, I was off and running.

Chapter 14

Ask any respectable, law-abiding Sat Nav and it would tell you that, thanks to the new-improved M74, the journey time from Linlithgow to Carmunnock was around forty-five minutes. And it probably was, if your assistant could work the Sat Nav app on her shiny new mobile phone, and you were not relying on a vague notion of where you were going and the Robbie Munro unerring sense of direction.

'You're not Andy,' Larry Kirkslap said, when, the eagle having eventually landed, he met Joanna and me in the opulent lobby of Carnbooth House Hotel. 'I was told my lawyer was here.' Kirkslap pointed a thick finger in my face. 'If you're from the Sun, I'm going to —'

'We're your new lawyers,' Joanna said.

Kirkslap lowered his hand, checked a chunky gold wristwatch. 'Are you with Mike?'

'Sort of,' I said. 'I'm Robbie Munro, and this is my colleague, Miss Jordan.'

I'd seen Larry Kirkslap on the telly many times; most recently during his month long trial. There was usually a video-clip on the news of him entering or leaving the High Court. I'd formed the impression that he was a great big tall man. He wasn't. He couldn't have been over five foot six in height, and yet his presence, call it charisma, was, like his bulk, immense. He shook my hand, took Joanna's and kissed it.

Once my assistant had extracted herself from his grip, Kirkslap swept a quiff of hair back across his head. Hair that was thick, expensively styled and... well, kind of orange. Kind of, because it wasn't a colour with which I or, I felt certain, Mother Nature was entirely familiar.

He must have noticed our stares. 'Don't,' he laughed. 'Supposed to be Autumn Hue, more like Iron Brew, eh?'

Kirkslap looped a long arm around Joanna's shoulders and led her, me following, from the lobby and into the cocktail bar. Short, stocky, plenty of orange hair: if they ever remade the stage musical of Disney's Jungle Book, the man was a shoo-in for the roll of King Louie. I liked him. I also liked his taste in women, for reclining on a huge cream settee in front of the magnificent fireplace, was an extremely attractive auburn-haired young lady, patiently awaiting Kirkslap's return with only a chilled bottle of Veuve Cliquot and a bowl of strawberries to keep her company.

'Now I don't want you looking at me,' Kirkslap said, and still on the subject of his hair, 'and thinking that I'm some sort of queer. There's a lot of them about these days. Brokeback Mountain. Put me right off Westerns that did.' The man was a walking breach of the peace. He put on a fake American accent. 'If I end up with a sore ass I want it to be from my hand-tooled, sliver-trimmed Mexican saddle and not from some sexually confused cowboy.'

I smiled professionally. Joanna licked a finger and wipe an imaginary stain from the sleeve of her jacket. Kirkslap made a woeful attempt at a serious expression, holding his hands up in mock surrender. 'Not that I have a bad word to say about the gays,' he said. 'Oh, no. In fact, lesbians star in some of my favourite movies. Them and custard.' He lowered his broad frame down onto the couch and patted the cushion. Joanna joined him, while I pulled up a leather armchair opposite. 'The hair was all Candy's idea. Part of my make-over.' He slapped a hairy hand on the thigh of the red-head and gave it a squeeze. She giggled, lifted a champagne flute to her lips and let a strawberry tumble out into her mouth. Kirkslap looked at Joanna and me in turn. 'Now what are you two having?' he asked, extending an arm towards the bar and a barman who was standing between two immense carved-wood, barley-twists either side of a fine array of single malts. Yes, it was only the back of five and I had an important meeting ahead of me, but was it ever the wrong time for an eighteen-year-old Bowmore? Joanna could always drop me off at the train station.

'I'm afraid this isn't a social visit, Mr Kirkslap,' Joanna said. 'We've got something very important we need to talk to you about.' She glanced meaningfully at Kirkslap's attractive companion. 'In private.'

I was about to explain that while those matters to which my assistant referred were indeed important, they could, nonetheless, be discussed over a glass of something peaty and old enough to vote, when Mike strode into the bar looking a tad flustered. He was clutching his iPad and towing a blonde-haired man behind him.

'Looks like the gang's all here,' Kirkslap said. He tapped one of Candy's shapely legs, and, taking the hint and the bottle of champagne, she got up and moved over to a table at the curved-glass bay window, overlooking the grounds. 'Mike, Mr Munro, I think you two know each other—'

'Oh, I know Mr Munro all right,' Mike said.

'What about you, Zack?' Kirkslap said. 'Zack Swarovski meet Robbie Munro and Miss...?'

'Joanna,' said my assistant. 'Joanna Jordan.'

I offered my hand to the blonde-haired man. 'Swarovski? Like the fake diamonds?'

'No - like the crystals,' he said. I could tell he was one unhappy American.

'Do I have you to thank for my little hold-up at Queen Street station?' Mike asked, quick on the uptake.

I had the sudden urge to stare up at the ornate cornicing and start whistling. I remained impassive.

'Do you know I was detained for nearly an hour?' he said.

Joanna came to the rescue. 'We thought we'd come through and tell Mr Kirkslap our thoughts on how to tackle the retrial.'

'Retrial?' Kirkslap spluttered. His early good humour evaporated and his complexion rose to that of the strawberry on which he was almost choking. 'What retrial?'

I gave him the Reader's Digest version of the earlier conversation with Mike at Linlithgow railway station.

Kirkslap spat the half-chewed strawberry into the soggy paper napkin that had been wrapped around the neck of the champagne bottle to catch drops of condensation. 'When's all this going to happen?'

'Soon,' I said, 'and the sooner you put a new defence team together...' I pointed at Joanna and then myself, in case he required clarification, 'the better. The mix-up with the jury and the oath gave you a second chance, nothing more. Don't forget they found you guilty. Unless someone can do better next time, your champagne and strawberry days are over.'

'And that's why you're here? You think you can do better than my present lawyer?'

'You don't have a present lawyer. Andy Imray's been sacked from Caldwell & Craig,' I said. 'He was their criminal defence department, now he's just another lawyer looking for a job.'

Mike pitched in. 'Mr Munro is a sole practitioner. We need a big city firm. We should stick with Caldwell & Craig.'

Kirkslap didn't take his eye off me. 'What do you think Zack?'

'I think Mike's got it right on this one,' he said.

Kirkslap shrugged. 'There's your answer, Mr Munro.'

'Caldwell & Craig?' I scoffed. 'with Andy away, they'll just delegate the case to some other minion. You had them act for you the last time, but in actual fact it was only one man: Andy Imray, a newly-qualified lawyer and a newly-qualified lawyer working in a big city firm is still just a newly-qualified lawyer. You need more experience on your side.'

'And you have that?' said the blonde-haired man.

'In spades.' It was an expression I knew Americans used a lot, or did in the movies. 'And I won't be working alone.

Joanna's an ex-Procurator Fiscal-depute. We can come at this case from all angles. Two heads and all that. We can go one better than the last time.'

'I didn't do so badly,' Kirkslap said. 'I mean – here I am.'

'The only reason you're not behind bars right now is because of a technicality.'

'A technicality that was exploited by a newly-qualified lawyer. The one from that big city firm.' Zack the blonde haired man pointed out.

'Yeah, and that newly-qualified lawyer learned everything he knows from me.' I turned to Mike. 'Show them.'

'Show them what?' Mike asked.

'That thing on your iPad. The newspaper report.'

Mike rolled his eyes, opened the app and flicked to the smoking jury report.

I took the tablet from him and handed it to Zack. He read the few column centimetres, shrugged non-commitally and handed the device to Kirkslap.

I pressed on, while he read, a smile growing on his face. 'I also have access to Scotland's finest Q.C.'

'And that would be?' Mike asked.

Fiona Faye was my first choice for senior in any High Court trial. Big, blonde and brassy, she had the knack of getting alongside the women jurors, and as for the men, they just wanted to lie down and have their tummies tickled by her. Fiona was a pussycat with the jury, but could rip into a careless witness like a sabre-tooth tiger. She was just the woman for this job.

'We already tried to instruct Fiona Faye,' Mike said. 'She wasn't available. Her clerk said she was 'clearing her feet,' whatever that means.' There must have been some serious feet-clearing going on for Fiona to have turned down such a high-profile and highly remunerative case. 'Miss Faye's clerk suggested Mr Staedtler and, fortunately, he was available.'

I had no doubt. The one thing you could rely on with Nigel Staedtler was his availability. It was his chief attribute. Rule one when instructing counsel: be wary of the constantly available. Rule two: never listen to the recommendation of an advocate's clerk. They punted those least instructed, and those least instructed were least instructed for a reason. Take, for example, Nigel Staedtler Q.C.; living proof that while ignorance of the law was no excuse, it wasn't necessarily an obstacle to a legal career. Staedtler's elevated position at the Bar had more to do with family and educational ties than ability. There were Silks and High Court judges swinging from every branch of the Staedtler family tree, and his educational tie bore the blue and white stripes of Edinburgh Academy.

'Then, my next choice would be Cameron Crowe,' I said, almost choking on the words. Relations between Crowe and me were usually in a state of flux, ranging somewhere between not very good and open warfare. After several years as a prosecutor, Crowe was once more back in the realms of the righteous, though yet to be raised to the rank of Queens Counsel; something that puzzled him more than it did others.

'The important thing is - is he any good?' Kirkslap asked.

'If you mean is he ten times better than Nigel Staedtler Q.C. who's currently instructed? Yes, he is good.' I could also have added that Cameron Crowe was obnoxious, self-important and, on occasion, downright malevolent, in fact, just the man to have on your side in a courtroom battle. 'If you're looking for someone to rip a highly circumstantial prosecution case to shreds, which you should be, Cameron Crowe is guaranteed to put the fear of death into any forensic scientist the Crown can throw at you.'

Kirkslap turned his gaze from me to his two colleagues.

Mike shrugged. 'It's your call, Larry.'

'I still don't like it,' Zack said.

Kirkslap stood. He took Joanna's hand and kissed it again.

'What are you going to do?' Zack asked. 'This is not just about you, Larry. There's the company to think about.'

Kirkslap waved to Candy, who tottered over on high heels. 'I'll make a decision in the morning,' he said, placing an arm around her waist. 'Until then - let me sleep on it.'

Chapter 15

'I hope I'm not disturbing anything.'

Thursday. Mid-afternoon. Joanna was sitting at Andy's old desk in reception, flicking through Danny Boyd's case file. I was standing beside her, hands planted on the desk, leaning over her shoulder and reading the disclosure statements that Grace-Mary had downloaded earlier from the Crown web-site.

I stood up straight and took a quick step back as Kaye Mitchell strolled in, fanning herself with a mobile phone. 'Jill sent me a picture this morning. Thought you might like to see it.'

She handed me the phone. On the screen was a photo of Jill in ski-gear, standing on a snowy mountain side. An equally ski-clad man stood at her side, one arm around my girlfriend's waist, the other brandishing a pair of ski-poles and looking pretty pleased about things in a devilishly handsome kind of a way. I had a horrible, queasy feeling in the pit of my stomach.

'This Josh seems to be a terrific sport,' Kaye said. 'I'll print that off for you, if you like. You can put it in a frame on your desk or something. I take it you still have a desk, and you two haven't decided to share?'

Joanna took the phone from my hand. 'They look very... cosy. Are you sure you're still going to —'

'So, Kaye.' I said, rallying from her exciting news about my girlfriend's dalliance with a handsome Swiss man on the side of an Alp. 'To what do we owe the pleasure of your company?'

But her reporter's instinct was not going to be so easily side-tracked. *'Are you sure you're still going to* what, Robbie?'

'Plead guilty,' Joanna blurted. She held up Danny Boyd's file. 'The evidence in the tomb raiders' case has just come in.'

Kaye raised an eyebrow. 'And?'

'And... well... it looks like the prosecution case isn't quite as strong as we'd expected.'

'Really?' The note of suspicion hadn't completely left Kaye's voice.

'That's right.' I took up from where my assistant left off. 'They've been charged with violating a sepulchre, but this is more like a fifty-two or a malicious mischief.'

'A fifty-two what?' Kaye enquired.

'A section fifty-two. Of the Criminal Law (Consolidation) (Scotland) Act nineteen ninety-five,' Joanna replied.

'Vandalism to you,' I said.

'Vandalism? How can it go from that sepulchre thing to vandalism?' Kaye wanted to know. 'I mean it's not complicated. A mausoleum is just another word for a sepulchre and they damaged it. What's not violation of a sepulchre about that? Seems simple enough to me.'

But it wasn't simple, and there was a century's worth of case law to show just how not simple it was. 'The thing is, Kaye, there is no property in a dead body in Scots law. So to stop people grave-robbing and meddling with corpses the common law of violation of sepulchres was introduced yonks ago.'

'And?' Kaye enquired.

Joanna picked up the threads. 'To be guilty you don't just have to damage the grave, you have to tamper with the body in some way. That's what Robbie and I were discussing. According to the evidence, the two Boyd boys damaged the mausoleum door and that's about all. Unless the Fiscal decides to amend to a much lesser offence, it looks like a not guilty on the charge as it stands.'

Kaye didn't look too pleased. 'So, Linlithgow's Burke and Hare...?'

'Sorry,' I said. 'You'll just have to do what you usually do on a slow news week, and slap something about the Gala Day Queen on the front page.'

Grace-Mary had gone out just after lunch to do the banking and, multi-tasker that she was, had taken the opportunity to do her weekly shop at the same time. 'You've a visitor,' she said to me, staggering in, laden down with carrier bags.

My brother strode into the now over-crowded reception, clamped a hand either side of my face and kissed the top of my head. 'Congratulations.'

'How—?'

'Dad phoned me. I'm on my way to show him my new car. Listen, don't muck about. You've made your mind up, just go for it or you'll get cold feet.' He looked out of the window. 'I was thinking you should have a Spring wedding. The weather's usually the best then. You know what Scottish summers are like. My producer knows a guy who can fix you up with a marquee. All you need after that is an outside licence, a buffet, some of those cocktail guys that throw the bottles around and a band. Whatever you do, don't let Dad talk you into booking the Red River—'

'You're getting married?' Kaye's steel-trap of a brain had sprung. 'Does Jill know?' She glanced down at the phone lying on Joanna's desk and then up at Joanna. 'I warned her about you hiring this floozy.'

Joanna folded her arms, lowered her eyebrows and gave Kaye the stare that had caused grown men to burst into tears in the witness box. The newspaper editor was impervious. You didn't work your way to the top in journalism without a certain thickening of the epidermis.

I pushed my way through the crowd in reception, went to my room and returned with the small velvet box. I opened it revealing the diamond ring. 'I'm marrying... that is, I'm hoping to marry Jill. I'm going to propose when she gets back from Switzerland, and I really don't want her to hear about it before I get down on bended knee. Understand?'

Kaye put thumb and forefinger to her pursed lips, twisted her hand and tossed an imaginary key over her shoulder.

Malky had noticed the photo on the phone. 'Who's this?' he asked.

'Josh,' I said. 'Jill's liaison officer, slash ski-instructor, slash fondue chef.'

'He's a bit gorgeous, isn't he?' Joanna said.

Malky looked closer. 'He's good looking enough, I suppose.'

'Good looking?' Kaye bared her teeth and growled. 'I could take a bite right out of him.'

'Yeah, well, looks aren't everything.' It wasn't every day my brother stuck up for me. 'Robbie has other attributes.' He didn't detail them. 'And he's got his own business.' He looked around the scene of clerical devastation that was the working hub of Munro & Co.

'Josh is vice-President of a multi-national pharmaceutical company,' Kaye added. 'He just missed out on the Swiss squad for the Winter Olympics in two thousand and two.'

Malky set the phone down onto the desk. There was only so much sticking-up a brother could do. 'You know, Robbie...?' He clamped a hand down on my shoulder. 'Maybe you shouldn't book that Marquee just yet.'

Chapter 16

Dubh Prais: a small basement restaurant on the Royal Mile, a cheese scone's throw from the Tron Kirk, just off South Bridge. I ordered the hand-dived scallops on a pea puree with coral jus for a starter. My companion, Larry Kirkslap, opted for pan-fried haggis with a leek and whisky sauce. I noticed his hair was darker today, a more standard ginger, but still much too vivid for a man of his age.

'Okay, here goes,' he said, cutlery poised. I could tell that while he might have been a sex symbol in the seventies, he'd had far too much to eat in the eighties. 'I've never had haggis before. I'm usually prawn cocktail, steak and chips, apple pie and custard.'

I wondered if the thought of life in jail had concentrated Kirkslap's mind and that's why he wanted to try new things. Not that they didn't serve haggis in prison, but if you're going to experiment with offal, HMP Shotts probably wasn't the best place to start. 'I'm a Scotsman who's never tried his national dish. Can you believe it?' Kirkslap leaned back in his chair to let the waiter once more fill his enormous wine glass with Chablis. The starters had just arrived. I'd not touched my glass. This was his second.

'Can I take it you've reached a decision on your choice of legal representation?' I said. When Grace-Mary had told me about the lunch reservation, I'd expected there might have been a message too. There hadn't. I had no idea why I'd been summoned. I could only hope. 'Is this meal a celebration or a consolation prize?'

Kirkslap held up his fork, a piece of haggis stuck on the end. 'Just a moment. If I don't do this straight away, I may never be able to pluck up the courage.' He screwed his eyes

77

tight shut, put the morsel of haggis into his mouth, chewed cautiously before opening one eye and then the other. 'Not bad.'

'Do you know what's in it?' I asked.

'I have a vague notion and I'd like to keep it that way - vague.' Kirkslap set his fork on the table and wiped his mouth with a large white linen napkin. 'I put my conservative taste in food down to married life.' He drank some more wine. 'My wife was a woman with a limited range of recipes.'

'Your wife, is she...?'

'Dead? Alas, no.'

Instinctively, I looked around in case anyone had overheard. Kirkslap's High Court trial had taken place only a little further up the Royal Mile and ended controversially a few days before. The chances were there'd be an action-replay in the next few weeks. 'Divorced then?' I asked, satisfied that the other diners were more engrossed in their food than our conversation.

'No such luck. Marjorie and I have an open marriage. So long as my wallet is open, we're married.' He finished the glass of wine. The waiter refilled it, put a dash in the top of mine and retired.

'And the girl at the Carnbooth?'

'A bit of fun. I think I deserve it. You might have handled lots of murder cases, Mr Munro, but you've never had to experience one from a seat in the dock. Makes you realise how important your freedom is.' Kirkslap sampled some more haggis. 'And as for my upcoming trial, I have some good news for you and some not so good news.' He drank more wine. 'Wonderfully crisp isn't it?'

It should have been at the price. 'How about you start with the good?'

Kirkslap pointed his knife across the table. 'I like you and want you to take on my case.' He put another forkful of haggis into his mouth, set down his fork and sat back, holding his rapidly emptying wine glass. 'The not so good news, is that, unfortunately, Zack doesn't.'

'Like me or want me to take on your case?'

'Both.' He wiped the blade of his knife on his napkin and dipped it into my coral sauce. 'Do you mind?' He sucked the sauce off the knife. 'What's in coral sauce anyway? Can't actually be coral can it? They probably call it that because of its colour. It's sort of pink. You get pink coral don't you? Good, whatever it is –'

The waiter had arrived to pour Kirkslap more wine. 'Double cream, shallots and the blended coral from the scallop, sir,' he said.

'Coral?'

'The roe, sir.'

I clarified. 'The wee orange bit. It's the eggs.'

Kirkslap made a face and glugged some more crisp Chablis. As we finished our starters, he detailed his business partner's problems with Munro & Co.

'Zack's worried. We're equal partners on P45 Apps. He's the brains. I haven't a clue about computers and gadgets. Zack lives and breathes that stuff, but the man's marketing ability is dire. He's practically a recluse. I hate to blow my own trumpet,' he laughed. 'What am I saying? I blow my trumpet like a colliery bandsman, but that's my point: I'm a born salesman. I could sell snow to Santa. Zack's not got a clue. If I go to jail, he'll be lost. It's no good making the product if you can't persuade somebody to buy it.'

'Then why don't you sell me to Zack?'

Kirkslap smiled. 'That's what I like about you – you're a trier. No, I'm sorry to say, Zack is one extremely stubborn individual. Persuading him is entirely down to you. He's based in Glasgow, but he's coming to Edinburgh this weekend. I'll arrange for you two to meet - the rest is up to you.' He popped another bite of haggis into his mouth. 'You know,' he said, chewing happily. 'I could actually get to like this stuff.'

High heels on the wooden floor behind me. Kirkslap stood, napkin still tucked into the neck of his shirt. It was Joanna. I'd dumped the Friday intermediate diets on her, and thought she'd still be in court. Kirkslap pulled her up a chair and ordered another glass.

'I'm really sorry to interrupt,' Joanna said, 'but I need to speak to Robbie about something extremely important.' She glanced around. 'I can't do it in here.'

Kirkslap smiled at her and then at me. 'If this is part of your sales pitch, it's not necessary.'

It wasn't.

'It's about Nathan Boyd,' Joanna said, when she'd managed to drag me away from the table and we were standing on the pavement outside the restaurant.

What was so important about Nathan Boyd that could keep me away from Melrose lamb cutlets, on a Skirley tomato and rosemary sauce? Besides, didn't we act for the other Boyd boy? Nathan was Paul Sharp's client. 'Can this not wait? Apart from the fact that I'm trying to secure us part two of the case of the century, my main course is going to arrive any moment.'

'I've had Mrs Boyd on the phone. She wants to speak to you. She's in a terrible state and I promised I'd get hold of you as soon as I could. I jumped on the first train after court.'

'She's a mother. It's her job to get in a state about her sons. Tell her not to worry. The case is almost guaranteed to plead out as a vandalism. It'll be fines or deferred sentences all round, and everyone will live happily ever-after.'

'Nathan Boyd won't.'

'Why not?'

'Because he's been murdered and Danny's gone missing.'

Chapter 17

It was a Saturday morning, but, with the events of the day before, I was certain Kaye would be at work. I was right. She was standing at the window of her second floor corner office, looking down the length of Linlithgow High Street, a journalistic bird of prey, sat in her eyrie, all set to swoop down on the next unsuspecting scoop.

'Looks like you found this week's headline,' I said.

She sniffed. 'I see. You're always complaining when I drop in to see you. Hitting me with all that solicitor/client confidentiality crap. Then as soon as I have some exciting info, suddenly I'm expected to sing like a linty.'

'I've brought you coffee,' I said. 'And a Danish. Peach.' I set my food offerings on her desk.

I'd tried to see Kaye the previous evening, but she'd been with the police until late on.

She turned around slowly. 'I gave the story to all the dailies. It's good to keep in with the big boys. Reevel what's-his-chops from Reporting Scotland is coming out to do a piece on camera.'

'Must have been pretty horrific.'

'Oh, just a little. You know what it's like when you happen to stumble across a massacre in a farmyard.' Kaye peeled back the lid of the paper cup. 'Did you remember to put sugar in this?'

I confirmed that I had. Kaye gave the coffee a cautious sip. She was obviously milking the moment. Wanting me to sit up and beg for details.

I sat down and waited. Joanna had already filled me in on the basics on the way back from my aborted lunch with Larry Kirkslap, the day before. Kaye had gone down to the

Boyd's small-holding, not that far from my dad's cottage, though set in an even more remote location. She'd wanted to speak to Mrs Boyd for some background information on her sons, no doubt intending to come over all sympathetic, but I suspected it had been a ploy to really ram it to the Boyd boys when they were eventually convicted. It wouldn't have mattered if the verdict had been vandalism; with liberal doses of journalistic licence, the two boys would have been labelled grave-robbers no matter the precise legal terminology. Things had clearly moved on.

'I was going to send one of the others,' Kay said. 'And then I thought, it was such a nice day, I'd go myself and stop off for lunch at The Park Bistro, down at Philipstoun, on the way. I had grilled tuna steak, couscous and roast vegetables. Lovely. I threw the lot up as soon as I got to the Boyd place and saw Nathan lying at the front door in a pool of blood. His throat had been cut. I mean *really* cut. I think it was the cat chewing his face that done me in.'

'What did you do?'

Kaye put a finger to the corner of her mouth and squinted. 'Hmm, let me see. Oh, yeah, now I remember. I turned around, ran to my car and overtook Jenson effing Button on the way back to Linlithgow!'

She took another sip of coffee, tore a piece off the pastry and popped it into her mouth.

'Is Mrs Boyd okay? Well, not okay, obviously, but not physically harmed?'

'She was out when it happened. Luckily the police got to her before she returned home.'

'And Danny?'

'Nowhere to be seen.'

'Is he a suspect?'

'Prime. Why wouldn't he be? Given that his brother was murdered and he seems to have scarpered.' Kaye leapt effortlessly to that particular conclusion with all the skill of a journalistic gymnast.

'Why would he kill his brother? What possible motive could he have?'

'They're a strange family. Boys who get a kick out of cracking open mausoleums must have some serious issues. Don't worry, they'll find him soon enough, and, when they do, it will be another nice story for me and a good piece of business for you.'

Or it would be, if Danny Boyd was my client. The Boyd boys belonged to Paul. He'd only cut me in on Danny in case a conflict of interest arose. First rule of client cut-ins: never steal the cut-in client, even if the next time he gets in bother he asks for you, no matter how tempting it is, you send him back to his original lawyer. Then again, most cut-in clients didn't go on to carry out a murder.

'Did the Police give you a clue where Danny might be?'

Kaye shook her head, mouth full. 'Can't have gone far. What's going do you reckon will happen to the violation of sepulchre case now?'

'Deserted, I suppose, or tagged onto a murder indictment.' Which reminded me. Had I been granted legal aid for the tomb case yet? I didn't mind the prosecution being chucked, but it was a fixed-fee job and I didn't want it binned before I was fully-lagged.

Kaye polished off the rest of the Danish pastry, screwed the paper bag into a ball and dropped it in her wicker waste-paper basket. 'Of course, the big news is you and Jill.'

'You haven't spoken to her have you?' I didn't trust Kaye to keep her big trap shut, then again, did I really want her to? Maybe she could give me a clue which way the wind was blowing.

'Not a word have I uttered. You're on your own with this one.' She turned to look out of the window again. 'Where do you think he is? Where do you go if you're sixteen, with no money, no car and have just brutally murdered your brother?'

It wouldn't be long before I found out.

Chapter 18

Kirkslap had arranged for me to bump into his business partner at a Sci-Fi Exhibition taking place at the Edinburgh International Convention Centre. I wasn't keen on the venue; not the best place to meet and discuss an upcoming murder trial I thought, but, as time was of the essence, I couldn't be choosy.

So, Saturday afternoon, I shouldered my way through crowds of fancy-dressed youths and older men in T-shirts and ponytails, past exciting displays of long-lost, but, apparently, not forgotten, TV shows, in search of a tall, blonde Californian. How hard could that be? I'd thought. In my experience you tended to hear Americans before you saw them; however, the Centre was so busy and so noisy with various theme tunes blaring out, that it took quite a while before I traced my mark to a Dr Who presentation that was set up in one corner of the arena. I wasn't a Sci-Fi fan. I particularly loathed Dr Who. Even as a child, watching a guy in Edwardian gear being chased about quarries by some blokes in rubber monster-suits had never appealed to me.

As it turned out, Zack with the even stranger second name was that most rare of creatures: a quiet American. Though he was against the idea of Kirkslap instructing Munro & Co. in the upcoming trial, he was perfectly charming. 'Dr Who, it's just the best sci-fi series ever, isn't it?' he said, taking my hand in a limp and disturbingly moist grip.

'Big fan,' I said. 'Who isn't?'

'How do you think the new Doctor compares with his predecessors?' He gazed up at a row of wax-work Doctors that stood in front of a host of assorted baddies and props from the long-running series.

Not so easy to answer. I was aware that the Time Lord shed his outward appearance every now and again, as a steady stream of actors became too big for their BBC contracts or decided, invariably too late, that they didn't wish to become type-cast, but, to the best of my, admittedly limited, knowledge, the metamorphosis always left behind the same smug, self-satisfied git.

'I think the new guy's great,' I said, hoping the line-up of past Doctors was chronological. I flapped a hand at the figure furthest away from the Doctor with the long white hair, who I was pretty sure was first off the assembly line. 'He's so…'

'Quirky?'

'Yeah. Very.'

'I think so too. They're all so very different aren't they? Each with his own idiosyncrasies. You know, I envy you. Must have been great to see those early episodes first time around. I had to make do with DVD box-sets as a kid. I've watched them over and over.'

Early episodes? How old did he think I was? How old was he? Beach blonde hair, freckles peeking from beneath a sun tan as faded as his jeans. When I'd first met Zack at Larry Kirkslap's secluded hotel, I'd assumed he was just a typical, rich, West-Coast, Yank; pumped full of lamb stem-cells; half-man, half-Botox. The closer I looked, the more I could see that he was a kid. He could only be twenty-five, twenty-six at a push. It made sense. When Kirkslap had his idea for an app, he was just a recently redundant door-to-door salesman. He wouldn't have had the money to go to a high-flying software design company. Much more likely that he'd plucked some promising student straight out of college.

Zack looked about the huge room. 'This is a top class venue isn't it? P45 has held the launch of a few of our new apps here. The management team is terrific, the kind of folk I like to deal with – professionals. No fly-by-nights.' Which brought him seamlessly to the subject of yours truly. 'Larry told me you were coming,' he said. 'I know you're here to put the strong arm on me about letting you take on Larry's case.'

There was a queue to see Joe 90's Rat Trap. Zack joined it. I followed.

'I've nothing against you, personally,' he said. 'Well, apart from the trick you played with Mike's iPad. You've no idea how attached he is to that thing. I had to drive halfway across town to positively identify him to the authorities. But, actually, it's not that. Well, not just that. I guess I'm a great believer that you get what you pay for.'

I was prepared to up my hourly rate to match Caldwell & Craig's if it made him feel any better.

He smiled at the suggestion. 'I have to say that I was shocked when Mike told me there might be a retrial. After court that day when Larry was freed, it was never mentioned. We just celebrated like crazy. Now it's all going to kick off again, right when we're trying to introduce some Disney characters to the P45 apps. There's no way Disney is going to touch a company that has a hooker-killing CEO on the Board.'

Hooker was a bit harsh. Depending on which newspaper you took, Violet Hepburn was either a female escort or a gold-digger. Still, I could see how Disney might be sticky about things.

Someone sat in the Rat Trap, and the skeletal steel cage began to spin accompanied by a psychedelic light show.

'All you have to do is say the word and I'll be right on the case,' I said, above the Joe 90 theme tune.

'I know you will. Maybe I'm being picky. Larry likes you. Apparently you remind him of himself. A scrapper he says. He liked the iPad stunt. Thought it hilarious.' Zack fixed me with his baby blues. 'I didn't so much.' The Rat Trap stopped spinning and there was a merciful break in the soundtrack. 'I notice you haven't denied it.'

'No,' I said, 'you've noticed I haven't admitted it.' The queue shuffled forward. 'So, if you don't select Munro & co., who will you instruct?' I asked, as though there wasn't a hundred firms to choose from.

'Caldwell & Craig again, or we could always give an Edinburgh outfit a try. Maybe an Edinburgh law firm would have more insight into an Edinburgh jury. In the States we have jury selection. It can go on for days. Here they pull names out of a goldfish bowl, and you're stuck with whoever you get. What kind of system is that?'

'A cheap one,' I said. The light-show switched on again, the music started and the Rat Trap began to turn, picking up speed. 'Choosing a local lawyer might be a good idea in the Sheriff Court. Never mind Doctor Who, the Sheriffs I know don't have idiosyncrasies: they have personality disorders. Knowing how they're likely to behave is an advantage. A jury is different. Like you say, you don't know who you're getting or how they're going to view things.'

'How many lawyers are in your firm?' Zack asked. 'Two? I want a firm that's got twelve, twenty, hell, two hundred lawyers, all working on the case around the clock.'

'And if you need a heart transplant who do you want? Two hundred doctors getting in the way of each other or one or two expert surgeons who know what they're doing?'

He laughed. 'Who are you? What are you? You're a small town lawyer. I need, Larry needs, the company needs, a big city firm with a marquee defence attorney —'

'Who's America's most famous ever lawyer?' I asked. 'Atticus Finch. A lawyer from the sticks.' Even I knew how stupid I was starting to sound.

'I don't know this Mr Finch,' Zack said. Perhaps if they ever made To Kill a Mockingbird into a video game he would. 'But we're in Scotland not the U.S.A. I want someone high-profile, someone important to head up a shit-hot defence team. Yeah, we may have instructed the wrong firm last time. We'll get it right this turn around. I'm sorry, but I'm looking for a big name. A go-to guy. Someone people rely on in times of emergency.'

What happened next could not have been better stage-managed had Gerry Anderson, creator of Supermarionation, been pulling the strings himself. The Joe 90 theme tune cut out mid-bar, as did the special effects from the various other demonstrations. Above the bemused chattering of the crowd, the loudspeaker system boomed. 'Attention. Would Mr Robbie Munro, that's Mr Robbie Munro, the lawyer, please attend the manager's office on level one as a matter of urgency.'

The announcement was repeated before the music and other sound effects were cranked-up again.

'What a place,' I said, followed by my best sardonic laugh. 'I wonder what bother they've got themselves into now. Still, duty calls.' I patted Zack on the shoulder. 'Enjoy Joe 90. And if Larry still wants me to act, and you change your mind, let me know as soon as possible. I'll try and keep myself available,' I smiled wryly and jerked my head in the direction of where I assumed the manager's office to be. 'Although you never know when something really important is going to crop up.'

And with that I set off for the manager's office, wondering what trouble I was in this time.

Chapter 19

A security guard was holding a phone out to me as I walked into the manager's office. The management team at the EICC was not in urgent need of criminal legal advice. The emergency was my dad.

'I think I've broken my ankle,' he said.

'How?' I asked, guessing his roof was somehow involved.

'I fell off the top of the ladder.'

'I thought you were going to get someone in to sort the roof?'

The only reply was a short grunt of pain.

'Okay, okay. I'll come see you. Where are you?'

'At the bottom of the ladder.'

'Why haven't you called an ambulance?'

'What if it's not broken? Could just be a really bad sprain. How would that look to folk? Me being carted off to hospital, sirens blaring, with only a sore ankle to show for all the fuss?'

'Don't move,' I said. 'I'll be there as soon as I can.'

I hung up and called an ambulance. Forty-five minutes later I was in the A&E Department at St John's in Livingston. Three hours later, I was back at my dad's cottage, and he was hobbling down the garden path on crutches.

'Are you going to get that door for me or what?' Many people would put my dad's crabbitness down to pain and suffering. Those who knew him wouldn't.

I opened the back door. He fended off my attempts to help him up the step, manoeuvred himself inside and sat down at the kitchen table, swinging another chair around so that he could prop his plastered leg on it. By the time he had thrown the crutches into a corner, I already had the kettle on. He'd been offered a cup of tea at the hospital, but they had only teabags which, according to my dad, contained nothing more than the sweepings off the tea factory floor. I scooped a couple of teaspoons of breakfast tealeaves into his treasured navy-blue enamelled teapot and then realised my mistake. My dad always insisted that the pot first be warmed with boiling water. A swift look over my shoulder suggested that he was too busy trying to scratch his leg with a pen down the side of his plaster cast to notice my faux pas.

'So where is he? You got him holed up in a safe house somewhere?' my dad asked.

In our wait at the hospital, we had more or less covered all the latest football rumours, and thus exhausted the favourite topic of conversation between Munro father and son. Somehow we'd moved onto my work, a subject I liked to steer clear off during chats with my dad; however, he'd learned of my acting for Danny Boyd, and word of his brother's murder was all over the local news.

'Don't be stupid. What would I want to put him in a safe house for?'

He cast the pen aside and ordered me to throw him a wooden spoon out of the drawer. 'He's your client. All your clients are innocent aren't they? You don't want to see the long arm of the grab him by the scruff of the neck.'

'I only get paid if he gets caught and ends up in court, Dad,' I said rising to the bait. 'I need my clients inside the criminal justice system before I can make any money. Me setting up a safe house for teenage fugitives would be like you, when you were a cop, not arresting a suspect and just short-circuiting matters by—'

'Giving them a right good thump and telling them to behave next time?'

Okay, it wasn't that good an analogy. I found a wooden spoon and rapped it off his plaster cast before handing it to him. 'Anyway, Danny Boyd's not my client. I was just borrowing him.'

'So whose is he?'

The kettle had almost boiled. I took down my dad's enormous cup and saucer from the kitchen cupboard and a mug for myself. 'He's Paul Sharp's.'

'So why are you acting for him?'

'Because Paul is, was, acting for his brother. He couldn't act for Danny as well, in case there was a conflict of interest.'

My dad was really going at it with the wooden spoon. 'A what?'

'In case they start blaming each other. What's a lawyer going to do then? You can't choose one client over the other, that's why each accused should be separately represented.'

'But brothers wouldn't blame each other would they? I mean you wouldn't rat on Malky if he was in bother would you?' Interesting how my dad, who generally thought it a citizen's duty to testify against a police suspect, labelled anyone who gave evidence against his eldest son a rat. 'It's all a legal aid dodge if you ask me. Two lawyers being paid instead of one.'

Please, not the legal aid lecture again. All those taxes he'd paid and for what? So that a whole lot of criminals could evade justice. For, as the Government and newspapers had brainwashed the general public into thinking, justice only happened when someone was convicted. A not guilty verdict was someone *getting off*.

'Academic is what it is,' I said. 'Nathan Boyd's dead, so there's only one lawyer being paid now – happy?' I sloshed some milk into his tea cup and my mug. 'And it won't matter if Danny blames his brother for the tomb-raiding, seeing as how Nathan will soon be buried in his own tomb.'

'I want to be burned.'

'That can be arranged,' I said.

He extricated the wooden spoon and set it on the table beside him as he readied himself to receive his cup of tea.

'Aye, well. Someone's bad luck is always someone else's good luck.'

'You should know,' I said. 'You've had a bit of both, today. Bad luck falling off the ladder and good luck that you still had my mobile phone on you. Any chance I could get it back?'

He frowned. 'I was thinking maybe I should be getting one of these,' he said, delving into a pocket and bringing out my phone. 'Living away out here. You never know when it might come in handy again.'

My dad had no need of the all-singing-all-dancing model that he was playing with, and which, along with Joanna's identical phone, was currently on the books as one of Munro & Co.'s few fixed assets. I could buy him a cheap one and he'd never know the difference.

'I'll buy you a nice new one for your birthday,' I said. 'Seeing how we'll have to put your surprise birthday party on hold for a while.'

'No, this one will do fine.' He shoved my former phone back into his pocket. 'Speaking of my birthday, Malky was through here the other day. He was showing me his new motor - German – but still it's very nice. Can go a bit too.' There wasn't a car built that couldn't 'go a bit' with my big brother behind the wheel. 'I talked him into taking me through to Jill's to water her plants for you and on the way he was saying something about a bottle of eighteen-year-old Springbank. I told him there was no need for expensive whisky if you and him were laying me on a party. I'm sure arrangements are well underway and I wouldn't want to disappoint everyone by calling it off. Not after all the hard work you will have been putting into it. Now where's my tea? I'm parched.'

'On its way,' I said, teapot poised over his cup.

'Good. Don't forget to rinse that pot out with hot water before you start brewing up.'

Chapter 20

Not unusually, Monday afternoon found me at the table in the well of the court, fighting to get my name down on the agents' sheet. There were thirty odd names on the official court custody list, and the defence lawyers found it more efficient to make up their own so that the cases could be called in batches. If not, those unfortunates who'd spent the weekend in the police cells would be dealt with alphabetically; which meant that if you were acting for a Mr Adams and a Mr Young, you were in for a long wait between clients. Better to get your name down first on the lawyer's list and be off in search of work that might actually pay; especially if your client was pleading not guilty. The Scottish Legal Aid Board only paid for guilty pleas at a pleading diet. Even then, with fixed fees, there was no point hanging around in court any longer than you had to. Defence agents were in private practice; time was money. The trouble was that the Procurator Fiscal, Sheriff and Clerks all operated on Civil Service time.

'What do you mean the cases haven't been linked yet?' Paul Sharp asked the Clerk, a plump girl with glasses who had a certain do-I-look-like-I-give-a-toss look about her. 'It's quarter past two. I've been waiting since twelve for this court to start.'

It was unusual to see Paul flustered, and even more unusual to see a defence agent showing annoyance towards a Clerk. The wrong side of the Sheriff Clerk's office was a dark place to be.

'Talk to the PF,' she told Paul. 'It's their side of the system that's down. I'm all set to go this end and so is Sheriff Brechin.'

Not that many years before, in simpler times, the local Procurator Fiscal's office would type up a complaint in triplicate. The principal was signed and given to the court, the second was served on the accused and a third was kept on the prosecution's file. Then someone had the great idea of centralising the process and giving computers a greater role. The result was squadrons of defence lawyers who used to be out by lunchtime, now hanging around court until late afternoon and not being paid for it. No wonder Paul was slightly grumpy, but the delay, I felt sure, wasn't the real cause of his bad mood.

'Heard anything from you-know-who?' he asked, after we'd decided to go down to the lobby for something to drink, while the PF's and Sheriff Clerk's computers tried to talk to each other.

'No, have you?'

Paul shook his head. 'Robbie,' he said after a short pause. 'You know how I cut you in on Danny Boyd? And, of course, he remains your client…'

I could see where the conversation was headed. 'Paul, there's absolutely no problem. He's your client. If Danny gets huckled for his brother's murder, as far as I'm concerned it's over to you.'

I could sense his relief. 'It's not the money. A murder case is more trouble than it's worth. All that hassle for legal aid rates, and you just know that if you get a guilty, some other lawyer is going to go through your file at a later date looking for mistakes for an Anderson appeal. It's just that a murder is... I don't know... interesting. A change from all the usual run of the mill crap that keeps us hanging about in this dump for hours every day, waiting on that bunch of numpties in there getting to grips with technology.'

'He didn't really have to explain. Murder was where it was at. No point studying for a medical degree and spending your career fixing sticking-plasters. As a law student, I'd always seen myself as a criminal lawyer, defending wall to wall murders, even though once in practice you realised that the client that made you money was not the occasional murder-accused, but the jaikie who was constantly in bother; the dripping roast. And the more lenient the country's sentencing policies became, the more often that roast dripped.

I knew we were in for a really long wait when I saw Hugh Ogilvie, the Procurator Fiscal, come down the stairs from the court and into the cafe. Paul and I had been careless enough to leave an empty chair at our table. On his way back from the serving counter, Ogilvie must have taken it as some kind of invitation to join us. He came over carrying a tray on which there was a small stainless steel teapot, a white cup and saucer and a tiny jug of milk.

'Ah, the life of a defence lawyer,' he said, pouring his tea; some out the side of the lid, hitting the table, some out of the spout, hitting the bottom of the cup. 'Sitting on your backside all day, milking the Legal Aid Board dry. Thought you might have been out looking for your client,' he said to me, mopping up a small lake of tea with a series of paper napkins.

'If you're talking about Danny Boyd he's Paul's client,' I said.

'Oh, jumped ship has he?' Ogilvie squidged the sodden napkins into a ball and placed it in the centre of the table next to the small vase with a plastic flower in it. 'If he's in touch, you can tell him the police would be very interested in having a chat.' He poured some milk from the jug and looked about for something to stir his tea with. Eventually he took a pen from his top pocket and used it. 'If he does, I'll say no more about the violation of sepulchre charge. It'll be...' He put his fingertips together and then drew them apart dramatically in an imaginary firework display. 'Gone.'

'He could be innocent, you know,' I said. 'Frightened and scared. Hiding out somewhere.'

'Very possibly.' Ogilvie was in full patronising mode. 'Probably all some terrible misunderstanding. Thought he was gutting a rabbit, but, no, it was his brother's throat.' He took a sip of tea. 'Easy mistake to make.'

Paul nodded. 'Or he could have witnessed the whole thing and done a runner.'

'Or been abducted by whoever killed his brother,' I suggested. 'Or he's dead in the bushes and his body's not been found yet.'

All excellent defences,' Ogilvie said. 'Especially the one about him being dead. Even I wouldn't prosecute a dead man, probably. I can see why you're both defence lawyers.' He just so needed a hard slap. 'However...' he finished the tea in one further draught. 'If it turns out that he's had a wee turn to himself, lost his temper and slit his brother's throat, then the sooner we have him locked up for life or packed away to the State Hospital in a strait-jacket, the better. Anyway, can't be sitting around here all day. Some of us have work to do.'

'Well could you try to do it a bit faster?' Paul said. 'We're not all killing time until our Government final-salary pension kicks in.'

'Ooh, Touchy.' Ogilvie pushed his crockery aside and climbed to his feet. 'By the way, Robbie, I heard about your former colleague's little triumph in the Larry Kirkslap case.' He picked up the blob of wet tissue and plopped it into his empty cup. 'Hope he enjoyed his fifteen minutes of fame, because I understand Mr Kirkslap had a little visit from the police to brighten up his Sunday afternoon.' Ogilvie shoved his chair under the table. 'I think we can safely say that his next jury will be well and truly sworn in...' He started to walk away, then turned around with that smile I'd always wanted to wipe from his face with the aid of a baseball bat. 'And that no jurors are going out for a smoke before the guilty verdict.'

Chapter 21

West Lothian's Civic Centre in Livingston was described as 'stunning' on its own web-site. Other, more accurate, descriptions that didn't feature were: cold, depressing and soulless. The biggest public sector partnership of its kind in the UK, it housed the Divisional Police Headquarters, the Sheriff and Justice of the Peace Court complex, Council Headquarters, the Procurator Fiscal's office, the Scottish Children's Reporter, Lothian and Borders Fire and Rescue Service and the West Lothian Community Health and Care Partnership. That meant a lot of employees, a lot of official visitors and lots of parking spaces for everyone; everyone except defence agents who, if they intended to stay more than forty-five minutes, and didn't want to defend themselves on a parking charge, had to abandon their car somewhere else.

By the time I had put through my final custody, marked up bail appeals for those deemed unsuitable for release by Bert Brechin, which was most of them, and posted those appeal forms under the, now very closed, door of the Sheriff Clerk's office, it was nearly six o'clock. And it was raining. I walked, collar up, head down, out of the building, through the grounds of the Civic Centre, across the bridge over the River Almond and into the car park of Livingston F.C. which was the nearest available parking facility for second class citizens such as myself.

Wet and tired, I drove back to Linlithgow, amazed at how knackering it was to sit about all afternoon with only the occasional interlude during which you required to spout a lot of nonsense to a man in a wig, in the hope that another man could go home and not have to spend his next few weeks in a cell with only a stainless steel loo, a kettle and psychotic roommate to keep him company.

I had my immediate future all mapped out. I was going home, I was going to have something to eat, quite possibly something alcoholic to drink, and then crash out. In the morning, I'd lie in until eight, then make my way to Perth Sheriff Court, and the trial of a dangerous driver. All I needed was to make a small detour via my office to collect the case file and I could head straight for The Fair City, first thing.

Back at Munro & Co.'s headquarters, I was pleased to see that Grace-Mary had predicted my intentions and the Section 2 file was waiting for me on my chair, a yellow-sticky adhered to the front cover. My secretary's scribbled order, under the heading in capital letters: URGENT, was that I should give Joanna a call. I had her number on my mobile. I reached into my pocket, but, of course, the phone was in my dad's pocket, not my own. All I had was my SIM card. Having been unable to wrest my ultra-hi-tech phone from my dad, I'd taken the SIM with a view to buying another phone for myself. I'd given him a pay-as-you-go SIM with a ten pound top-up. I reckoned it would last him a year. I could phone my dad on his landline and try and talk him through how to find Joanna's number on the mobile. There lay madness. Taking the file for the next day's trial, I headed for home to seek out my old coal-fired cell-phone. If I could find it and pop in my SIM, then I could give Joanna a phone while I boiled some pasta in a pot. It seemed like a plan until I arrived at my flat to find Joanna parked outside.

'What's the matter?' I asked, as I led her through the front door and into my sitting room. A pizza box lay open on the floor beside a couple of crushed beer and a pair of socks that had not yet made their way to the wash basket.

Joanna looked around. 'And I thought your office was untidy.' She moved a set of Playstation 3 controllers from the cushion to the arm of the sofa and sat down. She had with her one of those flight-cases with the long handle and wheels. I hadn't asked her why yet. She wrinkled her nose. 'What on earth is that smell?'

'Homemade pesto,' I said, with a degree of pride. 'Jamie Oliver was making it on telly the other night and I suddenly realised I had most of the ingredients. Jill gave me this basil plant that I keep in the kitchen, I've got olive oil and garlic and...'

'Pine nuts?'

'Peanuts. Same sort of thing.'

'Parmesan?'

'Yes. Well... cheddar.'

'What's it taste like?'

'Do you want to find out? I've got a big bag of spaghetti somewhere.'

'Another time, perhaps. Right now there are more important things to do than eat.'

I batted my eyelashes. 'Really, Joanna, I'm practically engaged.'

Not everyone finds my attempts at humour amusing, and most of them are women.

'Larry Kirkslap has instructed us,' she said. 'We've got the case.'

If this was my assistant's attempt at humour, it wasn't funny. 'Yeah, right.'

'No, really.' Joanna was beaming. 'He was served with his indictment—'

'Yesterday, I know. Sorry, go on.'

'Kirkslap's business partner, that guy, Zack, he was at the office this afternoon while you were at court. He brought the indictment with him. When I couldn't get hold of you by phone, I was starting to panic until Grace-Mary stepped in and told him that she would make sure you had the case file in your hands this evening.' Joanna unzipped the flight-bag. 'She had Zack sign a mandate and sent me through to Caldwell & Craig's for the papers. Maggie Sinclair didn't like it, so I called Zack and he had Mr Kirkslap speak to her directly. After that I had the stuff in no time at all. They even gave me this smart wheelie-case. Do you think they'll want it back?'

'Keep it even if they do,' I said. I could hardly believe it. Had Zack actually been taken in by my summons to the manager's office at the EICC? Was he really so Gullible? Possibly. He was a twenty-something who still watched Dr Who and would queue up for a shot on Joe 90's transmogrification device.

'Great.' I took the first of the dozen or so folders that came out of the case. It had a label on the front that said: 'Civilian Statements' and must have been easily six inches thick. I decided to give one or two of them a shufty before I got creative in the kitchen.

'Grace-Mary told Zack that you'd have the papers read and be up to speed by noon tomorrow at the latest - even if you had to work around the clock.' She pulled another folder from the case and balanced it on her knee. 'If we start now we can have this done by the morning.'

'But what about my trial in Perth?'

'Grace-Mary's phoned the PF and had it adjourned. A local agent will make the motion. The witnesses have been countermanded and the client knows about your sudden illness.' Joanna opened her equally thick folder marked: 'Cellphone Analysis'. 'We're going to need some paper to make notes as we go along.'

'And coffee,' I said.

Joanna agreed. 'Yeah, lots of coffee.' She, picked up the socks with two fingers and hurled them into the furthest corner of the room. 'But no pesto.'

Chapter 22

Murder cases are not usually that complicated. Murders are mostly assaults that go tragically wrong, and the perpetrators, even if they do their best to tidy up after themselves, invariably leave lots of clues lying around for nosey scene of crime officers to find. Larry Kirkslap didn't appear to have been any different. Around 6 a.m. and with my espresso machine wondering what had hit it, Joanna and I had more or less managed to sketch out the basis of the Crown case.

Kirkslap had first met thirty-six year-old Violet Hepburn when out celebrating P45's latest app launch with a trip to Karats, a champagne bar in Glasgow City, around Christmas 2011; nearly a year before Violet went missing. Twenty years his junior she'd taken to him right away, and although no-one knew what she saw in the stout, loud-mouthed, fifty-six-year-old millionaire, the couple had dated on and off for several months in a relationship that had met their respective expectations, with foreign shopping trips and stays in five star hotels.

Kirkslap had ended the relationship sometime during the summer of 2012. The witness statements didn't say exactly why; however, the general consensus was that as sales of P45 Apps increased, so did Larry Kirkslap's attractiveness to certain factions of the opposite sex, and he simply got tired of Violet and traded her in for a string of newer models. By all accounts, he'd had a showroom full.

Which took us to the last day Violet was seen by anyone. It was Wednesday, 31st October 2012. Records showed that Violet's credit card was used around half-past two in the afternoon and with that information the police had managed to pick her up on the city centre CCTV. After that she hadn't been seen again.

Joanna picked up a thick folder and started to leaf through a bundle of phone records containing details of all calls to and from Violet's and Kirkslap's respective mobile phones, going back to when they'd first met. There were hundreds of pages to sift through and she gave a little whoop of joy when she came across a month by month summary showing only those calls and text messages between the two: those from Kirkslap to Violet highlighted yellow, those from Violet to Kirkslap in red. It was very noticeable that, as 2012 had trundled on, the amount of yellow highlighting diminished as the red increased. The summary sheet for May was a sea of crimson. If Violet had been a man she would have been accused of tele-stalking.

'Sad, how some men treat women,' Joanna said.

It might have been sad if we were looking at the end of a love affair. We weren't. It was simply the unilateral termination of a business relationship. One Violet hadn't wanted to end.

'How much red highlighting do you think there would be on that page if Kirkslap had no money?' I asked.

'I suppose.' Joanna extracted a piece of paper from the bundle in her hand. 'Did you know that Violet had four Highers and a degree in business studies? What was she doing throwing herself at a lecherous old man like Larry Kirkslap?'

She'd left out the word 'rich' from her description. The statement I'd read from a barman at Karats was that Violet had been a regular, always on the lookout for the well-heeled gent. She and the other women who gathered at the city centre champagne bar could spot a fake Rolex a mile off and identify an Armani suit by the smell of the thread.

'Apart from the morality of it,' she continued, 'which is not for us to judge, going off with strange men, even if they can afford to buy you nice things, is an inherently risky business. They're going to want something for their money. That sort of career is always going to have some extremely dodgy moments.'

If by dodgy Joanna meant deadly, then she was right in Violet Hepburn's case; however, there was a possible line of defence there.

'If she saw a lot of men, that makes for a lot of possible suspects,' I said. 'There could be men she's ditched when someone richer came along, men whose pride has been hurt, men out for revenge. We can use that. No need to delve into her sexual past, the court won't allow that, but the jury will read between the lines. Jurors love playing Sherlock Holmes. As far as I can see, Kirkslap was the only person in the frame at the last trial. No wonder the defence bombed. If we can fire in an incriminee or two, it'll give everyone something to think about.'

'Great idea,' Joanna said in a tone that suggested the opposite. 'Except every man that Violet dated since High School has been questioned by the police. That's a complete dead end of a defence. She threw down the sheaf of papers. 'Ever think you'd have been better off letting Kirkslap go elsewhere for representation? Be careful what you wish for, I say.'

It must have been the fatigue talking. Let a case like this slip though my fingers when I could charge a proper hourly rate? 'Stop thinking like a PF and being impressed at how wonderful the Crown case is. Find an angle on this, something we can throw at a jury.'

'Give 'em the ole razzle-dazzle? Well, it's going to have to be very razzly and incredibly dazzly.' The sheaf of papers in Joanna's hand had dwindled to two pages. 'Take a look at this,' she said. A text message from Kirkslap mid-September.

- *Don't ever embarrass me or my family in that way again. I mean it* -

Not so good. 'Anything after that?' I asked.

There was one final summary sheet. Two text messages, one highlighted red: Violet to Kirkslap on the afternoon of 1st November 2012.

- See you at eight xxx -

The other highlighted yellow: Kirkslap's reply.

- Looking forward -

I took the page from Joanna. It didn't make sense, and, yet, it was those text messages, the last in the logs requisitioned from Violet's mobile phone company, that encouraged the police to search Kirkslap's lodge in the country. It was at that address they'd found Violet's phone as well as traces of blood on the hall carpet and, just to top it all, blood in the boot of Kirkslap's car.

'It was only a few smears,' I said, when Joanna reminded me of the DNA results that estimated the chances of the blood being anyone other than Violet's at one billion to one. 'We're not talking about pools of blood.'

'And of course there's the speed camera, clocking Kirkslap on his midnight road-trip through the Trossachs. Oh, and no-one has seen Violet since.'

I needed more coffee. And breakfast.

I was in the kitchen when the phone rang. 'Get that, will you?' I called through to the living room. Who could it be? Too early for Grace-Mary. The only person I knew who'd be up and about and phoning me at that time of the morning would be my dad. 'Wait!' I yelled. I clattered the frying pan down on the gas hob. Last thing I wanted was my dad asking why *some strange woman* was answering my phone. The main reason my dad disapproved of my relationship with Jill, was that he was sure I'd cock the whole thing up in some way. I darted from the kitchen and made it into the next room just as Joanna was replacing the receiver.

'That wasn't my dad was it?' I asked.

'No,' she said.

That was a relief.

'I think it was Jill.' Joanna fashioned a sickly smile.

I cleared my throat. 'What did she want?'

'I don't know.' The pallor of my assistant's complexion was not, I was sure, entirely down to sleep deprivation. 'After I told her who I was she hung up.'

Chapter 23

I distinctly remembered Jill telling me who her new employers were. Unfortunately, I may not have been giving her my full attention at the time. That it was a pharmaceutical company with headquarters in Switzerland and she was going off to work in Berne for a month and a half, had been as much information as I thought necessary or, indeed, could absorb, given that Jill had thought the best time to impart this important information was during the live transmission of a major football match.

I would have phoned her, but her number, along with that of just about every other person I knew, was on the SIM card in my suit pocket and I couldn't find my old mobile anywhere.

'You can have mine. I can do without for a day or so. Just don't respond to any texts from someone called Mark,' Joanna said.

I think she felt a little guilty, even though it wasn't her fault that Jill had called or that my girlfriend may have misread the situation.

I took it anyway and shoved in my SIM card. It was the back of seven and we'd eaten breakfast and drunk more coffee while talking over Larry Kirkslap's upcoming murder trial.

'I'll leave you to it,' Joanna said, collecting her things. I told her to go home for a few hours' sleep. We'd meet up at the office around lunchtime and organise a consultation with Kirkslap either later that afternoon or in the evening. 'I'm sure Jill will understand,' Joanna said, as I showed her to the door, 'and if there is anything I can say to her that you think will help...'

I said there wasn't and played the whole thing down.

After she'd gone I tried to phone Jill. No reply. Then I remembered I was phoning her old mobile phone, the one she'd forgotten to take with her. I left a message anyway. It showed a degree of willingness and I didn't want to say more in case, when she did hear it, she thought it suspicious that I was denying an affair I hadn't actually been accused of.

I was tired, but there was no way I could sleep. It might have been the caffeine or the evidence in the Kirkslap case buzzing about my head, or, most likely, the worry that Jill might think that I was two-timing her; whatever, I was awake and that wasn't going to change for a while.

After a shower, a shave and a fresh shirt I was off to Auld Reekie, hoping I was far enough from Perth so that no-one from that court would see the allegedly ailing Mr Munro bounding up the one hundred and eighteen stone steps of Advocates Close, two at a time. On my way through on the train, I had phoned Cameron Crowe's clerk to be told he had a deferred sentence calling that morning, and the best place to catch him was at the Lawnmarket, first thing. And so, my initial bounding having reduced to a stagger, I emerged from the Close entrance onto the High Street, heart pumping, breathing like a dirty phone call and fixed my gaze further up The Royal Mile.

Inside the Lawnmarket building, I didn't bother to check the courtrooms. It was just after nine and nothing happened very early or quickly in the High Court of Justiciary. Instead, I clambered a further two flights of stairs to the Advocates' robing room. Trips to the High Court were always aerobic occasions.

'What do *you* want?' said an unmistakable voice from behind The Herald newspaper, at the far end of a huge mahogany table. The hands either side of the broadsheet gave the pages a flick of annoyance. The only other occupants of

107

the room, two other junior counsel at a long sideboard helping themselves to coffee, looked towards the newspaper and then at me and grimaced in sympathy.

'I'm here to see you,' I said. 'With instructions.'

Crowe turned down a corner of the paper. 'Speak to my clerk,' he said over the top of it.

'Why? We're both here now.'

An immense sigh escaped from behind the headlines. 'Because that's how the system works. You speak to my clerk, she'll check my diary and *if* I'm available she'll ask you to forward the bundle and then, perhaps, we can consult. It's worked very well for hundreds of years. I'm told Walter Scott used it to great effect.'

I had to keep reminding myself that with Fiona Faye unable to act, Cameron Crowe was Kirkslap's next best chance of an acquittal.

'Larry Kirkslap,' I said.

The paper shook slightly. 'What about him?'

'He's been re-indicted,' said one of the two juniors, dropping coins into the ceramic sugar bowl that collected the coffee money.

'And is looking for counsel,' I said.

The junior counsel who had avoided paying for his coffee laughed. 'Doubt it. Nigel Staedtler's got his mighty talons well and truly wrapped around that brief. Instructed by some corporate clowns who didn't know any better, and he's using Lucy Locke for a junior. Nice bit of eye-candy for the Judge.'

'Those corporate clowns were Caldwell & Craig,' I said to the front and back pages of the still wide open Herald. 'They don't have the case anymore. Guess who's the ringmaster now?' The newspaper stiffened. I continued. 'Staedtler's out and I'm thinking of instructing a senior junior. Someone who knows how to tear into an expert witness.'

Crowe gently closed the newspaper, folded it once, twice and laid it on the table in front of him. He looked at me expressionless.

'Let's go for a walk,' I said. Crowe's deferred sentence was calling at ten, so we had a good half hour.

'What's the catch?' he asked, as we crossed the cobbled street and stepped over the black link chain into Parliament Square. 'No catch,' I said.

'Then, why me?' He stopped in the centre of the square next to a group of bored pigeons. 'If you think this is going to get you Brownie points next time I'm prosecuting one of your malodorous clients, you can—'

'Okay, I get it.' I kept walking, scattering the birds. 'You don't trust me.'

'Or like you,' he said, catching me up.

By now he should have noticed the lack of Valentine cards he'd received from Munro & Co. the previous month. The fact remained: I'd brought him the brief of his life on a silver platter and we both knew he was going to accept it. 'Well we're both just going to have to try and get along,' I said. 'If nothing else for the sake of the client whose instructions I have worked extremely hard to secure. Okay?'

'I don't buy it, 'Crowe said. 'Obviously, I agree, Nigel Staedtler's an oaf who couldn't cross-examine a puppy in a pile of poo, but there are plenty of highly competent seniors who'd bite your arm off for the case.'

'Are you trying to talk me out of this? Because, if you are, I won't need much persuasion.'

Crowe was silent. We'd worked together at Caldwell & Craig in my early days, when he'd been in charge of my training. Crowe, the doesn't-suffer-fools-gladly senior court associate, and me, the know-it-all legal trainee, had never really hit it off. Then, of course, there had been the infamous incident when he discovered me in a drunken embrace with his then girlfriend, Fiona Faye, and later when my then ex-girlfriend, Zoe had signalled her rejection of Crowe's amorous advances with a knee to the chuckies. He didn't like me and the feeling was mutual. No wonder he thought there had to be a catch, but there wasn't; however, Crowe was quite correct about one thing: I did have plenty vastly more experienced counsel to choose from. Ones who, like Fiona, could cross-examine victims without alienating jurors, sweet-talk police officers, charm judges and present a stonking jury speech at the end of it all. Strangely, none of that really mattered in Kirkslap's case. The victim was missing, presumed dead, there was little dispute on the evidence of any of the civilian or police witnesses and what eventually went to the jury depended on one thing: how good a job the defence made of demolishing the Crown's forensic evidence. Cameron Crowe was obnoxious, but he was smart. He could take apart an expert witness like a schoolboy pulling the legs off a spider. I'd witnessed him on many a previous occasion make a thoroughly prepared forensic report look like a failed third-grade science project.

'I'll ask you again,' Crowe said. 'Why me? Has Fiona fallen out of favour? I thought you and she were the dream-team?'

'We are,' I said. 'But Fiona's not available.'

Crowe looked at me.

I held his gaze for a while. 'I take it you are?'

He almost smiled. 'If I'm not I will be.'

We walked on into Parliament House to check Crowe's diary. His clerk flicked over to the following week. 'I'll need to shift a few things around,' she said. 'If the preliminary hearing is Friday, when do you expect the trial to start?'

'The preliminary hearing can't be this week,' I said. 'The indictment has only just been served.'

'I know,' the clerk had lowered her voice, 'but the Crown shortened the induciae for the new trial so the prelim's been brought forward too.' She looked down at the diary.

'When did this happen?' I asked. I thought she said Friday afternoon, but her voice was so soft I could hardly hear what she was saying.

Crowe had noticed his clerk's strange behaviour too. 'What's the matter with you?' he asked.

110

She glanced up and looked over his shoulder. A dark shadow loomed over even the tall frame of Cameron Crowe. The high and mighty Nigel Staedtler Q.C. pushed between myself and Crowe.

'What's this all about?' he demanded of the clerk who didn't answer.

'We're discussing the Larry Kirkslap case,' I said. The way the Q.C. was now glowering down at me I thought I should say something. 'There's going to be a change of counsel for the re-trial.'

'Says who?'

Before I could reply with a, 'says-me,' Staedtler turned his disapproving gaze on Crowe. 'A word. Now.'

The two advocates took a few steps away for the sake of privacy, although anyone within a twenty metre radius would have had no difficulty over-hearing their conversation. Whatever their respective advocacy skills, they'd learned how to project their voices to the back rows.

'Look here,' Staedtler said, 'Lucy is my junior. She knows the case inside out, and it's only fair to give her another crack.'

Evidently, word of the change in agency had not quite filtered through to Kirkslap's old defence team. It was about to.

'There's going to be a new defence team for the re-trial.' Crowe said. 'I'm going to take a fresh look at the evidence —'

'I'll decide who my junior is, who do you —'

'Think I am?' Crowe said into Staedtler's increasingly purple face. 'I'm the new lead counsel.'

There then followed a verbal exchange which, had two of my clients carried on in that way, would undoubtedly have been considered a breach of the peace. But this wasn't a couple of neds fighting over a bottle of Buckfast. It was learned counsel disputing ownership of a valuable brief and, watching Crowe in action, treating his more senior colleague with unconcealed contempt, only vindicated my decision to instruct the Prince of Darkness.

'Ask Miss Locke to deliver a set of papers to my box by the end of the day,' Crowe said. 'I see you've somehow managed to let the Crown shorten the induciae leaving very little time to prepare before the preliminary diet.'

'That's because I don't need time to prepare!' Staedtler replied. 'I am fully prepared!'

'Yes,' said Crowe, 'but I'm preparing to *win*.'

'How dare you!' Staedtler pulled Crowe back by his shoulder. 'You think you can step into this case on the say-so of that jumped-up, legal-aid shyster?' Staedtler jerked a thumb in my direction. At least I assumed it was my direction, my being the only jumped-up, legal-aid shyster in the immediate vicinity.

I thought Crowe wavered slightly. He looked around at me, a worried expression flitted across his face. Did he think I was on the wind-up? I went over and pulled him away. 'I'll have a set of papers couriered to you this afternoon.'

Staedtler lumbered off, muttering something about the Dean and bloody upstarts.

Crowe watched him go. 'Man's an idiot. Four days to prepare?'

When the dust had settled, a phone call to the Clerk of Justiciary confirmed that, in his zeal to get the show back on the road, the Lord Advocate had argued for a shorter than usual notice period before the statutorily required preliminary hearing. It was a request to which the court had been happy to accede.

'A preliminary hearing on Friday, and I haven't seen so much as a copy of the indictment yet. I'm beginning to think I should let Staedtler keep the brief. Who've we got for the hearing?'

Crowe's clerk checked the court list for the week. 'Lord Haldane.'

'Could be worse.' Crowe said. 'We can ask for things to be knocked on a month or two. Haldane's not so bad if you know the right strings to pull.'

'Do you think Staedtler even bothered to challenge the request for a re-trial?' I asked Crowe, after we'd put a pen through the next four weeks of his diary and were walking past St Giles Cathedral on the way back to the Lawnmarket.

'Probably not, but would have been a waste of time anyway.'

'What about the adverse publicity? How can Kirkslap expect a fair trial when his name and the guilty verdict have been plastered across the newspapers?'

'That would cut no ice with their Lordships. The Court ballsed-up the case last time, the Lord Advocate is annoyed, that means the Government is furious. The judiciary will be gagging to make amends.'

'And the prejudice caused by the reports in the media, which every potential juror will have seen...?'

'There's not a perceived unfairness which the Appeal Court thinks cannot be remedied by proper directions from the trial judge. Handy when you're a prosecutor, not so good on this side of the fence.'

'On the defence side of de-fence?'

Crowe curled a lip. Maybe it wasn't just females who didn't appreciate my humour. 'The judge will tell the new jury to put out of their minds anything they may have heard or read about the case and to concentrate their deliberations only on the evidence put before them. I'd quite like to know what that evidence is likely to be.'

We stopped outside the front doors to the Lawnmarket, next to the statue of David Hume. Dressed in toga and sandals, the philosopher's right big toe was shiny from people, accused and counsel alike, rubbing it for luck before they went inside.

'How long are you going to be with your deferred sentence?' I asked. 'If you like, I can wait and we can grab a coffee at Florentine's while I tell you everything I know about the case. We could discuss it over an espresso.' I laughed. He didn't.

'Let me make one thing abundantly clear,' he said. 'I'll accept your instructions, but I still don't like you.' He walked away. The glass doors of the court parted as he approached. 'Have the papers with my clerk by lunch.'

Chapter 24

The only set of papers I had for Kirkslap's case was the one I'd received by way of mandate from Caldwell & Craig. The papers would have to be copied a couple of times and properly bound. For Grace-Mary that meant getting out the needle and pink string; ring-pull binders just wouldn't do.

Off the train, and on the way back to the office, I stopped at my place to collect the brief, only to discover a suitcase inside the front door and another in the hallway.

'That you, Robbie?'

I went through to the livingroom to see my dad, propped on one crutch and studying a hairbrush that Joanna must have left behind. It had long plastic teeth with styling bumps at the end. Ex-cop, Alex Munro, had evidently deduced that the device would have been of little effect on my short back and sides.

'What's this doing here?' he asked, holding up prosecution label number one - a hairbrush.

There was a perfectly innocent explanation.

'Jill's,' I said. 'What brings you here and what's with all the suitcases?' My dad pulled some hairs from the brush and studied them closely. Brunette, just like Jill's. Only if he started to measure the length of them would I really be in trouble. 'I'm sure she wouldn't mind you borrowing it, though,' I said.

He grunted and set the brush down again on the coffee table. 'Got the roofers in. All my stuff is happed-up and the place is covered with tarpaulins.' He hobbled over to the couch, let the crutch fall and dropped into it. 'Where's the controls?'

We hunted around until we found the remote wedged underneath him.

'So, how long are you planning to stay?' I asked, as though the answer was of little import.

'Long as it takes,' was the best I could get out of him.

Twenty minutes later, I left him with tea and toast, taking the Kirkslap papers with me and reeling from the shock of my unexpected house guest. A drop of rain spat down the back of my neck. Did roofers work in the wet?

Joanna was there when I eventually made it to the office. Kirkslap had called, she'd assured him that preparations were well underway and a consultation had been set up for six-thirty that evening. I told her that I'd formally instructed Cameron Crowe as counsel.

'He doesn't like you,' she said.

'I know. Don't worry, it's purely personal.'

We cleared my desk for the first time probably ever and set about making up a new brief. There was no point chucking absolutely everything the Crown had disclosed into a brief, and so Joanna and I separated out what we had decided were the relevant papers, while Grace-Mary stitched them into neat bundles, each with its own index. We had bundles for Police statements, civilian statements and precognitions and for the various forensic reports and the transcript of Kirkslap's interview with the police.

There were also some DVD's with no descriptions, only Crown label numbers on them. I expected they would be the video versions of Kirkslap's police interviews and perhaps a film tour of various loci, including Kirkslap's lodge where the murder was supposed to have taken place, zooming in on the bloodstained carpet and car boot. There might also be footage of the route taken by Kirkslap on his late-night road-trip, all as tracked via the GPS chip on his mobile phone.

'We should really watch these,' Joanna said. She was right, but we only had a couple of hours before we were supposed to consult and, as Grace-Mary pointed out, certain technological advances had yet to reach the offices of Munro & Co. It wasn't a huge problem for me. I used to take Crown DVD's home and watch them there. I suggested Joanna do the same.

'I'll stay here and finish off the rest of the paper work. Be back for six at the latest.'

She held out her hand. 'Key?'

'You won't need it. My dad's there just now. He's broken his leg and is convalescing. It's no problem, he's perfectly harmless.'

Grace-Mary suddenly felt the need to clear her throat.

'He's fairly harmless,' I corrected myself. 'Just tell him who you are and that he's to stop watching day-time TV or his football DVD's and let you use the telly. If he doesn't like it, tell him I said he can take up his crutches and hobble off to a hotel.'

'Yeah, like I'm going to say that,' Joanna said, pushing the brown, padded envelope that held the DVD collection into her giant handbag. 'Anyway, I'll bet he's perfectly charming.'

'Joanna's never met your dad, then,' Grace-Mary said, after my assistant had left, tossing me another neatly-stitched bundle headed: *'Speed Camera and Vehicle Reports'*.

Attached to it by a short treasury tag was an A5 book of photographs, with the Scottish Police Service crest on the blue cardboard cover with the words: Semper Vigilo underneath.

There were several photographs of the speed camera in situ, and two showing the rear of a vehicle. The first of those was of a black Audi Q7, the second a close-up of the registration plate.

'So what's the story,' Grace-Mary asked, as I handed her the final pile of documents to go under her needle. 'Just how guilty is he?'

The short answer was, very, but I made do with, 'too early to say, really. Looks bad at the moment, but I have yet to weave the old Robbie Munro magic.'

Grace-Mary sucked the end of the pink string, closed an eye and pushed it at the eye of the flat-blade needle. 'Make stuff up you mean? Like you usually do?'

'What I do is seek out and compile an alternative view of the facts and present them to the jury.'

'An alternative to the truth?'

'Quid est veritas?' I find that a good way to end an argument, especially one you're liable to lose, is to lapse into Latin. Unfortunately, not when the person on the other side is my secretary.

She hit back with a quote from the Bard. 'The truth will out.'

Not if I could help it, it wouldn't. 'You want me to have a go at that?' I asked, as Grace-Mary failed yet again to thread the needle.

'No, I'll manage.' She took off her glasses and pushed them onto the top of her head. The next attempt also failed. 'I've been pushing this needle through so much paper today that my hands are shaking,' she said, lining up another charge at the needle-eye. 'I'm glad this is the last one.' Her glasses fell off her head and onto her chest. The gold chain around her neck to which they were attached became caught in her hair, and she spent a moment disentangling it before taking up the needle again.

Watching my secretary, combing her hair flat with her fingers, I suddenly remembered Joanna's hairbrush.

'When those are finished, call a courier and have them sent to Cameron Crowe's clerk at the Advocates' Library,' I said, grabbing my jacket from the back of a chair.

'Cameron Crowe?' I heard Grace-Mary say. 'You're kidding right?'

But I was already in the corridor and running down the stairs.

Chapter 25

'You two having fun?' I walked into the livingroom to find my dad seated on the sofa, his stookie resting comfortably on a cushion on the coffee table. By the looks of the glass of whisky in his hand, he'd found the bottle of ten year-old Talisker I'd inadequately concealed behind a family-sized cornflakes packet in one of the kitchen cupboards.

Joanna was sitting in an armchair with the TV remote in one hand and a cup of coffee in the other. Both she and my dad had their eyes fixed on the screen as they watched the blurry image of shoppers going in and out of somewhere that I eventually recognised as the Buchanan Galleries in Glasgow. The date and time at the bottom of the screen showed 14.23 hours on 31st October 2012.

'We're just watching the last pictures of that woman your client murdered,' my dad said. 'Out shopping one minute and then...'

'And then what?' I asked.

'We haven't got to that bit yet.' He took a drink of my whisky, staring straight ahead at the CCTV footage. 'Aye, the Talisker ten. Not a bad drop, but it's nothing on the eighteen.'

'Nothing like the price either.' I had a quick look around to see if I could spy Joanna's brush. I couldn't. I caught my dad glancing at me out of the side of his eye. I'd seen that look before. 'What have we learned so far?'

'Nothing we didn't already know,' Joanna said, 'although it's all much more real when you see it on television and don't just read it in statement. This is the last anyone ever saw Violet Hepburn.'

'Where is she?'

Joanna had to rewind and play a few times before I could pick out a head in the crowd. The face was only on screen for a second, but her parents and a video identification expert were all satisfied it was Violet Hepburn, buying make-up from a cosmetic counter at John Lewis, around two-fifteen. The CCTV showed her leaving the Galleries just a few minutes later and blending into the crowd on a dull and dreary Monday afternoon in late October.

'If it wasn't for all the brollies, they might have been able to follow her a bit better,' my dad said.

'And that's the last anyone saw of her?'

'Apart from your client when he murdered her,' my dad said, rather predictably. He drank some more whisky.

'You'd have thought a neighbour might have been able to narrow the times down more accurately,' Joanna said. 'No-one seems to have noticed anything strange until the Friday night when there was a disturbance outside her house. Some neds found an on-line grocery delivery outside Violet's door and started chucking it about. One of the neighbours called the cops.'

'When was the order placed?' I couldn't remember seeing that in the papers I'd read.

'First November. It was the last purchase she ever made with her credit card.'

'What did she buy?' my dad asked.

'Ignore him,' I told Joanna, 'he thinks he's still a cop.'

'And why was she having home deliveries?' my dad asked. 'Did she work?'

'Not really,' I said.

'Scrounger, then?'

'No, I don't think she was signing-on,' I said in defence of the deceased.

'Miss Hepburn was what you might call a good-time girl, Mr Munro,' Joanna said, probably thinking that references to 1940's melodramas might aid my father's understanding of the late Violet's occupation.

'A prozzie was she?'

'Did you not read all about the trial in the paper, first time round?' I asked.

'I wasn't really paying that much attention.' My dad read newspapers from the back pages forward and usually stopped when he came to the crossword. 'But I don't remember anything being said about her being on the game.'

Joanna corrected him 'She wasn't a prostitute, Mr Munro. She made friends with rich men and they bought her gifts, clothes and jewellery. She didn't necessarily have to perform, you know... sexually.'

My dad finished his drink. I'd have to find a better hiding place for that bottle. 'Is that a fact? Don't suppose those rich guys would chip in for a present for me, do you? I've got a birthday coming up.'

It was nearly five and we still had to get back to the office, collect our set of papers, make sure that Crowe's brief had been couriered and then head west for the consultation.

'Mustn't forget this again,' Joanna said, after we had packed away the DVD's into the brown Jiffy-bag.

The whole point of my going home had been to avoid any reference to the hairbrush. I'd become so engrossed in Violet Hepburn's last movements, as shown on TV, that I'd completely forgotten. Joanna went over to the mantelpiece and retrieved her hairbrush. Her actions didn't go unnoticed by a certain ex-cop.

'Can I pour you another wee drink before I go?' I asked him. He didn't reply. My dad ignoring the offer of a fine single-malt? Not good.

'No, hen,' he said to Joanna, an edge to his voice, looking at me all the time. 'That's Jill's brush, you know, Jill, Robbie's girlfriend.'

'Don't think so,' Joanna said, 'I've had it for years.' She gave the brush a quick once-over out of politeness. 'Nope, definitely mine. I left it here this morning. We had quite a night of it last night. I was totally shattered this morning. Still am.' She stuffed the brush along with the envelope into her handbag.

'Right,' I said. 'I've got a business meeting tonight so just make yourself something to eat from whatever's lying around, and I'll see you later. No need to wait up.'

But, by the look on his face, I thought he probably would.

Chapter 26

Larry Kirkslap's home would have been more accurately described as a bachelor pad, were it not for the small matter of his marriage, twenty-six years previously, to the long-suffering Marjorie. It was a Fyfestone and timber lodge, built into the side of a hill on the fringes of the Loch Lomond and Trossachs National Park, with no neighbours within sight and deer in the garden.

Despite some seriously fast driving, it had taken Joanna and me the best part of an hour to find the place, situated as it was somewhere between Aberfoyle and Kinlochard, two towns that shared a horse. When we arrived, Kirkslap, Zack and Mike were waiting for us.

'The moment I set eyes on it, I knew it was the place for me,' Kirkslap said. 'It's out of the way and yet only an hour from Glasgow and not much more to Edinburgh.'

Why wasn't the man worried? I'd be a wreck. He'd been found guilty once, probably would be again, and yet he was relaxed and pleased to show me and my assistant around a lodge thats interior design fell somewhere between Laura Ashley and Harry Lauder.

'Shot that beast myself,' he said, patting the antlers on a stuffed stag's head that was fixed to the wall, half-way down a flight of tartan-carpeted stairs. 'Plenty of good hunting up here. You could easily live off what you kill. Nothing like a nice piece of venison is there?' He gave Joanna the vegetarian a knowing nudge. 'Sadly, I had to surrender all my guns when all this nonsense over Violet Hepburn kicked-off. Haven't shot anything in months.'

'Can we get started?' Mike was as keen as I was that Kirkslap curtail the guided tour so that we could talk business. The preliminary hearing was only two days away. We were supposed to be able to tell the court we were ready for trial. Some kind of defence would have been nice too.

When we did gather to talk about the case, I made it clear from the outset that I did not approve of meetings with anyone other than my client. Solicitor/client confidentiality didn't extend to business partners and well-wishers. Anything stupid or incriminatory that Kirkslap said, would go no further than Joanna or me, but, if a sneaky Prosecutor got wind of a free-for-all consultation of the type that had been lined up for that evening, in theory, all non-lawyers present could end up on a Crown witness list.

'You're forgetting - I am a lawyer,' Mike said. We were all seated in the den, a log fire blazing in the hearth. He laid his iPad case on his knee, opened a word-processing app and prepared himself to take notes. 'Not a criminal lawyer, but I consider myself part of the defence team.' All eyes turned to Zack.

'Fine,' he said, pulling himself out of the armchair he'd not long sat down in.

'No, let Zack stay,' Kirkslap said. 'This case is just as important to him as it is to me. If I go down for this, so does he. So does all of P45.'

I wasn't there to question Kirkslap's high opinion of himself; however, I did have a feeling that, with his track record, Zack would manage to keep things afloat, and that, notwithstanding the young American's PR shortcomings, if need be there would be others available to step into Kirkslap's shoes and front the company.

Joanna took out notepad and pen as I began to summarise what I knew of the prosecution case, highlighting the negatives.

It took a while.

At the end, there were several important pieces of damaging evidence that Kirkslap just couldn't explain.

'We need answers,' I said, for the umpteenth time. '*It wisnae me,* is not going to cut it as a defence.'

Mike stirred the dying embers in the grate with a poker and lobbed on another couple of logs from a stack by the hearth. 'All right, Robbie. There's no need for that tone.'

I didn't take my eyes off Kirkslap. He couldn't take his eyes off the drinks cabinet, though I'd told him there would be no alcohol consumed during our consultation. 'Joanna's going to give you a list of the points that caused the most trouble during the first trial.' From our perusal of the papers, Joanna and I had hurriedly prepared a document containing the edited highlights of the Crown case. From that we'd compiled a list of the most important blocks of circumstantial evidence on which the prosecution case had been constructed. We needed explanations from our client in order to remove as many of those blocks as possible, and thus undermine the Crown case.

That was the plan. Unfortunately Kirkslap wasn't a great help. After a couple of hours discussion we had barely managed to dislodge a single brick from the wall of evidence that stood between him and an acquittal.

'You're giving me homework?' Kirkslap stared glumly at the sheet of paper Joanna handed to him via Mike.

'We must know where you stand on these important questions, Mr Kirkslap,' Joanna said. 'Read them over. Think about them carefully. Just take your time—'

'And let us have your answers by tomorrow afternoon,' I said.

Kirkslap made a low growling noise in the back of his throat as though he was wondering why he bothered to hire lawyers if he had to do all the work himself.

Mike looked at his watch. 'I think we've gone as far as we can tonight.'

Everyone stood except for Kirkslap. He was still staring at the sheet of paper in his hand; a breakdown of the case against him. I hoped it was slowly dawning on him how much work was required for his defence to succeed, and how much that defence, whatever we eventually came up with, relied upon him to produce some credible answers. I wasn't asking the world. Not even the truth. Some half-believable lies would at least give us something to work with.

'The preliminary hearing is at two o'clock on Friday,' I reminded everyone. 'We're going to meet at the consulting rooms at one four two High Street at noon, so that we can have a chat with counsel before the case calls. They won't make this a floating trial, there are far too many witnesses. They'll probably book it in for sometime in May, possibly June. That will give us a good two or three months to be ready.'

'That long?' Zack sounded disappointed. 'I just wish we could get it over and done with. All this uncertainty is causing havoc with our stock price.'

'Thank you for your heart-felt sympathy,' Kirkslap told his business partner.

'You know what I mean, Larry. Shares in P45 have been on a roller-coaster ride for months now. If we're going to further expand we need finance. The banks won't come near us the way we are right now.'

'If the trial is not going to be for months, what's the big hurry in me handing my homework in?' Kirkslap asked, sheet of paper in hand.

'For one thing, counsel will expect to know the answers to all these questions so he can prepare a defence statement for Friday's hearing, and, for another, depending on what your answers are, we're going to need time to investigate and shore up some weak areas of the defence.' If there was a defence.

I couldn't believe that Andy had let the case go to trial in such a half-baked state. As far as I could make out, defence counsel's tactics had been to sit back and see if the Crown could prove its case. Well it could, it had and would do again if nothing were done about it.

Zack went over to Kirkslap and gave him a friendly shove on the shoulder. 'You know I'd ditch the whole business if I could make this thing go away for you, Larry,' he said.

Kirkslap grunted. He was just a big baby. He looked the part; big and brash, and he could definitely talk the talk, but just how intelligent was he? I remembered his smiling face as he exited the High Court on the day his first trial was deserted. Understandable and expected of someone who has been freed after undergoing the most traumatic month of his life, and yet, that had been his demeanour all through the proceedings. The man had more front than Buckingham Palace, sailing through life expecting things to fall into place for him. Up until now they had.

Mike gestured for Joanna and me to follow him.

'I might not be able to come up with all the right answers,' Kirkslap called after us. 'But in case you're wondering, and seeing how you haven't bothered to ask, I didn't kill Violet.'

I turned around and walked back into the room. 'Then who did?' Perhaps I'd expected too much, thinking he might come up with an alternative scenario to that already sketched by Her Majesty's Advocate.

He blinked a few times. 'Someone else... I suppose.'

Chapter 27

Tuesday had been busy enough; Wednesday was even worse. There were trials, deferred sentences and custodies all calling at Livingston, and from mid-afternoon onwards my diary was packed with clients who'd been bumped while I'd focussed my attention on the Kirkslap case. Now that the brief was prepared, in the hands of counsel and I'd consulted with the client who was aware of those issues urgently needing addressed, I had some breathing space until the preliminary hearing on Friday.

Joanna was sitting at her desk in reception, sorting the mail, when I went to give her some final orders for the day ahead.

'I want you to have Grace-Mary give you the files for all the intermediate diets coming up in the next fortnight. Make sure we've sent out disclosure letters on them all, download any statements that have come in from the PF and then check to see if we need to draft any section one-forty-nine-Bs. You know what Brechin is like - he's the only Sheriff in Scotland who insists on those being lodged.

Throughout this little speech, Joanna was nodding continually, whilst generally ignoring me as she sifted through the yellow wire basket, selecting correspondence that needed a reply from that needing filed or binned.

I was leaving when I found my path blocked by a purse-lipped Kaye Mitchell. 'Care to tell me what's happening?' asked the newspaper editor. 'Between you and Jill,' she added, although I'd already guessed the reason for her stern expression.

I really had no time to discuss my troubled love-life and, yet, at that precise moment Kaye was the only connection I had to the object of my affections.

'A misunderstanding,' I said.

'Is that right?' she said, staring down at Joanna.

'Yes, it is right,' my assistant replied, neither looking up nor pausing in her letter sifting. 'So you can stop looking at me like that.'

'Oh, well then, that's fine, Robbie.' Kaye made as though to leave. 'I'll let Jill know, shall I? That when she phones you, early morning, and the call is answered by another woman, young enough to be your—'

'Wee sister?' I suggested.

Joanna grimaced and dropped into the bucket some glossy leaflets inviting the lawyers from Munro & Co. to exciting and expensive CPD seminars in London on subjects I'd never heard of.

'But not in an incestuous way,' I corrected myself, making matters worse.

'Good. Glad that's settled,' Kaye said. 'I'll tell Jill she can rest assured there is absolutely nothing to worry about and that it's all been a big misunderstanding.'

I only knew two certain ways of placating irate women and both of them were chocolate. I had a box somewhere from a grateful client. The last person seen in charge of them had been Grace-Mary, who was in the next room wielding a red pen over my monthly figures.

'Robbie and I worked all night on Monday preparing a defence brief,' Joanna was telling Kaye when I returned with the box of chocs.

I opened the box and offered it to Kaye.

'Preparing a brief. That what they're calling it these days?' She helped herself to a strawberry cream. 'Robbie's idea of a brief is something scrawled on the back of a beer mat. This is Mr Seat-of-his-pants we're talking about.'

'A brief for the Kirkslap case,' I said.

Kaye stopped mid-chew. 'Kirkslap? Who? *Larry* Kirkslap?'

'You've heard of him, I take it. His story was in some of the *quality* papers,' Joanna said.

'You're acting for Larry Kirkslap?' is what Kaye said. *'You're acting for Larry Kirkslap, do you expect me to believe that, and is that really the best lie you can come up with?'* was what it sounded like.

'Didn't you know his case has been re-indicted?' I asked. Kaye's blank expression was answer enough. When I thought about it, why should she have? I hadn't heard any mention of it on the news or read about it in the newspapers.

'When was this decided?' Kaye demanded, inserting another soft centre.

'There was a hearing last Friday,' I said. 'I don't think there was a decision until late-on and the indictment wasn't served until Sunday.'

'How come this is the first I've heard of it?' Kaye asked herself. She thought about it over a Turkish delight. 'If it was too late for the Sundays maybe they're saving it for this weekend.' She looked up from her contemplations. 'When is he next in court?'

'Friday.'

Kaye smiled. 'That would make a lot of sense. Grab a few photos of Kirkslap going into court, then slap the story on the front pages next Sunday morning. They'll all be in it together, the Herald on Sunday, SOS, Sunday Mail, and to think I handed over everything I knew about the Boyd murder to them on a plate.' She looked at her watch. Nine-fifteen. The Linlithgow Gazette came out on a Friday, with a deadline of noon, Thursday; bags of time to scoop the lot of them. She reached up and ruffled my hair.

'And if Jill calls you, you'll tell her about the misunderstanding,' I said, as she spun on a heel. 'And tell her to give me a call. I don't have her new number!' I yelled after her as she made off at speed.

Ten minutes later I was on the High Street, outside the newsagents, wondering whether it should be crisps or a Mars Bar for breakfast. The phone in my pocket buzzed.

'Is that you, Mr Munro? It's me, Danny.'

'Where are you?'

'I need to see you.'

'You need to see someone all right, but it will have to be Mr Sharp. He's your lawyer.'

There was a pause while Danny absorbed this information and then ignored it. 'Do you have GPS on your phone?'

'Probably,' I said. 'Somewhere.'

He reeled off a sequence of numbers. 'That's where I am. If you can't find it on your phone, use Google Earth.'

He either hung up or lost what had been a fairly weak signal. I'm not sure when I forgot the numbers he'd given to me. It was at some point after I started looking for a pen and sometime before I'd finished jotting them down on the back of my hand. I tried to phone the number on the screen and was put through to his answering service. I left a message for him to call back and went off to court.

Upon my return to an afternoon of clients, I tried to call Danny again without any success. I had the same result when I phoned Malky to talk about the surprise party, and remembered he'd be on air with his early-evening, football phone-in show. I decided to work on for a while, chiefly because I wasn't looking forward to going home to face the one-man firing squad that was my dad, over what Joanna kept referring to as Hairbrush-Gate. When I pointed out it was her forgetfulness that had caused me the grief, she offered to come home with me and explain things to my dad.

'Thanks, but I can handle him,' I said, paying no heed to Grace-Mary's stifled snigger. Bad enough having the staff make fun of you without them fighting your battles as well.

I worked on for a while longer, even catching up with things that were only urgent and not yet critical. At eight I

131

went down to Sandy's for something to eat and at nine, when the café-owner started sweeping up around me, I went home to be confronted by my dad.

'Where have you been? Malky's been here for half an hour,' he said, as though I'd kept royalty waiting.

'I would have been here even sooner, but I forgot Dad was staying here and went to his new place,' my brother said. 'See you've got Spanish roofers on the job - Juan Guy.'

The Munro humour was in the genes.

'You've got one person on the job?' I said. 'That's going to take ages.'

My dad disagreed. 'Not any one person: Arthur Campbell. I want someone who knows what they're doing.'

That would be Arthur Campbell, all right. He was a master stonemason and restorer of ancient monuments. If Stirling Castle ever needed repointed, he'd be the first person called. Asking Arthur to re-slate a cottage roof was like asking Michel Roux junior to whip you up a cheese and ham toastie. He wasn't old enough to be a school chum of my dad's, so I could only assume he was one in the long list of people who owed my dad a favour from his days in the Force. What had Arthur done, I wondered, to which Sergeant Munro had turned a blind eye? For him to be doing the old man's roof, it would have had to have been something fairly serious.

'He'll have it sorted in no time at all. And it'll last. When Arthur Campbell does a roof, the rest of the building can collapse but the roof stays up.'

'And how long - exactly?' I asked, when he'd quite finished laughing at his own joke.

He wiped a tear from the corner of his eye, riffled his moustache with a finger, composure regained. 'A week, ten days.'

'What!'

'He's got other jobs to go to as well.'

'But ten days?'

'Call it two weeks, tops. Now can we discuss what Malky's come all this way to talk about?'

He made it sound like the special-one had circumnavigated the globe and not just hammered twenty-five miles down the motorway in his new 3 series.

'We can't hold the party at Jorge Kleinman's place,' Malky said, when we were seated in the livingroom. 'He's just not for having it, and, anyway, it's too far away. You'd have to lay on a fleet of taxis.' He looked around. 'This place is way too small and if your cottage doesn't have a roof, Dad, I say you hire a function suite.'

'The West Port Hotel has a room,' I said, and there being no other alternative venue that was within easy reach of Linlithgow, Malky agreed to book it for the following Friday night.

That settled, my brother went off to make himself some toast. He came through a short time later with the phone Joanna had loaned me. I'd left it charging in the kitchen. It was lit up and buzzing. 'New mobile?' He lobbed it at me. 'Nice.'

It was Danny Boyd. 'I thought you were coming to see me?' he said.

'Sorry, I didn't catch those numbers you gave me.'

'Five, three—'

'Just tell me where you are.'

'What if someone's listening in?'

'Then they'll be noting down the numbers too and will know better than me what to do with them.'

There was a short pause while young Danny processed this information. 'Do you know the Refuge Stone?'

I didn't.

'You've got a car, right?'

I did.

'Drive up to Cockleroy. Do you know where that is?'

Everyone in Linlithgow knew Cockleroy, the extinct volcano that lay a mile or so to the south.

133

'Go straight on by. There are woods on both sides, don't take the turn for Torphichen and you'll come to a farm on the right hand side. Go past that for—'

'Is this really necessary?'

'Go past the farm and after a wee bit there's only trees on one side of the road. When the trees end, park there and walk down the track on your right. I'll find you.'

'Listen, Danny. If you'll just—'

'And bring food. I'm starving.'

Chapter **28**

The Refuge Stone turned out to be a six foot standing stone in the middle of a field. By the time I'd found it, and Danny Boyd had found me, it was getting on for dark, and the fish and chips I'd brought for him were cold.

'Follow me,' he said, getting stuck into the fish supper. We set off down an endless, bumpy track until we came to the ruins of a walled garden and a derelict outhouse, not far from Lochcote Reservoir, obscured by an entanglement of trees and bushes. Any glass in the windows was long gone, and through the disintegrating frames and into the dilapidated building grew a snarl of weeds and bramble briars.

We came to a door. A few flakes of blue paint remained on its exterior and there was a large gap at the bottom where the wood was rotten and chewed. Danny pushed it open. Inside, the only source of light was a fire, more smoke than flame, encircled by a ring of stones. A battered, soot-stained tin can sat in the centre, steaming gently. Danny ate the last chip, screwed up the fish-supper paper and chucked it onto the smouldering heap of twigs and leaves, some far too green to burn. In the brief burst of illumination that followed, I could see he had cleared an area, ten feet by ten, and that there was a sleeping bag and holdall of clothes at one end of it. 'Thanks,' he said, after a long pull from the bottle of Irn Bru I'd brought with me. He took another drink, burped, wiped his mouth. 'I've been boiling water from the reservoir.'

He crossed to his sleeping bag and sat down on it. I perched on a segment of partially demolished wall.

'You want to tell me what this is all about?' I asked.

'I'm hiding.'

I'd worked that out for myself. 'You can't stay out here in the wilds, drinking loch water out of a tin can forever.' Danny's only response was to hug his knees closer to his chest. 'Your mum's bound to be really worried,' I said. The fire was giving out little heat and a chill wind whipped the back of my neck. 'Danny, you asked me to come and see you. Well, here I am. Talk to me.'

'When's Nathan's funeral? Has it been yet?'

'No, and I don't know when it will be. Could be some way off yet.'

'Will you come and tell me when it is?'

'Look Danny, this is stupid. You're going to have to hand yourself in sometime.'

'Hand myself in where?'

'To the police.'

'Why?'

'Because you... because they think you killed Nathan.'

Danny leapt to his feet. 'What?'

'Why else would you be on the run?'

'They think I killed my own brother?'

'Didn't you?'

'No!'

'Where were you when Nathan was killed?'

'Taking samples of jam and stuff for my mum to the new farm shop up at Aberdovan. I never got back till about tea-time and there was polis everywhere. I could see Nathan lying, covered in blood. They were taking photos of him. I knew what had happened, so I came up here. This is where we used to camp out when me and Nate were ferreting. We kept a stash of food here. Beans and that. There's none left now.'

'Then come back to town with me. We'll this sort this out and get you back home.'

'I can't.'

What was wrong with the boy? 'Then why am I here?'

'I want you to find out how I can get rid the curse.'

136

'What curse?'

'The one on that tomb.'

Was he talking about the attempted break in at the Binny mausoleum?

'I told Nathan no to go there, but he wouldn't listen.'

'What are you talking about? A curse? That's rubbish. Do you think your brother got killed by a ghost or something?' I didn't want to make fun of the boy; however, the wind was really picking up and it had started to rain. My back was getting wet and my clothes were filling with reek from the damp fire. 'Come on. I'll take you home. You can stay the night in your own bed and we can speak to the police in the morning. Actually, not me. Mr Sharp's your lawyer. I'll contact him and—'

'You're my lawyer.'

'It doesn't work like that, Danny. You went to see Mr Sharp first, it's like an unwritten rule us lawyers have.'

'I don't care, I want you to be my lawyer. Anyway, it doesn't matter. I'm staying here. I'm not ending up like Nate. Find out what I have to do to make things right. I can live without food for a few days more.'

'You're being stupid, Danny. If a curse can get you at home it can get you anywhere.'

'Not if it doesn't know where I am. Not if I keep on the move.'

I wasn't having this conversation. 'Look, I've no idea how you make things right with a curse. It's all superstition. Someone real killed Nathan, and the longer you stay in hiding the more the police are going to think it was you.'

Danny climbed into his sleeping bag. He was going nowhere.

'At least let me tell your mum where you are and that you're okay.'

Danny shook his head. 'I don't want her involved. Just find out what I need to do. I won't be able to call you again because my phone's just about out of batteries.' He lay down and turned onto his side, facing the wall. 'I'll wait here until you come back.'

Chapter 29

'How did you sleep?' Thursday morning, I brought my dad his breakfast on a tray. He was using my bed and I had been decanted to the sofa.

He looked at the bowl of porridge. 'You've got it all wrong, son. I like my porridge lumpy and my mattress smooth.'

Cracking jokes, first thing in the morning. Not like him.

'That the tie I got you for your last birthday?' It was and I'd been wearing it off and on ever since. The pattern wasn't that great, but it was made of some indestructible material that repelled all kinds of spillages. 'I've always had good taste,' he said. 'What have you got on today?' Showing an interest in my business: even more unusual.

'Oh, same old, same old.' I would have looked at my watch if I had one. Not that I was in any hurry. I only had a few last minute things to do for Kirkslap's preliminary hearing the next day, as Joanna was going to court to deal with the remand court that morning. 'Right, I'll be off then. Busy day ahead. Take it easy. No need to be getting over-energetic, you want to let that bone knit. I'll maybe come back and see you at lunchtime.'

But probably not. I almost made it to the bedroom door.

'Joanna get her hairbrush okay?'

'Yeah, I think so.'

'It wasn't Jill's after all, then?' he said casually; way too casually.

It was either now or later. There was no escape. 'Okay I didn't tell you the whole truth about that.'

'You lied.'

'I thought it would be easier to make something up rather than start with a big explanation when none was needed.'

'Lied to your father.'

It wasn't like it was the first time. 'Yes. Sorry about that. It was just—'

'Don't give me any of your lawyer excuses. If I find out that you're cheating on that lassie. My best friend's daughter—'

'There's nothing going on between me and Joanna. She stayed over-night on Monday because we were working on a case.'

'D'ye expect me to believe that?'

'Dad, I love Jill. You know I'm going to ask her to marry me. Joanna is a work colleague. If it had been Andy staying over, and he left his comb lying about, you wouldn't be accusing me of anything would you?'

He took a spoonful of porridge, chewed for a moment.

'Well would you?'

He sniffed and chomped on another spoonful. 'Aye, well, Andy never had a pair of legs like yon.'

I laughed. He joined in. I sat down on the edge of the bed.

'Dad, what do you know about curses?'

'What kind of curses?'

Bad ones obviously, but there was no need to be facetious when we were getting along so well. 'You know my client, Danny Boyd?'

'You mean Paul Sharp's client, don't you?' His memory was as good as ever.

'He thinks he's cursed,' I said.

My dad leaned forward and had me push another pillow behind his back. 'You know where he is?'

'We've been in communication, let's leave it at that. The point is, he's not handing himself in. He thinks his brother's murder was because of them breaking into that mausoleum, and he's staying in hiding, more worried about a curse than the cops.'

'Killed by a curse? Think up that defence yourself?' My dad finished his porridge and wiped his moustache with the square of kitchen roll I'd provided. 'I've got news for you – it's not going to work.'

'Seriously, dad. What can I say to him? He won't come out of hiding until I find a way to stop the curse. It's no good me telling him it's all bollocks.'

'Maybe it's not. I don't suppose you can go breaking into tombs without expecting bad luck to follow.'

'That's a bit superstitious of you,' I said.

'Tell that to Lord Carnarvon. One minute he's digging up Tutankhamen, the next they're digging his grave. And,' he said forcefully, lest I come in at that point and suggest it was all nonsense, 'the rest of his archaeology team all got bumped off one way or another. I saw it on the Discovery Channel.'

'Dad, we're talking about a forgotten wee mausoleum on the outskirts of Linlithgow, not the great pyramid of Giza. It's about two miles from your house and I'll bet you never even knew it existed.'

'Oh, I see. Pure coincidence is it. That mausoleum is hundreds of years old and the first person who tampers with it...' he banged a fist down onto the tray, striking the handle of the spoon that was sticking out of the bowl, sending it spinning across the room and against the wall. 'Ach, on you go. Believe what you like,' he said, as though I were flying in the face of over-whelming evidence; not an entirely novel experience for me, it had to be said, 'but there are tombs all over the place if you look hard enough. There's Forbes's mausoleum in Falkirk at Callendar Park, there's the Dunmore mausoleum in Airth. I think there's one at The Binns too, and Greyfriars Kirkyard is full of them, so is the Necropolis up at Glasgow Cathedral. You can hardly chuck your bunnet without it landing on one.'

'So?'

'When do you ever hear of one being broken into?'

'Apart from the one down the road from you?'

He shook his head at my patent stupidity. 'That's what I'm saying. Break into a tomb and bad things will happen to you – that's why no-one does it. You'd need to be a daft laddie like that Boyd boy. There's nothing inside apart from dead men's bones and every chance that you're going to get a very unpleasant comeuppance.'

'So what's the answer? What do I tell him? What's worse? The curse or the cops?'

My dad took the tray from his lap and set it to one side. He swung his plaster-cast leg out of bed. 'Tell him he's stuffed whatever he does.'

Chapter 30

'Mr Crowe,' Lord Haldane, adjusted his spectacles, folded his hands on the bench in front of him and peered down to his left at counsel for the defence. 'It is of no concern to this court should your client choose to switch horses mid-stream.' The High Court judge brushed a hand down the starched-white fall that draped from his wing collars over his silk cape, two red crosses visible either side of his chest. 'This defence has been prepared and ready for some considerable time, indeed, Mr Staedtler advised the court so himself, only a week ago.'

'My Lord, Mr Staedtler's concept of preparedness does not coincide with my own; furthermore, I received the papers in this case only—'

'If *senior* counsel tells this court the defence is prepared, then it's prepared, Mr Crowe. Your apparent inability to properly organise your affairs is a problem for you to resolve, and does not represent a cogent reason why I should grant your motions to continue this preliminary hearing and postpone the fixing of a trial date.'

'M'Lord, in my respectful submission—'

'The answer is no, Mr Crowe.' The judge looked benignly down to his right where sat the Lord Advocate's depute. 'Miss Faye?'

Fiona Faye rose to her feet in a swirl of black silk gown and frilly-white blouse. Now I knew why she had been unavailable for Kirkslap's original trial. Fiona had moved to the dark side. Crown Office. She was already a Q.C. Clearly someone, somewhere, had enticed her to Castle Greyskull on the promise of high office if she did the right thing. 'If it please the court, I understand your Lordship's clerk has identified a week on Monday as a suitable start date for trial and I can confirm the Crown's readiness to proceed.'

'Very well,' said Lord Haldane, 'now if there are no further motions...'

There were, but it was clear any requests from the defence weren't going to find favour with the judge.

'Court!' called out the macer, and we all stood. Lord Haldane bowed. Fiona bowed back. Cameron Crowe barely lowered his chin.

'What's got into Haldane?' I asked Crowe, as we exited to meet a worried looking Kirkslap on the marble landing outside Court 3. At the foot of the brass-banistered staircase, a knot of journalists had formed, notepads at the ready, and beyond, at the front door to the building, television cameras.

Crowe swiped the horse-hair wig from his head and gripped it tightly by his side. 'Someone's got to him. He's had a word from on high to get this trial restarted, which means that we're going to trial in a week's time, come hell or high-water.' He turned his attention to the client. 'Mr Kirkslap, time is rapidly running out. You are going to have to come up with a lot more information than you have already and quickly.'

During our consultation earlier that morning, it had become increasingly clear that the accused had done very little of the homework he'd been set by Joanna a couple of evenings before. There remained holes in his defence through which the Crown would be more than happy to drive an evidential coach and horse.

Crowe fixed Kirkslap with his evil eye. 'Mr Staedtler might have been happy to sit back and enjoy the scenery while the Crown literally threw everything at you but the kitchen sink - I don't work that way.'

'I don't think you mean, *literally*,' Mike said, arriving with Zack.

'I was using literally, figuratively,' Crowe said. 'Now if we can stop picking holes in my grammar and start filling a few of the gaping holes in the defence, Mr Kirkslap might not spend the rest of his life behind bars.'

I gave Joanna a little, told-you-so look, in vindication of my choice of counsel.

'And as for you,' Crowe pointed a finger in my face and bared his fangs. 'You are going to drop all your sordid little legal aid cases and concentrate solely on Mr Kirkslap's defence. Understand?'

If this had been one of my sordid little legal aid cases, Crowe might very well have been eating his horse-hair bunnet by now, but for what I was charging my time out to Kirkslap's company, I could take the occasional kick in the shins from counsel. I gave my assurances and waited with Crowe, Joanna and Mike at the top of the stairs while the dour-faced directors of P45 walked down them to meet the press. I would have liked to have gone with them. If you can't afford a cheesy TV advertising campaign, the next best thing is to get your face on the local news beside a high-profile accused.

'I'm not joking,' Crowe said, as though I might have thought he'd been having a laugh. 'There is a great deal of work to be done and little time in which to do it. That man is impossible. I've never heard anyone talk so much and yet reveal so little useful information.' I found that hard to believe from someone who spent so many years at the Bar. 'If we're going to win this case, we're going to need to give the jury some alternatives.'

'*An* alternative,' Mike chipped in. 'You can only have one alternative...'

He tailed off as Crowe cleared his throat impatiently. 'If I'm going to have to surf the wave, make that a Tsunami, of Prosecution evidence in this case, I want to throw some other options to the jury. I need someone —'

Joanna beat me to it. 'With a motive?'

'The one thing in Kirkslap's favour is that he has no motive for killing Miss Hepburn, so, as you say,' Crowe

145

condescended, 'finding someone with a motive would be ideal. Unfortunately, men kill women for all sorts of reasons, frequently on the spur of the moment and sometimes for no obvious reason at all. One thing we might be able to use is the fact that most murdered women are killed by men they know; most likely someone with whom they are, or have been, in a relationship.' Sounded quite a lot like the Violet/Kirkslap set-up to me. 'Yes, a motive would be excellent, but, perhaps, that's being a tad over optimistic. I'd settle for someone, preferably crooked, who knew Violet and had the opportunity to kill her.'

'The last defence team looked into her previous relationships in some detail and there's nothing of any interest,' Joanna said.

'Mr Crowe's not talking about Violet's past boyfriends and romantic liaisons,' I said.

Crowe agreed. 'We all know what kind of person she was—'

Joanna cut him off. 'What kind of person is that?'

'A glorified call-girl,' Crowe said. 'Someone out to make money from men, and not too fussy what she had to do to earn it. For a woman like that, violence is an occupational hazard.'

'She was only doing what she had to, to get by,' Joanna said.

Crowe's smile was little more than a baring of teeth. 'How very sisters-are-doing-it-for-themselves of you.'

'It wasn't as if Violet was hanging around industrial estates, shouting at men in passing motors,' I said.

'That's right,' Mike chipped in. 'She was one of the regular girls at Karats. They don't let just anyone in.'

'I'll take your word for that,' Crowe replied. 'Say what you like, our Miss Hepburn was a hooker. A high class hooker, perhaps, but such a woman is always going to meet unpleasant people. We need to dig up...' he grinned horribly at Mike, 'not literally, an alternative suspect. At the moment

Kirkslap is isolated. No man is an island, but in these proceedings our boy is Ben-bloody-becula.' He jabbed a finger at me again. 'I want you to find if there was someone unsavoury who knew Violet in her *professional* capacity. We'll put that person on a witness list and lodge his schedule of previous convictions. If we can muddy the waters enough, I guarantee that there are some on the jury who'll think that a woman who uses her physical charms to sponge off rich men, has got what was coming to her. Most of those will be women. I find that female jurors can be highly judgmental of their own gender.'

How Crowe had come to that conclusion, I didn't know, but his plan came straight out of the Robbie Munro book of smoke and mirrors. Maybe we weren't so unlike after all.

'Where did you say Violet plied her trade?' Crowe asked Mike.

Mike opened his iPad case. It was a handy device. You never knew when it was going to come in useful. In a few deft manipulations he had brought up the web-site for Karats champagne bar, all turquoise and gold graphics.

Crowe took a fleeting look at the electronic tablet, then seized hold of my bicep and ushered me further along the landing, our backs to Joanna and Mike. 'We both know you have a certain knack when it comes to rooting around in the dirt,' he said. 'Do what comes naturally, but do it quickly.'

Chapter 31

I was thoroughly scrubbed and dressed in my best, grey suit over a black shirt that Jill had bought me in advance of my birthday. I didn't come any smarter than this, and yet the doorman still took a good, long look at me, from polished shoes to new haircut, before somewhat grudgingly pushing open the smoked-glass doors to Karats Champagne Bar. The plush interior was replete with turquoise fabrics and gold fitments. Suddenly, I had a deep longing for the bare, reclaimed-timber floor, painted wood-chip walls and water-stained ceiling of the Red Corner Bar, where I usually found myself at some stage of a Friday night; more often than not to prise my dad loose from a bar stool and sling him into a taxi; however, this Friday night was different. This Friday I was suited, booted and hefting an enormous wedge of expenses, courtesy of the accused in the case of Her Majesty's Advocate –v- Larry Kirkslap. My business account would describe the trip as an evidence-gathering mission.

I took a deep breath and, as I walked through the candlelit bar, piano-player crooning Paul Anka in a far corner, I realised that I wasn't under, but over-dressed. Any dress-code applied to women only. The male occupants of the velvet-lined booths were not only a lot older than me, but casually attired; chino's and checked shirts or, at best, rumpled suits seemed to be the order of the day. I could sense disappointed stares from the group of bored-looking, mahogany-tanned women, gathered by the powder-room as they watched me walk up to the bar, my best clobber semaphoring the fact that I wasn't rich, that I was trying too hard. More was less here. I should have come in dressed like a scruff and the girls in the slinky evening gowns and tight-fitting dresses would have been all over me.

'What can I get you sir?' asked the barman, leaning across a beaten-copper counter top, so highly polished it shone like gold.

I pulled out a wallet that was straining at the seams. 'This is a champagne bar, isn't it?'

The barman perked up a little at that and slid a menu across the counter at me. I hadn't realised there were so many varieties, all listed in order of price. Obviously no-one bought the cheapest and the clear sign of a cheapskate was to order the second cheapest on the list. I selected the Perrier Jouet Belle Epoque 2002. I'd no idea if it was any good. I liked the name and it was sufficiently mid-table to be reassuringly expensive. 'Two bottles,' I said, I hoped, airily, looking around the dimly-lit room. The booths along the walls were all occupied. I pointed to an empty table in the centre of the room. 'I'll be sitting over there.'

The pop of the first champagne cork was like a starting gun to the bronzed women in the corner, two of them broke loose from the pack and came over to me. I could imagine Kirkslap and his colleagues, Mike and Zack, at their celebration night here, back in December 2011, commandeering a corner booth, ordering a dozen bottles of vintage Bollinger and waiting as Violet and the other would-be prospectors wiggled and giggled their way over.

My girls were called Molly and Candy, blonde and brunette. They were young, pneumatic and smelt as lovely as they looked. They sat down either side of me. No sooner had they done so than the waiter arrived with two more glasses. He poured each of the ladies a drink and we clinked glasses. I had the strangest feeling that I'd seen Candy before, though I doubted we moved in the same circles; I certainly didn't remember her from a Friday night at the Red Corner Bar.

The night drove on. The young women were delightful company and became even more delightful as we started on the second bottle of champagne. They were witty and intelligent, never letting the conversation flag for a minute, never failing to laugh at my jokes. There was a moment, shortly before I ordered another bottle of champagne, and as I stuck the second dead Frenchman nose down into the ice bucket, when I thought of Jill. I hadn't spoken to her in a week. Since her phone call on Tuesday morning, the one that had been answered by Joanna, I'd tried every number I had to call her. I'd sent emails, left messages on switchboards, answering machines; and nothing. Was she dodging me? Who did she think she was, going off in the huff? I'd done nothing wrong. I wasn't the one away on skiing trips with hunky Swiss guys. I looked at my gorgeous bookends and wished they were gone and that Jill was there instead. What a night that would have been; just me, my wife-to-possibly-be, champagne and someone else's money.

I beckoned to the barman with an upraised index finger and while I waited for the next bottle to arrive, Molly and Candy excused themselves and floated off in the direction of the powder room.

'I think you might find it more comfortable over here, sir,' the waiter said, arriving with bottle three in a new ice bucket, and, taking his advice, I followed him to the velvet warmth of a recently vacated booth.

The waiter brought over fresh glasses and was peeling the foil from the top of the bottle when Candy returned minus Molly. She didn't say anything about her friend's departure. I wondered if the girls had arm-wrestled for me in the ladies' room. Or maybe I'd passed some kind of nutter test, been weighed in the balance and found harmless. That was good. It was also good from the point of view that, if such precautions were taken, it meant that there were some dodgy characters about. The gorilla at the front door wasn't there to beat off the hordes of punters who were fighting to get in to spend two hundred quid on a bottle of fizzy French wine. When it came down to it, no matter how much I was enjoying myself, I was there for a reason. I wanted to know the names of any men who had ever been considered a cause for concern or were downright dangerous. In my short time in the bar, I'd already noticed a face I recognised: Tam 'Tuppence' Christie, sharing a booth with a male acquaintance and three young ladies in brightly-coloured, tight-fitting clothing. Tuppence was an ageing Glasgow gangland figure. I was uncertain as to the source of his nickname; however, his notoriety was such that, if he were even loosely associated with Violet Hepburn, it would open up a whole avenue of defence that had not previously been explored.

'Tuppence come here often?' I asked.

Candy smiled and changed the subject. 'La Belle Epoque,' she said, tilting her head to read the label on the champagne bottle, as the waiter twisted off the wire cage and prised out the cork with a satisfying pop.

'The Beautiful Era,' I translated.

'France eighteen ninety to nineteen fourteen.' She'd mentioned earlier that she was a student. History probably. A subject that got more difficult with every passing day. 'Also a female trio with the Seventies hit, Black is Black,' she added. Perhaps with the average age of Karat's clientele it was handy to know something of classical music. Certainly the man on the ivories hadn't ventured this side of the Eighties.

The waiter wrapped a white cotton napkin about the bottle and began to pour. Candy drew a finger down the sleeve of his jacket as, having filled our glasses, he withdrew from the table. He returned a few minutes later with a small glass bowl of strawberries.

'I hope you don't mind,' Candy said, which I took to mean, *I hope you don't mind paying for these, because you are.*

Champagne and strawberries. It was then that I realised where I'd seen Candy before: that afternoon I'd met Kirkslap at Carnbooth House. It was the hair that had fooled me. It had been auburn then; tonight it was a deep chestnut. I felt awkward for the first time since walking into the bar. I'd hoped to casually drop Violet's name into the conversation, find out a little more about her and glean some information that, with a twist here and a little innuendo there, could be put to good use in Kirkslap's defence. Did Candy recognise me? Would she know what I was up to?

She seemed to read my mind. 'Why did you lie earlier?' She asked, dropping a strawberry into her champagne. It hovered for a moment on a billow of golden bubbles before sinking slowly to the bottom of the flute glass. 'When you said you were a pools winner.'

'What I said was that I'd had some luck with betting on football.'

'And have you?'

'As a matter of fact I have,' I said, though the tenner I'd eventually squeezed out of Grant Goodwin's wallet, despite the Sheriff Clerk's valiant efforts to keep it there, was long spent.

'But you're really a lawyer. One of Larry Kirkslap's lawyers.'

I ate a strawberry. Might as well since I was sort of paying for them.

'Can I take it you're here on business not pleasure?' she asked, chewing up my cover story like the strawberry I was enjoying.

I stalled, wondering how to play this without ending up with a glass of champagne over my new suit and the doorman introducing my face to the pavement. 'If it is, it's the most pleasurable business I've ever been on,' I said.

'Does Larry know you're spying on him? Or are you spying on me for him?'

'Larry doesn't know I'm here and, no, he hasn't asked me to spy on you.'

'But I take it you're spending his money?'

'It's a dirty job,' I said.

She smiled. I relaxed, called over the waiter and ordered an eighteen year-old Talisker. Might as well find out if my dad was right when my client was paying for it.

'So why are you here?' Candy asked.

'I'm digging.'

'Aren't we all?' She played with the gold chain around her neck on which was set a single diamond, twice the size of the one in a certain velvet box at the bottom of a drawer in my office.

'Not for gold,' I said. 'For information on Violet Hepburn.'

'Dirt, then.'

'Is there any?'

Candy didn't reply, just lowered the level of her glass with a delicate sip.

'I'm not trying to blacken Violet's character,' I said.

'No?'

'All I want is—'

'Someone else to pin the blame on?' She was definitely not daft.

'Obviously you don't think Larry Kirkslap's a murderer,' I said. 'Not if you're happy enough to keep his company.'

She shrugged. 'A murderer? No. Did he kill Violet? Perhaps. Larry may seem like a big pussycat to you, but he likes things to go his own way. If they don't, believe me, he'll let you know all about it.'

'Got a bit of a temper has he?'

'I saw Larry lose it once and it was quite frightening.'

It wasn't what I'd come to hear. 'You probably come across a lot of men like that in your line of work,' I said. 'Men who are angry and violent when they don't get their own way.' I glanced over at Tuppence Christie and his party.

Candy set her glass down firmly on the table. 'My line of work?'

Touchy. I swiftly moved away from that topic and asked her to tell me about Kirkslap's temper tantrum.

'It was not long after his daughter's wedding.'

I hadn't known Kirkslap had a daughter far less a married one. 'When was this?'

'Last September, anyway, it was weeks after he'd stopped seeing Violet. She turned up unannounced at the reception, drunk and upset. She caused a major scene and had to be carted off. A few days later Larry went to her flat with his lawyer. The lawyer threatened an interdict. Larry threatened something slightly more permanent than a court order.'

'How do you know all this?'

'I was there. I'd started to see Larry back and forwards, and Violet asked me round for a drink. She wanted me to take a step back, give her a free run.'

'She must have really liked him.'

Candy drained the last of the champagne, tilting her glass so that the strawberry fell into her mouth. 'Violet was a lovely girl,' she said, chewing slowly, 'but she was getting on; thirty six on her last birthday.'

Same age as me more or less. 'She'd had a good innings then,' I said.

Candy didn't miss the sarcasm. 'I don't mean it like that.' She allowed me to replenish her glass. 'Violet wasn't old, old. It's just that... well you've seen the other girls here.'

'Can I ask how old are you?'

She was twenty-five. Two years younger than Joanna. Ten years younger than Jill.

'I think she saw Larry as her last chance at a real high-roller. The pair were practically inseparable for six months. I actually believe she heard wedding bells. Dumb. That's not what this place is about.'

I'd assumed it was exactly what Karats was about.

'Do you know what we do here?'

'I have a rough idea,' I said.

'I don't think you do.'

'You're gold-diggers. Looking for rich husbands.'

She sighed. 'We're not here to form long term relationships. We meet men, we're nice to them and in exchange they buy us nice things. They're not looking for anything permanent, we shouldn't be either. No-one's forced to do anything they don't want to. As soon as I've paid for my education, I'm out of here.'

'Unless you end up like Violet. Come on, who else did she know? Tuppence? Some of his pals?'

Candy took a quick sideways look in the direction of the gangster and put a finger to my lips. 'I like you, Robbie,' she said. 'I like your spit and sawdust haircut, your off-the-rack suit and the way you throw other people's money about, but it's time you were going.' She removed her finger and stood, looking from me to the smoked glass doors and the dinner-suited monolith beyond.

I stood too. The waiter appeared instantly at my side with a turquoise leather folder. He handed it to me. Fifty quid for strawberries. The whole bill came to seven hundred and forty eight pounds including a very unoptional-looking, optional gratuity.

'Who picks the strawberries for you - the Queen?' I asked him.

Candy no longer found my sense of humour quite so charming. I peeled off eight hundreds, stuffed them inside the folder and handed it to the waiter who received it with a polite nod of the head. 'I'll wait for my change,' I said to his back as he walked away. 'And a receipt.'

'Classy,' Candy said.

'Anything else you can tell me about Violet,' I asked. 'Any other men lose their temper with her?'

Candy looked around. 'It's not a good idea to go around asking those kind of questions,' she said, satisfied no-one had overheard. 'The men who come here rely on a degree of discretion. Not everyone has such an open marriage as Larry and Marjorie Kirkslap.

'And you'd be happy to cover up for them, even if they'd murdered your friend, for the sake of being discreet?'

The waiter returned, laid the turquoise folder on the table beside me and marched off again. Candy moved closer, made a show of hugging me, before dismissing me with a peck on the cheek. As I made to leave, she lifted the diamond solitaire from her chest. 'If you really want to know, why don't you ask Larry Kirkslap? He'll tell you how discreet I can be.'

Chapter 32

'He threatened to kill her?' Crowe asked incredulously.

Wednesday morning, four days since my trip to Karats, a section 67 notice had been served giving intimation of a new prosecution witness: Mike Summers. The notice had been faxed to my office, still the Crown's preferred means of communicating urgent messages, and I had arranged an emergency, late-afternoon consultation with Cameron Crowe at The Lord Reid Building on the High Street, Edinburgh. Mike was also present by video-link via his and Crowe's respective iPads.

'Mr Summers, I understand the police have been to see you,' Crowe said, once I'd filled him in on the background.

'Monday afternoon,' Mike admitted.

'And you told them everything?'

'I couldn't very well lie.'

'What did you say - exactly?'

'That I was only there to warn Violet that if she didn't stop bothering Larry, I was instructed to commence court action against her.'

'What kind of action?'

'Interdict, non-harassment, something like that. To be honest it was a sabre-rattling exercise. I don't know much about civil litigation. I shouldn't have let Larry talk me into it, more importantly, I shouldn't have let him come. He was drunk and got completely carried away.'

'So how do the police know about this?'

I knew the answer to that one. 'One of Violet's friends from the champagne bar was there as well,' I said. 'A girl called Candy.' I went on to tell all that I'd learned at my Friday night visit to Karats.

Crowe looked at me like I was insane. 'You knew about all this and never told me? You knew that Kirkslap threatened Violet Hepburn and then covered it up by bribing this Candy woman with a diamond necklace? When were you going to tell me?'

I wasn't. The plan was to keep it as quiet as possible. I didn't see how it could have helped my client's chances of acquittal, and, if Candy could be discreet about it, so could I.

Crowe turned his iPad around to face the other way. 'This is down to you,' he hissed. 'You were supposed to dig up dirt on the victim, not on the client.' He turned the iPad back to face us. 'When did he give it to her?' Crowe asked the computer screen.

Mike looked puzzled.

'The necklace. Was it before or after Violet went missing?' Crowe asked him.

'What's the difference? Oh, wait a minute, I think I see where you're going,' Mike said.

Crowe was seething. 'It's not a case of where I'm going. It's a case of where the Crown will go. If Kirkslap tried to silence this woman after Violet went missing, it looks highly suspicious.'

Mike thought about it and then shook his head. 'I couldn't say. It was definitely after he threatened Violet, but whether it was after Violet went missing I don't know. You've got no idea how Larry throws his money around. He could have given it to her anytime. It's probably not the only gift he's bought her. He's seen Candy a few times. For all I know he's still seeing her.'

'Not for very much longer,' Crowe said.

What had I said that had annoyed Candy so much that she'd picked the phone up and called the police? What about her self-proclaimed discretion?

'What's our next move?' Mike asked.

158

'You don't have one,' Crowe told him. 'You are now officially on the Crown witness list. I'm afraid your involvement in further defence discussions is over.'

iPad Mike looked like he was going to protest. With a rub of his fingers across the screen Crowe made him and any objections disappear.

'Can I expect any more surprises to result from your defence preparations?' he asked me.

If pedantic Mike had still been on the screen, he might have pointed out that by their very nature surprises were never expected - unless they were surprise birthday parties for my dad.

We left the consulting rooms and exited onto the cobblestones of the Royal Mile, which was the usual bustle of locals, lawyers and tourists. When I had entered, only half an hour earlier, the weather had been sunny with jumpers. Now it was overcast with overcoats.

'All I'm asking,' Crowe said, 'is something, anything, that might suggest, just for one second, that Larry Kirkslap isn't the guiltiest man alive. Is it too much to ask? At this rate he might as well plead guilty and ask the court to give him a discount on the punishment element of his life sentence. Be better than nothing.'

Perhaps for Kirkslap it would be, but not for the Munro & Co. bank overdraft.

'Don't even mention that option to the client at our next consultation,' I said. 'There's no way he'd plead guilty and we'd be booted into touch and replaced by a new defence team in two seconds flat. Do you know how difficult it was for me to secure this gig? Kirkslap thinks I'm a real trier, a winner. He says I remind him of himself.'

'Why, who have you killed recently?' Crowe said.

It was his little joke. One that brought back bad memories for me.

'When do you want to consult with the client?' I asked, changing the subject.

'Is there any point? He never tells us anything.'

It started to rain. We were both heading for the train station. Crowe had a meeting in Glasgow, and the next train to Queen Street stopped at Linlithgow. Neither of us had raincoats. We scurried across the High Street, through Jackson's Close, over Cockburn Street and commenced the descent of the steps at Fleshmarket Close. We didn't talk. All the way to Waverley Station I tried to think of something to say, some new plan of attack.

When we entered the concourse, the train was waiting to leave and I knew we would part company once aboard. Counsel always travelled first class. It was one of their conventions, like wigs, brass collar studs and opening the door for colleagues who had called at the Bar before them. It was also a good way of shaking off annoying clients and instructing agents.

We walked through the ticket barrier. 'The trial is on Monday,' Crowe said, as though I needed reminding that the trial of the millennium, my millennium at any rate, was just a few days away. 'I have a lot of work to do before the trial starts. I don't think I need see you or the client before then.'

'Is there anything you want me to do?' I asked.

Crowe put a finger to his lips and pretended to think hard. 'Yes, seeing as how, so far, all you have managed to do is provide the Crown with their missing motive - try not to do any more serious damage before Monday. Do you think you could manage that?'

At that moment I could also have managed to push him under the wheels of the train now arriving at platform 13.

On-board, I eventually found a seat that wasn't occupied by someone or their shopping. I had a twenty-five minute journey; ample time to run through the Crown case as I expected it to unfold in the weeks ahead.

Violet Hepburn had been in a relationship with the accused; of that there was no doubt. The Crown had lodged Kirkslap's credit card statements, hotel bills, jeweller's invoices, there was even CCTV evidence from Karats where'd they'd originally met and frequented on numerous occasions thereafter.

On 31st October 2012, Violet went shopping in Glasgow city centre. On 1st November, she exchanged text messages with Kirkslap, arranging to meet him later that day. She left bloodstains on Kirkslap's hall carpet and in the boot of his car and was never seen again. In the early hours of the morning of 2nd November, Larry Kirkslap had gone for a drive into the heart of the Loch Lomond and Trossachs National Park; hundreds of square miles of unspoilt countryside; excellent terrain for those looking to make a body disappear. On both legs of his journey a mobile traffic camera had clocked his car speeding.

When interviewed by the police, Kirkslap had been unable to keep his mouth shut and, to summarise, his explanations for these choice cuts of evidence were: 'I don't know why Violet arranged to meet me or why her blood is in my house and in my car, and I didn't go for a late night drive.' Not surprisingly, that defence strategy had failed to raise a reasonable doubt in the mind of the jury. This time around, thanks to me, there was even more evidence in the form of a threat by Kirkslap to kill Violet and possibly an attempt to cover that up by bribing a potential witness.

The upcoming retrial offered some limited scope for a change in the line of defence. This time Kirkslap would go into the witness box and use his oily charms on the jury; trouble was, he wouldn't have much to say. According to him, that first of November he'd stayed in alone all evening watching TV. He hadn't gone out until around eight o'clock the following morning. He didn't have any ingenious alibi defences or explanations why he went sightseeing in the wee small hours of the night, but at least he could look a jury in the eye and tell them he was innocent. That had to be worth something.

Deep down I knew it wouldn't be enough. There was one question a jury would need answered satisfactorily if it was to acquit. If Kirkslap didn't do it, who did?'

If my client could even cast a reasonable aspersion, he might be in with a chance.

Chapter 33

'Motive is everything.' My dad was in the kitchen stuffing clothes into the washing machine when I returned from Edinburgh. I didn't normally discuss my cases with him, then again, he didn't normally do my laundry.

'That's the problem, Dad. The only person with a motive is Kirkslap. He was being pestered by Violet Hepburn, stalked even, and had already threatened to kill her if she didn't leave him alone.'

'And did she?'

I wasn't sure. I should have asked Candy. Should I try to contact her again? So far, she wasn't on the Crown witness list, which meant that she had tipped off the authorities anonymously. If, because of me, she ended up for the prosecution, Crowe would go crazy. As things stood, I just knew he was going to stick me with the blame when the guilty verdict duly arrived. There had been plenty prosecution evidence at the last trial, now I'd gone and added an extra piece.

'There must be lots of reasons why a girl like Violet could have come to a sticky end,' I said, 'and yet we don't even have a potential suspect, far less a motive to pin on someone.'

'Don't start with the suspect. Start with the motive.' My dad pulled a pair of jeans out of the wash basket and held them up. 'How long have you been wearing these for? Is that blood or pizza?'

'Is that how you did it when you were a cop?' I asked, not really wanting to discuss my soiled clothing.

'No, cops always take the easy route first, mainly because it's usually the best. When a woman gets killed you start with the nearest and dearest. If you work your way out from there you'll never need to go much further than the husband or boyfriend. Sometimes it's a son. It's almost always a relationship issue and that relationship issue is usually to do with sex.' He cleared his throat. 'Not necessarily in the case of mother and son, but you get the idea. Basically, with women it's all to do with relationships.'

'Kirkslap was in a relationship with Violet Hepburn, or had been.'

'There you go, then.'

'I was sort of presuming my client to be innocent, Dad.'

He shoved my dirty jeans into the washing machine. 'Then you'd better find someone else she was in a relationship with.'

Easier said than done. 'And if I can't?'

'Find a different motive.'

'Like?'

'Money. If sex isn't the motive, it's money. At the end of the day murder comes down to either sex or money.'

Given that my dad had been a uniformed police sergeant, and that Linlithgow was not exactly a murder capital, I often wondered if his detective expertise came more from reading Ian Rankin than from actual experience; just as his own inability to swim had never stopped him from teaching me and Malky. I could still remember my brother and I lying across kitchen chairs, doing the front crawl with my dad, who couldn't swim the length of himself, telling us not to worry, and that it would be a lot easier when we were in the water.

'What about drink? That can lead to murder.' I said.

'Yeah, all right. Drink too.'

'Jealousy?'

'That's usually to do with sex.'

'Drugs?'

'Again, that's about money.'

'Racism, bigotry?'

'All right, all right. I'm just saying, that when it comes to murder the big two are sex and money. If you don't think Kirkslap did it, follow the money.'

From the wash basket he pulled my best shirt, the black one I'd worn to Karats the previous Friday. He gave it a flap. 'I wish you'd stop pulling your shirts over your head when you take them off.' He held it up. 'Have you even worn this? Doesn't look like it needs washed.' He unfastened the buttons and must have noticed the label – Armani – a fashion house even he'd heard of. 'What are you doing with a good shirt like this?'

'What's the matter? Am I not allowed expensive clothes? What am I supposed to put on when I'm going somewhere nice?'

'Where do you ever go that's nice?'

'It was a present from Jill.'

He put the shirt to his nose, sniffed. 'Is that Jill's perfume on it too?'

The CID never knew what they'd missed.

'It's a long story. I was on business.'

'Doing the business, you mean.' He chucked the shirt at me.

'It's not what you —'

'If I ever find out that you've been two-timing that lassie, you'll be defending me for murder, after I've killed you.'

There was no talking to him and I had other things to do that evening. I tossed the shirt back into the wash-basket, went to the fridge. There was nothing there but an egg, some cheese that had gone penicillin and a carton of full-fat milk, the only kind my dad would use in his tea. 'I'll explain it all to you later.'

'What's wrong with right now?'

'I'm too busy right now.' I grabbed my coat.

'Going somewhere nice?' he asked.

'The supermarket. I'll not be late. Will you be here when I get back?' I thought I'd throw that little dig in. A reminder that he was my guest. I snatched my car keys from the fruit bowl on the kitchen table.

'Robbie, there's something I should tell you,' he said, suddenly on the defensive. 'About my roof. Arthur's going on holiday.'

'When?'

He looked at his watch. 'About an hour ago.'

'You book a roofer, and before he's so much as dressed a slate he's jetting off to the sun? You didn't pay him in advance did you?'

'Don't be daft. His brother's had a heart attack.'

'His brother lives in Linlithgow Bridge. It doesn't have an airport.'

'Very funny, no, his brother's got a timeshare week in Salou he can't use. Arthur didn't like to see it going to waste.'

That meant I'd have my lodger for at least the next seven days, and that was just while we waited for sun-worshipping Arthur to get back on the tools. After that it would be the same again or longer before my dad's cottage had a lid on it. I didn't say anything. It wouldn't have made any difference, and his revelation had got us off the subject of Jill and the lingering scent molecules of Candy's perfume that a bloodhound wouldn't have noticed.

We looked at one another, each assessing the situation. Was the whole perfume scandal something my dad had used to take the heat out of the news that he'd be staying on a further fortnight? I wasn't taking the chance. 'You're welcome to stay however long you want, Dad, you know that.'

He grunted. 'Thanks son.'

I walked to the back door.

'By the way, did you know you were running a wee bit low on whisky?' he said.

I didn't. I had a couple of good bottles at various stages of consumption - or I did have the week before, when my dad came to stay.

'How low?' I asked.

'About as low as you can get and even lower by the time you get back from the shop.'

Chapter 34

Car boot full of groceries, I took the back road to Bathgate, parked at the edge of the woods and walked down to the derelict outhouse where I found Danny Boyd, sitting in a corner wrapped in his sleeping bag. It had been exactly a week since my first visit to his make-shift camp site. The circle of stones held nothing but some blackened twigs and a pile of empty tin cans nestled in the ashes.

I set down two carrier bags. From one I took out a six-pack of cola. I tore open the cardboard case, removed a can and gave it to the boy. He ripped open the ring-pull and drank the contents in one go.

'Where have you been?' he gasped, wiping his mouth with the back of a grubby hand. The whole place stank of smoke and rancid teenager. I should have brought a bar of soap and told Danny to take it for a swim in the nearby reservoir from time to time.

'I've been working, Danny. I'm in the middle of a big murder trial.'

'What about the curse?'

'I've talked to an expert. He says that Scottish tombs don't have curses.'

'They do. I know they do. What else have you got in the bags?' he asked.

'Milk, bread, cheese, various tins and some other stuff.' I threw him a pork pie and he set about it immediately. 'Some tombs in Scotland might have curses, but according to my expert it's just the Egyptian curses you have to watch out for. He reckons you'll be fine.'

'Did you tell him what happened to Nathan?'

'I did, and he said it can't have had anything to do with an ancient curse. Did Nathan have any enemies?' I remembered what my dad had said about murder motives. 'Did he owe anybody money?'

Danny shook his head, took another bite of pork pie.

'There's matches in there too.' I gave one of the bags a prod with my toe.

'What happens if I go home?' He ate the last morsel of pie and rubbed his hands on the sleeping bag.

'You'll be questioned by the police about Nathan's murder.'

'They still think it was me?'

'The police always take the easy route,' I said, quoting my dad. 'They'll start with you and once they're satisfied you didn't do it they'll move on.'

'When will they think it wasn't me?' Danny pulled over one of the carrier bags, rummaged inside and produced a box of matches. He screwed up the greaseproof paper that the pork pie had come wrapped in and stacked some of twigs around it inside the stone circle.

'I have no idea what evidence they have. They will definitely want to speak to you. The fact that you've done a runner doesn't look good, and if there is any more evidence pointing to you then they can put you on a murder petition. They don't need much evidence to do that.'

'Will I go to jail?'

'Bail is difficult, not impossible. The trouble is you're on bail already, and only from a couple weeks ago. The chances are that you'll be remanded.'

Danny sparked a match and put it to a corner of the greaseproof paper. It took light quickly. He fed it from a little pile of wood he had gathered. 'I'm not handing myself in if I'm going to jail,' he said, once he had a good blaze going.

'Well you can't stay here forever,' I said.

'I'm not. I'm going to move up to the woods at the back of Beecraigs reservoir.'

Some criminals fled to Brazil. Danny's idea of doing a runner was to camp out in a country park about three miles from his house.

'And how long do you think you can live rough for? The rest of your life? It's not like the cops are going to forget about you after a few weeks and then you can go home again.'

He sniffed, stared at his grubby hands.

'And I'm not a grocery delivery service. I can't keep bringing you supplies,' I said, sounding more like his dad than his lawyer.

'Do what you like. I never asked you to come back.'

'Actually, you did.'

Danny bowed his head. 'I'm sorry,' he said. 'It's good of you to bring me all this stuff. I've had no food or matches for two days now. It's been freezing up here at night.'

The food I'd brought him, if rationed properly, could have lasted three or four days, but he was a sixteen year old with nothing to do all day. I estimated the whole lot would be scoffed in half that time.

'I'll come back and see you at the weekend,' I said. 'Think it over. Even if the police do detain you, you'll have a lawyer at the interview, and if they have no evidence they'll have to let you go.' I looked around at the dank walls, the window spaces through which a twisted mass of bramble briars climbed and at the cobweb-strewn ceiling that gave me the creeps. Give me a cell in Polmont Young Offenders', Playstation, SKY TV and three square, any day of the week.

I was leaving when I saw a light in the field. In the dark it was difficult to make out how far away it was. My first thought was the police. I ducked back inside the building and told Danny.

'Could be the farmer,' he said.

'What farmer?'

'There's a farm up the road a bit.'

'Has he been down this way before?'

He hadn't. Apart from me, Danny had seen no-one for nearly two weeks. I wasn't taking any chances of being caught harbouring a fugitive. 'Get your stuff, we're leaving.'

Danny picked up the two carrier bags in one hand and the holdall in another. He asked me to gather up his sleeping bag. I lifted it with two fingers. It was damp and stinking. I threw it into the corner again, took the carrier bags from him and we set off in the dark, taking a route across the fields towards the road, perpendicular to that of the approaching light. After we'd traversed less than fifty bumpy yards, I nudged Danny and whispered to him to halt. The terrain underfoot was rough. We couldn't see our own feet. The light was gaining and we were making far too much noise. I set down the carrier bags and the two of us crouched behind a crop of gorse bushes that sprouted from a section of collapsed dry-stane dyke. Together we strained our eyes to see who it was approaching the ruins of the walled garden. There was only one source of light, a torch, and by its faint beam it was just possible to discern a shadowy figure. Ten yards or so from the outbuilding, the light stopped moving. It went out. We waited, scared to make the slightest sound. A creak of hinges. Faint light from the remains of the fire framed the shape of a man in the doorway. We crouched lower, holding our breath, faces in the wet grass covering the rutted earth. I knocked over a carrier bag. Bottles clinked. In the still of the night I might as well have rung a bell. The torch switched on again, beam shining straight at us, not powerful enough to pick us out, I hoped. In my reclined position, I reached into one of the bags, pulled out a bottle of lemonade. Back-handed, I hurled it as far as I could to my right. It smashed a distance away. It was a diversion tactic that might have worked in the movies: not in real life. There was a moment of hope when the torch beam flicked in the direction of the noise, but it was soon shining in our direction once more, a disc of light on a black background, growing larger with every step the man took. Whoever it was couldn't see us yet, all the same he'd be on us in no time.

I jumped to my feet. 'Run!' I yelled at Danny. I didn't need to tell him twice. The torch began to swing wildly from side to side as the man picked up speed. I started to run after Danny, and with my first stride turned my ankle. I staggered, fell onto my knees. The pain in my ankle coursed up my leg, causing me to cry out. There was no way I was outpacing torch-man now. My only option was to dive into the bushes, lie still and hope that he would run past me in the dark. As for Danny, he was on his own. He was young with a good head start. I turned, hobbled towards the gorse, ready to plunge into the foliage when my good foot stood on something hard. A carrier bag full of groceries. The light stopped. The torch light dipped. I glimpsed another dimmer source of light in the darkness; the reflection from the broad blade of a knife. A very big knife. The man was close, no more than thirty yards. I could hear him breathing hard. There were only a few fronds of broom concealing me from him. I bent over, snatched the other bottle of lemonade from the carrier bag and threw it at the light. It missed by a fraction, veering off to the left of my target. The man moved closer. In an instant I had a tin of beans in each hand. The first hit him, I didn't know where. The second elicited a curse. Encouraged, I fired a salvo of cola cans, following up with a carton of milk and some apples, more hitting home than not and yet inflicting no real damage. It was the tins of tuna that saved me. Although I could see only the yellow glow of the torchlight and a blurry figure behind, a yelp of pain told me I'd been right on the mark with the first. I rummaged in a carrier bag. There was definitely a second tin somewhere; they'd been two-for-one.

The light was really shifting now, as the man charged through the undergrowth. He'd be on me in seconds. I found the tin, kissed it and sent it off into the darkness. Like the shot at goal that you just know is going to hit the back of the

172

net the split second it leaves your foot, the tin flew from my hand. The resulting clunk had to be metal meeting skull. The light fell and went out. Something heavy hit the ground and began to groan. David –v- Goliath: the young shepherd boy had finished off the job by beheading the giant with his own sword. I wasn't quite up for that. My ankle had stiffened and the pain eased slightly. As quickly and as quietly as I could, I limped away.

Chapter 35

'It's not broken.' My dad the non-doctor seemed fairly certain of his diagnosis. 'Just a sprain.' He'd found a bag of frozen peas in the depths of the freezer compartment of my fridge and strapped it onto my ankle with a tea towel.

I'd been through the 'how did it happen?' interrogation session with him and come up with a believable enough story that also explained my muddy shoes and grass-stained trousers. In my parallel universe I had been down at his cottage, checking that Arthur had left the place secure, and had tripped when shifting some scaffolding poles that had been left lying on the back green.

The beauty of it was that it was almost true. From the wilds of West Lothian I'd found Danny waiting for me by the roadside and he'd helped me back to my car. I'd agreed that even if my expert was right and there wasn't a curse, there was definitely someone out to get him. Why? Neither of us could say, but lack of motive didn't make the danger any less.

It was downhill all the way to Linlithgow. Painfully, I engaged the clutch, put the car in third gear and, using only my uninjured right leg on the accelerator and brake, drove to my Dad's cottage.

'Will he not mind?' Danny asked, looking up at the scaffolding, erected against the front elevation of the building and the tarpaulins that covered the roof, each sheet held down by batons of wood, lashed to the rafters.

'He won't find out,' I replied. 'You can stay here over the weekend, but on Monday...' No, Monday wasn't any good. It was the first day of Larry Kirkslap's retrial. I couldn't be elsewhere, even if it was to advise a murder suspect. I'd have to cover at least the first couple of days before I could slip

174

away and let Joanna stand in for me at the High Court. 'On Wednesday I want you to hand yourself in to the police.'

'I don't want to go to jail.'

'If you do, it will not be for long and you'll be safer in there until we find out what's going on.' He didn't answer. I let him in the back door. Everything inside was covered in sheets and the floor was carpeted with old newspapers or rolls of plastic. I gave him a carton of milk and a loaf of bread from the groceries I'd bought for myself. 'There are plenty of tins in the cupboards. If you're cooking, keep it simple. Just heat something up in a pot and wash up after yourself. Don't make a mess. Use the spare room. There's a wee telly in there you can use, but make sure the curtains are closed and turn the volume low. Keep the door locked, don't answer the phone and keep out of sight during the day. I don't think anyone will come by except maybe the postman. He'll know that my dad's away just now and get suspicious if he notices anything.'

Having given Danny his instructions I left him to it. I really hoped I could trust the boy. I knew I should have driven him to the police, but he'd begged me not to and it would make my life a lot easier if I could keep him on ice for a day or two. I'd have to speak to Paul Sharp about who was to represent the boy and I had a busy few days coming up as Kirkslap's trial neared.

'So everything looks okay at my place?' My dad was limping around the kitchen, storing the groceries, occasionally pausing to critically examine my purchases. I was pretty sure that the putting away of foodstuffs would come screeching to a halt the moment he came across the bottle of Bowmore I'd bought and hidden in a carrier bag below a pack of toilet rolls.

I assured him that everything was fine, removing the bag of frozen peas before frost-bite set in.

The phone rang while my dad was questioning my choice of breakfast cereal. It was the Scottish Legal Aid

Board's call centre. Up until the recent past, if a suspect wanted a lawyer notified of his arrest or detention he'd tell the police who were duty bound to contact the solicitor in question. For the Scottish Government that had been far too simple a procedure. Now all such calls were relayed via SLAB, even where the suspect wasn't eligible for legal aid. By the introduction of civil service efficiency measures, what had once been a single phone call had now been increased to four. The police phoned SLAB, SLAB phoned the lawyer, the lawyer phoned the police who by that time were usually busy processing some other detainee and arranged to call back the lawyer later – often much later, which led to many a restless night as lawyers waited for the phone to ring. Usually it didn't, until the moment they'd dropped off to sleep again.

I took the details, phoned the police and was put through to the custody sergeant at Stewart Street Police Station, Glasgow.

'Mr Kirkslap wants to see you before we interview him,' the sergeant said.

'What's the charge?' I wanted to know, still scarcely able to believe it.

It was a breach of the peace allegation. Kirkslap had paid a visit to a Miss Candice McKeever that evening, better known to me as Candy from Karats, and there had been much shouting and banging on her front door. Obviously, Kirkslap had been made aware of the latest evidence in his High Court case. I just hoped he wouldn't follow the tracks back to me. This new matter would be classified as a domestic incident and as such zero-tolerance. The prisoner would be going nowhere except court tomorrow, even if, as I would advise him, he made no comment when interviewed. Unfortunately, I couldn't drive with my ankle. My dad was getting ready for bed. I was going to ask him to drive me and then I caught sight of his crutches in a corner of the room and remembered his own injured leg.

'You've got to be kidding me,' Joanna said.

I wasn't. 'Kirkslap's been lifted for a domestic. I've injured my leg and I can't drive.' I knew I sounded pathetic. 'Do you think you could nip down there and tell him to keep his mouth shut? They'll keep him in. You'll have to break the news to him that bail is going to be very difficult tomorrow.' I couldn't think of any Sheriff who, when faced with a man already on bail for allegedly killing one woman, would grant bail for a threatening visit to the door of another.

Joanna agreed to go. She lived to the west, and midnight trips to police stations were part of defence agent's job.

My dad had found the whisky. 'Bowmore? You're a good lad.' He favoured me with a smile. The mere sight of an Islay malt could have that kind of drastic effect on him. He opened the bottle. 'I'll just have a wee half before I go to bed. It'll ease the pain in my leg and help me sleep.' He poured himself a generous measure and swirled the glass.

The phone rang again. Joanna, I presumed. It wasn't: it was Jill.

'You were expecting someone else?' she asked.

'Jill,' I managed to gulp, 'How are you? I thought you might be—'

'Joanna?'

'Well... yes, she's—'

My dad took the phone from me. 'Hello, Jill. How's Switzerland?'

The two of them chatted for a while, mainly about my dad's leg, Jill's plants and the weather in Berne. Eventually they came around to the subject of me.

'He's fine,' my dad said. 'Well, not fine, he's hurt his leg too. No, nothing serious. Not a break or anything; just twisted it. You can ask him yourself.' I waited to be passed the receiver. It never came. 'Yes,' my dad continued, 'Robbie's was on the phone to his assistant about some crook. Robbie can't drive because of his sore,' with two fingers on the hand not holding the phone, he made quotation marks in the air, 'leg. No, he's not been up to much. Living quiet.

177

Missing you of course.' I should have bought my dad whisky more often. 'I'm staying here while my roof's being sorted, so I can keep an eye on him. Came for a rest and ended up being a home help, washing, ironing... I know I shouldn't, but Robbie's hopeless and I wasn't about to let him anywhere near that nice shirt you got him with a hot iron... the Armani one... that's right, the black one... I think he had it on last Friday night... I don't know where... Glasgow... I think... business...' My dad was beginning to flounder. He'd be no match for Jill if she really started to cross-examine and he knew it. He looked at me, out of his depth; Luke Skywalker about to take on Darth Vadar and realising that he hadn't charged his light-sabre.

I seized the phone. 'Hi Jill... Yes, I know the shirt was for my birthday, but I had this do to go to and nothing nice to wear—'

'I haven't told her about the perfume,' my dad said in too loud a voice.

I put my hand over the mouthpiece and told my dad to back away slowly and drink his whisky. Had Jill heard my dad's dismally awful sotto voce remark about the perfume? I needed to think fast. Then again, why should I? Jill was the woman I was going to ask to marry me. I didn't usually lie to her, or, if I did, she always found out anyway. Most importantly, I'd done absolutely nothing wrong.

'What do were you at?' Jill asked. One false word and she'd gut me like a herring.

'It wasn't a *do* as such. I was working. Do you remember that big murder case that Andy had?' she did. 'Well I've got it now.'

Jill was hugely unimpressed. 'And where does your Armani shirt come into it? You've had big cases before. I don't remember you wearing anything smarter than your usual creased suit and an M&S shirt.'

178

'I had to interview a witness.' I cleared my throat. 'In a champagne bar. It's for rich people and I didn't think they'd let me in wearing my usual work clobber.'

'A champagne bar? Who were you interviewing in a champagne bar?'

'Just a witness.'

'A female witness?'

I had to agree.

'Does she work in this champagne bar?'

'Sort of... not exactly.' Cross-examining was a lot easier than being cross-examined. 'Look Jill, I'd like to tell you everything, but it's to do with a murder trial starting on Monday and—'

'What was Alex saying about perfume?'

'I can't really talk about it. Everything's very hush-hush, need to know, privileged communings...' I was running out of clichés. Time to go on the attack. 'How's things your end? I saw the postcard you sent to Kaye with you and Hans—'

'Josh.'

'On the piste. Did you have a good time?'

'I'd love to tell you, Robbie, but you know what the world of international pharmaceuticals is like. Everything is terribly hush-hush.'

I was never so pleased to hear my doorbell ring. I made my excuses to Jill and handed the phone back to my dad despite his frantically shaking head.

At the door I was met by two ludicrously young PC's. One male. One female. I immediately thought of Danny Boyd, hiding out at my Dad's place.

The policewoman did the talking. 'Robert Munro?'

'Yes.'

'We'd like you to come with us.'

Chapter 36

DI Dougie Fleming looked like he'd got out of bed especially for the interview. Not that it mattered; no amount of beauty sleep was going to make any difference to that face. Upon my arrival at the charge bar, I'd been advised that I was there under suspicion, along with Andy, of having wasted the time of the police by making a false report about a stolen computer tablet. Whether Fleming had disturbed his slumber, or if he was working nightshift anyway and had just let me stew for an hour or two, he was intent on wasting even more police time by asking me questions.

'No comment,' I said to the latest in a series of questions.

Sooner or later Fleming would get the idea. For now he was in full interrogation mode. 'We know it was either Imray or you who made the call,' he said, which, like being interviewed at all, was generally a good sign, because if the cops did actually know who it was and had sufficient evidence, they wouldn't be trying to wring out an admission.

'Do yourself a favour. Tell us what you know and we can help you.' Fleming's sidekick was so bored he was talking like a British TV cop show. In a minute he'd be asking me to make a clean breast of things or turn Queen's evidence.

'No comment.'

'We've got your pal next door,' Fleming said.

I could only presume he meant Andy. My former assistant wouldn't be best pleased, but no matter how upset he was with me I knew he wouldn't stray from the Munro & Co. policy of omertà.

'And we've got a tape recording of the call to the British Transport Police.'

What they didn't have was any video evidence of the call. I'd checked for CCTV cameras before I made it.

'The one where you or your pal pretends to be Sheriff Albert Brechin.'

'We've got the pair of you bang to rights on this one,' said the other cop.

Even Fleming was getting fed up with his colleague's clichéd interruptions. He gave his corroborating officer an I'm-asking-the-questions look, then leaned across the table at me, red in the face.

'We've got evidence that you were at the train station and the recording will do the rest,' he said.

They might have someone to say I was at the station, they might be able to link the call to Andy's phone, but, other than that they had a recording of my Sheriff Brechin impersonation, one I'd always felt was highly authentic, right down to the cocked-eyebrow expression of disbelief that he gave jurors, while listening to defence evidence. I couldn't see a team of forensic voice analysts being assembled at public expense to scrutinise vocal wave-lengths, or whatever it was they did, for the sake of a prank. Wasting the time of a couple of British Transport cops? It would have been a light relief for them; a change from scraping suicides off the tracks.

'Well?' Fleming asked, more in hope than expectation.

'No comment.'

'We've already contacted the Sheriff, he doesn't even own an iPad.'

Brechin probably thought an iPad was a patch pirates wore.

'Shall we call it a day at that, Inspector?' asked the bored detective.

Fleming couldn't help a quick exasperated glance up at the camera in the corner of the room that was preventing more robust forms of questioning. 'The time is three forty-four on Thursday the fourth of April, two thousand and thirteen. This is Detective Inspector Fleming terminating the

181

interview with Robert Alexander Munro.' Without another look in my direction he got up from his seat. 'Get him out of here,' he said to his colleague.

I met Andy outside the police station. He'd remained silent, and so it looked like I was in the clear. Unlike me, Andy hadn't insisted on being detained and had gone to the station voluntarily so he had his car with him. He agreed to give me a lift. I was expecting to be on the receiving end of some flak.

'I should have stuck you in just now,' he said. 'I told you it was a stupid idea at the time.'

'It worked,' I said.

'Oh, yeah, it worked for you. You're all right. You've got a nice high profile murder trial. I'm on the buroo.'

'You'll find something,' I said.

'What's Kirkslap's view of it all?'

What did Andy want me to say? That his former client was pining after him? He wasn't.

'Kirkslap was lifted tonight,' I said.

'What for?'

'Did you know that Kirkslap had threatened to kill Violet?' He didn't. 'What about the diamond necklace?'

'What diamond necklace?'

'Kirkslap gave one to the other girl who was there to shut her up. I can't believe you didn't find out about her. If word gets out that her silence was bought it'll be a disaster.'

'What girl?'

'One of the girls from Karats. She was there when Kirkslap threatened Violet. He bribed her to keep quiet, she hasn't and last night he went round to her house and started banging on the door. He's been arrested for a breach and got no chance of bail.'

'First I've heard of it or of anyone being bribed,' Andy said. 'When's this supposed to have happened?'

I would have liked to have known that myself, but I didn't want to go anywhere near that question in case I got the answer I didn't want, and it too became public knowledge.

Andy dropped me off at my house, where I heard my dad's snores before I found him asleep on the couch. The TV was on with a late night repeat of a documentary about Army recruitment policy, or, since the cuts, the lack of one. It hadn't always been so. I'd had a young client, not long out of school, who'd been enticed to join the Argyll's with the promise of passing his HGV. A year or so later, with a category E on his licence, he hadn't been too pleased to find himself, not driving a truck for ASDA, but trundling through some of the scarier neighbourhoods in Afghanistan.

My dad stirred when I switched off the TV. I prised the empty whisky glass from his hand and set it down on the arm of the sofa.

'They let you out, then?' he asked, sleepily.

'All a big misunderstanding.'

'Aye, Robbie, you've always been terribly misunderstood.' He yawned, leaned forward and I helped hoist him to his feet.

After he'd gone to bed, I sat down on the still warm couch. The bottle of Bowmore had got a bit of a fright. I found it stuffed down the side of a sofa cushion. I wasn't tired and I thought a nightcap would help. I was reaching for my dad's glass when I heard a buzzing sound and saw my mobile phone on the coffee table flashing. I hadn't taken it with me. The first thing the cops did if you were detained and had a mobile phone in your possession, was go through it and read the texts, phone logs and contacts. If they found anything remotely interesting you'd never see it again. By the time I'd picked up the phone it had stopped. I had two missed calls: one from Joanna and one from my dad's house. I checked the answering service. The only message was from Joanna. She'd met with Kirkslap and sat with him through his police interview. It didn't sound as though things had gone too well. She expected he'd be appearing in court later in the day. As I was wondering about the call from my dad's house, the phone started buzzing again. My dad's number. I answered straight away. It was Danny Boyd.

'I've got to speak to you urgently,' he said. It was three o'clock in the morning. I asked him if it could wait.

It couldn't.

Chapter 37

The curtains were drawn and not a chink of light escaped my dad's cottage. I parked out front and limped to the back door, dodging scaffold poles, wooden batons and pallets of slates that had been indiscriminately stacked in readiness for Arthur the roofer's return from sunnier climes.

On the way down the side of the building, I tapped on the window of the spare room where I expected Danny Boyd to be. I thought he might welcome me at the back door. He didn't. I tried the door handle. The door was unlocked. I pushed it open, stepped inside. The kitchen light came on, blinding me. After the second or two it took my eyes to adjust, there in front of me stood the giant that was Deek Pudney. The sight of Deek standing in my dad's kitchen was bad enough, worse still was the handgun he held at his side. It was huge. A Desert Eagle. It would have taken most men two hands to lift the thing. Deek raised the gun and pointed it straight at my head, so quickly I was unable to react. Bam! More light; this time inside my head. I reeled backwards, crashing into the side of the door. In that moment I was sure I was dead, and yet how could I be thinking at all if I had a bullet in my brain? I don't know how long it took me to come to my senses. Dazed, I put a palm to my forehead. Blood, and then pain. A great deal of pain. I looked up at Deek, my head throbbing, my eyes watering. The handgun was at his side again. Next to him stood another familiar figure: Jake Turpie.

He shoulder-barged into Deek. 'I told you to give him a fright, not knock his head off.'

If I hadn't been in such a state of shock, I could have confirmed, on Deek's behalf, that I had been given a fright all right. One I would relive for a long time to come.

'It's this thing,' Deek said, holding up the enormous pistol, like it was a toy. 'It weighs a ton.'

'Look what you've done to his head, eejit.' Jake prodded the ever increasing bump in the centre of my forehead where the muzzle had struck me. 'Get him a cloth or something.'

'Jake?' I just about managed to croak.

My landlord pulled up a chair and sat down on it, legs crossed on the kitchen table. Deek handed me a tea towel.

'Put some water on it first,' Jake told him, and seconds later a soaking-wet towel was slapped into my trembling hands.

'Anyway,' Jake said, when satisfied I'd received the appropriate first aid. 'The point is, that's how easy it would have been. Consider us quits.'

'Quits?' My brain was constructing whole sentences, and yet my mouth was capable of uttering only one word at a time.

'Aye, quits. Win, win. You're not dead and I'm expecting my rent paid as usual.'

I began to wonder if I'd had that nightcap after all and was asleep on my couch. *'What?'*

Jake brought a leg down from the table and kicked a nearby kitchen chair towards me across the Lino. 'You know you're not exactly Mr Popular with certain people.'

I sat down. 'Who?'

'People who'll pay to have you killed. I was asked to set you up. I said no.' He looked around my dad's cottage. 'This would have been a great place to do it, though.'

He paused. Waiting for me to say something it seemed.

'Thanks.'

He grunted.

What was Jake's game? Was this all some elaborate set up to save him three months' rent? I squeezed out some water from the sodden tea towel into the sink and sat down again, the towel clamped to my forehead. It felt better - slightly.

Who knew? In a day or so I might feel able to string two words together.

'If you're wondering: the boy's gone,' Jake said.

I'd totally forgotten about Danny Boyd. He was the reason I was there and now he was... 'Gone?'

'Naw. Not *gone*, gone. Gone. As in he's not here anymore. I let him go. You and the boy were a package deal. I couldn't very well have him done in and not you. I wouldn't have been paid. You're a lawyer. You know what contracts are like.' Jake stood. 'Right. That's me. I'm off.' He walked to the door. 'I'll send Deek along later for the rent. This month's and next's in advance.' He beckoned to Deek to follow.

'Wait.' I gave the lump on my head a final press with the damp towel and then threw it onto the draining board. I went over to the big white Belfast sink and ran my head under the tap.

'What is it now?' Jake asked.

'Who wants me dead?' I asked, after I'd had a long drink from the tap. I rubbed my hair with the tea towel, trying to avoid the painful bump on my forehead. 'Come on, Jake. I deserve to know who's trying to kill me.'

'I can't tell you that,' he said.

'Why not?'

'Because I don't know.'

'Somebody does. The person who told you about the contract does. That name would do for a start.'

'Sorry.' Jake opened the door.

'If I'm dead who's going to be your lawyer. Who else would have got Deek off?' Just about anybody with a law degree, but Jake didn't know that.

He turned to Deek. 'Put that gun away and let's go.' He stepped out of the back door, Deek following close behind.

'I thought you were a business man,' I called after him. 'You're not looking at this from a business angle.'

Jake reversed back through the door, bumping into Deek. 'What angle?'

'Munro & Co. has a lease with you. We shook on it. Twenty years - remember?'

'So?'

'So, we're only three years in. Someone kills me and the lease is over. With me gone, who do you think is going to take that dump on the High Street off your hands?' I now had Jake's attention. 'Seventeen years is… two hundred and four months. Multiply that by my rent and that's how much you lose if someone fulfils that contract.'

Jake said nothing, but by the lowering of his brow I could tell he felt a faint stabbing pain in his wallet.

'I still can't tell you,' he said, after a while. 'You know how these things work. It's a sub-contract. A chain. I only know the next link up.'

'That's all I want to know. Tell me who it is and I'll work my way upstream from there.'

Jake shook his head. 'Can't do it.'

I was going to start on my, if-I'm-dead-there's-no-rent-for-you, line of argument again, but if Jake thought about that too much he might realise that if I was going to be killed by someone else, there would be no rent anyway, and he might as well collect on the contract himself.

He pulled the semi-automatic out of Deek's trouser belt and held it out to me. 'Do you want this to keep you company?'

I had the crazy idea of taking the gun, pointing it at Jake and asking him for the name he wouldn't reveal. 'No thanks,' I said.

Jake shrugged, as though he'd done all he could. 'Then stay on your toes. You're no good to me dead.'

Chapter 38

I was showered, shaved, dressed and away before my dad surfaced the next morning, thus avoiding any interrogation over the bump on my head.

Joanna arrived dead on nine, looking fresh, cheerful and exactly how I didn't feel.

'I got him out,' she said. 'Kirkslap. I got him out on police bail. He's to attend Glasgow Sheriff Court on a bail undertaking in three weeks. It'll have to be knocked on, of course, because he'll still be in the middle of his murder trial. What happened to you?' She came over for a closer look at my injury. 'One raised contusion, two centimetres in diameter, with a central superficial laceration. Where did you get it?' she asked, as though I'd picked it up while I was out shopping.

'Someone wants to kill me.'

'Are you serious?'

I pointed at my forehead.

'Who?'

'No idea. That's the problem. All I know is they're after Danny Boyd too.'

Grace-Mary arrived for the day, popping her head around the door to my room. 'Morning all.' She looked at me and frowned. 'What did you do to your head this time?'

'You still got your coat on?' I asked.

She stepped through the door and with a flowing gesture of her hands revealed that she was indeed wearing a raincoat.

'Then nip down to Sandy's. Coffee for me and Joanna, whatever you're having, and cakes for us all. I'll have a doughnut. Actually, better make that doughnuts.'

'I love it when you're all masterful,' Grace-Mary said, taking a rain-mate out of her pocket.

Grace-Mary out of the way, I told Joanna all about Danny Boyd.

'You're going to have to go to the cops,' she said. 'Today. Right now.'

'What about Kirkslap's case?'

'I can deal with that. I'll give Cameron Crowe a call and see if there's anything else he wants us to do.'

Joanna went to the window and looked out at the rain drenched High Street. 'Why do you think they let Kirkslap out? I was sure that bail would have been opposed and he'd be a custody today.'

I tried to think it through. If Kirkslap had appeared in court, no matter if he'd pled guilty or not guilty, the story would have been all over the newspapers. 'Maybe the Crown didn't want to take any more chances,' I said. 'There has been enough publicity already and it's something of a jinxed prosecution for them as it is. Could be they didn't want to run the risk of the defence raising a preliminary issue that even more media-coverage would mean that Kirkslap couldn't get a fair trial.'

'Yes,' Joanna said. 'That could be it. Or it could be because I'm such a great lawyer.'

By the time the coffee and cakes had been scoffed, the day's work was sorted and divvied up between us. I would go to the Sheriff Court, deal with the few procedural diets we had that morning and call into the police station while I was there. I wouldn't mention Jake Turpie, but I would let them know what I could about Danny Boyd in the hope that they might redouble their efforts to track him down.

So, off to court where the bump on my head provided a source of amusement and light relief for many of my fellow defence agents. The day dragged on. Albert Brechin took a proactive interest in intermediate diets; one which his brother and sister Sheriffs generally didn't share. He liked to quiz

190

everyone at great length, prosecution and defence alike, as to their state of preparedness; mainly, I was sure, because he didn't want the Crown to overlook something that might later come between the accused and a conviction. By the time he had finished scrutinising each of the sixty or so cases on the roll, it was late afternoon. Paul Sharp had the last case to call and I waited for him outside the courtroom.

'What are we going to do about Danny Boyd?' I asked him, as he took off his gown, rolled it up and stuffed it along with his files into a large leather holdall.

'I thought we'd had this discussion,' Paul said.

'Yeah, but—'

'Have they caught him?' Paul eyed me suspiciously.

'No, but it's a matter of time, and then what?'

'Do you mean, who's going to act for him? You or me?'

I confirmed that was indeed what I meant.

'I thought we'd already discussed that.' Paul hefted his holdall and walked with me along the corridor. 'The Boyd boys both consulted me about the mausoleum case and although I cut Danny out to you, he was really my client to begin with.'

'And so was Nathan,' I reminded him. Would Paul act for one client accused of killing another? It wasn't the sort of dilemma that would have kept me awake at nights, but Paul was the kind of guy who wrestled with such abstract concepts as professional ethics. He mulled it over as we walked out of the door at the end of the corridor, and onto the landing at the top of the stairs.

'I suppose Nathan was my client, but only for a very short time. The case against him hasn't gone ahead. It can't. He's dead.'

'Even then, you don't think there might be a conflict of interest if you act for the person accused of his murder?' I asked.

Paul smiled. 'If there is, he's unlikely to complain to the Law Society. You can keep the grave-robbing case, though.'

I shook my head. 'I think you should have that as well.'

'No, really, keep it. After all, I cut him out to you for that one. Fair's fair.'

'I'd rather not,' I said.

By this time we had reached the foot of the stairs and the lobby of the Civic Centre. Paul looked at me. 'You're not in the huff about this are you?'

I assured him we weren't going to fall out over it.

'That's fine then. So keep the mausoleum case. A fixed fee is a fixed fee.'

It was financial logic with which I could hardly disagree, still I had to refuse.

'You definitely *are* in the cream-puff,' Paul said.

'I'm not. I don't want Danny Boyd as a client—'

'Robbie—'

'Because,' I pointed straight ahead to the Divisional Office of Lothian & Borders, scarcely twenty paces away. 'If he's my client, I can't go over there right now and grass him off to the police.'

'You must like it here.' The sergeant at the front desk was the same one who'd taken my details when I'd been detained the night before. He was just coming on duty again and getting himself organised, when I limped through the door. 'Forget something?' he asked.

I pointed at the bump on my head. 'I slipped and fell when being interviewed by Inspector Fleming. Is he around?'

I could tell the sergeant wasn't sure if I was joking or not. He lifted the phone and a minute or so later the florid features of Detective Inspector Dougie Fleming hove into view. 'What do you want?'

'To help the police with their enquiries,' I said.

'Please. Don't make me laugh. I've got chapped lips and no lip-salve. What happened to your head?'

'I slipped. That's not what I'm here about, though. I want a word in private about a client... a former client of mine.'

Fleming looked at his watch as though he had a pressing engagement. Probably with a pie and a pint. 'I can give you five minutes.'

'It won't take that long,' I assured him, as he led me to one of the interview rooms. 'It's about Danny Boyd.'

'Who?' He held the door open for me.

I walked past him into the room and sat down. 'The boy whose brother, Nathan, was murdered.'

'Are you talking about the tinks from down by Philipstoun?'

'I know where Danny is. He's been hiding out in the Bathgate hills. You should find him somewhere in the woods up at Beecraigs.'

'Fascinating.' I noticed that Fleming hadn't come into the room. He was still at the door, leaning on the handle. 'Anything else?'

'Is that not enough to be going on with?'

'And why would I be interested in some boy holidaying in the woods?'

Because you're scouring the country looking for him as a murder suspect, was what I was going to say, but didn't. 'Aren't you looking for him?'

'We were until we found out he'd been at the opening of the new farm shop up at Aberdovan from early doors. When someone has a dozen alibi witnesses, including the Provost, we tend to discontinue that line of enquiry.' He raised his eyebrows. 'Now, before you start getting all comfortable... I'm a busy man.'

'But—'

'Any more and I'll do you for wasting the time of the police – again. Understand?'

I didn't. But I left anyway.

Chapter **40**

Mrs Boyd was a big, strong woman with red, raw hands and hair like a stook of wheat. She invited me into what she called the parlor; a small, spotlessly-clean room that smelled of home-baking. Roses on the wallpaper matched the furniture, and the cheap ornaments scattered here and there gave the place the appearance of a gypsy caravan. Mrs Boyd excused herself to go stir a pot of jam. She opened the door to the kitchen and a warm waft of air blew into the room.

I looked for somewhere to sit. The sofa was occupied by a dog of some indeterminate variety. Though it was old, it felt obliged to give me a brief but well-mannered wag of its wiry-haired tail. I didn't disturb it, opting instead for an armchair next to the fireplace in which a beech log smouldered gently, and where I sat happily engulfed in the gloriously sweet smell of simmering jam.

Mrs Boyd returned in a few minutes, wiping her hands on her apron. She shoved the dog off the sofa and sat down, hands clasped between her knees. 'You must think I'm terrible, Mr Munro. Me making jam and my own son, dead just a fortnight ago and not yet buried.'

I didn't know what to say, so I tried to rearrange my features into a non-judgemental, sympathetic sort of an expression.

'I was in bed for a week after it. My sister came to stay for a few days. Sadie got me up and about. She lost her man last year and said the best way to get by was to try and keep yourself busy. If you stay in bed...' She pulled a handkerchief out of the big front pocket of her apron and blew her nose. 'All you do is lie there and think.' The tears came in huge sobs. I was hopeless in those sort of situations. Should I go over and sit beside her? Put an arm around her? What could I say? So, I said nothing and just sat there until Mrs Boyd returned the hanky to her apron pocket, gave each eye a final wipe with the back of a hand and looked up at me with a crooked, strained smile.

'I'm sorry,' I said. 'Why don't I come back later? It's too soon for you.'

She wouldn't hear of me leaving until I told her why I was there.

I wanted to ask her if she had any idea why Nathan was killed, but I couldn't launch straight into that, nor, in her present state, was it advisable to let her in on my theory that I believed the person who'd killed her older son was also after his brother.

'Danny's safe,' I told her. 'I've met him a couple of times recently and he's fine.'

She got up, came over, pulled me from my seat and hugged me like a sack of spuds.

Once she'd released me, I pressed on with more good news. 'I've also spoken to the police. Danny is no longer a suspect. At the time of the... at the time of Nathan's death he was at the Aberdovan farm shop. The police have checked that.'

Mrs Boyd's eyes filled with tears again. 'Where is he? Did you not tell him to come home?'

'I've been trying to. The problem is, he's living rough and moved on somewhere else.' The woods around Beecraigs Country Park covered many hectares of West Lothian countryside. If that was where the remaining Boyd boy had gone, the chances of finding him, if he didn't want to be found, weren't really all that good, even if I spent all that drizzly Saturday looking. And did I want to find him right then? Somebody wanted to kill Danny. If the boy came home, he might very well end up like his brother. For the time being he was safer hiding out amongst the trees.

Mrs Boyd sat down again.

'I never thought for a second that Danny would of hurt his brother,' she said.

'Do you know who might have?' I asked tentatively.

'I told the police that I thought Nathan must have been trying to stop someone breaking in here.'

In here? What for? To steal a few pots of jam or some home-baking?

Mrs Boyd's bottom lip began to tremble. 'Me and Danny were both out. Maybe somebody thought the place was empty and...'

'Mrs Boyd...' On closer inspection she wasn't much older than me. 'What's your first name?' Unfortunately it was Hughina and I wished I'd never asked. Was that even a name?

'My dad was called Hugh,' she explained. 'He wanted a boy. Folk just call me Ina.'

I was glad to hear it. 'Were your sons into drugs or anything, Ina?' Drugs were a chart-topping reason why people in Scotland were murdered. It seemed to me like a reasonable question, and though I tried to ask it as gently as possible, Mrs Boyd was outraged.

'I'm sorry,' I said, after she'd calmed down slightly. 'I didn't mean to be rude. It's just that—'

'They're both good boys.' She snorted. 'Drugs. As if.'

Not drugs then. 'Can you think of any other possible reason someone would want to kill Nathan? Did Nathan owe anyone money?'

Apparently he didn't.

'Was there a woman involved? Maybe somebody else's wife,' I suggested cautiously.

Mrs Boyd bit her bottom lip and shook her head.

There had to be some reason why the Boyd boys should be targeted. I'd tried drugs, money and sex. What else was there?

'I know that you'll think this a bit crazy,' I said, when I'd run out of possible motives, 'but Danny thinks he and

Nathan were cursed when they tried to break into that mausoleum.'

Mrs Boyd's face tightened. 'I warned them. I warned them both when they started going out looking for tombs. I told the pair of them they could explore if they wanted, but to touch nothing.' She stood. 'Mr Munro, I've never offered you a cup of tea.'

'I'm fine.' I was wasting my time. 'I'd better go. Let you get back to your jam.'

'Do you like jam?'

Everyone liked jam didn't they?

She took me through to the kitchen, a much larger room than the parlor with an immense gas range on which two big jam pots burbled and blubbed, half a lemon partially submerged in the centre of each batch of molten strawberries. 'What's your favourite?' Mrs Boyd pulled open the double doors of a cupboard on the far wall. It was stacked with row after row of jam jars, each with a plastic cover over the top, held on by a red rubber band. Homemade paper labels proudly proclaimed: *Mrs Boyd's Finest Preserves*. A row of rhubarb and ginger caught my eye. My dad's favourite. Might as well keep in with him. We'd yet to discuss the state of my forehead, and my planned walking into a door story was unlikely to meet with critical acclaim.

Mrs Boyd wrapped a jar in a brown paper bag. 'I'm not a superstitious person, Mr Munro. I just know what is best for my boys. Nathan is... was... a clever boy. He did well at school. He kept all the books for the family business. He wrote all the letters and used to get much better deals than I could from the garden centres.' Tears began to well once more. She took the hanky from her apron pocket and dabbed her eyes. 'We've got a computer for printing labels and doing letters and stuff. Nathan wanted the internet. I didn't like the sound of it, but we got it anyway and the two of them were never away from it. Have you got children, Mr Munro?'

I confirmed the absence of heirs.

'Well, when you do have, you'll be able to tell when something's not right. Even though my boys never said nothing, I knew something was wrong. Then I found Danny was getting threats.'

This was more like it. 'Who from?'

'Other kids, making fun of him. Calling us gypo's and pikey's. Sending him emails and telling him to kill himself. The school called it cider-bullying. Said it was a big problem these days for kids. It wasn't a problem for me and my boys much longer. I pulled the plug on that internet. Problem solved.'

Some playground taunting was hardly going to result in Nathan's throat being slit and a contract being put out on his brother and his brother's lawyer.

'I didn't like them doing all that tomb searching. Those people have been dead for years. Just because they're forgotten doesn't give anyone the right to go disturbing them.'

I had to ask. 'What people?'

'Nathan got a list off the internet. There are tombs all over Scotland. In places you'd never think. I told him... I told him... leave them alone.'

I could tell she was about to burst into tears again. I didn't want to be there when it happened. The dog wandered through to see what all the fuss was about. Mrs Boyd shoo'd him out again.

'Find Danny,' she said.

I reached out for the brown paper bag. 'Thanks for the jam. My dad will love it.'

Mrs Boyd kept a tight grip on it. 'Don't let anything happen to my boy.'

I didn't intend to. Danny and I were inextricably linked by way of a contract out on our lives. I was certain that if something bad happened to him, it would happen to me.

Chapter 41

I took off my mud-caked boots and left them at the door. Six hours straight, traipsing around Beecraigs Country Park, trying to find someone who was doing his damnedest not to be found.

'You're back then?' my dad said, without diverting his gaze from the TV. Sunday night; a divorced detective with a drink problem, whose wife still secretly loved him, was driving around in an interesting car, solving crimes to the astonishment of his colleagues who hated and yet secretly admired him. Given that he rubbed his superiors up the wrong way so often and continually flouted the rules, the only mystery for me was how he'd been made inspector. Clearly, unlike most other major organisations, sooking-up to the top brass counted for nothing in the Police Force.

'Manage not to bump into any more doors on your travels?' my dad asked, as I padded past him, through the livingroom to the kitchen.

I ignored the jibe. 'I'm having a beer, do you want one?' A question I should have asked before I opened the fridge door. 'That was a six-pack when I left this morning,' I said, sitting down beside my dad on the sofa, clutching the last bottle of beer.

'Well your whisky ran out earlier today,' he replied, as though somehow the bottle of Bowmore I'd bought just a few nights before had evaporated.

I took a swig of lager. 'Can we watch something else? You don't even like cop shows.'

'I know, but I've got a theory about this series.'

My dad had a theory on most things. 'You don't mean to say that this disillusioned detective who goes about being gruff and horrible to everyone is really a diligent officer with a heart of gold?'

'Actually, it's not my theory, it's Vince's.'

Vince Green was not only the late father of my girlfriend, Jill, but former best friend of my dad. If he'd had a theory I'd better take it seriously.

'Go on,' I said.

I used to watch this show with Vince. He could guess the killer every week without fail. We used to have bets on it. I lost fortunes to him. I even told him once he should join the polis as a consultant.

'You sure you weren't watching repeats?'

'No, he told me afterwards how they write the scripts for these things. He had an old army pal who went on to work on the telly. I think he was a stunt co-ordinator or something. Anyway, he told him all about it. You see, you can't have the killer being somebody who suddenly appears at the end. That would be like cheating. You have to have seen them during the show sometime, understand?'

I was with him so far.

'Well, you know how the detective goes about interviewing folk? It's always the third suspect who's done it. If it was the first it would be too obvious.'

'What about the second?'

'It's always the third, all right?'

I took another mouthful of beer. 'Is that it? That's the theory? Seems simple enough. Did you never catch on.'

'Until someone tells you, it's not that easy to work out. The first two suspects always have motives. The third doesn't really have a motive until you find out what it was right at the end and it all becomes clear.'

'So who did it?' I tilted the neck of the bottle at the TV. 'That guy with the cravat looks a bit dodgy. What is he? An antiques dealer?'

'Auctioneer, but it's not him. He's only number two.'

The whole show was number two so far as I was concerned. I finished the beer in one more long gulp.

'Did you not find him then?' my dad asked.

With five beers in him as well as the rest of my whisky, he was in talkative mood. 'I'll not disturb you. Watch your programme. I'm going for a shower to wash off the muck and midges.'

'It's okay, I don't mind having a wee chat.' He pressed the mute button on the TV remote. 'Number three'll not be on until after the adverts. Tell me, what's so important about this Boyd boy? If the polis aren't hunting him, he'll come home soon enough. You can call off the search. I mean it was a nice pot of jam, but that's two days you've been looking for him. There wasn't even that much ginger in it. It was mostly rhubarb.'

'I think he's in danger.'

'Because of what happened to his brother? You don't even know what that was all about. Could have been anything. A housebreaking gone wrong or something.'

'There's nothing in the house to steal unless you're a jam thief. There has to be more to it. I spoke to his mum. She was going on about the Boyd boys being cyber-bullied.'

'That's not real bullying,' my dad said, after I'd enlightened him on the meaning. 'When I moved to Linlithgow, early Sixties, there was a bully at our school, Big Dowzer. He used to take bottles of juice off his classmates, drink them, pee in the bottle and then make them buy them back with their dinner money. Now that's proper bullying. Not some kids on the computer slagging-off your trainers.'

I could never imagine my dad as a schoolboy. 'Dowzer ever sell you a bottle?' I asked.

'Tried to. He was a big laddie and I think all his life he'd relied on his size to scare everyone else. Not sure if he'd ever actually been in a fight, before.'

'Before?'

'Before I kicked him up and down the playground one afternoon. I got into bother for that.'

'The belt?'

'Oh, aye, of course the belt, but his parents called the polis. I was summoned to see Sergeant MacKenzie. Everyone knew Sergeant MacKenzie. I think there was just him and one other cop in the town back then. I went down to see him thinking I was getting sent to the borstal. So did your Granny. He made me sweat in a cell for I don't know how long. I was only fourteen. By the time that cell door clanged opened and I saw him standing there in full uniform, I was more or less resigned to a life behind bars.' My dad levered himself up from the sofa.

'Where are you going?' I asked.

'The toilet, before you go for a shower and spend the rest of the night in there.'

'But what happened? Sergeant MacKenzie? What did he do?'

'He gave me a police recruitment leaflet and told me to come back and see him when I left the school. Best advice I ever got.'

The phone rang. It was Jill. 'Caught you in, have I? Not out and about on important legal business in a champagne bar?'

I could tell by the sound of her voice that she was kidding, sort of, and for the next half hour we had our first proper conversation since Jill had left for the land of the Toblerone, four and a half weeks before. It was great just to hear her voice. I could have talked on, but my dad came and took over. Though I could only hear one side of their conversation, it started off about me and the state of my flat and quickly reached what appeared to be general agreement on my lack of domesticity. From there they covered a range of topics including my dad's pending birthday celebrations.

'Will you be back for the party, pet...? No, it's a big surprise... The boys are laying it on for me.... Aye, it's top secret... I'm having it at the West Port... Next Friday night... My birthday's not actually until the Saturday...'

And so it went on until discussions led predictably to the acquisition of a bottle of whisky from Duty Free. My dad wasn't fussy, although he had heard good things about the Springbank eighteen year-old, but Jill needn't think she had to go to all that expense just for him, he said, with a highly voluntary, involuntary, grunt of pain, before going on to update her on the condition of her plants and his heroic watering thereof, because I was too busy, and him with his leg in plaster.

I left at that point. When I returned he was dozing on the couch and the credits were rolling. He stirred when I sat down beside him and tried to locate the remote. 'Big case starts tomorrow, eh? Have you a clean shirt? You'll probably be on the telly. I don't want you showing me up on the news in a grubby shirt.'

'Clean shirt and clean pants too - just in case I'm in an accident.' I found the remote. It had fallen on the floor and rolled under the sofa. 'So, whodunit?' I asked switching over to the news.

'The wife.'

'Was she number three then?'

'I don't know. I missed some of the programme when I was on the phone to Jill. Must have been, though. She did it after all.'

Perfect logic. 'Not very original,' I said. 'The wife being the murderer? Don't need a theory to work that out.'

He extracted the Sunday newspaper from the side of the sofa cushion an announced that he was off to bed.

'Unless it was supposed to be a double bluff,' I said.

'I suppose that could be it.' He levered himself upright. 'To make you think it couldn't be her because it was so obvious that the jealous wife would be the killer.'

He said something else. I wasn't listening. He was right. It was obvious. The jealous wife. Kirkslap was married.

204

According to him it was an open marriage. Did Mrs Kirkslap think the same? I'd read volumes of statements. From the woman at the cosmetic counter who'd sold Violet Hepburn her last tube of lipstick, to the scene of crime officer who'd cut holes in the carpet at the lodge to remove the traces of blood, to the traffic cops who'd stationed the mobile speed camera that had caught the accused's car on its late night tour of the Trossachs, and, yet, there was one important person whose views did not appear to have been canvassed. One person whose evidence could have been crucial, depending on whether she wanted the accused convicted or acquitted. Why, when we were on the eve of the trial, had no-one taken a statement from Mrs Larry Kirkslap?

Chapter 42

What was the most effective way to lead a Crown case? An insecure, inexperienced prosecutor usually started right at the beginning, leading every adminicle of potentially incriminatory evidence available. It might seem the safest way to go, but it could also seriously bore a jury and, of course, every witness the Crown called was potentially, under the right cross-examination, the makings of a reasonable doubt for the defence.

Today would be different. Cameron Crowe sat to my right, Joanna on my left, and across the well of Courtroom 3, Edinburgh High Court, sitting beside junior counsel and a solicitor from Crown Office, was Fiona Faye Q.C.

Fiona was neither insecure nor inexperienced. I knew exactly how the prosecution would play the re-run of H.M. Advocate –v- Lawrence Kirkslap. This time around, the trial would last nothing like four weeks. With Fiona it was all rapier, she left the bludgeon to others. The blade was in and the defence bleeding-out before the accused even knew he'd been stabbed.

Fiona believed that the road to a conviction started with the creation of a strong first impression. No tedious formalities. Present the jury with the best stuff first. Get them on your side straight away. Add to that a strong finish and that's all a jury would remember, needed to remember. What happened in the middle only confused them and confusion in a jury could lead to a nasty case of not proven. Fiona would start and finish strongly, while keeping the beginning and the end as close together as possible. I predicted we were in for a whirlwind of a trial. A trial with the evidence whittled to the minimum. No fat, just the solid bones of strong Crown case.

And my prediction that the Crown would hit the jury hard and fast was proved correct. Once his Lordship made great show of well and truly swearing-in the jury, Fiona kicked off the trial with one of juiciest morsels of evidence available: the bloodstains.

First up to bat was a scene of crime officer. Using books of photographs and police video footage that, as uncontroversial evidence, had been agreed in advance, he talked us through the layout of Kirkslap's country lodge and adjacent garage, paying particular attention to blood staining found on the hall carpet and in the boot of Kirkslap's black Audi Q7.

Although there was no cross-examination of this routine evidence, the careful leading of it, together with the empanelling of the jury and reading of the Joint Minute took us, with perfect timing to one o'clock and lunch. The next witness was a forensics expert who spoke to the DNA analysis of the bloodstains and explained that the odds of the blood not being the deceased's were astronomical.

The day ended. Without the defence having fired a shot, Fiona had left the jury with a first, and, no doubt, lasting impression of Violet Hepburn's blood being found in strange and highly incriminating places, for which, as the jury would find out soon enough, the accused had no reasonable explanation.

'You've got to hand it to her, Miss Faye certainly knows how to capture a jury's attention,' Joanna said. After a brief consultation with Kirkslap and Cameron Crowe we were walking down the High Street towards Waverley Station. On the way we passed by Royal Mile Whisky's flagship store, a bottle of Springbank 18 year-old in the front window, a reminder of my dad and a surprise birthday party which as yet was a surprise to everyone apart from him.

'Crowe will get stuck in about the forensic scientist in the morning,' I said.

'He can't stop it being Violet's blood. If only Kirkslap could come up with an explanation about why it was there, or why he was out driving late at night, or why he arranged to meet a woman he had already threatened because she was stalking him. Or why—'

'And if he did?' I said. 'If he did come up with some reasonable explanations for it all. What then? Violet would still be missing, presumed dead.'

'If Kirkslap didn't do it, somebody else did,' Joanna said.

'Brilliant. I knew I'd hired you for a reason.'

Joanna swivelled ninety-degrees, striking me a friendly straight arm to the shoulder with the heel of her hand. 'I meant somebody else who made it look like it was Kirkslap.'

'Do you ever watch TV detective shows, Joanna?'

'Now and again.'

'My dad's got this theory that it's always the third suspect whodunit. Last night it was the jealous wife.'

'And?'

'And, I think we should speak to Mrs Kirkslap. I'm told she wasn't at court today.'

'And I've been told she's not the slightest wee bit jealous.'

'Could all be a front. You know what women are like.'

Joanna, wrinkled her eyes. 'Tell me.'

'They're devious.' I remembered the recent blow to my shoulder and took a swift step out of arm's reach. 'Or they can be. Some of them. Not all and without prejudice to present company,' I thought it best to add.

'Really?' Joanna seemed hugely under-whelmed. 'Is that the best you can come up with?'

'What other theories have you got?' I asked.

'Just one,' she said. 'That our client is a murderer. And not a very good one.'

Chapter **43**

Thanks to the prompt end to the court day I was able to return to the office before five where I left Joanna to sign the mail and deal with the collection of yellow-sticky notes, mainly phone-backs, that, in usual fashion, Grace-Mary had left stuck to my computer monitor.

Routine tasks thus delegated, I crunched up the driveway of chez Kirkslap, officially titled Addison House, shortly before six, where I was met by the lady of the manor who showed me through to what I assumed was the library, due to all the shelves with books on them. It's not every house that has one.

Marjorie Kirkslap, née Addison, sat down opposite me on a Chesterfield, the green leather faded and cracked. If I owned the Kirkslap heap, I might have been tempted to keep the books, but throw out the ancient furniture and stick in a snooker table.

'I don't know how right and proper this is,' she said, like there was a difference between the two. 'After all, you're my husband's lawyer—'

'And I thought you might like to know how the trial is going. I noticed that you didn't make the court today,' I said.

Actually, it was first time I'd clapped eyes on Mrs Marjorie Kirkslap. She was tall and thin, hair either not yet grey or expertly dyed and cut short. Although she had the merest dab of powder on her cheeks and only a hint of colour on her lips, if I hadn't known she was nearly sixty, I would have guessed her age to be easily ten years younger. She was wearing a shapeless brown woolly jumper with a mustard cravat tied around her neck, tan slacks and, on her feet, a pair of ox-blood brogues. She looked at me, wondering why I was really there, too polite to accuse me of anything. I'd have to be careful. Even if I wasn't there to confront her, in the library with the candlestick, I did hope to glean, by way of stealth cross-examination, anything upon which I might base my jealous wife theory.

She pulled back the sleeve of her pullover and looked at the tiny face of a delicate gold wrist watch and then checked it with a monstrous marble mantel clock above the fireplace. 'Lovely isn't it,' she said, mistaking my, how-could-anything-be-so-hideous, look for one of admiration. 'Edwardian. French movement.' I adopted an expression which I hoped made me look like I knew what she was talking about.

'It was a gift,' she said. 'From the Queen.'

At least she was engaging in conversation. Not about anything I was interested in, but it was a start.

Further along the mantelpiece was a photograph of a man in some kind of uniform, holding a feathered hat under one arm, a sword in an ornate gold scabbard at his side.

'My father. That photograph was taken back in the early seventies when Charles Hope took ill.'

This time my face could register only a blank.

'The Marquess of Linlithgow. He was Lord Lieutenant of West Lothian for twenty or so years. He was unwell for a time and father stepped in for a few official duties. We used to fly the Lion Rampant from the top of the house. It's one of the privileges.'

It was all highly edifying, but not what I'd come to learn. I wanted to know more about the famous open marriage of the Kirkslaps and just how much of a two way street that was.

'I'm an Addison,' she said. 'We've been landowners here for hundreds of years. My father was a Baronet. Did you know?' I didn't. 'The Baronetcy was created, or, more likely, purchased, back in the seventeenth century. My older brother holds the title. He lives in Canada now.' She smiled. 'It's down to me to stay home and keep the family crest polished.'

She looked set to divulge some other fascinating historical fact when an elderly man appeared in the doorway carrying a galvanised tin bucket. It looked heavy.

'It's gone six, Marjorie,' he said. 'Are you forgetting that important phone call?'

Really? I was getting done over by the important phone call routine? Did she actually expect me to fall for that? She stood. I had the distinct impression that my hostess didn't really care whether I did or not. She was leaving. She'd been stalling all along, feeding me the Addison family history while waiting for this chance to escape.

'You will excuse me,' she said, leaving me no choice than to follow her to the library door, and the tin pail carrying old man. She put out a hand. 'Lovely to meet you. I'm sure you will do your very best for Larry, won't you?'

'This way, sir,' said the elderly man, gesturing open-handed down the hall towards the front door.

'Worked here long?' I asked, as he led the way to the front door, still carrying his shiny bucket.

He laughed. 'Oh, I see. You think I'm the butler. No such luck. I'm Gordon - that's Marjorie's Uncle Gordon. If I was the butler at least I'd get paid.'

'Let me get that.' I took the bucket from him as he switched it from one hand to the other. It was unexpectedly heavy. I felt a twinge in my greatly improved ankle, still the pain would be worth it. If I couldn't get anything useful from Kirkslap's wife, maybe I could interrogate this old duffer into revealing something interesting. 'Where to?'

He thought for a moment and then smiled. 'To feed the duke and duchess.'

I followed him out of the house, across some garden ground and over a dyke to a small track. Set back from it were some sandstone blocks and other materials beside a partially completed structure that looked like it was going to be some kind of outhouse.

I enquired about the building work, but the old man, who wasn't the most talkative, just grunted and marched on, with me following and the bucket of grain, bread and wriggly maggots, growing heavier with every step.

'You're Larry's new lawyer, then,' he asked, eventually, as we trudged forever onwards and, usually, upwards. 'What happened to the last one? Inman or Irving or —?'

'Imray?'

'That's the chappie. Where's he this weather?'

Uncle Gordon nimbly jumped a burn. I almost did too, but my heel slipped on the grassy bank, dipping into the water, soaking my sock.

'You've met Andy, that is, Mr Imray, then?'

'Yes, he was up here before the first trial. Asking a lot of impertinent questions about Marjorie and Larry.'

I wasn't sure what to say. I'd been hoping to ask a few myself.

The duke and duchess, it turned out, after what must have been a half-mile limp down the track, through a gate, over a stile, over another stile, across a burn and up a hill, were a peacock and peahen, shacked up amidst a small copse of trees. Sweating, breathing hard, my left sock squelching gently, I set down the bucket. 'So, Lawrence and Marjorie... where *did* it all go wrong?'

Uncle Gordon didn't reply, just reached into the bucket and threw great handfuls to the birds.

'Shame when a marriage takes a nose-dive, isn't it?' I thought those old boys liked nothing better than a chat and a bit of gossip, but Uncle Gordon's only response was to scatter more feed mixture.

'How did Marjorie take it? All Larry's fault, I suppose. Success gone to his head.'

The old man finished scattering and dusted off his hands. With a green, welly-boot he pushed the bucket onto its side and emptied out the rest of the contents onto the grass, amongst which I noticed two building bricks. No wonder the bucket had been so heavy.

'Know where your car is from here?' Uncle Gordon asked, sitting down on the trunk of a fallen tree and taking out his pipe.

I confirmed that I could probably locate my vehicle without too much difficulty.

He packed the bowl with tobacco he'd teased out from a well-worn leather pouch.

'Good,' he struck a match and gazed out at the rolling West Lothian countryside. 'You can bugger off back to it then.'

Chapter 44

Car heater on full blast to dry my wet clutch pedal foot, I drove straight from the seat of the Addison family Glasgow, phoning Andy on the way to tell him that I'd meet him in a pub in the Merchant City we both knew well.

'What's the emergency?' he asked. We took our pints and managed to find some elbow room further down the bar.

'Why didn't you tell me you'd already been to see Marjorie Kirkslap?' I said. 'There's nothing in the case files about her, no precognition, no attendance note, nothing.'

'You've been then?'

'Yes, I've been. Fat lot of good it did me. I thought I might be on to something there.'

Andy sipped the head of his pint. 'What happened to your head?'

'I slipped. Don't change the subject.'

'Okay, yes, I went to see her.'

'Why?'

As it turned out my jealous wife theory had not been an entirely novel one. Andy had gone with the same idea.

'I pretended that I was looking for an alibi for Kirkslap for the night of the first November. I knew Kirkslap had already told the police he'd been alone at his lodge all night, but I was really trying to find out where his wife had been.' Andy smiled. 'Clever, eh?'

'Go on.'

'She was in Magdeburg. That's in Germany. She had been over there all that week with St Michael's choir. I don't think she sings, more of a sponsor. Anyway, they were on some kind of tour and singing at the cathedral on All Saints Day. She didn't even return to British airspace until bonfire night.'

'And that fact wasn't deemed worthy of so much as an attendance note on the file?'

'What was I supposed to do? Leave a note saying, checked out the wife's alibi - she never done it?'

My still damp foot, sore ankle and aching bucket-carrying arms weren't yet prepared to forgive Andy his oversight. I drank some beer, refreshed some brain cells, killed some others. 'What difference does it make if Marjorie Kirkslap has an alibi? I can't see her personally bumping off Violet and then making the body disappear. She would have paid somebody to do that.'

Andy had to agree it was possible, except... 'You can't just Google hit-men. You need contacts.'

'There are people out there happy to take on the work,' I said.

'Yes, and you know who some of them are because you've been a defence lawyer for yonks. I wouldn't know who to get in touch with - how on earth would someone like Marjorie Kirkslap?'

He was right, which made me realise that whoever was after me and Danny Boyd must have connections. The only person who could point me in the right direction was Jake Turpie. Suddenly, sitting there in that pub in Glasgow, I felt very vulnerable.

'You okay?' Andy asked. 'You look like somebody just walked over your grave.'

'Or through my mausoleum,' I said. I told Andy about my bumping into the barrel of Deek Pudney's Desert Eagle, about Danny Boyd and the contract supposed to be out on my client and me.

'Doesn't make sense,' Andy said. 'Who'd want to kill a sixteen year-old boy just because he vandalises ancient tombs for a hobby? And why kill you? What have you done? You're usually acting for killers. They should want to keep you alive.' He took another drink of beer. 'You'll need to go to the police of course.'

215

'And say what? That Jake Turpie told me there's a contract out on me? Do you think he's going to help the police with their enquiries? No, I'm going to have to work on Jake and get him to tell me who's behind it or see if he'll put a stop to it. I've already explained that if I'm bumped off he'll have to whistle for his rent.'

We'd almost finished our drinks when Andy mentioned the Kirkslap case again. 'I heard the Crown got off to a flying start. It's not going to be any easier this time, you know. Not with the new evidence about the threat being made against Violet. I remember you telling me about that. What I didn't know was that they were calling Mike Summers as a witness.' He smiled. 'That's not going to help.'

'Who told you about that?'

'Just someone I know.'

'A lawyer?'

'Not quite yet. Candice is a paralegal doing the part-time law degree at Strathclyde. She's—'

'Candice?'

'Candice McKeever.'

Was Andy referring to brunette, legs that go all the way down to the ground, all-round-gorgeous Candy from Karats Champagne Bar?

'I don't know. It could be her,' Andy said. 'She did say that she sometimes worked in a bar. But a gold-digger...?'

'How long has she been with Caldwell & Craig?'

Andy thought about that while he shouted us up another round, a pint for him, ginger beer for me. 'Must have been shortly after I arrived. She was working more or less full-time on the Kirkslap case. She never attended any of the consultations, but she did take a few statements and helped a lot with the admin: photocopying, collating papers, that sort of thing. I thought she was really nice. How do you know her?'

'Because she's a potential witness.'

'What? In Larry Kirkslap's case? Don't think she'll be able to help much.'

'Not a defence witness. For the prosecution. She was there when Larry Kirkslap went round to Violet's house and threatened her. She's the girl whose silence was bought with a diamond necklace. I told you about her already.'

'You never said anything about it being Candice. Are you sure we're talking about the same person?'

'No,' I said. I downed the glass of ginger beer in a oner. 'But I'm going to find out.'

It wasn't that far to Karats, even with a wet foot and a limp. When I got to the steps leading up to the entrance, it was the back of seven and the street lights were coming on. The doorman came down them to meet me. He was wearing a turquoise baseball cap with a monogrammed gold 'K' on the front and mirrored sunglasses.

'I don't think so, sir,' he said.

'What do you mean, you don't think so? Do you know who I am?' I thought the old, *do you know who I am?* Might be worth a try. It wasn't.

'Yes, I do,' he said, jerking his head at the CCTV cameras on the wall, 'and I've been told not to let you in.' He tapped a Bluetooth earphone. 'Sorry.'

'Well, will you find out if Candy McKeever is in there and ask her to come out?'

He wouldn't. He seemed quite certain about that.

'Do you have a number for her?'

The doorman had returned to the small landing at the top of the steps and was now looking, side to side, up and down the street, anywhere apart from at me.

There was no point arguing. The doorman didn't look like the kind of guy who'd be likely to indulge in reasoned debate, and, in any event, it was a Monday night. I didn't know if Candy would be there or not. She might have been at home, curled up in front of the TV or out zimmer-shopping with her latest sugar-daddy.

I'd have to try and contact her via Caldwell & Craig tomorrow. Time was fast running out, and I would like to have known what she was playing at before Kirkslap's trial progressed much further. If she was the same Candy McKeever who'd accused me of lying to her, why had she hidden from me the fact that she too had been working on Larry Kirkslap's case?

The smoked-glass doors opened and out strolled Tuppence Christie.

He looked down at me. 'Problem?' he asked the doorman, who assured him there was none. 'Good,' he said, and, with a young lady on either arm, came down the steps and into a Merc that had appeared from nowhere.

'Tuppence come here often?' I asked the doorman, as the limousine pulled away.

'Mr Christie is the proprietor,' he growled.

'Taking some work home with him tonight is he?'

'You're a funny guy.'

I was getting nowhere in my search for Candy. Tuppence Christie's connection with the champagne bar was interesting, though. If he was the proprietor, there had to be a lot of nutters coming and going. Acquaintances of his with plenty of drug money. A rich nutter was a nutter nonetheless. If we'd had weeks or months to prepare for the retrial instead of a few days, it might have been possible to make something of that information, but I doubted there was much that could be done at this late stage.

I started to walk away.

'Be seeing you,' the doorman said.

I doubted it. But I was to be proved wrong.

218

Chapter 45

'Tell me, were you asked to examine any other samples of blood from Mr Kirkslap's lodge?'

Tuesday morning and Cameron Crowe's cross-examination of the Crown forensic expert was underway.

'Yes, we were given several samples to test.'

'How many?'

The forensic scientist referred to the document in front of him: Crown Production fifteen, a laboratory report compiled by him and a colleague. 'Nine in all.'

Fiona had only led evidence of two blood samples the previous day. Some of the jurors shifted, interested.

'Nine?' Crowe turned his head to the jury box and looked at them when he asked his next question. 'And how many of those nine samples do you say belonged to Miss Hepburn?'

'Two.'

'Ah, yes,' Crowe said, as though it was a minor matter he'd almost forgotten about. He picked up his copy of the report, donned a pair of tortoiseshell-framed spectacles and read, 'on the hall carpet and in the boot of the car.' He whisked off his glasses again. 'What about those seven others?'

'Three belonged to the accused. The other four samples were found not to be relevant. One of them turned out to be a drop of rabbit blood on the kitchen floor.'

The expert smiled. Cameron Crowe didn't. In a few more questions, Crowe elicited that the three samples belonging to Kirkslap were all found on a towel in the bathroom next to the sink and were consistent with him having dabbed his face after shaving.

'Leaving the rabbit to one side for the moment,' Crowe sneered, 'tell us about the other three samples. Perhaps the ladies and gentlemen of the jury would like to decide for themselves how irrelevant they are.'

It was a minor dig, but a good jury point nonetheless. No witness, however well qualified, should tell a jury what is or is not pertinent. It didn't do the defence any harm to align itself with the jurors, give them their place, remind them how important they were. The subtext was that the defence lawyers were there on the side of justice and wouldn't let the Crown decide what the jury should or shouldn't hear. The defence would make sure the masters of the facts heard all the evidence; not just the edited highlights.

'Well? Did you find out who the other samples belonged to?' Crowe asked. 'The *irrelevant* ones?'

Crowe was really milking it. Whatever information now came out would seem to the jury like details the Crown had tried to hide.

'The other samples came from a Mr Eric Spalding.'

'And where were they found?'

The expert again checked his report. 'The police label on the samples given to us stated, 'carpet beneath window sill in bedroom one'.'

'And do you know this Mr Spalding?'

'No, I don't'

'But you know what he does for a living?'

'I believe he's a joiner.'

'And do you know how his blood came to be there?'

'The police told me—'

'One moment please,' the judge interrupted. 'Mr Crowe, it sounds very much as though you are attempting to lead hearsay evidence.'

It not only sounded like it, he definitely was.

'My friend hasn't objected.' Crowe looked across the table at Fiona.

Fiona couldn't object. If she did it would look like she was trying to conceal something else from the jury and, when the evidence eventually did come out, it would seem all the more important because of it. She smiled at the judge and shook her head. 'No objection, M'Lord.'

Crowe didn't wait for the go ahead from the bench. 'The police told you that Mr Spalding was a joiner and that he'd recently fitted a new bedroom window at Mr Kirkslap's lodge - is that correct?'

The expert agreed that was the information he'd received.

'And it is generally accepted that his blood is on the carpet because he injured himself with a chisel or similar instrument, is it not?'

The judge looked impatiently down at the Crown side of the table, expecting an objection, but Fiona stared stalwartly ahead.

'So what you are saying is that there would appear to be an innocent explanation for the blood on Mr Kirkslap's shaving towel?'

'Yes.'

'And there appears to be an innocent explanation for Mr Spalding's blood on the bedroom floor?'

'Yes.'

'And for all you know there may be an innocent explanation for those bloodstains you have attributed to Miss Violet Hepburn?'

The expert didn't answer, but the slight shrug of his shoulders would have been enough for the jury.

'For the tape, please,' Crowe said.

'Yes,' said the expert.

'Just as well Mr Spalding hasn't gone missing too or this would be a double-murder trial,' he said, flashing a wry expression at the jury.

'Are you quite finished, Mr Crowe?' the judge asked.

He wasn't. 'Your expert analysis...' Crowe held the report up to the witness and looked at it as though it were a filthy rag, 'doesn't even tell us if the rabbit was murdered. Does it?'

The expert gave him a don't-be-ridiculous look.

Crowe threw the report onto the table and walked over to the witness box. 'Well, does it?'

He held the expert's stare until the latter said, 'no,' and then about-turned, strode back to his seat and sat down with a flap of his gown.

The judge looked down at Fiona Faye, who was doing an excellent job of trying not to appear fazed. 'Lunch?'

Joanna met one of her old friends from the Fiscal Service and went off for a sandwich. Crowe disappeared, probably to hang upside down in a cupboard for a while, following his prolonged exposure to daylight. Mike, now a Crown witness, was not supposed to communicate with the defence before giving his evidence. That left just myself, my client and Zack. The previous day we had adjourned to Gordon's Trattoria, an Italian restaurant only a hundred yards or so from the court, further down the Royal Mile, and I was looking forward to a re-run of the Penne Tre Figlie; however, I noticed that Kirkslap was hanging back, pacing the lobby at the top of the stairs.

Zack came over to me. 'Larry's not happy,' he said. 'No, better upgrade that to furious.'

I couldn't understand it. Cameron Crowe had made a great start to the defence case. He'd taken a serious bite out of the first chunk of circumstantial evidence. If Kirkslap was to be acquitted the defence would have to take each piece of incriminatory evidence and hang a reasonable doubt from it. Crowe had done that extremely well with the bloodstains; one of the Crown's most important strands of evidence; Fiona Faye's opening gambit.

'No, he's very pleased with Mr Crowe. He's not pleased with you going to visit Marjorie.'

Word travelled fast within open marriages.

'I had a good reason.'

'You had a hunch,' Zack said. 'Like Andy did. It was made very clear to him that Marjorie was strictly out of bounds. No meetings, no interviews, no publicity.'

'I'm trying to do my job,' I said.

'Do it. Just don't include Marjorie Kirkslap in it.'

Who was this twenty-something to tell me how to do my job? What did he know? He made stupid games for a living; ones that stupid people bought and lost their money playing. I walked past him to where Kirkslap was gazing up at the abstract tapestries on the wall outside Court 3.

'After court today we're having a meeting,' I told him. 'No Zack, no Mike, no counsel, just you and me.'

He was going to say something, but my phone buzzed and I turned away to take the call.

Malky.

'I forgot to book the West Port for dad's birthday,' he said.

'Well book it now.'

'I can't. Someone's got it for a twenty-first. What are we going to do? The party's supposed to be Friday night.'

Chapter 46

The Scotsman Hotel on South Bridge is the former headquarters of the Scotsman newspaper, before its move to Barclay House on Holyrood Road. Kirkslap had taken a junior suite, situated high on the north-west corner of the building. A plaque beside the door told me the immense, wood-panelled room had once been an editor's office.

We sat in chairs at a tall window with a fine view over Waverley Station, across Princes Street Gardens to the Scott Monument.

'Drink?' Kirkslap set a glass on the bureau desk beside me, along with a selection of single-malt miniatures from the mini-bar. Judging by his own glass and the number of tiny dead soldiers, he'd started early. It wasn't five o'clock. Court had finished for the day less than an hour ago.

I helped myself to an Ardbeg.

'Islay?' Kirkslap said. 'Never really got a taste for it. They say it's peaty. Tastes more like TCP to me.' He raised his own glass of vodka. 'Here's to Cameron Crowe.'

'I think he'd rather be toasted with blood,' I said.

Kirkslap laughed. 'He is a cold bastard right enough? Doesn't smile much and when he does, never hits his eyes, does it?' He took a drink. 'Still, better on our side than theirs, eh?'

There was no point going around the houses. I was there to find out what Kirkslap's big problem was with me going to see his wife. I still had to go back to the office and make sure that the day to day business of Munro & Co. wasn't too neglected, and then there was my extreme concern over the contract out on Danny Boyd and myself, not to mention my dad's surprise birthday party. The surprise being that it didn't look like there was going to be one.

'I went to see your wife yesterday and you're not pleased about it,' I said. 'Why?'

'Why did you go? This whole affair has nothing to do with Marjorie. She's a very private person, a very proud person. This business with me, all the publicity, it's really getting to her.'

I could understand that. Marjorie Kirkslap was a throwback. From our brief meeting I had the impression of a woman determined to continue her family's small place in history; the Baronetcy of the Addison's, West Lothian's second most-titled family. But there was more to it than that, I was sure of it.

I opened the miniature and poured it into my glass. 'You didn't give evidence in your last trial, why not?'

'Mr Staedtler advised against it.'

'Well, you're giving evidence in this one.' There was a plastic bottle of spring water on the desk. I opened it and added a thimbleful to my malt.

'That's my decision to make,' he said.

'Some people say that the definition of madness is doing the same thing over and over again and expecting a different result.'

'It's hardly over and over.'

'Sitting back and hoping the Crown can't prove its case isn't enough,' I said. 'It's a strategy that didn't work last time and it won't work this.'

Kirkslap cracked open another miniature. 'Mr Crowe has done more in one day to discredit the Crown case than Staedtler did in the whole of the first trial.' He poured his drink and raised his glass to me. 'I've you to thank for that as much as anyone.'

'There are a lot more days still to go,' I said. 'Lots more damaging evidence to come out. Crowe can only try to muddy the waters. It's not going to be enough for the jury.

They've already read the newspaper report that you were found guilty last time. The judge can direct them to put that out of their minds, but how exactly do they do that? Put yourself in their shoes. What would you need to hear before you could return a verdict of not guilty or not proven?'

Sulkily, Kirkslap put the glass to his lips.

'Larry, you have to stand up in that witness box and tell the jury that you didn't do it. You have to tell them exactly what happened on the night of first November, but first of all you have to tell me.'

Kirkslap's face was red, his forehead sweaty. 'I'll tell you what happened,' he said, quietly. He held up his now empty glass. 'This happened. Drink happened.'

'And your visit to Candy McKeever's the other night? Were you drunk then too?'

'Blootered.'

'And the trip to see Violet when you threatened to kill her?'

'I can't remember a thing about it.'

'And the first of November two thousand and twelve?'

'Did I text, Violet? I could have. Did I kill her? What do you want me to say? That I didn't? I'm sure I didn't. I know I wouldn't have. Can I remember if I did...?' Kirkslap put his head in his hands for a moment and then looked up at me, the whites of his eyes red and watery. 'Are you sure you want to put me in the witness box?'

Carefully, he lined up the four remaining vodka miniatures on the desk beside us. When they were arranged in a neat row, he took the first and threw it at the nearby drinks cabinet. The miniature bounced off unscathed. The next three weren't so fortunate; they smashed, one by one, spraying glass and vodka everywhere.

When he reached for my half full bottle I grabbed his arm. 'Enough.' I held his arm pinned to the desk until his livid face returned to its more natural ruddy hue. I stood and started to clear the glasses and empty bottles from the desk.

As I did, I looked out of the window. Princes Street Gardens were only a short stroll away. 'Get your jacket,' I said. 'We're going for a breath of fresh air. You're going to tell me everything.' I took the plastic bottle of spring water and handed it to him. 'And if you feel like lobbing a bottle about - use this.'

Chapter 47

Upon my return home that evening, I was met by my dad, bearer of glad tidings. Arthur Campbell's wife had caught some kind of virulent tummy bug in the time-share pool. They'd had to cut the holiday short, Arthur had managed to spend a full day on the cottage roof and work was progressing apace.

'So, what's the schedule for my birthday party?' he asked, washing a pile of dirty crockery at the kitchen sink. 'Everything going according to plan?'

I'd spoken to Malky again on my way home from Edinburgh. He'd invited all the usual suspects, ordered balloons, bought drinks, arranged snacks and booked both members of the Red River Trio. All that was needed now was somewhere to put everything and everyone. That was down to me, Malky said, seeing how he'd done everything else. Once I'd secured a venue I was to tell him and he would ring round the guests at short notice; my dad's pals were highly flexible where free drink was concerned.

'So far so good,' I said.

'Malky get the West Port okay, did he? Who's all going?'

'Do you want this surprise party to retain the faintest tinge of the unexpected?' I went over to the cooker and inspected a pot on the hob that contained a blob of congealed mince. 'This my tea?'

'It'll be fine if you heat it up. There wasn't enough tatties. Oh, and suet.'

'What about it?'

'You don't have any. How am I supposed to make dumplings without suet? And Jill called,' he said, as I replaced the lid and put a light under the pot. 'I told her you were working late. She's going out somewhere tonight. She'll call again tomorrow. Something important. She didn't say what.'

What could Jill want to tell me that was important? The tall figure of Josh, standing on the side of a snowy Alp, flitted through my mind. 'Did you get a number for her?' He hadn't. 'Try and remember to ask her if she phones again when I'm out, will you? Or tell her my mobile number, so she can call me on that.'

He put the last soapy dish on the draining board. 'How's the case going?'

'So much for your jealous wife theory,' I said.

My dad dried his hands on a towel and chucked it onto the back of a chair. 'What jealous wife theory was that then?'

'From that TV show the other night.'

'That wasn't my theory.'

'Well, whoever it was, it was rubbish. Turns out the least likely candidate for murdering Violet Hepburn was Mrs Kirkslap. Wait a minute, how many spuds did you have? I was sure there was quite a lot left, I bought a big bag a couple of days ago.'

'There would have been plenty, but you had a visitor and she stayed for her tea.'

'Stayed for my tea, you mean. Who was it?'

'Your wee assistant, Janey.'

'Joanna?'

'Nice girl. There's definitely not anything funny going on there between you two is—'

'No, Dad. There's not.'

He held his hands up, head height, palms facing me. 'Okay, okay, I didn't think there was. I told Jill that when she phoned.'

'You what?'

'I was only trying to help.' There was a knock at the door. 'That'll be Janey. She nipped along to Cabrelli's to get us

229

some ice-cream for pudding. I should have told her to get you some.'

After a very small plate of mince and no ice-cream to follow, I raised the subject of Kirkslap's trial when a news report came on TV, with a video clip showing the accused leaving court. They were still using the one from the earlier trial: Andy Imray proudly by Kirkslap's side, trying to look all serious and lawyer-like, when he'd probably wanted to give a big cheesy grin to the camera.

As I soon discovered, the reason Joanna had come to see me wasn't just to eat my evening meal. She'd had a phone call from Cameron Crowe before she'd left the office. He knew about Mike being called as a witness, but not about Kirkslap's recent arrest for an alleged breach of the peace at Candy's house. We'd forgotten to tell him.

'He didn't know until I mentioned it, and now he's sure Fiona will find a way to bring it to the attention of the jury,' Joanna said. 'He was also going his dinger about Kirkslap. He says he can't keep shovelling smoke and needs the client to give him an actual line of defence to put forward.' Joanna licked the last of the ice-cream off her spoon and placed it in her empty bowl. 'I've to tell you, to tell Kirkslap, that his memory better start improving fast. Crowe wants an hour by hour, minute by minute account of the evening of first November.'

'That's not happening,' I told her. 'I had a meeting with Kirkslap tonight. He's a very heavy drinker, and, like most nights, he was rubberoid the night Violet went missing. He went hunting with Mike in the afternoon and stayed in alone that evening, he says. Just him, a movie and Mr Smirnoff. He never saw another living soul from about seven o'clock until eight the next morning, when he was picked up and whisked off to a business meeting in Edinburgh.'

'That's more or less what he's said all along,' Joanna pointed out.

'So how does any of that rule out the jealous wife theory,' my dad said.

'Do you want the long or the short version,' I asked.

He opted for the short.

'She's not jealous.'

Joanna asked for the longer version.

'During our chat today, Kirkslap told me that he takes the blame for what happened between him and his wife.'

'What did happen?' Joanna asked.

'He made a lot of money and suddenly found himself irresistible to certain women. Violet was the first gold-digger. His wife found out, told him to leave. He's pretty sure she's found somebody else now and the bottom line is that she doesn't want him around. The way he tries to protect her from the mess he's got himself into, I'm not entirely convinced that the feeling is mutual; however, they've made their bed.'

'She could still be jealous,' my dad grumped.

'Then she'd have to spread that jealousy around a lot of women, not just Violet Hepburn,' I said.

'Why don't they divorce?' Joanna asked.

'It's complicated. When Larry and Marjorie married, her old man, Baronet Addison, was suspicious and there was a pre-nup. I don't even know if those sort of agreements are competent under Scots law, but it stipulated that if they divorced, Kirkslap was to get nothing from Marjorie.'

'Does she have anything?'

'She owns the Addison estate which covers a fairly large chunk of West Lothian. There's the big house, some woodland and a few farms that pay rent. She lives there with an uncle. Her brother emigrated years ago. He took his inheritance early and in cash. When her father died, Marjorie was left the estate.'

'Kirkslap's a multi-millionaire,' my dad said. 'What's he wanting with a big old house and some countryside?'

'Like I say, it's complicated. A couple of years ago, in happier times, when it looked like P45 Apps Ltd would really start to take off, the company had cash-flow problems. Those were eased when Kirkslap persuaded Marjorie to mortgage the house. The money was paid straight from her account into P45's. The company has the capital, the bank has the security.'

'But wouldn't she get half of Kirkslap's share in the company if they divorced?' Joanna asked.

'Kirkslap says his wife has taken advice on that, several times. Some say she'd get half his shares, others that the pre-nuptial agreement works both ways. It would make for an interesting and highly expensive Court of Session action, which neither party would like to lose.'

'So it really is an open marriage?' Joanna said.

'Looks like it. Marjorie has absolutely no motive for killing Violet. She would have been better killing Kirkslap. That's proper revenge and she would probably inherit his share in the company.'

Joanna sighed. 'Let's face it. Kirkslap is as guilty as hell. He might as well plead.'

I wasn't having such defeatist talk. Time for a morale booster. 'Maybe you'll change your mind about that when I tell you that following my discussion with Kirkslap tonight, he's agreed to pay a whopping win-bonus for a result.'

My dad grunted. 'Might be easier just to pick six numbers for next week's lottery.'

'Your dad's right, Robbie,' Joanna said.

'Not necessarily. Violet's body has not actually been found. It's not even certain that she's dead.'

'Come off, it Robbie.'

'Come off what? We're trying to create doubts here. With a jury, anything is possible. Kirkslap was only convicted on a majority last time.'

'Probably fourteen to one,' my dad said.

'And don't forget there's additional evidence this time - the threat Kirkslap made against Violet before she went missing.' Joanna didn't have to remind me.

I wasn't put off. 'When there's no body and the case is purely circumstantial, there's always a chance. A lot of the damaging evidence could be there by coincidence. Coincidences do happen.'

'Trust me,' my dad said. 'When there's a rich guy involved, there are no coincidences.' He pulled himself out of the sofa, collected the dirty dishes and took them through to the kitchen. When he returned he had three whisky glasses.

'What are those for?' I asked. 'You drank the last of my whisky the other day.'

He smiled. 'Don't kid a kidder. I saw that bag you were trying to hide from me when you came home.'

The man was an expert at finding things that weren't lost. After Malky's call, and with no obvious birthday venue available, I'd lashed out on a bottle of Springbank 18 year-old as a fall-back. *Sorry, Dad, there's no surprise party but, Ta-ra, a bottle of expensive whisky.*

'That's not for just now,' I said, failing to stop him from going into the hall where I had tried to conceal the carrier bag behind my briefcase. 'I mean it Dad.'

Too late. His hand was in the bag and the boxed whisky was out.

'Springbank? Now you're talk... What's this? The eighteen year-old?' His moustache turned down at the edges. He might never have made detective, but Sergeant Alex Munro had worked this puzzle out.

'Joanna,' I said, in an effort to limit collateral damage. 'Let me get your coat.'

Chapter 48

Day three of HMA –v- Kirkslap. Joanna had been dispatched to Livingston Sheriff Court and a trial, while I swanned around up at the Lawnmarket. We'd agreed to alternate roles, but I really wanted to be there that Wednesday morning because Fiona Faye, in an attempt to regain any lost ground from the day before, was about to spring Mike Summers on the jury.

'Court!' Lawyers and those in the public benches rose to their feet as Lord Haldane was led onto the bench. The macer, black suit and gown, white shirt, white bow-tie, hooked the silver mace of office onto the wall below the Royal Coat of Arms and pulled back the big chair for the judge to sit down.

Cameron Crowe gave me a sideways glower. 'This is all your fault, you know?'

As everyone sat again, I turned to take a look at Kirkslap sitting upright in the dock, looking unperturbed as ever, but pale by his standards. The man was a born salesman and he was about to start another day of selling his innocence to the jury.

Mace, Judge and jury duly ensconced, Mike Summers was brought to the witness box. He had brought his iPad with him and was made hand it over to the court officer before raising his right hand to take the oath. I wasn't looking forward to this, and it turned out to be a lot worse than I'd expected.

'Idiot,' Crowe said, stalking past me and out of the court around eleven-thirty. The jury was led away for a coffee break, coinciding with the end of Fiona Faye's examination-in-chief of Mike.

Kirkslap was let out of the dock and I met with him and Zack outside the court. His fellow director had sussed the judge's habit of breaking for elevenses, left early and brought back coffees for us all. Kirkslap looked like a man who was needing his. How many more miniatures of Russian fire-water had bit the dust after I'd left him the previous evening?

'Mike's really done a job on us,' Zack said, taking the lid off his tall cardboard cup.

'Not his fault,' Kirkslap said. 'He can only answer the questions they put to him. I'm the one to blame.' He looked at me. 'Does this mean Mike can talk to us again; once he's given his evidence?'

It was possible for a witness to be recalled after he'd testified, but I expected the judge would allow Mike to be excused, and then he could return to the defence fold.

Zack sipped his coffee, if that's what it was. It was very creamy on top and smelled of caramel. 'I don't know if we want him back in the fold. You ask me, he answered some of those questions too well.'

'At least, we never heard any evidence about the other night,' I said. 'About you going round to Candy's house.'

'Me and my temper again,' Kirkslap said.

You and the drink, I thought, glancing around quickly, smiling as though Kirkslap had told a joke, trying to see if anyone had overheard. 'Do not mention your, you know what again.'

'My what?' Kirkslap asked.

Zack tried to help. 'He means your temp—'

'That's right. Let's not mention it again,' I said, drowning him out. How had these two ever set up a multi-million pound business?

'Why did you go round?' I asked Kirkslap in a low voice, hoping he'd follow suit with his reply.

'I got a call from Candy. She said she had some important information that would help me in my trial. I took a taxi all the way to her place and then she refused to let me in. Just left me on the doorstep, while she started accusing me of murdering Violet. She was doing as much shouting as I was. I don't know who called the cops. It was nothing. Just a bit of an argument so far as I can remember.'

There was no mileage to be had in telling Kirkslap how stupid he'd been. 'I'm just glad that they didn't call her to back up Mike's evidence,' I said, taking a cautious sip of my ridiculously hot Americano. 'With any luck Crowe will take the edge off his evidence. Hopefully, Mike will be happy to assist his cross-examination in any way he can. Play things down.'

Kirkslap wasn't listening. 'What do you mean about Candy backing up Mike's evidence?'

'About the time you went round to see Violet, with Mike. You know the…' I mouthed the word, threat.

'Candy was there? I know I was drunk, but why would Candy have been at Violet's? They hardly knew each other.'

I took Kirkslap by the arm and led him aside. The landing outside Court 3 was fairly busy with spectators from the public gallery milling around. Many eyes on the man of the moment. 'You bought her a diamond necklace. Told her to be discreet.'

Kirkslap looked at me as though I were mad. 'It's possible I might have bought her some bling, but, if I did, it had nothing to do with Violet or being discreet.'

'I spoke to Candy. That's what she told me.'

A bar officer poked her head out of the door to the court. When she eventually spied us in the far corner, she came over and told us the court would resume in five minutes.

'Why would Candy say that?' Kirkslap took my hand that was holding the coffee and sniffed the top of the cardboard cup. 'You sure that's just coffee you've got in there?'

At the recommencement of hostilities, Cameron Crowe managed to do a rough patch-up job on Mike's evidence. After that we heard evidence from one of the traffic cops who had set up a mobile speed camera on the B829, a mile west of the small town of Aberfoyle. Kirkslap's car had been clocked speeding, not once, but twice in the early hours of 2nd November: forty-eight one way and forty-five on the return leg, one hour and fifty minutes later. The final witness for the day was an expert in forensic geography. Just in case anyone was uncertain of his authenticity, he had on a corduroy jacket with leather elbow-patches.

The witness was asked about the land around the Trossachs and Loch Lomond, and he spoke at length about the rough and wild terrain, the many riverbanks, lochsides and marshes all criss-crossed by a spider's web of country roads, tracks and thoroughfares, readily accessible to an Audi Q7. Crowe's objection that the witness was an expert in geography, not off-road vehicles, was acknowledged by the judge, but the evidence allowed.

Once the groundwork was laid, the witness was asked by the Crown to give his opinion on the area a car might cover over a certain period of time, using Aberfoyle as the centre. He was asked to discount thirty minutes from the one hour fifty minutes spoken to by the traffic cop; a time the Crown felt reasonable for someone to dig a shallow grave. That left one hour twenty minutes. Assuming both legs of the journey took the same time, that meant an outward trip of approximately forty minutes. Forgetting the sort of speed Kirkslap's car was actually clocked at, and taking an average of only twenty miles per hour, the expert calculated that given the many routes available, had her body been in the boot of the SUV, the final resting place of Violet Hepburn could be anywhere within an area of five hundred and fifty six square miles.

'And if we increase the average speed to, say, thirty miles per hour?' Fiona asked.

The expert made a few more calculations on his notepad. 'We'd be talking about an area of one thousand two hundred and fifty six square miles.'

It was schoolboy arithmetic that didn't need an expert to testify to it; however, it was a damaging sequence of evidence. In any missing-body murder trial, jurors must wonder why, with all the searching that's taken place, no-one has stumbled across the victim's remains. This jury now had a good idea.

Mr Geography's evidence finished at three-thirty. The judge thought there no point in calling another witness so near the end of the court day and the jury was sent away early.

I bumped into Fiona Faye on her way to the advocates' robing room.

'Hello Robbie, listen,' she said in a mock-conspiratorial tone, making a show of looking around to make sure no-one was over-hearing. 'If Kirkslap pleads to the murder, I'm prepared to drop the two speeders.'

I left her, still laughing at her own joke, to go find my client, but Kirkslap had no time to talk. There were business matters to attend to and he and Zack were going off to be reconciled with Mike. There was nothing like getting your priorities right. Why bother to talk to your lawyer about the case that might send you to prison for life when there was money to be made? I had a feeling Zack was behind their hurried departure. I knew P45 Apps Ltd was taking a real financial hit because the young software designer was forever going on about the tumbling share price. Now wouldn't be a good time for Marjorie Kirkslap to seek a divorce, even if she were entitled to one-half the value of her husband's stock.

I set off alone down the Royal Mile towards Waverley Station. All the way back to the office, I couldn't stop thinking about what Kirkslap had said. He couldn't see any reason why Candy would visit Violet at her home. Mike had said Candy was there. Candy had told me she'd been there. Had she been there? Did it matter?

I phoned Karats. Not Robbie Munro: an imaginary Professor Docherty, lecturer in jurisprudence, who required urgently to speak with Miss Candice McKeever about a late dissertation.

'Oh, it's you,' she said, when I'd revealed my true identity. 'I heard you were trying to see me on Monday night. What do you want?'

'To speak to you about Larry Kirkslap and why you said you were there when he threatened Violet.'

'What about it?'

'Why would you say you were there, when you weren't?'

There was a long pause before Candy said, 'give me your number and I'll call you back.'

Chapter 49

Candy was scared about something. She didn't want to meet anywhere there was a chance of us being seen together. I suggested my dad's cottage. It was well out of the way and for now uninhabited. I gave her the address and what I thought were good directions. She declined, saying that it was too far away, and she thought she'd get lost finding it; so we arranged to meet in a lay-by on a B road off junction 5 on the M8. I knew the area fairly well as it was not far from Shotts Prison.

After nearly half an hour waiting in the cold and the dark, only one other vehicle passed by. I was about to give up when my phone buzzed. I thought it might be Candy, lost and looking for directions. It wasn't: it was Mrs Boyd. The signal on my mobile wasn't good. The gist of the call was that Danny had been to see her. Even through the crackles on the line she sounded happy. She'd told Danny it was safe to come home, that the police were no longer looking for him, but he'd just taken some supplies and left again, not saying where he was headed. She wanted me to do something. I'd already spent much of the previous weekend tramping around Beecraigs Country Park; what more could I do? Eventually the bad connection saved me and we were cut off.

Headlights. A car pulled up in the lay-by behind me. Once I'd alighted, I could see it was a dark-coloured Range Rover. Not the sort of vehicle I expected Candy to be driving. Who else could it be? I got out and walked over to the passenger side of the vehicle. The window slid down and I peered in. It took a moment or two for my eyes to adjust and realise I wasn't looking at Candy, but at Tam 'Tuppence' Christie. I recoiled, bumped into something large. The doorman from Karats. No turquoise baseball cap or mirrored sunglasses tonight. He had a slight cut across the bridge of his nose and two fading black eyes. I was more interested in the knife in his hand. He placed the point under my chin.

'Get in the car,' Tuppence said.

I got in the car.

'Now, give your mobile to the big man.'

From the front passenger seat, through the open door, I handed the doorman my phone. In doing so, I had a better view of the knife. It was huge: a hunting knife; razor sharp on one side, a jagged edge along the other. He dropped my phone on the ground, crunched it under his shoe and then hurled it deep into the North Lanarkshire countryside.

'Put your seatbelt on,' Tuppence ordered.

I had intended leaving it off to increase my chances of an escape.

'Now!'

I did what I was told. As soon as I had, the doorman seized my hands, wrapped an electric cable-tie around my wrists and pulled tight.

This wasn't good. 'Where—?'

'Shut it. You'll know when we get there.'

I shut it and ten minutes later we got there, wherever there was.

I was pulled out of the car by the doorman, who remained at my back, while Tuppence Christie led the way up a Tarmac path to some prefabricated steel buildings. Weeds grew everywhere, and there were one or two burnt-out cars, one with a small tree happily living inside it. A surveyor's sign, a large corner chunk missing, looking like it had been blasted off by a shotgun, advertised the area as a rare development opportunity.

Although it was very dark, both men seemed to know the way well. Soon I was shoved inside one of the buildings, via a metal door inset in a much larger roller-shutter. Tuppence had a small LED torch on his key-ring. He switched it on once we were inside and closed the door. The place was big and empty, about the size of a five-a-side football pitch, high ceiling, concrete floor, the only furniture a work bench against the wall, next to the door. Tuppence took a box of matches from a drawer in the bench and managed after several attempts to light a small gas camping lamp that made a valiant effort at illumination, casting our tall shadows up the ridged steel walls.

The doorman produced the knife again. I backed away. He shoved me. I took a further few steps away from him and then noticed a pool of darkness on the floor. At first I thought it was an oil spillage, but the edges were too well defined, rectangular, like a grave for a giant.

'What's this all about?' I said, trying to gain some control over the situation. The doorman shoved me again, ever closer to what I could now see was a vehicle inspection pit.

'Do like he says,' Tuppence ordered.

The doorman hadn't actually said anything, but his actions spoke louder than words. I knelt on the cold floor and lowered myself as best I could, hands bound in front of me, the four feet or so into the inspection pit.

Tuppence was pleased. 'Good.' He relaxed, looked around, smiling. 'Haven't been to this place in ages. Used to come here all the time. Had my own set of tools, hooks on the walls, everything.'

He wasn't talking motor repairs.

'I won't need any of that stuff for you, though, will I?' He didn't wait for an answer. 'All I want is some information.'

It didn't sound so bad. I'd tell him whatever he wanted to know and we could be on our separate ways. No harm done. Why didn't I believe it?

'Where's the boy? Simple question.'

To which I had an equally simple answer. 'I don't know.'

With an air of great patience, Tuppence squinted through the gloom at his watch and then up at the doorman. The big man went over and removed a jerry can from under the work bench. Without further instruction he returned to the pit and poured the contents over me. The petrol splashed off my head and shoulders, puddling at my feet. I jumped back, trying to dodge the flow, choking, putting my clasped hands over my face and mouth. When the pouring had stopped, I looked up to see Tuppence gently shaking the box of matches.

'I don't really need your help. The boy can't stay hidden forever, but it would make things a lot easier for everyone if you'd co-operate.'

I'd loved to have co-operated. I knew I couldn't. I ran to the other side of the pit and had almost clambered out when the doorman ran around and kicked me back in. I landed, slipping and falling on the petrol-soaked filth that was caked on the floor of the pit.

'Okay,' I said. 'I'll tell you what I know. First of all, you tell me why you want him.'

Tuppence ignored the question. He pushed open the matchbox with the tip of a finger and removed a single match. He leaned the tip against the sandpaper side. 'Where is he?'

I remembered what Jake Turpie had told me. Danny Boyd and I came as a package. I licked my lips. They stayed dry. 'If I tell you will you let me go?'

'Sorry,' Tuppence said. 'I can make it quick,' he tilted his head towards the doorman and his obscene hunting knife, 'or slow and horrifically painful.'

I wasn't leaving that pit alive. The realisation ripped at my insides, vision blurring, breath coming quick and shallow. Was this it? Was I really about to die? I thought of my dad and Malky, but most of all about Jill and the velvet box in the drawer of my desk.

The flare of the match was like a spark igniting my brain. Tuppence was old. Providing I could keep away from the matches, I could take him, hands tied or not. The problem

243

was his big pal. My chances of over-powering him were not at all good. If I did nothing, they were non-existent anyway.

Heart thumping, blood rushing in my ears, I ran, slipping and sliding, to the far side of the pit. The doorman lumbered around to meet me. I launched myself out of the hole in the ground, crashing into his legs, hoping to knock him off balance, make him stumble, anything that might give me a chance to get out of that building and into the black safety of the night. The doorman struck out with the knife, narrowly missing me. I rolled around on the concrete floor, thrashing my legs, scrambling to get away from him. Jumping at last to my feet, I tried to get my bearings. A striking match. Tuppence stood between me and the door, a lit match in his hand. How flammable was I? The petrol had soaked into my clothes, the fumes were mostly away. If the choice was possibly being set on fire and definitely being gutted, it was one I was able to make in a split-second. I feinted left, ran right. Tuppence threw the match. I don't know if it went out or missed. All I knew was that I was no flaming torch and the door to safety was just yards away. I ran to it and found the handle. I tried to take hold of it, but couldn't part my hands wide enough to take a grip. Frantically, I tried to turn it with the tips of my fingers, still wet and slippery with petrol.

Suddenly, I was no longer upright, my legs cawed from beneath me. I fell to the concrete floor, landing heavily on the base of my spine. Winded, I looked up, grimacing through the pain. The doorman stood over me, knife gripped in his hand.

The big man grabbed me by the front of my jacket and lifted me from the ground. He threw me back into the room and towards the hell hole in the centre.

I stumbled and fell. The fight had left me. I gasped for breath.

Tuppence joined his henchman. Again he sparked a match, holding it in front of his face. 'I'm going to ask you one more —'

CLANG! I'd never had a fright like it. Well, perhaps once, and the same person had been responsible then. Tuppence dropped the match. He and the doorman spun around, so, like me, they were facing the door; the now wide open door which Deek Pudney had just thrown open. He strode towards us, Desert Eagle at his side.

'You're Jake Turpie's boy,' Tuppence said. 'What are you doing here?'

Deek raised the automatic.

Tuppence laughed. 'Tell your boss he's too late. He had his chance.'

Deek looked at me. 'Get out.' The barrel of the semi-automatic flicked to the inspection pit and back to Tuppence and the doorman. 'You two, get in there.'

'It's Deek isn't it?' Tuppence said, not moving, smiling, as though this was a chance meeting in a pub.

'Get in,' Deek said.

'Ask him why he wants to kill me,' I said.

'I told you to get out,' Deek said.

'No, no, let him speak,' Tuppence said. 'I'm sure we can sort things out.'

The doorman shuffled his feet, moving sideways, in some kind of doomed to failure, out-flanking manoeuvre. Deek brought him back, front and centre with a waggle of the Eagle.

'I'll tell Mr Munro, here, what he wants to know and we can all go home. How's that sound?' Tam Christie seemed intent on changing his middle name to 'Reasonable'.

'Fine by me,' I said.

Deek sighed. 'Go on then, tell him.'

'Mike Summers.'

iPad Mike wanted me dead? 'Why?'

'He's answered your question now get out,' Deek said.

'Look, Deek, I need to know why.' I stared into Tuppence's eyes. 'Who's Mike Summers to you and why does he want me and Danny Boyd killed?'

245

Tuppence shrugged.

'You've got your answer, now get out,' Deek growled.

I left. Legs shaking, I was wandering around in the dark, looking for Deek's car, when I heard two gunshots. Then another two.

The door to the building opened. Deek walked out, silhouetted by an orange glow, accompanied by the smell of burning petrochemicals.

'How did you know?' I asked him, as he cut the electrical tie around my wrists with his own lock-knife. I was shivering and it wasn't just because of the cold and my damp, petrol-soaked clothes.

Deek wasn't in talkative mood. He never was. I could get nothing out of him from stepping into his white Transit van, until he pulled up alongside my car, still parked in the lay-by. I changed into a set of overalls in the back of the van, leaving my own clothes in a carrier bag for Deek to dispose of later. The overalls must have belonged to Jake; they were far too small for me. Fortunately, my dad would be in bed and I could sneak into the bathroom for a shower.

I wanted to thank Deek, but was unsure what to say and, anyway, the big man seemed neither up nor down about the whole terrifying affair. I was pretty sure I was still in shock.

I was about to alight when Deek reached forward to the where a bottle of Barr's Irn Bru lay sideways in the angle between dashboard and windscreen, amidst greasy, chip-wrappers and assorted crisp packets. From the debris he pulled a flat brown envelope. 'Jake said I was to give you this.'

I opened it. A bill of advocation. Someone at Crown Office had decided, belatedly, to appeal Deek's acquittal from the smoking-jury trial. It would never be successful. It was just another example of the Crown's wish to have Scotland's three verdicts: Guilty, Not Guilty and Not Proven, reduced to two: Guilty and Give Us Another Go.

'Nothing to worry about,' I assured the man who had just shot dead two people, torched their bodies and was now taking a long pull from the bottle of Irn Bru. 'Tell Jake I'll deal with it.'

Deek screwed the cap back on the bottle, slung it onto the dashboard again and wiped his mouth with the back of his hand. 'He knows you will.'

Chapter 50

There was no way I was sleeping that night. The adrenalin was coursing through my body like it was being fed by hosepipe. I felt nauseous, my hands trembled and I had a heartbeat like a dance-music drum-machine.

I'd showered, scrubbed the dirt and oil out of my fingernails, washed my hair three times and yet the smell of petrol still lingered in my nostrils, each whiff flashing me back to the inspection pit and Tam 'Tuppence' Christie smiling down at me, a box of matches in his hand.

Around dawn I had calmed down slightly, my brow not quite so clammy, my heart beating a slower rhythm.

Mike Summers wanted to kill me. Me. His old University chum. What had I done to deserve that? How did he have connections to a high-level gangster like Tuppence Christie?

By the time my dad was up and about making breakfast, I had come to a series of conclusions.

'You awake yet?' My dad asked, wandering into the livingroom, bread knife in hand, his striped-pyjamas/paisley-patterned dressing gown combo producing a strobe effect to my sleepy eyes. He stared down on me, lying in my sleeping bag on the couch. 'You look terrible.'

His sixth sense could kick in at any moment. I didn't want him asking awkward questions. Attack was the best form of defence. '*You'd* feel terrible after two weeks sleeping on a sofa.'

'Toast and egg do you?' he asked, and not waiting for an answer padded back through to the kitchen.

I was up and dressed and drinking coffee by the time my dad had finished scrambling the eggs.

'I'm thinking of going down to the cottage today,' he said. 'I phoned Arthur last night and he reckoned he'd be finished by tomorrow afternoon.'

'That's quick. Sort of.'

'Malky says you've had problems with a venue for the party.'

By which I took it my brother had told him we didn't have a venue and pinned the blame for that on me.

My dad seemed surprisingly calm as he confirmed my suspicions. 'Malky says he's ready to go. He's just waiting on you to say where it's to happen. It's good to know that one of my sons is taking my birthday seriously.'

'You're sixty-seven, so what?' I snapped at him. I couldn't help myself. My nerves were frayed and the coffee wasn't helping. 'I'm sorry, Dad. Of course your birthday is important. It's just that I've—'

'Got more important things than me to worry about. I know that.' He sniffed, picked up his dirty dish and dropped it into the sink.

'It's not that,' I said, although it was.

'No, no, I understand perfectly well. Your criminals come before me, always have, always will.'

If it hadn't been for the intervention of one of my criminals the night before, he'd be one son down on his current total. But I couldn't confide in my dad. What had happened had to remain between me and Deek and Jake Turpie.

My dad turned the hot water tap on full and squirted far too much washing-up liquid into the sink. 'Jill phoned again last night,' he said, over the roar of the water hitting the basin, bubbles billowing everywhere. 'Somebody else you've been doing your best to ignore recently.'

How did Jill always manage to miss me? It was almost like she was doing it on purpose. As a long distance romance we were a disaster, but there was only one week to go. If I could keep alive until then. What should I do? Was it fair to propose marriage when I knew there was a contract out on me? Should I mention it to her? What good would it do if I did? So many questions. All I knew was that I missed her so much.

'Well? What are you going to do about the party?' my dad asked. He was really starting to annoy me. If Jill had been home, she'd have seen the funny side of the non-surprise, surprise party. She would have had the whole thing sorted out in no time and my dad eating out of her hand; Munro men and the wrapping of them around her little finger being just one of her many talents.

'If your cottage is nearly ready, why don't you have the party there?' I said. 'That was the plan all along, wasn't it? Me and Malky could come along nice and early and help you with the furniture, blow up some balloons. You can leave before the guests arrive and come back at eight. Surprise!'

He didn't disagree, mulling it over, arms up to the elbows in soapy bubbles. 'You'd need to be there for about four at the latest. That would give us time to get the place back into order.'

'It's a date, then,' I said. He didn't reply so I took that as a sign of contentment. 'What did Jill want?'

'She's your girlfriend. She wanted to speak to you, of course.'

'When she phoned last time she said she had something important to tell me. Did you remember and ask her to leave a number?'

He'd forgotten.

I still didn't know what Jill's important news was. I was wondering about that and a lot of other things when I arrived at the office at half-past eight. Grace-Mary wouldn't be in until nine and Joanna was going straight to the High Court. I checked the diary. Thursday: remand court day. Five deferred sentences. I called Paul Sharp and explained that I was bogged down with Kirkslap's trial and asked him to cover court for me.

That out of the way, I had a great deal of thinking to do. Maybe it was years of court work, thinking on my feet, but I thought better pacing the room.

First things first. There was no reason to disbelieve Tam 'Tuppence' Christie's last words. Mike Summers had put a contract out on me. Why? Who was I to him, apart from a long lost University acquaintance? I stopped pacing and found myself at the window looking onto the High Street. Two steady streams of traffic heading in opposite directions, a few folk under the bus stop shelter outside the Auld Hole in the Wall pub.

There was no reason Mike would want to kill me in particular, so it all had to do with Danny Boyd. After all, weren't we part of a package? Who was Danny to Mike? Who was Danny to anyone? He was just a boy who ran messages for his mum and raided old tombs for a hobby, and, yet, there was some kind of link between him and me and between us and Mike. A link so potentially damaging to Mike that he wanted to kill us both.

Grace-Mary arrived. 'Get your files okay? I left them on your chair.'

I told her I was giving court a miss, and asked her to fax over the copy complaints to Paul Sharp's office.

'Having the day off are you?'

'Not exactly. Things to do, people to see.'

'Like who?'

'Like Jake Turpie. The rent's overdue.'

'I thought we had three months free?' Grace-Mary said.

'Change of plan. What cash have we got?'

'I don't even want to know,' she said, returning with the contents of the Munro & Co. safe and slapping it into my hand. 'There's enough there for this and next month.' She left the room again.

I closed the door. Peace restored. Back to the link. The link that bound me to Danny Boyd, the link that bound Danny to Mike Summers. And then there was Nathan. I had

251

to assume he'd been murdered by Tuppence Christie's doorman, on the instructions of Mike Summers and for the same reason he wanted Danny dead. Danny, who thought his brother and he were cursed. If I was to solve the puzzle I had to find the boy. He'd been to see his mum recently. Maybe she would have a clue where he was now.

At the Boyds' smallholding, there was no answer to my knocks. I tried the handle on the front door. It was unlocked. I pushed it open. I could hear the sound of someone working in the kitchen. From its vantage point, sprawled across the couch, the old dog lifted an eyelid, twitched an ear and then went back to sleep again.

'What a fright you gave me!' Mrs Boyd exclaimed, when I entered the kitchen to find her sitting at the table surrounded by heaps of green apples, chopping knife in hand.

I apologised.

She stood, set down the knife and wiped her hands on her apron. 'Have you found Danny? Is he all right?'

'I'm sure he's fine. I just want to know if he said anything the other night that might make it easier for me to find him.'

Danny hadn't said a lot. Just told his mum he was okay, taken away some food and fresh clothes and said not to worry, that he wasn't far away.

'Does he know that the police aren't looking for him?'

She nodded. 'I told him. He's not worried about the police. It's the... you know...'

'The curse?'

She nodded again.

'You said Danny kept a list of tombs he'd downloaded from the internet. Do you know where it is?'

She showed me through to a bedroom. Two single beds, mismatched furniture, posters on the wall. In the corner was a computer, printer attached. After a great deal of searching for printouts from the internet we could find nothing. At last Mrs Boyd went over to a corner of the room. There was no central heating, just a convector that had probably been a hi-tech appliance in the 60's. She moved it out of the way and lifted the edge of the carpet. 'The boys don't know, I know,' she said. 'I never look. Well hardly ever.' She prised up a loose floorboard. Inside there was a well-worn lads' mag, a jar containing some money, mainly coins, and an A5 spiral bound notebook.

I took the notebook from her. There was nothing written on the cover, but inside, on the first twenty or so pages, was detailed, in painstakingly-neat print, facts about ancient Scottish tombs from all over Central Scotland and the Lowlands. Each tomb had a page to itself, listing the precise location, name, number of deceased and any associated family mottos or facts of special interest. The last entry was for the Binny Mausoleum. Beneath the heading was a date - the night that Nathan and Danny Boyd were caught and arrested.

'I was sure there was a lot of other stuff the boys printed off the internet,' Mrs Boyd said. 'There was one web-site they were always on. I could hear them chatting about it. It wasn't a big secret or anything. I didn't really like it. It was all a bit creepy. I just thought it was boys' stuff and if it kept them out of bother...' she tailed off, probably realising how wrong she'd been. One son dead, the other running scared of some ancient curse; that was quite a lot of bother actually.

After promising to do my best to secure the safe return of her remaining son, and taking the notebook with me, I left Mrs Boyd to her apples and made the short journey to my dad's cottage where Arthur Campbell was hammering away at the roof.

'How's it going?' I shouted up to him.

He stopped what he was doing and drew a forearm across his sun-tanned brow. 'I'm getting there. Did Alex send you out here to spy on me?' he laughed. 'He's a terrible man, your old boy.'

'Think you'll have it done for tomorrow?'

'Should do. I've got one of the lads coming off another job to help me this afternoon, so we'll have the slates on today. Then all there is to do is to re-attach the guttering, point the chimney and sort the lead flashing.'

When he started on about soffits and water-gates, I decided it was all getting too technical for me and volunteered to make him a cup of tea. Internally, the place was much as I'd left it. Danny Boyd had been a tidy tenant. I checked the spare room. You'd never have known he'd been there. The only sign of occupancy was a black bin liner of rubbish which I put in the wheelie bin outside. At least something was coming together. The cottage was small, all on one level, with only three rooms, excluding kitchen and bathroom. If we got an early start at it, the place could easily be in order for the birthday party the following night.

Back in my car, I looked at the notebook again and the blank entry under the Binny Mausoleum heading. Ecclesmachan was only a two minute drive away. There was a series of country walks available and I took the one in the direction of Binny Craigs, until eventually I found the mausoleum, almost completely overgrown and carved into the rock face. Along the stone arch above the door was carved an inscription stating that the tomb had been consecrated by the Bishop of Edinburgh on 25th October 1873, and below, on the blocked up entrance, the minor damage caused by the Boyd boys was still clearly visible. Other than that there was nothing at all unusual. And yet the damage to this tomb and the criminal proceedings which had followed, were my only links with Danny Boyd; a boy I'd never set eyes on until I'd met him in court four weeks before. I stood there, staring at the solid concrete door that was covered in ivy What did Danny and Nathan Boyd know that Mike Summers wanted silenced? He had already had one brother killed and wanted the same for the other – and me. If I was on the same contract it had to be because Mike thought whatever Danny knew, he had told me. What was that? Unless I tracked Danny down, I was never going to find out.

Chapter 51

On the way back to the office from Ecclesmachan, I took a detour into Jake Turpie's yard, where I found him berating a group of men whose work ethic he was calling into question, punctuating his remarks by cracking a short length of scaffolding pole off the roof of a crumpled Corsa.

I knew most of Jake's employees, a cash-in-hand, hard-living group who were no strangers to the court and viewed by me as an important part of the Robbie Munro pension plan. Once the men had set about their business again with renewed vigour, Jake tossed the pole aside and marched off. I caught up with him at the foot of the flight of shoogly steps leading up to his HQ: a dilapidated wooden structure, guarded by a scruffy, wild-eyed mutt.

Jake held up a hand when he saw me approach. 'Say nothing.'

'I just came to pay the rent,' I said, handing over the cash. Jake stuffed it into a pocket of his dungarees. 'And to say that I've got those court papers from Deek. I'm not expecting the Crown appeal to go ahead. Once someone who knows what they're doing has a proper look at it, the whole thing will be ditched.'

Jake signalled his approval with a grunt, turned and began to climb the steps.

'Jake, about—'

'I told you—'

'I only wanted to—'

Jake came down the steps and put his face in my face. 'It never happened, all right?'

'The bodies...' I hissed.

He stepped back, baring teeth like a row of condemned buildings. 'Deek's away tidying up the mess right now.' He gave the impression that his minder was whisking a feather duster about, rather than collecting the burnt remains of Tuppence Christie and his doorman for onward disposal. At least Deek know what to do. When it came to disappearing bodies, his boss had written the book.

'Are you expecting any repercussions?' I asked. Jake looked about in an exasperated fashion, before coming to the conclusion that the easiest way to get rid of me was to talk. He grabbed one of my arms and dragged me across the rutted landscape, down an avenue of piled-high, scrap cars. 'I'm not expecting any bother. *The height of tuppence, he'd shoot you for thruppence,*' he snorted and spat. 'The man was a legend in his own mind. No-one's going to find him, and no-one's going to care.'

That solved the mystery of the deceased gangster's nickname, but I was still worried his disappearance might be traced to me via Jake. 'Somebody must know that he called you,' I said.

'So? A lot of people call me. I buy and sell cars.' Jake sold second hand cars. He didn't sell brand new Range Rovers like the one that had transported me to deepest Lanarkshire, or the Mercedes I'd seen Tuppence getting into outside Karats. 'Satisfied? Can I get back to work now? Please tell me you're not going to ask me to try and find out who put the contract out on you.'

'I know who.'

'That right? Then you know more than me.'

'What I want to know is why.'

Jake kicked a stone with a steel toe cap. It bounced along the hard packed dirt and collided with the near-side wing of a battered Peugeot. 'I was offered cash to set you up. You and the boy together. I wasn't interested. After I tipped you off, I had Deek keep an eye on you. And now I'm happy...' he tapped the rent money in his pocket, 'and you're happy. Everyone's a winner.'

He made it sound like a game show. Would I still have been a winner had Tuppence's price been right?

'And you-know-who didn't say why he wanted you to set me up?' I said.

'I never asked. I just thought you must have narked someone off.' Jake came to a halt. Gave me a light slap on the cheek. 'You're good at that. Now, was there anything else?'

There wasn't.

'Good,' Jake said, 'because some of us have work to do.'

We turned and started walking down the way we'd come. As we neared Jake's HQ, one of his men was leaving in an allegedly white Ford Transit van. Jake slammed a hand against the side panel and it stopped. The driver rolled down the window.

'Have I got to do everything around here?' Jake asked him. He reached into the pocket not containing Munro & Co.'s rent and pulled out a crumpled, oil-stained tissue. He went over to a rain-filled pot-hole, of which there were many, dipped the tissue in the muddy water and splattered it against the front number plate of the van, partially obscuring the middle digits. 'Eejit. The M9's got average speed camera's the length of it.'

'Does that work?' I asked.

'How many speeding tickets have I brought you recently?' He battered a hand on the van's bonnet and stepped to the side as it drove off. 'You'll still need to watch yourself, mind,' Jake said. 'There are other contractors out there.'

It was something I was well aware of. Tuppence Christie's contract had been terminated. Would somebody else pick it up? Until Mike Summers realised what must have happened, I had some time.

'One more thing,' I said. 'How easy is it to change the number plates on an Audi?'

'Thinking about getting a proper car? I've an A4 in the pound. Clean motor, only got twenty K on the clock. Or it will have. I could let you have it for—'

'I've got a car. Just answer my question and I'll leave you alone.'

It was an offer Jake couldn't refuse. 'Is it UK or Euro plates you're fitting.'

I had no idea.

'If it's Euro's you're going to need a bracket and you'll have to drill mounting holes in the corners. If it's standard UK, you can go with the bolts and plastic caps, but double-sided tape is just as good and makes a cleaner job.'

'I only want something temporary. It's just for one trip.'

'I've got more tissues and there's plenty of puddles about,' he said.

'I don't want to conceal the numbers, I want to make them look like somebody else's. Just for the night.'

'Then any double-sided tape will do. The cheaper the tape, the easier to rip off in a hurry. Most people use 3M command strips. They're good but a nightmare to come off again.' He shoved the dog aside with a leg, and started up the steps. 'If you need a getaway driver, let me know,' he said, half-jokingly and disappeared inside his wooden HQ.

Chapter 52

Joanna trooped into the office shortly before five that afternoon. She took the working brief for Kirkslap's case from her handbag and thumped it down onto my desk.

'All yours,' she said.

'How'd it go today?' I asked.

'Quickly. I can't believe how fast the Crown case is going. We had six witnesses in and out.'

Six witnesses in one day was insanely quick for the High Court. Fiona Faye was really rattling though the Crown case. She would know from having read the transcripts of the previous trial that the defence was short on explanations for a lot of the damaging circumstantial evidence, and hoped to fire it at the jurors thick and fast, while they remained interested.

Joanna recapped. 'There was the girl on the cosmetics' counter at John Lewis who sold Violet lipstick,' Joanna said. 'She knew Violet quite well, even knew the shade of lipstick she liked. Then a CCTV operator talked us through Violet leaving Buchanan Galleries on the afternoon of thirty-first October, followed by a phone expert speaking to the text from Violet arranging to meet Kirkslap the following night and his reply. And that was us just at lunchtime. In the afternoon a guy from the credit card company said that they had authorised payment for an on-line order for a home delivery of groceries. The order was made around mid-day on First November for delivery to Violet's house. The next witness was a cracker, though.'

'The mobile phone tracker?'

'Afraid so. Former Edinburgh University professor, now a consultant on mobile technology and running his own informatics business.'

With a little help from the phone companies, this latest expert had been able to say with certainty that Kirkslap's mobile phone had been in the general area of Violet Hepburn's apartment around six on the evening of 1st November and then later at Kirkslap's lodge, before going for a tour of the countryside in the early hours of the following morning.

'The entire workforce of P45 Apps have iPhones,' Joanna said. 'The battery doesn't come out and even when it runs down it still sends out signals for a few hours. Big Brother is watching you as long as you have that thing in your pocket.'

It was terribly damaging evidence, but I had been expecting it. 'How did Crowe cope with it all?'

'As well as could be expected. Better, in fact. He came off sounding more like an expert than the expert, going on about triangulation and interference and false signals. It was going fairly well until the final witness.'

'The cop who found Violet's phone down the side of the couch in Kirkslap's sitting room?'

Joanna nodded.

'How did the jury take it all?'

'Hard to say, but they were definitely listening.'

Never a good sign.

'By the way, where is my ex-phone?'

Joanna's former phone was in a thousand tiny pieces, somewhere outside Shotts and the one before that was in my dad's possession.

'I lost it,' I said.

'Too bad for you.' Joanna opened her handbag, took out a phone, identical to her last. 'Grace-Mary got me a new one.' She waggled it at me, teasingly. 'And you're not getting your hands anywhere near it. You'll just have to learn to be more careful.'

It wasn't just the loss of the actual phone that bothered me. It was the SIM card with all my contacts.

'What kind of phone are you going for this time?' Joanna asked. 'Same as the last two? Three phones in a month? Samsung must really love you.' She looked at hers. 'This is a great phone. I've only learned how to use about fifty per cent of the functions.'

That was approximately forty per cent more than I had. I could make phone calls and send texts, that was about it. 'Might as well get the same one as you,' I said. 'Keep the Munro & Co. corporate identity.'

'You should put a tracking app on it. That way I could know where you really are when you say you've been held up in court, and I have to see your Friday afternoon clients.'

'Wouldn't do any good,' I said. 'I'd just leave the phone in my locker in the agents' room and go to the golf course anyway. Big Brother might be watching, but that's not to say he's looking in the right place.'

Joanna's cheerful expression changed when she noticed mine had. 'What's the matter?'

'Are you thinking what I'm thinking?' I asked.

She wasn't, but she soon would be.

Chapter 53

Cameron Crowe was never pleased to see me, but he was even less so than normal when, later that Thursday evening, Joanna and I turfed up at his apartment, a fine example of Georgian architecture and part of the beautiful circular terrace that was Moray Place in Edinburgh's New Town.

'Very well, then. Tell me what's so bloody important?' he said, after I'd persuaded him we had extremely urgent news, and he'd reluctantly allowed us into his drawing room. It was seven o'clock. Crowe and a glass of brandy had been watching yet another TV debate on the pending Scottish referendum.

Crowe dragged himself across to the corner of the room. 'Independence,' he said. 'Serve us right if we get it. Democracy - eight stupid people telling two clever people what to do.' He switched off the television and ordered us to sit.

'It's about a possible line of defence,' I said.

'Please don't tell me you have some kind of cunning plan,' he said wearily.

Joanna read my mind. To Crowe I'd always be a red rag to a bull. I sat back.

'What if Kirkslap is innocent and was fitted up by someone else?' she said.

'Who?'

'Mike Summers.'

'His lawyer and business partner, Mike Summers?'

Joanna nodded.

'Motive?'

'We're working on that.'

Cameron puffed out his cheeks and blew, flubbering his lips. 'Let's have it.' He took his balloon glass from the arm of his chair, swirled and took a sip. 'Let's have your theory.'

'Okay.' Joanna sat forward in her chair, hands clasped in front of her. 'Mike Summers killed Violet Hepburn. We don't know why, yet,' she said, hurriedly, when it looked like Crowe was about to interject, 'and then disposed of her body.'

'Where?'

'Somewhere as yet unknown.'

Crowe winced.

Joanna continued. 'And then sent a text from her phone to Kirkslap's to make it look as though they were going to meet up the next day.'

'Would you listen to yourself?'

'It makes sense. Why would Kirkslap arrange to meet Violet if he'd already made it very clear that their relationship was over?'

'Perhaps he had certain needs,' Crowe said. 'Any port in a storm and all that.'

Joanna ploughed on regardless. We'd talked about it all the way through in the car. 'You know Kirkslap's side of things—'

'Quantum valeat,' Crowe said.

'He was at a business meeting with Zack Swarovski until late-afternoon on thirty-first October. He'd had a drink at lunch-time, so Zack drove him home in the evening. They watched a movie, Zack left late and next day Mike arrived and he and Kirkslap went off shooting furry animals.'

'Yes, yes, I know all this.' Crowe sipped some more brandy, while taking a glance at the blank screen of the television as though he longed to hear more on the benefits of Scottish independence from the First Minister of a Government intent on destroying the last vestiges of Scotland's once proud legal system.

Joanna was not to be put off by Crowe's impatience. 'They come back from the hunt late afternoon, Mike leaves and Kirkslap settles down for a night of television and heavy drinking. Nothing unusual happens, then, the following morning, Zack and Mike collect him and whisk him off, hangover and all, to yet another meeting, this time in Glasgow.'

'I understand all that. I just don't believe it and neither will the jury.'

Joanna sat back and held up a finger. 'What if by the time Mike went to see Kirkslap on the first November, Violet was already dead? What if he didn't go home after the hunt, but borrowed Kirkslap's car?'

'Did he?' Crowe asked.

I pitched in at this point. 'We can't say. What we do know is that Larry, Mike and Zack all drive the same make and model of car. How hard would it be to have new number plates made up and slap them on with double-sided tape?'

Crowe closed his eyes, kneaded his brow between thumb and forefinger. He was tired. Four days of making bricks without a straw of a defence had obviously taken its toll. Now he was being asked to enter the Munro & Co. alternate universe.

Joanna took over again. 'Mike borrows Kirkslap's car, or puts dodgy number plates on his own or something, then, having swapped iPhones with Kirkslap, goes for a late drive, making sure he can be traced not only by the phone, but by a speed camera that anyone who was caught by the first time, would surely have noticed the second.'

'And the blood stains?' Crowe asked.

'Easy to leave behind if you have already killed Violet.'

'And Violet's phone at Kirkslap's lodge?'

'Ditto.'

'What about the threats Kirkslap made to Violet?'

I'd been thinking about that. 'Kirkslap has no recollection of ever having gone to Violet's, far less making threats. It was something Mike told him had happened, and he believed it because on the night it's supposed to have occurred, like most nights, he was drunk. Mike simply fabricated it to beef up the Crown case this time around. He roped in Candy McKeever to make it look to us like she was the source of this new piece of damaging evidence, not him.'

Crowe sneered. 'So she's in on it too? What about his wife? What about Swarovski or whatever his name is?'

Was Zack in on it too? I knew how my next words would sound. 'We can't entirely rule Swarovski out yet either.'

Crowe downed the rest of his brandy and stood up. 'This is ridiculous. I can't go making accusations of murder against everyone who knows Larry Kirkslap, purely on the basis of your creative imagination. I can't even raise the subject of incrimination, because we've never given notice of an intention to do so. What's more, one of your imaginary incriminees, Mike, has already testified and been excused further attendance. Don't you think it'll look a tad strange that I never took the trouble to ask him any obvious questions such as, by the way, are you the murderer?'

The period of time from the end of that sentence to our arrival on the New Town pavement could be measured in seconds, not minutes.

'He's right,' Joanna said. I could tell that her excitement during our earlier discussions had begun to fade. 'There's only one person who had any motive to kill Violet and that was Kirkslap. It was obviously a volatile relationship; on one minute, off the next. Kirkslap's got a temper, there's been an argument and whammo!' she slammed a fist into her open palm. 'The reason he's botched everything up; taking his phone with him, leaving bloodstains, getting caught, not once but twice by the same speed camera, is because he was drunk.'

Crowe had really done a job on her.

'You've said it to me before, Robbie. Murders are usually assaults that go badly wrong. That's why the cops play the odds. The most obvious suspect is usually the person who did it. Why on earth would Mike Summers or Zack, for that matter, want to kill Violet Hepburn? They're not killers.'

What Joanna didn't know was that I firmly believed Mike was a murderer, not by his own hand, perhaps, but he had ordered the death of Nathan Boyd and tried to have his brother and me killed. The dying words of Tam 'Tuppence' Christie had satisfied me on that count.

'One's a lawyer, the other is a software designer,' she said, talking herself out of our earlier defence strategy, such that it was. 'Both men owe Larry Kirkslap their careers. They have absolutely no motive.'

Follow the money my dad had said. Even though he was an expert on many subjects about which he knew very little, this was the first time he'd ever advised me on a possible defence. What if he was right? Follow the money, find a motive, find the killer.

We reached my car. 'Joanna,' I said. 'What do you know about corporate law?'

'I got the University of Glasgow prize for company law.'

'Did you, really?'

'No.'

'Then we're going to have to rely on my expertise,' I said.

'But you don't have any.'

'I think I may have enough to find a motive.'

'Really? A motive why Mike Summers would kill Violet?' Joanna opened the car door and climbed in.

'No.' I started the car engine. 'A motive why Mike would want to send Larry Kirkslap to prison.'

I drove from New Town to Old and parked in Chamber Street, outside Old College, from where it was a short walk to the Scotsman Hotel. After some unsuccessful knocking at the door, we had a porter allow us entry to Larry Kirkslap's room and found him sitting on a chair at the big window, in a state of such inebriation that he couldn't understand what I was asking him, far less why I was asking it.

'Really, Robbie is this worth it?' Joanna asked, attempting to revive Kirkslap with a cup of coffee she'd made using the in-room facilities. 'I'm not trying to be cheeky, but you don't know anything about company formation.'

'When I was at Caldwell & Craig we were a limited liability partnership, not a company. We didn't have shares as such, but the members' agreement did have certain provisions about what would happen in the event of wrong-doing. I'd like to know what happens to Kirkslap's shares if he goes to prison.'

'Won't his wife get them?'

'If he died, then I'm sure they would go to whoever inherited his estate and that would depend on whether he left a will or not. What I want to find out is who gets his shares if he goes to prison.'

We waited with Kirkslap for around two hours, Joanna topping him up with black coffee at regular intervals.

Eventually we gathered from him that there had been a share agreement, but that he didn't have a copy. The papers had all been drawn up by Mike a few years back. He could remember that the shares were split forty-seven, forty-seven, between the two directors, himself and Zack, with the six per cent balance going to company secretary Mike. He couldn't provide any more details than that.

Around ten o'clock, when Kirkslap returned from a trip to the bathroom, sat on the bed and started chuntering on about how much he loved Joanna and, more worryingly, me, we put a pillow under his head and threw a quilt over him. By the time we'd put on our jackets he was snoring.

'So much for that idea,' I said.

'Are company share agreements public documents? Can we order a copy up from somewhere?' Joanna asked; a question to which neither of us knew the answer. She looked at her watch. I offered to drive her home. She declined. 'If I run, I can catch the ten-thirty to Queen Street.'

I accompanied her the few hundred yards to the station concourse, discussing the next day's schedule. It was my turn to sit in on Kirkslap's trial: day five. Joanna would cover the intermediate diets at the Sheriff Court.

'I'll go straight to Livingston in the morning,' she said, 'but I'll take a look when I get home and see what I can find on the Company House web-site. There must be some way to get a copy of that agreement without Mike Summers knowing.'

I thought so too and, forty minutes later, I was well on my way to Addison House to find out if I was right. The way I saw it, if Marjorie Kirkslap had granted the bank a security over her estate to inject capital into P45 Apps, she must have had a lawyer draw up the deeds. For conflict of interest reasons, she would have had to have sought independent legal advice. Whoever that was, it couldn't have been anyone connected to the company, so that ruled out Mike Summers. Could I persuade Marjorie to give me her lawyer's name or even call them for me?

It was worth a try I thought, and then, with half a mile to go, I began to wonder if I was doing the right thing. Should I wait until the morning? How would Marjorie view my prying into her personal affairs? If I'd been given the bum's rush on my last visit, I was unlikely to meet with a more cheery welcome at eleven at night.

It was as I crept the car up the drive towards the big house, still in two minds whether to go through with my visit or not, that I saw up ahead, parked outside the front door, a black Audi Q7. Immediately, I brought my car to a halt and switched off the headlights. I reversed back down the drive to the road. Change of plan.

Chapter 54

I drove straight to my office. Joanna had left our set of papers on the desk. In amongst them I located Zack Swarovski's precognition. At one point we'd thought about using him as a witness to confirm that he'd picked up Kirkslap the morning after the disappearance of Violet and that he'd seemed perfectly normal. Perfectly normal for Larry Kirkslap, on any given morning, being hung-over.

The precognition had his name, address, mobile and home number at the top. I called the landline. All three P45 officials owned a black Audi Q7. If Zack answered his house phone it was safe to assume it wasn't his parked up at Addison House.

After several rings I'd almost given up, when Zack answered. 'Yeah?'

Was Zack involved with Mike? I was prepared to take the chance he wasn't. 'I'm really sorry to bother you Zack —'

'Is that you, Robbie? Do you know what time it is?'

I told him I did and that I wouldn't be calling at that time of night unless it was extremely important.

'I'm really tired,' he said. He sounded like a wee boy. I imagined him standing there in his Dr Who pyjamas. 'I was at court most of the day and had a lot of work to catch up on when I got back. I've a whole load more to do first thing and that's before I take Larry to court in the morning.'

I expected that Zack had a struggle every morning rousing Kirkslap, far less dragging him up Edinburgh High Street to the Lawnmarket.

'I don't want to keep you out your bed,' I said. The truth. 'I had a meeting with counsel tonight.' The truth. 'And he wants to see a copy of P45's share agreement, don't ask me why.' Two out of three wasn't bad.

I could hear him sigh. I held my breath.

'I've got it somewhere on the system. Give me your email address and I'll send it over,' he said.

I gave him the details.

'And don't phone me if you have any questions. Save them for the morning.'

I suppose the thing about being an IT expert is that you can do computery things very quickly. By the time I'd booted-up my own PC, the email from Zack had arrived in my Inbox. Hurriedly, I clicked on the attachment. It opened to reveal the share agreement; all fifteen pages of it. Corporate lawyers never liked to use one word when a dozen would do.

What I was looking for I found on page nine. As soon as I saw it, I knew for certain that Violet Hepburn's death had been all about sending Larry Kirkslap to prison.

In a way I could understand, not the killing of poor Violet, but, Mike's undoubted belief that he'd been shafted. The agreement had been prepared when the company was young, and, until Marjorie mortgaged her mansion, probably without much in the way of working capital; in reality, no more than Kirkslap's idea and the enthusiasm of a young software designer. Kirkslap and Zack might have founded the business, but it had been Mike who'd put the plan together. With his knowledge of intellectual property rights, he had protected the fledgling company's interests against competitors, negotiated contracts with the mobile phone companies and brought in the big social networking players. What was his reward for all of this? A handsome salary, no doubt, but, stock-wise, he was entitled to only six per cent. Six per cent of a multi-million pound company, it was true, and, yet, Kirkslap owned forty-seven per cent and what did he do for his money? He was a front man. A big, warm-hearted, gregarious ambassador, who, having made his money, was happy to womanise and drink himself into oblivion most nights, to the detriment of the business.

I read on. *In the event of the expulsion of any Director by operation of clause 14, the whole interest and shareholding of such Director shall accresce to the remaining shareholders per capita...*

I turned to clause 14. It stated that expulsion of a Director would follow automatically upon any criminal activity that led to a period of imprisonment exceeding sixty months.

What it all meant was that, while upon the death of a P45 director his shares would be transferred to his legal heirs and successors, in the event of serious wrong-doing, the offending director's shareholding would be transferred, not proportionally, but equally, between the remaining shareholders.

Had Kirkslap and his young American software designer read past page one of the agreement before signing? Did Zack Swarovski even know the difference between per capita and pro rata? Zack's idea of a classical education was probably limited to playing retro-computer games like Space Invaders.

Whether or not the directors of P45 knew it, if Kirkslap was convicted and sent to prison for life, one half of his shares would be transferred to Mike Summers, boosting his holding from six to twenty-nine and a half per cent. That equated to several millions of pounds and was, I was sure, to Mike's way of thinking, a more equitable division for the work he'd put in. It was a redistribution of wealth that Larry Kirkslap would pay for by going to prison. Violet Hepburn had already paid for it with her life.

I printed off a copy of the share agreement and put it with the rest of the case papers. It was a further step in the right direction, but not enough. 'Mike the murderer' was a fine theory; nonetheless, still just a theory. Forgetting, for a moment, the procedural difficulties of putting it before a jury, there were clear evidential problems. Crowe was right.

Trying to incriminate Mike on the proof available would look like a defence that was clutching at straws.

So far as I could see, Mike's plan was airtight. He was safe, and yet obviously he didn't share that view. If he wanted to kill me, he had to think that I had prejudicial information. Information that would give my theory actual substance and put him firmly in the frame for Violet's murder. What did I have that made the case I'd cobbled together against him a stateable one? What proof did I have? It had to be a witness. It had to be Danny Boyd.

Chapter 55

Friday. Day five of Larry Kirkslap's trial, and Fiona Faye had lined up another batch of witnesses to whiz through. Before the jury was led on, she dropped the bombshell that the Crown expected to close its case on Monday or Tuesday at the latest. By expert pruning and efficient examination-in-chief, she had crammed the prosecution case into six or seven days.

Fiona's first witness was the supermarket delivery man who'd left a box of groceries at Violet Hepburn's door, early evening on 1st November. The second was a neighbour to say that she had not set eyes on Violet since around the same date, which was unusual because Violet used to pop in for coffee every few days. The third was another neighbour who'd once seen Violet get into a black 4x4, though he was hazy on the exact date. And so it went on, the witnesses coming fast and furious. Fiona certainly knew how to show a jury a good time.

By three o'clock the procession was over. Pushing at something of an open judicial door, Fiona suggested an early finish.

When the jury had filed out, she advised the court that on the Monday she would be calling her final witnesses. In the morning we were to be presented with those witnesses who had collected various Crown productions: blood samples, mobile phones, credit cards etc. and relayed them for forensic analysis. It was essential to prove a chain of evidence, but routine stuff like that could be agreed by way of a Joint Minute of Admissions - if that's what Fiona wanted. It wasn't. Why simply read out the evidence to the jury? Much better to lead a string of police witnesses, each speaking to an important strand of prosecution evidence, in effect, summarising the Crown case in a stream of formal evidence so incontestable that it would be heard quickly and without cross-examination.

Thereafter, on Monday afternoon, Fiona intended to call Violet's mother. Her evidence wouldn't add a great deal to the actual facts of the case; however, it would be an occasion of high emotion and tears. Fiona could have easily brought Mrs Hepburn to the witness box that Friday afternoon, but to do so would have allowed the impact of the woman's evidence to fade in the jury's mind over a weekend.

'This case is proceeding like a runaway train,' Crowe said, throwing his horse-hair wig onto the table in the centre of the advocates' robing room. 'Do you realise that if everything goes to plan for Fifi she's going to wrap things up on Monday and I'll be expected to lead some kind of defence?'

Obviously, I did realise that, as I'd been sitting beside him in court when Fiona made her announcement.

'And what have I got?' Crowe demanded, again rhetorically. 'A client who knows nothing, can explain nothing—'

'We've got our phone guy...'

'Fantastic. The best we can come up with is a phone expert who might tentatively suggest that the other experts got it wrong on their mobile phone tracking evidence - big deal. Have you read his report? Fiona will tear him limb by limb and feed him to the jury in small pieces.'

'Mike Summers stands to make millions if Kirkslap gets the jail,' I said.

Crowe shrugged off his gown and ripped off his white bow-tie. 'Then I say congratulations to him.'

'No, really, if you look at the evidence, it's quite possible this whole thing is a set up.'

'By Summers? Please, not this again.'

From my papers I produced the copy of P45's share agreement. 'Take a look at this. Summers stands to make a lot of money out of a conviction.'

'It's rubbish,' Crowe said, not even glancing in my direction as he struggled with a brass collar stud.

'It's all we've got. It's our only chance of a win.'

Crowe gave up on the collar stud for a moment. 'Would you please stop? I'm not your pretty little assistant. You don't have to try and impress me. I told you last night this theory of yours was all a waste of time.'

'That was before this.' I waggled the agreement. 'This shows that if Kirkslap is sent to prison for over twelve months, one-half of his shareholding will be automatically transferred to Mike Summers. That leaves him with around a thirty per cent share in the company. Do you know how much money that is?'

Crowe looked down at me as though I were a form of infectious disease. He raised his chin. 'Would you?'

I unfastened the stud. Something about getting my hands close to Crowe's throat was quite appealing.

Crowe removed the rear stud himself, and tossed his detachable winged-collar onto the table. 'I spoke to Summers this morning, told him about your little theory.'

He hadn't, had he? He had.

'Summers told me that if it helped free Kirkslap, he'd allow his name to be dragged through the mud. He would deny everything, of course, but if we wanted to use him as a smoke screen, he'd be willing. Sound like a guilty man to you?'

'He's bluffing.'

'Whatever, I'm not using him. Where's his motive?'

Clearly, to Cameron Crowe I was of less import than a stubborn collar-stud. 'Have you even been listening to me?'

'What good is a shareholding in the company when the main man is in jail? Thirty per cent of zilch is still zilch.'

'But he won't be the main man for much longer. Kirkslap's a booze-bag. He's made his dosh. All he's interested in now is booze, birds and blasting the Trossachs wildlife. P45 will have to bring a new frontman in sooner or later. I think Mike wants to be that person.'

Crowe snorted. 'You really are pathetic, you know that?' He took off his starched white shirt and sprayed under his arms with a can of deodorant from his locker. 'You'd be happy to incriminate a fellow lawyer just to make yourself some extra cash, and to hang with justice and that man's reputation.'

Was it too late to sack him? Could I persuade Kirkslap and, I supposed Zack, to let me bring in another counsel who might have the guts to incriminate Summers? Supposing the client were amenable, who could I get to argue the extremely late lodging of a notice of incrimination and the recalling of a witness who'd already been excused, all in the face of stern opposition from Fiona Faye? Even if successful, it would all seem just too desperate.

'You're not denying it then?' Crowe said, slipping into a more casual white shirt and wrapping a black tie around the collar. 'I heard you'd managed to talk the client into agreeing a nice little win bonus, and now you're prepared to do anything to get your grubby little hands on it.'

'I'm sure the generous offer will extend to counsel. Why don't you try and earn it?'

Crowe smiled like a serpent, sliding the knot in his tie up to the collar. 'I intend to. You see, I have a cunning plan of my own.'

I'd thought that, for all his bluster, Crowe had been looking even smugger than usual. 'And that is?'

'Simple. We get Kirkslap to say he killed her.'

I clapped my hands together. 'Well done! Why didn't I think of that?'

'But,' Crowe continued, 'we say it was all a terrible mistake.'

I couldn't help but be intrigued. 'In what way?'

He stood to attention as though in the witness box and put his right hand up to God. 'She came to the house that night.' Crowe dabbed an imaginary tear from his eye. 'We'd both been drinking. We argued. She was leaving. I tried to stop her. She slapped me. I pushed her. She fell. Banged her head...' he paused for a moment, stopped staring at the imaginary jury and turned to me. 'That would explain the blood on the hall carpet.' He took up his witness pose again. 'I didn't know what to do. I panicked. I put her in the boot of the car and buried her somewhere in the countryside. If I'd planned the whole thing, invited her to my lodge to murder her, do you think I would have been so stupid as to be caught on speed camera, twice, or to take my mobile phone with me?'

'So where's the body?' I asked.

Crowe relaxed. 'Who cares? It's out there in the wilds somewhere. Kirkslap will have been too upset to know exactly where he dug the grave - if he did dig a grave. He might have just left the body above ground. Yes, that would be better. There's a lot of wild animals up there. Violet will be long gone.'

I pointed out the obvious. 'It's not really that good a defence. Is it?'

'No, but it's not murder. It's culpable homicide.'

'And attempting to defeat the ends of justice by concealing a body.'

'It's not life imprisonment. It's eight years, ten at the most.'

'It's not the truth.' Was that really me speaking?

'Who's to say? Just because a body goes missing, why should it automatically be murder? Why not culpable homicide? Or even accident? Kirkslap accidentally kills his girlfriend. What's he to do? His reputation, his standing in the community, his career, all ruined. So he panics. Perfectly

278

credible. Kirkslap boasts what a great salesman he is. Let's see him sell that story to the jury.'

It was clever. So clever that I was sure with a little persuasion Kirkslap would jump at it, put on a show and quite possibly escape a life sentence. Culpable homicide. It wasn't murder, but it wasn't an acquittal. Juries loved a compromise.

Crowe gestured to the door. I was leaving.

'So Kirkslap goes to jail and the world is Mike Summers' proverbial oyster, is that it?'

'That's about the size of it,' Crowe said. 'Who knows? If the jury comes back with culp hom you might get half your win bonus.' He ushered me out of the door. 'Oh, and as Mr Summers would be sure to advise you, there are no proverbial oysters, only allegorical ones.'

Chapter 56

It was half-five by the time I returned from the High Court. Joanna was waiting for an update. I told her of Crowe's plan and she agreed that there was something to admire in its simplicity, and in the fact that it could very well be true - almost.

When she left at the back of six, I remembered what day it was: the day of the big party. I phoned home. No answer. My dad must have left to go tidy his cottage. He and Malky had probably been slaving away for hours. I could picture his face if I arrived on the scene late and in my suit and tie.

There was a note on the telephone table when I got home: *Phone Malky.*

A quick shower, a change of clothes, I could be at the cottage around seven, help blow up a few balloons and be ready for the party starting at eight.

I was all set to leave and just going to phone Malky, as the note instructed, when there was a knock at the door. It was Candy. She slipped inside before I had the chance to ask her why she was there.

'You've got to help me,' she said.

Why she thought I would feel under any obligation, when I was fairly certain she'd set me up to be killed by Tuppence Christie, I wasn't sure.

'He's going to kill me,' she said.

'Who?'

'Mike Summers. Because of Violet.'

This was more like it. I invited Candy into the livingroom. She sat down in an armchair.

'Why should I trust you?' I asked.

'Because I'm here to tell you the truth. Mike made me tell you that Larry threatened Violet and that I was there. He had me phone in an anonymous tip-off to the police. Mike wanted to give evidence against Larry, but at the same time to make it look like he was a reluctant witness.'

I sat down on the couch where my dad normally sat. 'Go on.'

'He wants Larry convicted of the murder. It's all a fit up.'

'How do you know?'

'I overheard him speaking with the owner of Karats.'

'Who's that?' I asked innocently.

'Tam Christie. You saw him that night you were there.'

Was she telling the truth? Could it be she hadn't set me up with Tuppence and his doorman?

'Why did you not meet me as planned on Wednesday night. In the lay-by?'

'I got lost.'

I didn't believe her.

She could obviously tell. 'I was scared. All right? Tam Christie's a gangster.' Candy rubbed her brow. 'Mike's been spending a lot of time with him. I'm scared. I don't know what to do. I don't want to end up like Violet.'

Candy was shaping up to be the missing piece of evidence I needed to add to my Mike Summer's theory - if she was telling the truth.

'Why did you do it?' I asked.

'Mike asked me. He gave me this, not Larry.' She put a hand to the diamond pendant at her neck. 'I thought, who cares? I didn't know Violet that well, but she didn't deserve to die. I liked Mike and he said Larry was guilty. Everyone thought Larry was guilty. He said and did a lot of stupid things when he was drunk. Mike thought it was important evidence that the court should hear, but he couldn't come forward voluntarily. I was just trying to help. Then I heard him talking to Mr Christie about how he was fitting Larry up. I knew I'd made a mistake and could be in trouble. Now

Mike wants me to come forward and speak to the Crown. Give evidence on oath that I heard the threats. I don't know what to do.'

'You're a law student. Did you not think about all that before you lied to the defence solicitor in a murder trial?'

Candy looked up at me. Her mascara was holding up well, despite the tears running down her face. Quality cosmetics. Girls who worked at Karats were worth it.

'You worked with Andy Imray at Caldwell & Craig. How did that come about?'

She looked surprised that I knew. 'Mike arranged it. They were looking for a paralegal and he gave me an excellent reference.'

'When?'

'Earlier this year.'

'When in relation to Kirkslap's first trial?'

'Right at the beginning.' She didn't wait for my next question. 'He did it to help me out and he wanted to know how strong the prosecution case was. I thought he was just being nice to me and concerned for his friend.'

'And what did you tell him?'

'Not much he didn't know already.'

'Do you know somebody called Danny Boyd,' I asked. I looked her in the eye and she looked right back at me.

'No. Should I?'

I checked the clock. Seven-twenty. My dad's party would kick off in forty minutes.

I phoned Cameron Crowe's mobile. No answer. I left a message on his answering service, fairly certain that he'd recognised my number and bumped me. There was only one thing for it.

'This is really improper even by your standards, Robbie,' Fiona Faye said.

'I've found a new witness. An important one.'

'Then call her for the defence.'

'We can't.'

282

'Why not?'

'Because I don't think you or Lord Haldane will let us.'

'Go on, then. Tell me why not.'

'She's part of a proposed incrimination—'

'And you haven't so much as lodged a notice and, of course, your defence statement is completely silent on any impeachment defence. Tut, tut.'

'Speak to her, Fiona. That's all I ask. If you believe what she has to say, call her as part of the Crown case.'

'I'm trying to win. Why would I want to help by calling a potential defence witness?'

'Because you're prosecuting in the public interest, remember?' That was what the Crown always said to align themselves with the jury, but you seldom caught a Procurator Fiscal or Advocate Depute call a witness who was saying anything remotely favourable for the defence. 'Isn't getting to the truth the most important thing?'

'The truth? Robbie, is this one of those prank calls you're so famous for? Do us your Sheriff Brechin impersonation, will you?'

Fiona heard all the gossip.

'Okay,' she relented. 'I'm about to settle down with a warm husband and a glass of chilled Sancerre. I'll give you ten minutes if you're here before eight. Otherwise forget it.'

Chapter 57

We decided to take Candy's car. It was a red BMW, more likely than mine to make the journey to Fiona's place in Edinburgh within the next thirty minutes, mainly because it had fuel in it.

I climbed into the front passenger seat, Candy started the engine, and we had hardly turned onto the High Street when something jammed into the back of my neck. I half turned to see Mike Summers.

'Face front or I'll blast your head off,' he said. The words didn't suit him, but, still, they were clear enough.

'Where are we going?' I asked, my eyes firmly fixed on the windscreen.

'Don't worry, Candy knows where to take us,' Mike said.

At the east end of the High Street Candy pressed a button on the dash. 'At the roundabout take the second exit onto the B nine oh eight oh,' said an electronic voice.

We were taking the old Edinburgh Road. One I travelled a lot these days. A couple more robotic directions, and I had guessed where we were headed. Candy was a clever girl. She'd remembered our conversation of a couple of nights before, when I had told her my dad's house was unoccupied and well out of the way. I couldn't believe that I'd fallen for the same damsel in distress line in the space of a few days.

The car sped on. It was impossible to relax with a gun pressed against the back of my neck, but I did feel better now that I knew the uninhabited cottage Mike thought he was taking me to, was actually populated by twenty or thirty party guests of whom at least half were cops. I said nothing. Just sat there watching the headlights cut through the darkness on that windy road. Never interrupt your enemy when he is making a mistake.

A few more electronic commands and we were pulling into the small driveway at the front of my dad's cottage. The place was in darkness. The clock on the dashboard said seven fifty-five. The party guests would be inside now, hiding, awaiting the arrival of the man of the moment. Malky would have taken dad for a drive to kill time. They'd return at eight, all set for the big surprise. Not half as big as the one Mike and Candy were in for.

Candy alighted, came around and opened the door for me.

'Get out,' Mike said.

I turned in my seat, and, as I did, saw that whatever Mike had in his gloved hand, it wasn't a gun. I clenched my fist. As soon as both Mike and I were out of the car I was going to deck him. Heart pumping, muscles tightening, fists clenching. I was going to enjoy this.

How did I end up on the ground? How long had I been there? I looked up at the face of Candy, peering down at me. Mike joined her.

'Up,' Mike said, brandishing an object at me. A blue bolt of light flashed in the gloom.

We walked down the side of the house, Mike at my back, one hand gripping the top of my left arm, the other pressing the stun-gun into the side of my neck.

My foot struck something. We stopped. There was a stack of slates, as well as bags of cement and sand still lined up against the gable wall of the cottage. At the corner I could see scaffolding erected. The roof wasn't finished. The party venue, if there was one, was elsewhere. I remembered the message to call Malky. Why hadn't I done so?

We continued round to the back of the cottage. Candy tried the handle on the door. It opened.

'Careless,' Mike said.

Candy pushed the door open. I didn't remember going in, only finding myself on the floor, my limbs like jelly, Mike, standing over me, pointing the stun-gun from me to a kitchen chair. 'Sit.'

I could hear Mike clearly, I wasn't particularly dazed. I knew what was happening and what he wanted me to do, it was just that my body refused to respond.

'Sit!' he yelled.

Somehow I managed to drag myself off the floor and onto the chair.

'Where's Boyd?' Mike asked.

I shook my head. 'I really, really, have no idea.'

He must have believed me, for he turned to Candy and told her to find a knife. 'Bigger,' he told her, when she held out a small vegetable knife to him.

Candy rummaged in a drawer and found a large chopping knife. Like Mike she was now wearing a pair of cream surgical gloves .

I shifted in my seat, took my eyes off Mike for a second and wham! I found myself on the floor again feeling like I'd been poured out onto it.

'We'll do this now and get out of here,' Mike said. He was holding the stun-gun, keeping me at bay as though I were fit to do anything other than just lie there.

'Me?' Candy made a face. 'I'm not doing it.' She held out the knife to Mike. He took it, switching the stun-gun to his other hand. He looked down at me, a sick and worried expression etched across his face that couldn't have looked sicker or more worried than the one on mine.

The muscles in my arms and legs were slowly beginning to get their act together. Mike readied himself, gripping the handle of the knife tightly. I had to stall for time.

Mouth dry, I managed to croak, 'what's so important about Danny Boyd?'

Mike was not going to let himself be engaged in small talk. He took a deep breath, steeling himself to do what he'd rather have paid others to do for him. He gave the stun-gun to Candy. 'You zap him again,' he told her, 'I'll stab him.'

Candy hesitated. What was she thinking? That it was all right setting someone up; not so good if you had to be there when the blood was spilled? 'Mike...'

'Zap him!' Mike roared.

She came closer, the arm holding the zapper out-stretched, shaking.

My legs had regained some power, the strength in my arms was returning, aided by the flow of adrenalin. I tried to squirm away across the kitchen floor. Mike kicked me hard in the side. I grabbed his ankle, trying to trip him.

'Hurry up!' he screamed at Candy, wrenching his foot free from my grip.

As soon as she struck out with the stun-gun, I'd try to kick it out of her hand. I propped myself up on an elbow. I'd only get one shot at it. If those electrodes touched any part of my body, it was over. Once I was incapacitated, Mike would finish me off.

'Mr Munro?' The door from the livingroom into the kitchen opened and Danny Boyd stood there, hair tousled, face puffy, as though he'd just woken up.

Candy spun around. Danny took in the scene through widening eyes and slammed the door shut again. Seeing Mike distracted, I hurled myself at him. The knife ripped through the left sleeve of my shirt. I jumped back, grabbed a chair and, lion tamer-like, held him at bay. Mike feinted with the knife, but could get nowhere near me. He reached out and grabbed the stun-gun from Candy. Zapper in one hand, chopping knife in the other, he shuffled towards me. I backed away. There wasn't much room in the kitchen. Two steps and I was at a kitchen drawer. I wrenched it open, one hand rummaging about inside, the other jabbing the chair legs at Mike. I felt around, eyes fixed on stun-gun and knife. A fish slice, a wooden spoon, both useless. A rolling pin: better. I'd no sooner pulled it from the drawer than Mike, threw the

287

chopping knife at me. I had barely time to react. I dropped
the chair, flung my arms up to protect my head. The knife hit
the rolling pin, bounced off and clattered into the sink. Mike
lunged at me, blue lightning crackling. I kicked the fallen
chair. It struck one of his legs below the knee. Off balance, he
put out a hand to steady himself. Instead of touching the
wooden table top, he leaned heavily on a dirty coffee mug.
His hand skidded away. He fell sideways, hip striking the
edge of the table. As he tried to regain his balance, I struck
out back-handed with the rolling pin, catching him across the
top of his arm. Ignoring the blow he came straight for me,
bringing the stun-gun to bear. Before he could do so, I swung
the rolling pin again. It was supposed to knock his head off,
but my muscles were still recovering, the effort was weak
and I connected with little more than a glancing blow. As he
shimmied to avoid my next attempt, Mike's feet caught in
the fallen chair. He stumbled, toppled backwards and fell,
the stun-gun smashing on the hard floor.

Candy looked down at the zapper. The plastic casing had
split open, the innards scattered, a single nine volt battery
still attached by an electrical umbilical cord.

Blood oozed from Mike's nose. I raised the rolling pin.
'You wanted to find Danny Boyd? Well you have. Now you
can tell me why. Danny!'

The boy never appeared. I shouted his name again. Still
no show.

'Danny!'

The door to the livingroom opened slowly and Danny
Boyd came into the kitchen.

'I'm sorry,' he said. 'It was really cold and I—'

'Who's he to you?' I asked pointing the rolling pin at
Mike.

Danny stared at Mike for a while and then at me. 'I
dunno. Who is he?'

Despite his sore face and a flow of blood from his nose which he was trying to stem with the sleeve of his coat, Mike managed a smile.

I seized Danny by the back of the head and pushed his face down for a closer look at the fallen Mike. 'Who is he? This man is trying to kill you!'

'I told you I don't know!' The teenager broke free of my grip, stepped over Mike and walked out of the back door.

Mike watched him go and then clambered to his feet. He produced a white handkerchief, dabbed his nose and checked it for blood. Satisfied that things were drying up, he stuffed the hanky back into his pocket. 'That's that, then,' he said. 'I'll be off.'

I kept a tight grip on the rolling pin. 'You're going nowhere,' I said.

Mike laughed. 'What are you going to do? Call the cops? I'm the one bleeding here. I'm also the one with the independent witness.' He took Candy's wrist and pulled her towards him. 'By the way,' he said, when they'd taken the few steps to the door, 'you're sacked. I'll break the news to Larry. I can take things from here. Culpable homicide. He'll know it makes sense.'

Chapter 58

I was clearing up the mess in the kitchen when Danny Boyd re-appeared, sheepish and soaking wet.

'It's raining,' he said, unnecessarily. 'I've come back for my stuff.'

'Where have you been living?' I asked him, after he'd returned from the spare bedroom wearing a waterproof jacket and lugging a rucksack.

He jerked his head towards the door. 'Out there. Down by the canal. I've got a tent. Had a tent. It blew away last night. '

'It's all over,' I told him.

'But what about the curse?'

'There is no curse any more. That man just now, he was the curse. He had your brother killed. He wanted to kill you. He tried to kill me. Twice. But he's not interested in us anymore.' Whatever Mike had thought Danny knew, the boy obviously didn't; which meant he couldn't have passed the information onto me. Contract terminated. Mike had won. Whether Larry Kirkslap was convicted of murder or managed to silver-tongue his way to a culpable homicide verdict, he was going to jail for a long time and Mike was scooping one-half of his shares. 'You can go home now, Danny.'

I phoned a taxi and, after much persuasion, dropped Danny and his wet camping gear off at his home. I didn't go in with him. As the taxi pulled away again, Mrs Boyd came to the door and waved. Even the dog had dragged itself off the couch and was sitting on the porch, scratching an ear.

Back home, I found some money to pay the taxi and then wondered how I could find out where the party had moved to. Without my mobile and the numbers saved to the SIM card, I had no means of contacting anyone. I gave up at eleven, sat about until midnight and went to bed, shattered but unable to sleep, turning over and over in my mind the events of that night. I got up a couple of hours later and had a drink of milk. Then I realised I hadn't eaten in a while and put some bread in the toaster. While I was waiting for it to pop, a taxi pulled up outside and my dad and Malky rolled in.

The old man walked straight past me. He ran himself a glass of water and then without a word, or so much as a glance in my direction, went off to bed.

'Don't worry,' Malky said. 'You know what Dad's like, he's rubbish at staying in the huff. He always forgets that he's in the huff and starts speaking. By the time he remembers it's too late. Once you're out of the huff, re-entry is not really an option.'

I thanked him for his booze-fuelled words of wisdom and asked how things had gone.

'Yeah, it wasn't that bad. The party kicked off at eight and the buffet was scoffed by half-past. You know what these old guys are like. You'd think some of them had never seen a sausage roll before. Most people started to drift away about midnight. I wish I had. When you start thinking the Red River trio are playing in tune, you know it's time to go home.' He stared into the toaster to see if there was a problem. 'So, anyway where'd you get to?' he asked, satisfied on the ETA of the toast.

'Where did I get to? Where did the party get to?'

Malky laughed. 'You never turfed up at the little house on the prairie, did you? If you'd have phoned me, like you were supposed to, you would have found out.' The toast popped. 'One slice do you?' He took a knife off the draining board, butter from the fridge.

'Well? Where did it all happen?' I asked.

'Jill's.'

'Jill's? My Jill's?'

'Yeah. That Arthur bloke had another job he had to go to, or was short of materials or something. It was all last minute, and then I remembered…' He picked up one of the slices of toast he'd buttered and crunched into it. 'That time when me and dad were out there watering her plants... I thought, if Jill is away skiing—'

'She's working and you didn't have permission—'

'We tried to contact you,' he chomped. 'It's not our fault you never answer your mobile.' He took another bite. In a departure from the norms of polite company, my brother seemed to only speak when his mouth was full. 'Jill won't mind. If she does, you can put your foot down. You'll soon be master of the house.'

'Not if you've damaged her precious plants I won't be.'

He grimaced. 'About that. Jorge had a bit of a trip. Over a rug.' From recollection of Jorge Kleinman's footballing career he had a habit of falling over, especially in the opposition's eighteen yard box. 'He landed on something prickly.' Malky shoved the rest of his toast into his mouth. 'I think we managed to patch it all right. Jill will never notice.'

My dad came through. 'Will you two shut up? I'm trying to get to sleep.' He looked at my, as yet, untouched slice of toast. 'You having that?'

I stepped to the side to give him a free run at the toast on the bread board. 'Sorry about tonight, Dad. Something cropped up. It was really—'

'Important. Of course it was.'

'I'd have been there if I'd known where it was.'

'You should have phoned Malky.'

'I know. I went to the cottage. I thought you said Arthur would have the job done?'

Malky sniggered. Apparently, the thought of me turning up to a party at a derelict house, was pure comedy gold.

'Arthur had to go to another job.' He parted his moustache with a snort. 'A more important customer than me, obviously.'

'By important customer Dad means, a paying customer,' Malky said, dropping another couple of slices of bread in the toaster. 'Just as well I was there to save the day. That's me...' He tapped the side of a head from which far too many footballs had bounced. 'Always thinking.' He walked out of the kitchen.

Suddenly I felt quite tired; like I could sleep. And sleep. Where did Malky think he was spending the night? My dad had commandeered the bed and I had the sofa. The sofa?

I dashed through to the livingroom to find Malky already divested of most of his outerwear and snuggling down to sleep under my sleeping bag. He still had two slices of bread in the toaster. Had he meant to eat them or were they to lull me into a false sense of security? Could Malky really be that smart?

I found the bottle of 18 year-old Springbank and returned to the kitchen where my dad was finishing off my toast. 'Happy birthday,' I said. It had officially been his birthday for the past two hours. 'The distillery at Campbeltown has a tour. You can watch them making this stuff. Might be a good wee trip for us, once your leg is...'

'You didn't know I'd had the stookie off did you?'

I hadn't. Not until that moment.

'Three days that thing's been off and you've never even noticed.'

'I've been busy.'

'Well don't worry about me. I'll be out of your hair and back home, middle of next week. Just as soon as Arthur finishes building his latest castle or monument or whatever he's doing.'

All of a sudden, into my weary brain, came the picture of me lugging a bucket of grain past a pile of sandstone blocks in the grounds of Addison House. Where was Danny Boyd's notepad? I went through to the livingroom. Malky was already asleep and snoring, either that or doing an excellent impersonation so that he wouldn't be disturbed. I shifted his legs, found the notepad and flicked through the various entries until I came to one I'd seen before but that had never properly registered. Addison Tower. A mausoleum. What better place to hide a body?

Chapter 59

It was a cold, dreich, Sunday morning in April when we gathered outside the Addison family's ancestral resting place. It was called a tower, but was no more than fifteen feet high, the statue of a single weeping angel atop a domed roof of slate and lead. The door was solid oak, still in excellent repair, with three, broad, iron-studded hasps securing it to the door post by the same number of heavy-duty padlocks. The locks looked new. Too new for such an ancient edifice.

That early morning visit was my second trip to the tomb in as many days, for I had been there twenty-four hours earlier with Danny Boyd. The tomb was set back, well away from the big house, and we hadn't been disturbed by Marjorie Kirkslap or practical-joking Uncle Gordon.

Danny and Nathan Boyd had come to this mausoleum on 31st October 2012. I'd never had the notion to enter a mausoleum, not while I was still alive anyway, but, if I'd ever been so inclined, I was certain Halloween would be the one night at which I'd draw a line.

'It was Nathan's idea,' Danny told me. 'I was scared. We'd been in quite a few others, just for a look around, but we'd sealed them up again afterwards and never took nothing. We read about them on the internet, and there was this chatroom that had folk from England on it, saying we were lucky and that it was great fun. It was like a competition to see how many you could do.'

'And it was the curse that made you scared?'

'None of the others we done had curses. As soon as I read the history of this one I had a bad feeling about it.'

That Sunday morning, I read again the words inscribed on the lintel, just as I had the day before.

He that spares these stones be bleste
And curst be him who breaks my reste.

'Cheery, here, isn't it?' Fiona Faye was wearing a bright red raincoat, flanked by two uniform cops in standard-issue dark waterproofs.

Hugh Ogilvie hovered in the background, sulking under an umbrella, not amused at being bothered on a Sunday.

'You'd better be right on this one, Munro,' Cameron Crowe said. 'If this is some kind of wild goose—'

'It's not,' I assured him. 'Michael Summers murdered Violet on thirty-first October. He brought her here to this sealed mausoleum, knowing that it would not be opened again, since the Addisons were busy having another built elsewhere on the estate. He framed Kirkslap, leaving bloodstains at his home, taking his mobile for a spin—'

'I get it,' Fiona said. I'd had the same discussion with her the previous afternoon. She held out her crooked arm and let one of the cops support her as she tip-toed through the mud to the door of the mausoleum for a closer look at the padlocks.

Fiona had been highly dubious when I'd presented my theory to her the day before, and I'd been hindered slightly in that I had been unable to tell her everything for fear of being linked to Tam 'Tuppence' Christie's death, which, as yet, was still merely a missing person's report on the desk of Strathclyde Police. Knowing Tuppence's relationship with the polis, I didn't think they'd be looking too hard. It was only after I'd persuaded Fiona to make a phone call that things had really got moving. That call had been to SOCA, the Serious Organised Crime Agency. A member of the public or a defence agent could wait months, years, for information from the mobile phone companies. SOCA had the information I'd had Fiona ask for within three hours. Three hours to track the movements of three mobile phones and one iPad.

Candy McKeever's phone had made a call via the nearest base station to Violet Hepburn's home on the evening of 31st October. That call had been to Mike Summers. The phone had then travelled, along with Violet's phone, from Glasgow to Edinburgh the same day. Violet's phone had gone silent and not been reactivated until the following day when the text message had been sent arranging to meet up with Kirkslap. That text had not been sent by Violet. She'd been dead nearly twenty-four hours.

A data search showed that Mike's phone had remained in his house on Halloween night, but not his iPad. The tablet was alive, switched on and receiving signals via 3G in the vicinity of Violet's home on 1st November at the time the text to Kirkslap was sent, but, more importantly, it had been in the vicinity of Addison House shortly before midnight on 31st October.

Why had Mike taken it with him? It went everywhere. He never knew when it might come in useful. Well, it had now. Very useful. But not to him.

Candy had set Violet up. Mike had finished the job. Everything had gone according to plan - until he walked out of the mausoleum, out of a door he'd thought would not open again this side of the resurrection. On the other side of that sturdy old, oak door, Mike had expected to stroll into a fortune. Instead he'd stumbled into two teenagers trying to break in and to whom he'd given the fright of their lives.

It must have been a stressful few months for Mike, not knowing who these potential witnesses were. And then two lads had been arrested for an attempted raid on the nearby Binny Mausoleum. Violation of sepulchres, an unusual occurrence; it had to be the same two boys. If they started blabbing about other escapades and word of Halloween 2012 got out, someone might check the Addison Tower. Larry Kirkslap didn't have an alibi for the 1st November, but he wouldn't need one if it was discovered that Violet had been

297

killed the night before. Could the Boyd boys identify Mike? They had to be got rid of.

Fiona examined the locks, like me, recognising the newness of them. 'We're going to need a warrant to open this thing up.' She turned to the PF. 'Mr Ogilvie, better send your police officers round to see one of the local Sheriffs. This is Sheriff Albert Brechin's jurisdiction isn't it? Maybe you can rouse him from his bed.' Delicately, she tip-toed over to me. 'Unless...' she whispered in my ear, 'you can have him grant us one over the phone.'

Chapter 60

Violet Hepburn's body was found wrapped in a tartan travelling rug on the floor of the Addison Tower. The pathologists later concurred that she'd been strangled. One of her wrists was lacerated; enough of a wound for some blood to be collected. If kept moist or airtight, that blood could easily have been transferred elsewhere, such as to the boot of a car or wiped onto a hallway carpet.

When Larry Kirkslap turned up for day six of his trial on Monday morning, he was given the happy news that, yet again, the case against him was being deserted, this time simpliciter. Mike Summers, who had accompanied him to court, was arrested and charged with the murder of Violet Hepburn. Candy McKeever had been detained and questioned on Sunday afternoon. She had not exercised her right to silence, and had landed iPad Mike right in it. Candy might have been an excellent liar, but, when it came to telling the truth in order to save her own skin, she was good at that too.

Where did Marjorie Kirkslap fit into all this? Did she fit into it at all? I remembered the black Audi Q7 outside the big house the other night. The death of Violet Hepburn would have been mutually convenient for a jealous wife and a greedy business colleague. It would all make for an interesting trial. Not one in which Fiona Faye, Cameron Crowe or Munro & Co. would be instructed. I understood Nigel Staedtler Q.C. had declared his availability.

Tuesday morning: dull, miserable and pouring with rain. Joanna came into my room. It might have seemed like winter outside, but in her heart it was most definitely spring.

'Have you seen it?' she asked, excitedly.

I hadn't.

She dragged me and pressed my face against the window. One floor below us, the April rain battered against the roof of a brand new Mercedes SLK AMG Sport.

I was pretty happy about the win-bonus I'd received from Larry Kirkslap too. It was tax-free and could just about be squeezed into the shoe box under my bed. A bed that had recently been returned to its rightful owner.

Joanna released her hold on the back of my head and gave me a big hug. 'What a case! I never want to leave here,' she said.

I heard my secretary clearing her throat. A familiar enough sound and one that signalled all was not well in the Grace-Mary universe. We turned, my arm still around Joanna's waist, hers still around mine. They dropped quickly, perhaps too quickly, to our respective sides when we saw Jill standing there.

Call it male intuition, I could tell she wasn't happy. 'Hello Jill—'

'Do not *hello Jill* me.'

'I'll put the kettle on,' Grace-Mary said, performing a tactical retreat.

Jill took up position in the centre of the room. 'Why do you never answer your phone?'

'I've lost —'

'Did you not get the message that I was coming back two days early? I told your dad to tell you to phone me. I left hundreds of messages on your answering service over the weekend. You were supposed to pick me up at the airport.'

'I'm sorry Jill, I—'

'If you even had a web-site or something I could have emailed you. I've stood in the rain for an hour. I had to get a taxi.'

'Is it outside? Where's all your luggage?'

'Where do you think? At home.'

Oh, oh.

'My home which has burst balloons everywhere and a recycle bin full of empty beer bottles. And what on earth happened to my ivory pineapple? Oh, and I found this on my dressing table.' From her hand bag she removed a plastic bag with a half-eaten sausage roll inside. 'Explain.'

'There was a small family get together for my dad's birthday,' I said.

'At my house?'

'It's a really long story. I'll explain everything later. Come here.' I went over to her, arms wide open.

Jill let me hug her, but did not reciprocate. I tried to give her a kiss and was presented with a cheek, no lips. After a brief coming together she broke free. 'I can't believe that I'm away for six weeks and come home to find those plants that are not dying of thirst have been squashed, bakery products on my make-up box and now this.' Jill pointed at Joanna. 'My boyfriend canoodling with the staff.'

'We were celebrating,' I said. 'We've just won a big case. Come over here and see what Joanna's got.' I took Jill by the wrist and tried to pull her over to the window.

'No thanks,' Jill said. 'I can see what Joanna's got from here, thanks.'

I'd had enough. Time to go on the attack. 'Josh! What about Josh?'

'What about him?'

'Oh, I see.' I paced up and down, waving a hand. All I needed was a jury. 'It's all right for you to go off on skiing trips and late-night fondue parties with your work colleague, but I can't even give mine a celebratory hug after we've won the biggest case of our lives?'

Jill placed her hands on her hips. Five-foot two of righteous indignation. 'Josh is very nice and probably the gayest man in all Switzerland *if* it's any business of yours.'

I didn't get to where I was by not being quick on my feet. 'There you are then. A misunderstanding on my part, for which I apologise. Now, if you'd care to do the same, we can put this behind us and —'

'Oh, I'll put this behind us all right. In fact I'll put you right behind me!'

Jill turned on a heel.

'Wait!' Joanna yelled. 'No, really, wait,' she called again when Jill showed no sign of halting her march to the door.

Jill had to stop as Grace-Mary appeared in the doorway carrying a tray of steaming mugs.

Joanna went to my desk, yanked open the top drawer and pulled out a small velvet box. 'Here!' she chucked it at Jill who just managed to catch it as she turned around.

Jill opened the box. 'What's this?' she asked, not looking up.

'It's a ring,' I said. 'That's a diamond. One carat. Nearly. Do you like it?'

Jill stared at the engagement ring for an age. 'Yes... I do...' She tore her eyes from the ring and glanced, confused, from me to Joanna to Grace-Mary.

'Robbie wants to marry you, dear.' Grace-Mary gently prised the box from Jill's hand and replaced it with a mug of tea.

It wasn't exactly how I'd planned it, but everyone else knew - why not Jill too?

'What do you say?' I asked. 'Will you marry me, Jill?'

The look of anger had gone. Jill smiled. Nippy to sweetie in a personal best time. She took a slow sip of tea. 'Oh, probably.'

* * * * *

Author's Note:

I am sometimes asked where I get my ideas from. One of the benefits of being a criminal lawyer, and these days there are few, is the wealth of material that comes one's way.

Many of the scenes, characters and events in the Best Defence series are based on fact, some so weird that I can't use them because they would simply not be believed. One example being the time I was sitting in my car in the centre of Edinburgh, with a dud battery in my phone, wondering how I could contact Edgar Prais Q.C. with whom I was supposed to be consulting in Glasgow in about ten minutes time.

As I pondered how I'd get word of my delay to senior counsel, another vehicle collided with the rear of my car. Swapping details, I noticed the lady driver's unusual name and discovered that she was none other than the charming Mrs Prais, who not only had her husband's phone number, but allowed me to use her phone to call him (there was no damage done to either car, or, if there was, it sort of blended in with the other assorted dents and scrapes on each).

Such a coincidence just can't be used in fiction. While it's true – it's unbelievable. Trust me, it took some fine advocacy on my part to explain to Edgar what I was doing calling him from his wife's phone. Which brings me to the point of this note: the procedural blunders referred to in the above chapters, namely, the 'smoking jury' and the jury that was not sworn in.

The smoking jury incident took place at Falkirk Sheriff Court in January 2012; the accused, not represented by myself, but, by my friends and fellow defence agents, Gordon Addison and Kevin Douglas.

Although the Crown conceded the point at the trial, it later disputed the smoking jury decision and, in fine style, the Appeal Court decided that when the 1995 Act said, *'shall acquit'* it actually meant something else, and, having dug up some 16th Century authority, ordered the Sheriff not to acquit but instead to desert the case *pro loco et tempore*, thus, theoretically at any rate, allowing the Crown a second bite at the cherry. An opportunity of which it decided not to avail itself. HMA -v- Paterson XC83/12

The jury that was not sworn, sat in 1997 at the trial of my client Peter Arthur George Schroder who was charged with the murder of a teenage girl in Bonnybridge. The mistake was noticed shortly before lunchtime by Dorothy Bain, now Q.C., then recently called to the Bar and watching from the public benches. Whether the error was noticed by the defence team shall go unrecorded; however, once the problem had been brought to the court's attention by the eagle-eyed Ms Bain, the trial had to be recommenced with two witnesses being recalled to repeat their evidence to a now duly sworn-in jury. What would have happened if the error had gone unnoticed until after the trial, I don't know. I suspect that nowadays the appeal court might overlook such an error in correct procedure; however, due process seemed to be viewed a lot more stringently in those far off days. Mr Schroder was represented by Derek Ogg Q.C. who had not at that time taken silk.

WHSM
2014

THE BEST DEFENCE SERIES

#1 RELATIVELY GUILTY

Follow the trials of Scots criminal lawyer Robbie Munro as he joins battle in the fight for truth and justice - hoping truth and justice don't win too often because it's terribly bad for business.

A policeman with a caved-in skull, his young wife found clutching the blood-stained murder weapon; it all looks pretty open and shut until Robbie detects the faint whiff of a defence and closes in on a witness who might cast a precious doubt on proceedings.

So why is it, the nearer he gets to the truth and a possible acquittal, that Robbie's murder client becomes more and more eager to opt for a life sentence?

Short-Listed for the Dundee International Book Prize

#2 DUTY MAN

Justice is blind - which is handy because sometimes you need to pull a fast one.

Continuing the trials of Scots defence lawyer, Robbie Munro.

Local lawyer Max Abercrombie is gunned down in cold blood, and the historic town of Linlithgow is rocked by its first assassination in five hundred years. Robbie, Max's childhood friend, is duty-bound to act in the accused's defence, and when investigations reveal a link between his friend's murder and that of a High Court judge many years before, he wonders if his client might actually be an innocent man.

The more Robbie digs into the past, the closer he gets to the truth and the more the bodies pile up.

#3 SHARP PRACTICE

A good criminal lawyer seeks after the truth.

A great criminal lawyer makes sure the jury doesn't hear it.

Scotland's favourite criminal defence lawyer, Robbie Munro, is back and under pressure to find a missing child, defend a murdering drug-dealer and save the career of a child-pornography-possessing local doctor.

Add to that the antics of his badly-behaving ex-cop dad, the re-kindling of an old flame and a run-in with Scotland's Justice Secretary and you'll discover why it is that, sometimes, a lawyer has to resort to Sharp Practice.

#4 KILLER CONTRACT

It's 99% of lawyers that give the other 1% a bad name.

It's the trial of the millennium: Larry Kirkslap, Scotland's most flamboyant entrepreneur, charged with the murder of good-time gal Violet Hepburn. He needs a lawyer and there's only one man for the job – unfortunately it's not Robbie Munro. That's about to change; however, more pressing is the contract out on the lives of Robbie and his client, Danny Boyd, who is awaiting trial for violating a sepulchre.

Who would anyone want to kill Robbie and his teenage client?

While Robbie tries to work things out, there are a couple of domestic issues that also need his urgent attention, like his father's surprise birthday party and the small matter of a marriage proposal.

#5 CRIME FICTION

If the ink is in your blood...

Desperate for cash, Robbie finds himself ensnared in a web of deceit spun by master conman Victor Devlin. What is Devlin's connection with the case of two St Andrew's students charged with the murder of a local waitress?

Enter Suzie Lake, a former-university chum of Robbie, now bestselling crime fiction author, who regards Robbie as her muse. Lois has writer's block and turns to Robbie for inspiration. She's especially interested in the St Andrew's murder and wants some inside information. How can Robbie refuse the advances of the gorgeous Suzie, even if they threaten to scupper his pending nuptials? And yet, the more Robbie reveals to her, the more he finds himself in a murky world of bribery, corruption and crime fiction publishing.

#6 LAST WILL

Blood is thicker than water - but it's not as hard as cash.

The trial of Robbie Munro's life; one month to prove he's fit to be a father.

No problem. Apart, that is, from the small matter of a double-murder in which Robbie's landlord, Jake Turpie, is implicated. Psycho-Jake demands Robbie's undivided attention and is prepared to throw money at the defence - along with some decidedly dodgy evidence.

Robbie has a choice, look after his daughter or look after his client. Can the two be combined to give the best of both worlds? Robbie aims to find out, and his attempts lead him into the alien worlds of high-fashion, drug-dealing and civil-litigation.

It's what being a father/lawyer is all about. Isn't it?

#7 PRESENT TENSE

'Crime with an edge of dark humour. The Best Defence series could only come out of Scotland.'

Tommy Flanagan, Braveheart, SOA, Guardians of the Galaxy Vol. 2

Criminal lawyer Robbie Munro is back home, living with his widowed, ex-policeman dad and his new found daughter, Tina. Life at the practice isn't going well, neither is the love life he regularly confesses to his junior, Joanna. Then again, on the subject of Joanna, Robbie may be the last to know... When one of his more dubious clients leaves a mysterious box for him to look after, and a helicopter comes down with two fatalities, events take a much more sinister turn, and all of this is complicated by the rape case he has to defend.

ABOUT THE AUTHOR

William McIntyre is a partner in Scotland's oldest law firm Russel + Aitken, specialising in criminal defence. William has been instructed in many interesting and high-profile cases over the years and now turns fact into fiction with his string of legal thrillers, The Best Defence Series, featuring defence lawyer, Robbie Munro.

Based in Scotland and drawing on William's thirty years as a criminal defence lawyer, there is a rich vein of dry-humour running through the series, which he describes as an antidote to crime fiction that features maverick cops chasing a serial killers, and in it he emphasises that justice is not only about convicting the guilty, but also about acquitting the innocent.

William writes from the heart and from his own experiences. Robbie Munro, is very much a real life lawyer, juggling a host of cases, dealing with awkward clients and battling an at times Kafkaesque legal system, all while trying to retain some form of personal life. Notwithstanding their relatively light-hearted approach, the books deal with some very serious issues, each story raising an interesting philosophical or ethical issue. Though the plots are often complex, they are never confusing such is William's deftness of touch.

The books, which are stand alone or can be read in series, have been well received by many fellow professionals, on both sides of the Bar, due to their accuracy in law and procedure and Robbie's frank, if sardonic, view on the idiosyncrasies of the Scots criminal justice system.

William is married with four sons.

www.bestdefence.biz

21478478R00185

Printed in Great Britain
by Amazon